Praise for the Dam

'In *Caligula*, Turney uses fiction to challenge some of [the] lies that masquerade under the name of "history" ... [His narrator, Livilla] provides an energetic and intelligent eyewitness view of the imperial court and of the gradual decline of Caligula's rule ... A satisfyingly alternative look at Caligula, something perhaps better done in fiction than in academic history ... Great and enjoyable'

Mary Beard, *TLS*

'Caligula is a monster we all know and love to hate. Turney's novel challenges our prejudice, and sketches a more understanding view of the Roman Emperor ... Turney's version is an entirely plausible take on the sources. We pity the boy, even as we deplore the insane violence of the man. *Caligula* is an engrossing new spin on a well-known tale'

Antonia Senior, *The Times*

'Turney's masterful, persuasive writing makes you start to question everything you have ever read about Rome's most tyrannical ruler ... Finding humanity and redeeming qualities in one of history's most reviled villains is a bold move, but in Turney's hands, it pays off'

Helena Gumley-Mason, *The Lady*

'Inspired ... a mesmerising, haunting and disturbing portrait of Caligula'

Kate Atherton, *Sunday Express S Mag*

'Enthralling and original, brutal and lyrical by turns. With powerful imagery and carefully considered history Turney provides a credible alternative to the Caligula myth that will have the reader questioning everything they believe they know about the period'

Anthony Riches, author of the Empire series

'*Commodus* combines thrilling Roman spectacle, star-crossed young lovers, and poisonous palace intrigue into a compulsively readable drama ... A tense, taut, thrilling character study of one of Rome's most maligned rulers, transformed here into tragic hero'

Kate Quinn, author of *The Alice Network*

'Brilliant ... a gripping gallop of a read, impeccably researched, beautifully written, impossible to put down'

Angus Donald, author of the Outlaw Chronicles

'Gripping, emotional and authentic. The best Roman novel I've read in a long time. Turney is one of the best historical novelists out there'

Christian Cameron, author of *Killer of Men*

'Turney masterfully gives readers a new and illuminating look at Emperor Commodus, but also introduces us to the clever freedwoman who should have been his empress. Seeing imperial Rome through Marcia's eyes is a delight not to be missed, and Turney is at the top of his game'

Stephanie Dray, author of *Lady of the Nile*

'Commodus, son of Marcus Aurelius: mad, bad and dangerous to stand too close to according to history. Turney, however, does here what he did in *Caligula* – puts some humanity back in the beast of Rome. Warm and well written'

Robert Low, author of the Oathsworn series

Domitian

S.J.A. Turney is an author of Roman and medieval historical fiction, gritty historical fantasy and rollicking Roman children's books. He lives with his family and extended menagerie of pets in rural North Yorkshire.

Also by S.J.A. Turney

Tales of the Empire

Interregnum
Ironroot
Dark Empress
Insurgency
Invasion
Jade Empire
Emperor's Bane

The Knights Templar

Daughter of War
The Last Emir
City of God
The Winter Knight
The Crescent and the Cross
The Last Crusade

Wolves of Odin

Blood Feud
The Bear of Byzantium
Iron and Gold

The Damned Emperors

Caligula
Commodus
Domitian

S.J.A. TURNEY

DOMITIAN

CANELO

First published in the United Kingdom in 2022 by Canelo

This edition published in the United Kingdom in 2023 by

Canelo
Unit 9, 5th Floor
Cargo Works, 1-2 Hatfields
London SE1 9PG
United Kingdom

A CIP catalogue record for this book is available from the British Library.

Ebook ISBN 978 1 80032 672 9
Hardback ISBN 978 1 80032 904 1
Paperback ISBN 978 1 80032 933 1

This book is a work of fiction. Names, characters, businesses, organizations, places and events are either the product of the author's imagination or are used fictitiously. Any resemblance to actual persons, living or dead, events or locales is entirely coincidental.

Cover design by Sarah Whittaker

Look for more great books at www.canelo.co

Printed and bound in Great Britain by Clays Ltd, Elcograf S.p.A.

1

MIX
Paper from
responsible sources
FSC® C018072

For Harry. Dis Manibus, my friend.

Damnatio Memoriae

Upon the death of an emperor, it became practice for the senate to confer apotheosis upon his name, granting him divine status and a cult of his own. If the emperor had been despised, however, the senate could choose the precise opposite and vilify rather than deify him – *damnatio memoriae* (a modern term) would occur. Without hesitation or ceremony, the emperor's name was erased from all public inscriptions (a process known as *abolitio nominis*), his image would be scratched from frescoes, his statues smashed. Sometimes, even coins bearing his image would be defaced. The damned emperor was not only denied an ascent to heaven, but wiped from history. Such was the fate of the wicked, the unpopular, or the unfortunate.

Prologue

'Everything, *Domine*?'

'Everything.'

'Even the marbles, Domine?'

'*Especially* the marbles. Any you cannot refashion into my likeness, refashion into dust.'

I sat, pinching the bridge of my nose for a moment, as the workmen began their task. I could feel a headache coming on. I was not looking forward to the hammering and the dust, but this was something I had to force myself to watch. The first of the statues, gathered from around the Palatine, was carried to the centre of the room with some difficulty, and there placed upon a wide sheet. The sculptor looked at the figure captured in cold, white marble, austere face above a torso clad ironically in the togate pose of a senator. The orange-tinted paint of the skin and the purple of the robe had been roughly washed off to allow the craftsman a better view of what could be done with it, leaving almost-red streaks collected in the cracks and folds of the clothing.

I watched as the sculptor's eyes took in that wide forehead and the slightly receded hair, tastefully carved to be considerably thicker and curlier than its subject's true coiffeur. The nose was wide and long, though not unattractively so. Domitian was never unattractive, even when his hair began to recede. All around the room, copies of that familiar face looked back at me, accusing.

It was not my doing.

I felt the guilt, though, and perhaps things could have worked out differently. Still, he was gone, and in the forum below citizens and soldiers alike cried their mourning for their fallen emperor.

No one cheered for the new occupant of the throne, not yet, and I wondered if I would be reviled by the loyal people of Rome for what I must do. But it had to be done.

The sculptor shook his head, a decision reached.

'There is insufficient marble for a recarve, Domine. I think this was once a statue of the Divine Claudius, already reworked. If I try again, the head will be too small for the body.'

I nodded my understanding, a tacit agreement.

As the sculptor moved off to another statue, one of the workmen stepped forward to the unwanted marble. The hammer swung and I watched that face crack and shatter, the likeness of the young man I had known for most of his life falling away in pieces.

The last of the reddish paint, like deep rivulets of blood, gathered on the body of the statue, making it an echo of a butchered corpse. It made me shudder, for it brought me back to how it all ended.

I am Marcus Cocceius Nerva, Emperor of Rome, and this is how it began.

Part One – Corruption

*Every city contains wicked citizens from time to time and
an ignorant populace all the time*

—Livy: *The History of Rome, Book 45.8*

I

Pomegranate Street

Rome, AD 52

It starts with blood. It always does in Rome.

I was finally returning after a two-year sojourn in the provinces. My travelling companion was Titus Flavius Sabinus, a friend of some years, and he was as tired and travel-worn as me. The Flavii and my own family had ties stretching back several generations, and it was no coincidence that Flavius and I had managed to secure a military tribuneship, the first step on the ladder of public offices, in the same province and in the same month as one another.

I had served with relative distinction in the Twentieth Legion under the great governor Ostorius Scapula, slogging through the hills and valleys of western Britannia to bring the light of civilisation to tribes whose idea of culture was different colours of mud. Flavius had served with the Second during the same campaign. He and I had spent many a dreary day together enduring the endless rain, and many a soggy night drinking away our woes with the other tribunes in a warm, clammy campaign tent.

'Is it not a welcome sight, Marcus?'

I turned to Flavius. 'I'm not sure. I think I have grown to appreciate the simplicity of the military life. Commands given and carried out, everything working like a machine. As long as every gear turns, the whole thing works. Rome is… complex.'

'Better than the soggy hills of Britannia, surely, my friend?'

'Perhaps. But in Britannia, the only snakes are small grass snakes. Here they walk and talk.'

'Gods, but you're a delight sometimes.'

'Rome is a pit of serpents, Flavius, coils within coils all writhing with no apparent order or purpose until one is bitten without warning.'

Such was the Rome of Claudius, anyway. Both my own family, the Cocceii, and the Flavii had suffered times of disfavour and trouble, especially with that gilt harpy Agrippina at the emperor's side. Neither of us were under any illusion that we would be returning to comfort and simplicity, no matter how relaxed Flavius might sound. We had exchanged an enemy who ran at us wielding swords and screaming for an enemy who lurked unseen, ready to issue the accusation of *maiestas* and the appropriate death sentence at a moment's notice.

We entered Rome and climbed the Viminal towards my family's townhouse side by side.

We arrived at my father's house to discover the door wide open, something so unusual as to cause alarm.

'What...?' I began, but Flavius threw me a warning look, and we glanced around the street. The heights of the Viminal where the houses of the wealthy are to be found are not usually crammed with life like the streets closer to the centre, but had I been more alert as we approached, I might have noted the lack of any movement. I had the sense of being watched, of many pairs of eyes behind shutters, but no one stood in the street, not even beggars or drunks.

'Where is the doorman? Where are our slaves?'

Flavius and I dismounted, feeding the reins through the stone loops on the kerb and tying them there. Sharing a look once more, the hair rising on the back of my neck, we approached the door. There was no noise as we moved from the bright morning of the street into the shadow of my father's doorway.

The small shrine to the family gods lay on its side, marble figurines chipped and smashed where they had fallen. Orion, the family's bulky doorman, lay close by, a small pool of dark liquid about his head. Whoever had done this was fearless, for I had known the ex-gladiator all my life, and I had been certain that no man born of woman could best him.

My gaze slipped back to the door. Carrying a bared weapon of war is illegal within the city, but I was already regretting leaving the weapons on the horses, and from Flavius' expression he shared my regret.

A scream echoed across the house, and we exchanged another look, hackles going up, and stepped further inside, passing into the atrium. More shouts and screams came, then, and the sounds of violence. It was almost unheard of for criminals to risk breaking into the houses of the great, and so there was almost certainly something of import happening. Someone had overcome not only Orion, but the various heavy guards my father employed for his property, too.

My heart was pounding as we crossed to the doorway that led to the gardens, and a figure suddenly emerged through it, blocking our way. I froze in shock at the sight. A soldier armed for war, white tunic spattered with red, shield emblazoned with golden scorpions.

'Who are you?' demanded the Praetorian, lifting his crimson-coated blade to point at me and then my companion. The soldier's eyes were narrowed in suspicion. As I tried to find my voice around a mouth that had suddenly gone dry, a second soldier appeared behind the first, this one unarmed, but with a writing tablet in one hand and a stilus in the other. I am forever indebted to Flavius for his quickness of mind, for, as I floundered, my friend cleared his throat and pulled himself up, hands on his hips indignantly.

'I am Titus Flavius Sabinus, tribune of the Twentieth Legion, son of Titus Flavius Sabinus, ex-consul and former governor of Moesia, *soldier.*'

If the Praetorian was impressed, he gave no such sign. 'And your friend?'

'Aulus Flavius, a cousin from Norba. We are here to visit our friend Marcus Cocceius Nerva, the younger,' he added brazenly. 'Where is he?'

The Praetorian looked over his shoulder and his friend consulted the writing tablet in his hand, tapping it with the stilus. Finally, the second soldier shook his head, and the first nodded and turned back to us.

'Lucky for you, Flavii, you're not on the list. Nor is the young Cocceius you seek, but if you find him you might want to keep him away. This is an imperial proscription order, and things could get a little awkward here if he wanders by.'

I still couldn't find my power of speech, and although I'd witnessed the exchange, my eyes had never left the blood dripping from the point of the sword. *Whose* blood?

'I want to speak to your officer,' Flavius demanded, remaining haughty. It takes a truly brave man to make demands of a Praetorian. Indeed, the soldier was clearly surprised by such a bold statement.

'Run along, boy, before I add a few names to the list.'

Still staring at the blood running down that blade, I reached out and grasped Flavius by the sleeve. He kept his eyes locked on those of the Praetorian for a long moment, then seemed to realise that I was there and turned. He saw the fear in my eyes, I think, for he nodded, and we retreated from the house.

'What do we do?' I murmured as we emerged into the street. I was trembling. I was no nervous boy, but a man cannot find his household and family butchered without it shaking him to the core.

'We wait,' Flavius answered in a low growl. 'We watch.'

I followed him, hollow and aimless, as he retrieved our mounts and returned to the slaves and the horses. There, he located his sword among the packs and belted it on. There are prohibitions as old as Jove himself against drawing a weapon of war with violent intent within the city's ancient boundaries, but for a moment I seriously worried that my friend intended to face up against a unit of Praetorians. I was rather relieved when he kept it sheathed. 'Arm yourself,' he suggested. 'Just in case.'

'Your father must have done something,' Flavius said, finally.

'In this emperor's Rome you don't need to do something to be punished,' I noted rather bitterly.

'Even Praetorians need a reason to kill a nobleman.'

I shivered. 'It *is* my father, isn't it?'

Flavius nodded his head. 'There's only you and your father in the house who would be of note to the Praetorians, and you weren't on the list.'

I nodded. All I could picture now was my father's face, full of pride at seeing me in my bright new uniform, preparing for the journey to Britannia.

'If they don't want you,' Flavius reasoned, 'then it's not treason. And if that's the case, then you'll still inherit. At least the emperor is not taking the family's property.'

'Titus, that's not much of a consolation.'

We sat in silence then, watching the empty street and the dark maw of my father's doorway. My mind began to race. I would still have the family house, but clearly I wasn't going to want it for now. Flavius' father would undoubtedly give me shelter. He and my own sire had been friends and comrades for years, and the elder Sabinus' reputation meant that he was important enough that even Praetorians would think twice about insulting him. I would be safe with Sabinus and the Flavii until I discovered what had happened.

Finally, after an hour or so, the Praetorians exited the doorway, eight of them, all armed for war and spattered with blood. Without a single glance back, the soldiers marched off in the direction of the Palatine and their odious master. No Praetorian eye therefore fell upon the two young men sitting on the fountain a little further up and watching them.

Once they were safely out of sight, Flavius gestured to the slaves and we made our way back. The Praetorians had left the door wide open, and as I approached, I noted two figures in the vestibule. I knew not the name of the girl, for she was simply one of the nameless, faceless slaves that served the house, but my father's body slave Albinus I knew of old, and my lip twitched at the sight of him cradling his pulped and broken arm as he moved to close the door.

'Master Marcus?' the man managed, his face filled with a mix of fear, horror and now hope.

'My father?'

The slave failed to reply, but his eyes flicked back to the atrium, and so I pushed past him, Flavius at my heel. The small impluvium pool that gathered rainwater at the centre of the atrium's expensive mosaic floor was filled with pink water, fed by rivulets from the pile of abandoned bodies close by. A household almost entire, heaped up like the corpses of the penniless in the pits outside the city. Slaves and master alike piled in death. My father was just visible as a wispy grey head and a torn, bloodied, yet clearly expensive tunic, halfway down the pile. Just looking at the heap, I was already convinced that Albinus and the girl had been the only two survivors. Why, I could not imagine. The Praetorians had clearly had their fun with Albinus, and his arm would never work again. Presumably the slave girl had managed to hide throughout the ordeal.

'I will go to the palace,' I said, shaking, staring at that heap of dead flesh.

'What?' Flavius grabbed my elbow and turned me away from the sight of my father.

'I will demand an explanation.'

'Don't be a fool, Marcus. You'll just get yourself noticed. You probably escaped this because you were away in the army. If you march up to the emperor and make demands of him, how long do you think it will be before you're added to the top of that heap? Keep your mouth shut, accept what's happened, bury your dead and move on.'

'That's my *father*,' I hissed.

'No. That *was* your father. Come on.'

I resisted for a moment, but in truth I was still lost and horrified, and it was easy to be led, so I turned and followed my friend as he marched me back out of the house, pausing to give a few instructions to the house's two remaining slaves. Back in the street, he grabbed me by both shoulders. 'You're coming to my house. My father will know what to do.'

–

The house of Titus Flavius Sabinus sat on the wide Pomegranate Street, and I half expected to find that door similarly open, and blood pouring out from the Flavian household. I was relieved to find the place sealed tight and smoke belching from the chimneys above the house's baths. I was still shaking. No matter how much I tried to harden myself to what had happened, I couldn't quite stop the trembling. I was silent and cowed as we dismounted, and I stood, eyes lowered, as Flavius hammered the door knocker. The slave opened up, club in hand, and made cheery remarks at the sight of his master's son.

We were admitted and made our way through the house swiftly, escorted directly to the study of Sabinus. Flavius' father was seated in his office with his brother, the former consul Vespasian. The two men could hardly be less alike. Vespasian, the younger by a number of years, was short, stocky and bald with a tanned, weathered complexion, more resembling a farmer than a nobleman. His face was permanently creased into a wry smile, and he moved with animation always. Sabinus, the older brother, by comparison, was tall and narrow, with iron grey hair and a serious face. Indeed, their expressions were outward reflections of their personalities, for I knew Vespasian to be a man of sharp wit and easy humour, while Sabinus was a hard-working and serious, traditional man. Yet despite their differences they were close even for brothers, and woe betide a man that harmed one and turned his back on the other. It was this simple and straightforward loyalty that they had shared with my father, and one reason why our families were so close.

The two men looked up and Sabinus broke into a rare smile, rising from his seat.

'Welcome home, my boy,' he announced, then caught the clearing of his brother's throat as Vespasian nodded past my friend, at me. Sabinus' smile slipped away and was replaced with his usual seriousness as he halted halfway to embracing his son and noticed for the first time the second figure just outside the doorway.

'Marcus Cocceius Nerva,' he said, his voice cracking just slightly, the only betrayal of any emotion.

I bowed my head to my elder respectfully, but he shook his own. 'No standing on ceremony here, young Marcus. Come in. I am afraid that I have bad...' He paused, catching sight of my expression, perhaps noting that I trembled still. 'You already know.'

'We called at the house of Marcus' father on the way,' Flavius explained. 'Father—'

'I know. It is truly unfortunate timing that you should arrive so soon. I was not expecting you before the kalends.'

'Better now than a few days ago,' noted Vespasian from the other side of the table. 'Then he might have been part of it.'

Sabinus nodded. 'Quite.'

'What happened?' I managed, my first words since we arrived, dragged out through a dry throat and over a trembling lip.

'Your father has always had an unfortunate tendency to tell things how they are,' Sabinus said. 'Something he shared with my brother,' he added, eyeing Vespasian. 'Your father took it upon himself to make certain suggestions to the emperor. Suggestions of a... a matrimonial nature.'

'He denounced that heifer Agrippina,' explained Vespasian flatly, earning a warning look from Sabinus.

'The palace has ears everywhere, brother. Watch that tongue and remember what's just happened.'

'So my father insulted the empress,' I said.

'More or less.'

'Some spurious charges were levelled,' Vespasian added. 'Nothing serious enough to drag the family down, for that would likely have created unwanted backlash in the senate, but sufficient to demand that he take his own life.'

'He was not given such a noble opportunity,' Flavius spat.

'I can imagine,' his father nodded, then turned back to me. 'Your house is not safe, young Nerva. Be welcome in mine. I have room for you as long as you wish to stay, and be reassured that while I might share your father's misgivings, I am a careful man, and this place will be safe for you.'

I thanked the man and stood back, allowing him a happy reunion with the son he had not seen for two years. My head was still reeling. I had no plan, no direction and no goal. It had been my father's web of contacts that had secured me my tribuneship and he would have expected me to spend a few years now acquiring clients and contacts of my own, growing my relationship within the circles of Rome and the court before landing a position as quaestor. I had no desire to move within the court now. Indeed, I had no idea *what* I was to do.

At least, whatever happened, I would be safe within the household of the Flavii.

II

A dangerous woman

Rome, AD 54

I spent the next year and more living in the household of the Flavii, which tightened the bonds between my own line and theirs ever further. Never once did Sabinus make me feel beholden for his generosity, and I was welcomed as one of the family. I came to know not only Flavius and his father, but also his brother Vespasian, whose own house lay just a little further up the same road, and whose son, Titus – a solid young man only recently out of childhood who twitched and nagged at his father for a posting to the tribunate – reminded me much of myself at his age. Vespasian's daughter, Domitilla, was a quiet girl who kept to herself.

Though I knew little of him yet, I became accustomed also to the sight of Vespasian's younger son, Domitian, a toddler who seemed ever to be in the way and whose birth had brought forth in his mother a long-term malady that weakened her constitution and saw her largely retire from public life.

Fourteen months had done nothing to lessen the spite I felt for Agrippina. Indeed, over those months I had come to know what it meant to move in court circles, and I began to understand just how dangerous she was. Sabinus had spoken many times of Claudius, his unexpected rise, and of how far he was from the fool people thought him to be. Of how he had played the cripple and the drooling idiot to survive the machinations of his wicked family, and had risen from that obscurity to mastery of the world. And then, in hushed tones, of how, in his dotage, the old emperor had fallen under Agrippina's spell, and was now little more than a puppet dancing her dance.

I had railed against her and planned her downfall over those first days in the house on Pomegranate Street, and only the steadying influence of Sabinus and Flavius kept me from doing something stupid. In the end, I simply put my father's affairs in order. We had a small, nondescript funeral, sufficiently minor not to draw imperial attention, and he was interred in the family mausoleum. Unwilling to live in the shadow of that pile of corpses, I sold the house to a senator for a fraction of what it was worth, assuming I would buy another when I needed it. Sabinus helped me with everything, good man that he was.

It took half a year for me to settle back into the life of a nobleman in the city, and even then I did so more as a member of the Flavian house than of a noble line in my own right. I was twenty-three summers then, and still more than a year from taking my next step on the career ladder, and so alongside Flavius I began once more to connect with the city of my birth. I attended palace functions on rare occasions, for Agrippina disliked the Flavii, and especially Vespasian, but sometimes societal strictures demanded our presence despite her bile. I met the emperor twice during that year, and it struck me both times how frail and old he looked, compared with the man who had been conqueror of Britannia a decade earlier. I did sometimes find myself wondering if, when his time came and his son Britannicus took the throne, I would be able to tether my cart to that dynasty. I would need *some* sort of imperial patronage if I were ever to achieve the sought-after rank of consul, after all.

Given the rarity of our visits, it came as something of a surprise when we received our invitations to dine with the imperial family just before the ides of October. Sabinus noted wryly that the invites had come in the name of Tiberius Claudius Caesar Augustus Germanicus, with no mention of his wife Agrippina at all.

Intrigued, we gathered in our best togas, slaves rushing around us, straightening and brushing, adjusting the hang of the weighty wool garments. Sabinus and Flavius, Vespasian and myself. Four invitations. None for Titus, which came only as a relief to his father, but caused a fit of petty anger in the young man, given that I, a guest in the house, had been selected over him. Leaving Titus to stomp impotently around the house, making his infant brother laugh, we entered our litters. A veritable army of slaves and guards with ash clubs surrounded the four vehicles as we were borne aloft and carried through the evening streets, down the slopes of the Quirinal, across the forum and up to the Palatine and the great palace Tiberius had built there.

At the monumental doors, guarded by shiny Praetorians, the litters disgorged their loads. Slaves and servants made last-moment tweaks so that we were presentable, and we were escorted into the palace.

Through rooms of impressive marble and bright mosaics we strode, past busts and statues of gods and of members of the imperial household back to the great Caesar himself, until we were left outside the doors of the imperial banquet chamber, awaiting the signal to enter. I found myself musing on the situation. The harpy empress was said to hate Vespasian so much over some slight from their youth that she had announced she would boil him alive before deigning to speak with him. It seemed exceedingly odd that we were here at all.

'Why have we come?' I asked finally, as we waited.

'Pardon?' Sabinus frowned at me.

'If the empress hates us so much, then this is the most dangerous place for us in the empire. Why have we come?'

Vespasian was the one who answered, his mouth twisting into an ironic smile. 'Because even if you're chained to the floor, when the emperor invites you to dine, you go.'

Sabinus nodded. 'I made discreet enquiries among friends, and it would appear that we alone were invited by the emperor personally. The other guests' presence was demanded by Agrippina.

One wonders whether the empress is even aware that we are coming.'

That chilled me. Springing such a surprise on such a dangerous woman might well have repercussions. We had no further time to discuss matters, though, for at that moment an announcer stepped out, noted who waited in the antechamber, and then paced into the hall, slaves pulling the doors wide, intoning our names with any appropriate honorifics in a deep and sonorous voice.

Sabinus, as the elder of the gathering, strode in first, bowing low. Had the emperor been close enough to speak to, he would have kissed Claudius' cheek, as one did, but it was clear from the moment we entered that the occasion was not going to work like that. The emperor was already reclined on his couch at the top of the room, the empress by his side. His son Britannicus and his stepson Nero reclined nearby, both with bored expressions. Our own couches were indicated some way from the imperial position, yet to my surprise still relatively close. I had expected, given our unpopularity, to be placed at the very bottom end, far from imperial favour. Still, we were too far from the emperor to elicit more than a bored nod.

The main food had not yet been brought out, just a few appetiser courses lying on silver platters around the tables, and we were not the last to arrive. The various luminaries present were generally milling around the periphery of the great room, under the watchful eye of the Praetorians, as naked flautists filled the hall with a gay little melody, and two dwarves, depilated and oiled, wrestled on a balcony for the entertainment of the guests. Sabinus and Vespasian told Flavius and I to mingle, to make small talk and move about the room, but not to engage the emperor or empress or either of the sons, and to steer clear of any talk that might be divisive. Until we knew why we were here, we were to be careful, non-inflammatory and, to all extents, invisible. 'Try not to be here' was the order of the evening.

Flavius and I did just that, passing the time of day with minor nobility and senators but otherwise drawing no unnecessary attention to ourselves. We drifted towards the flautists, shapely women all, and then swiftly moved off at a tangent, Flavius' hand on my elbow. When I enquired as to why, he pointed at a well-dressed and hook-nosed man involved in a tedious-sounding conversation.

'Faustus Cornelius Sulla Felix, the emperor's son-in-law.'

Nodding my understanding, I veered away. I tried not to engage anyone in conversation at all, which was quite easy given my lack of direct connections with any of these people. When Flavius was called over by a young acquaintance busy espousing the merits of the green team at the races, he gave me an apologetic look and moved off, and I was alone, drifting like a fallen leaf in a swollen stream, eddying in corners and washed up occasionally to lean against walls.

How I found myself back in the proximity of the flautists I have no idea, but find as much I did, and as I listened, appreciating the melody, my eyes fell once more upon the emperor's son-in-law, but this time I was surprised to find him away from others and engaged in quiet debate, with Vespasian of all people. My nurse as a child abhorred my habit of eavesdropping, and had tried to knock it out of me, but to this day, I stand by that bad habit as the very best way of finding out what is truly going on. I drifted across to a slave with a krater of wine and acquired a drink in a position where, if I strained, I could just hear the two men's conversation.

'All the world can see he's not well, Cornelius.'

'He has fears, Vespasian. Fears that certain powers mean to see him fade further, and rapidly.'

'Speak plainly, Cornelius.'

The nearby wine slave was shooed away and the two men, ostensibly alone now apart from the flautists, and clearly unaware that I listened on the far side, lowered their voices to little more than a whisper. I strained harder, trying to block out the music.

'She means to make her son Claudius sole heir, you know?'

'Nero? But Britannicus has priority. He's the emperor's direct blood. And they share his will.'

'Gods, Vespasian, look at how far she has come. Can you imagine even for a moment that she will stop now and accept Claudius' natural son as the next emperor? No, she means to put Nero on the throne, and he alone. Britannicus will be lucky not to find himself face down in the Tiber.'

'What has this got to do with us?'

I saw, then, Cornelius Sulla looking about furtively. Miraculously he seemed to miss my lurking shape, and turned back to Vespasian. 'Claudius is not as frail and daft as she thinks. He has one more trick to play yet. A will needs to be witnessed by seven adult male citizens. There are seven of us here not invited by the empress. Your party, myself, Publius Suillius Rufus and Lucius Vitellius. Tonight, Nero is disinherited. Britannicus will be made sole heir.'

'Gods,' Vespasian breathed, and then went on to say something else in a hiss, but I was sadly distracted then, for Flavius appeared from nowhere, calling to me. Cursing his timing, and aware that I was clearly lurking, I hurried away before Cornelius Sulla realised I had been listening, and joined Flavius, who wore a curious smile.

'You won't believe who I've found.'

'You won't believe what I just heard,' I replied earnestly. If what Cornelius Sulla had said contained any truth, then we were walking into the deepest of pitfalls. The empress already hated the Flavii. If we were instrumental in stripping her son of his inheritance, she would stop at nothing to see us boiled to death.

'The emperor,' someone suddenly shouted across the room.

The murmur of conversation around the hall died away in an instant, the flautists warbling off into silence. I knew that something was seriously wrong in an instant, for the guests were motionless, trying to see what had drawn their attention, but at the far end of the room, Praetorians were on the move. Flavius and I scurried across to a small set of steps leading up to a bronze statue of Atlas, and climbed all three in order to see over the heads of the gathering.

My eyes widened at what I found. At the head of the table, the emperor was convulsing on his couch, shaken wildly with spasms, his face taking on a horrible grey pallor, froth and yellow liquid pouring from his lips across his arm and chest. Even from a distance I could see odd dark lumps in the pale vomit, and my eyes slid down to the bowl of mushrooms on the table beside him. Clearly, they were the culprit. Had it been some accident? If so, the timing seemed impossibly lucky for the empress.

Praetorians were around the imperial family, then. Britannicus was on his feet, shouting at his father in a desperate tone, soldiers were sent to find a physician, and the Praetorian prefect, Burrus, was by the empress. If anyone present was labouring under the impression that this was simply an accidental illness, they need only look to the imperial family. Claudius, foaming and convulsing as his son screamed at him, unable to help. But Agrippina sat still, watching her husband, while her son Nero actually wore a small, smug smile. Had I still for even a moment believed that this was not premeditated, that notion would have been brushed aside by the fact that Prefect Burrus, rather than rushing to the emperor's side, or to his son Britannicus, had cleaved to Agrippina.

This was a coup – a murder… an *execution*. Not even a subtle one.

Tonight the emperor had planned to change his will. Nero would have been ousted, and Britannicus given sole inheritance. Instead, tonight the emperor was dying and the two joint heirs would find themselves under the wing of the dreaded Agrippina. What that meant for the Flavii I could hardly imagine.

As we watched the disaster unfold, I became aware that Sabinus and Vespasian had threaded their way through the crowd to stand beside us, the four of us a small, unpopular island in this sea of Agrippina's chosen.

'Say nothing. Do nothing.'

I nodded at Sabinus' sage words as we stood, still and silent. Praetorians appeared from one of the doors. Slaves were all around the emperor now, trying to ease him, to help in some way, at least to clean some of the mess. A medicus was dragged into the room.

The man, a swarthy figure in a rich tunic, was wild-eyed and in a near panic, as would be any man called upon to attend a dying emperor. The medicus, his leather satchel of supplies and tools at his side, was pushed out in front of the convulsing Claudius, a Praetorian at each shoulder.

Prefect Burrus exchanged a final few words with the empress Agrippina, and then stepped out to face the medicus, who was opening his satchel and running through muttered lists of what might help.

'An emetic,' the physician said, almost breathless. 'There may still be time with a strong enough emetic. I think I have...'

'The emperor is dead,' Burrus said in a flat tone, looking directly at the medicus across the shaking form of Claudius, the emperor visibly refuting the pronunciation as a fresh wave of yellow burst forth from his mouth.

'If I have mustard water, and I combine it with copper vitriol, which I carry, I can...'

'The emperor is dead,' repeated the Praetorian prefect, one eyebrow rising meaningfully.

The medicus frowned, looking back and forth between Burrus and the shaking form of the emperor, then to Agrippina, reclining calmly nearby, and then around the room, almost as if begging someone to come to his aid.

'There probably isn't time, now, to...' the medicus began, but then caught the look on Burrus' face and took a deep breath, straightening. 'Such convulsions as you see here are the body's natural reaction to the illness which has robbed our noble emperor of his life. This is but an echo of living movement, and soon he will be still. The great Claudius is no more,' he announced, with a panicky look.

The whole room stood in an uncomfortable silence, then, watching the 'dead' emperor as he busily passed away before us. It took more than a hundred heartbeats yet before Claudius let forth a plaintive yelp between fountains of yellow vomit and then collapsed like a decayed building falling in on itself and lay still on his couch.

Still, we remained silent and motionless. This was, even with my limited experience of the court, easily the most dangerous moment in my life. One wrong move now would lead to a swift demise. A woman who would so brazenly murder an emperor before so many witnesses would hardly baulk at ordering the death of a family she already hated.

'Perhaps we can get out of here without being noticed?' Flavius murmured. Even as Sabinus shook his head, I realised the truth of it. Every door to the room was sealed and guarded by half a dozen armed Praetorians. The room was tense, awaiting some new command, and it would take only the word of Agrippina to turn this banquet into a bloodbath.

As slaves gathered around the emperor, crying and wailing, raising their hands to the sky and begging Jove for his mercy, finally Agrippina rose from her couch. Burrus was behind her again now, a visible reminder of her *imperium* in the absence of her husband. She was the daughter of the great Germanicus, the sister of the emperor Gaius Caligula and both niece and wife to Claudius. No woman since Antonia or Livia could claim the power she commanded. The room remained silent, and even the wailing slaves, crying and mourning as was naturally expected of them, toned down their grief to make way for the empress's voice.

'The emperor is dead. He has suffered a weakening constitution for many months, and his physicians have warned him away from rich foods more than once. Good living has taken my husband from me.'

I caught sight, out of the corner of my eye, of Britannicus, then. The natural son of Claudius with his previous wife, the natural heir to the empire, was under no illusion as to what had just happened, and what it meant for him. I felt for the young man then, for the empress had torn his father from him just as she had torn mine from me little more than a year ago. I was impressed with Britannicus. He seethed and boiled over with accusation and hatred, yet he had the good sense to say nothing and stand still.

'Fortunate is the empire,' Agrippina went on in a businesslike manner, 'that the emperor's passing was so widely witnessed, and there can be no doubt over the succession. My husband's will, lodged with the city records for years now, names his heirs Britannicus and Nero as joint successors. Of course, with Britannicus still bearing the bulla of childhood, the burden of empire must naturally fall to the eldest heir.'

I watched Claudius' true son trembling with rage even as he stood motionless and silent. Had that been me, I doubt I would have managed to restrain myself so, even as an adult, let alone as a youth. In a brief moment of selfishness, I saw my future consulship at the behest of Britannicus evaporate, and a future of trying to remain unnoticed under the empress and her own son rise. I watched that empress, tense, as her gaze played across the gathered luminaries. Most of them were her creatures already, perhaps invited here purely to play witness to the 'innocent' demise of an ailing emperor, but her eyes fell first upon Publius Suillius Rufus and then Lucius Vitellius, shifting to Faustus Cornelius Sulla Felix and then finally to the small gathering of Flavii. It was impossible to miss both the challenge and the threat her gaze levelled at the seven of us. This entire room had witnessed a murder and was expected to speak of it only as an unhappy natural demise. If just one of us raised a voice in dissent, it endangered the succession, and would begin rumours and trouble all across the city. Of course, the speaker would live to regret it for only a matter of hours.

As the silence dragged on, Agrippina finally nodded her satisfaction. Nero, I noted sourly, had not stopped eating grapes throughout the entire nightmare, as though this were all some play put on for his benefit. The empress took a long, slow breath, and gestured to the Praetorian prefect.

'Burrus, have the announcement made from the palace balcony, and make sure that the news is relayed into every forum and to every street corner. By the time the *acta diurna* is released in the morning, I want every soul in the city to know of my divine husband's unfortunate passing, and the advance of Nero Claudius Caesar Drusus Germanicus to the purple.'

The prefect bowed to her and hurried out. As the room now began to move once more, voices rising in the murmur of low conversation, a small squad of Praetorians carefully and reverently shuffled the dead emperor onto a stretcher and bore him from the room, while slaves worked to clear the mess he had left.

No one moved, there was just the low hum of nervous conversation filling the hall.

Finally, Nero, pausing, rolling a grape between two fingers on the way to his mouth, cleared his throat. 'You are all aware that the main course is yet to come. This *is* a party, after all.'

There were a few trickles of nervous, forced laughter, and at the insistence of the empress, the guests were seated. The soaking couch was removed from the head of the table and a new, soft one placed there. Nero wasted no time wandering around to plonk himself now at the head of the feast, as though his adoptive father had not died in that very spot mere moments ago.

As the Flavii and I took our places obediently, wishing in truth that we were almost anywhere else in the empire, I looked across to Sabinus.

'Why has she made no move against you?'

'What do you mean?'

I fretted. 'If the empress harbours such anger against the Flavii, why not act upon it now? The emperor would have stopped her, but she is unrestrained now. Given what she has just done, taking against us would hardly make anyone blink.'

Sabinus nodded. 'The empress is inscrutable, and shrewd. Perhaps she sees some value in us yet. She is also wicked, so perhaps she intends to play with us as a cat with a mouse. Whatever the case, Rome has become all the more dangerous now.'

I nodded, watching the slaves beginning to bring out the food.

I was not hungry. Certainly I was going to skip the rest of the appetisers.

I had totally gone off mushrooms.

The death of Claudius ushered in a new era of tension and danger for those families who had already incurred the wrath of Agrippina, for, unfettered by the restraints of a powerful husband, that dreadful woman now exerted an almost total control of the city and the empire. Nero, though emperor in name and at a healthy adult age of seventeen, was little more than a mask worn in public by the real power, his mother.

She was always shrewd, and never more so than in the days following her husband's demise, for she continued to play off one power or family in Rome against another, maintaining a balance, always with her at the top.

We did not speak of the events of that dreadful evening that changed everything; for half a year it remained unmentioned, as though talking of such things might draw unwanted attention. I remained an honoured semi-permanent guest of the Flavii, spending time at the houses of both Sabinus and his brother Vespasian. I watched Flavius' cousin Titus come into his own, already a powerful young man, and I watched the Flavii somehow manage to remain strong and safe, despite all that went on around us.

Gradually, as Nero became more and more insistent on controlling the reins of state himself, struggling to draw the power away from his mother, we found things a little easier, some of the pressure taken off us. By the time Nero had reigned a year, the Flavii were feeling more ignored than endangered. Not that we were ever truly safe, as occasional incidents reminded us.

One summer night the emperor argued with his mother over some grand and lavish notion of a great party in the palace, with a theme based upon the tales of gods and heroes from the old Greek tales. In a move simply designed to aggravate her, Nero held the party anyway, against her wishes, and invited Flavius, Titus and me to it. Within an hour of the invitation reaching us, a second missive from the palace suggested that it could be a fatal move to accept the invite. We were caught in a hard place, forced to either refuse an emperor or defy an empress.

Nero was something of an unknown, but we all knew what Agrippina was capable of, and so we politely declined the party invitations, citing a family crisis. For five days, Flavian slaves went missing about their work and turned up on the doorstep dead, yet dressed as Achilles, or Odysseus or Ares, in case we had somehow missed the point. The lessons soon ended when Agrippina set herself against us once more and, consequently, Nero threw his support behind us. I was granted the position of quaestor, a step up on the *cursus honorum*, as part of his maternal defiance. I began to see that possibly Britannicus being shuffled out of the way might not mean the end of a career path for me, and yet Nero was ever opposed by his mother, and so perhaps I would still struggle, even with the emperor's support.

The year that followed was little better, for with the increased struggle for power between the emperor and his mother, the Flavii and I found ourselves increasingly used as pieces in their game, and a careful balance was required to avoid proscription from one side or the other. Sabinus and Vespasian, their older sons and I, all worked at keeping the *familia* safe from such wiles, and I was so involved in this that I was largely unaware of Vespasian's second son, Domitian, who was growing up with alarming speed, unnoticed by much of the household.

He was largely kept out of such family affairs. At approaching five years of age, he was too young to involve in the dangerous machinations and politics of the palace anyway, but also his father had promised his mother while all this was going on that their younger, and apparently more gentle, son would be shielded from the worst of it. Domitian was spending most of his time with his nurse, Phyllis, and we'd assumed that was the end of it.

But we were wrong, and I realised that one afternoon as we discussed the latest problem and how to work our way out of it without falling foul of Nero or Agrippina. Needing to visit the latrine, I left the room and the private discussion and, as I opened the door, did so straight into the face of the young boy who had been crouched beside it, eavesdropping.

Domitian. I was not sure whether my authority in the house of the Flavii was sufficient to scold one of their children for them, even when he was clearly doing wrong, and I dithered for a moment, closing the door behind me.

'What were you doing?' I asked, one of those stupid questions to which the answer is plainly obvious.

'No one tells me anything,' he said in reply. Blunt. Straightforward. Honest.

I found that I actually had no adequate reply, and I mumbled some vague admonishment about manners as I hurried off for a piss. But I had become aware of Vespasian's other son, that moment, and of how inquisitive, devious and bright he could be even at five. I made a point of watching him as the seasons rolled around, and my opinion of the lad only deepened. After that first time I never again found him eavesdropping, but I would wager a small fortune that every time I found him looking innocent he had been doing just that, unobserved. Often I found him near a statue of Minerva in the atrium. Innocent enough, for sure, but also the hub of domestic life, with a view of more or less the whole house.

A little after his sixth birthday, there came a confirmation that he was still learning that which was officially kept from him, and it was something of an insight into him again that he allowed me to know that on purpose. I was lounging in the warm bath of the family balneum when the lad came in and slipped into the water opposite.

'Will my father be killed?' he asked. I blinked at the blunt manner of his question. And I did not know how to reply. It was a constant threat, of course. As long as Agrippina remained with any thread of power in her needle, we were all at risk.

'Why do you ask?'

'What was it like when it happened to *your* dad?'

There it was: the proof he was still listening in. That was a subject of which I never spoke in public, only discussing it late at

27

night after too much wine, and usually only with Flavius. How often had he listened in on my own private discussions? I was angry at him for that, and yet the worry in his face stopped me bringing him up on it.

'I do not wish to discuss it. And with the goodwill of the gods it will never happen to your house.'

'Could you have stopped it?'

'What?'

'You weren't there. If you were, could you stop it?'

I sagged back against the side of the pool. 'When an emperor – or an empress – sends out that order, there is no power in the empire that can stop it.'

He registered the truth of this, and perhaps my answer is somewhat at the root of what was to come. Certainly I did little to diminish his curiosity and the deviousness with which he acquired information.

III

Scion of the Flavii

Rome, AD 58

Another year of Nero's reign passed with tension, but no disasters. Though Agrippina retained her bile for the Flavian house, her son, the new emperor, seemed not to care about the feud, and maintained the same sort of bored politeness towards my friends as he did to the rest of Rome's upper class. Agrippina's destructive influence waned as the months went on, for Nero was becoming less and less enamoured with his mother's controlling nature. The rift that had opened between them was becoming a chasm.

I was, I admit, pleasantly surprised by Rome's new ruler. From what I had witnessed during the demise of his predecessor, I had expected an indolent and cruel emperor. Nero was, as stories continue to dictate, something of a hedonist. The years that followed Claudius' death were characterised by lavish parties, such as the one whose invite we had declined, and the ever-deepening aggrandisement of Nero's dynasty and its connection to Rome. But despite his love of art, music and debauchery, I cannot fault the young man as an administrator. Under his aegis, Rome thrived and the machinery of empire continued to turn in order. Of course, much of that success should be accorded to Seneca, the emperor's former tutor and advisor of the time, but selecting the right men for the task and allowing them to do their job is half the battle in any position of authority. Oh, he took the precaution of making sure that Britannicus, his step-brother, crossed the final river to the world of shades, but only a fool took the throne and left a sibling with a better claim alive to fester, and few blamed him for that. And with Nero's support in my career, I was hardly going to miss his brother.

With this settling of matters, and apparently no immediate overt danger to myself or my Flavian allies, I moved away from Sabinus' *domus* once more. I acquired a good house on the Quirinal not far from the Flavii, I made connections and friends, became a regular courtier, took on well-connected clients, and began to climb the cursus honorum once more. I served as an aedile, and Flavius served in a similar role. In short, I began to make my way.

I maintained my connection and close relationship with my friends, though. Two years into Nero's reign, Flavius took a wife from the Cornelii, much to the delight of all. Sabinus and Vespasian, in the absence of my father to make such suggestions, continued to put forth names of well-connected girls that might grace my own house, though I continually swept such things aside. It was not that I disapproved of marriage, and not that I preferred the company of the male specimen, though such leanings were far from unusual among my class. It was simply that I was not interested in matrimony or female relationships. I think that I had always assumed it would happen when I needed to consider dynastic options, but it never seemed to be the right time. And so, as Flavius settled into married life, I continued to move in the court. On one occasion it was even suggested that I wed Vespasian's daughter Domitilla, now a demure young lady of thirteen, but in the end she was betrothed to the brilliant but headstrong young general Petilius Cerialis.

Sabinus, enjoying surprising favour from the new emperor, largely to spite his increasingly powerless mother, had taken on the position of urban prefect, controlling the cohorts that acted as Rome's home guard and police force, a prestigious and powerful command. Vespasian lived a quiet life, remaining careful not to become too noticeable, lest Agrippina move against him with that authority and power she could still muster. Titus had gone off to Germania to serve, finally, as a tribune in the legions, and his younger brother, Domitian, was now a precocious seven-year-old who I met frequently now during my visits to the houses, and who repeatedly surprised me with questions as he had that night in the baths. Every seven-year-old asks questions, of course, but not usually insightful ones that make one think hard before providing an answer. I became increasingly aware of this unusual youth, though I was yet to realise just how sharp, and perhaps how dangerous, he could be. That, I discovered one balmy spring night in the year of the consulship of Nero and Messalla.

I had been invited to one of the emperor's soirees once again, along with the Flavii, a move Nero made, as usual, deliberately to aggravate his mother, and one that this time we could hardly refuse. With Titus away, there were four of us, Sabinus, Flavius, Vespasian and myself. As always, Vespasian made a very successful attempt to blend into the background, keeping clear of Agrippina, who moved around the palace like a trireme on a war footing. Sabinus, being now in one of Rome's chief roles, was constantly sought after by social-climbing senators, and therefore so was his son. I was left about my own business, and moved through the swirling eddies of Rome's elite, making polite conversation and discussing inanities as though they were matters of state. Something like an hour of such activity began to wear on me, and I became bored. I tried to draw Flavius out to slip away and visit the Subura, where there was real entertainment to be had, rather than oiled eunuchs, bawdy poetry and endless flute melodies from naked trios. Sadly, Sabinus' recent elevation had made Flavius an important friend to have, and the crowds of tedious nobles flocking to him removed any chance of my friend and I escaping.

It took some doing to extricate myself, in fact, but finally I managed to slip away from the entertainments and leave them to it. I was of peripheral importance at such an event, after all, and was content I would not be missed. I had been announced, and it was known that I'd attended, which satisfied societal requirements.

I left by one of the palace's lesser doors to avoid fuss, receiving respectful nods from the Praetorians on guard as the slave opened the door. The night was warm and the sky a pleasing indigo colour, dotted with high, wisping cloud. The city was alive with lights, especially here in the heart of Rome; great torches and lamps burned on the Capitol, the sacred heart of the empire blazing golden and glorious. I walked for a change, to savour the night. I did not, of course, wave away the slaves and guards. Only a fool walks the streets of Rome alone at night.

I breathed in the calm, the quiet, as we threaded our way down the Palatine and across the forum. Here and there, as we passed through the less salubrious parts of the city, my guards moved more to the alert, stepping ahead to clear drunkards and trouble-makers off the street, and my slaves hurried forward constantly, making sure that the street was clear of ordure, one man with a brush carefully sweeping any mess into the gutter to prevent me soiling my boots. I enjoyed the walk, and in a little over half an hour I was climbing the Quirinal, closing on my house on the Vicus Bellonae, an area of the city so filled with parks and gardens it almost felt like open countryside. On the way, I passed the houses of my Flavian friends, close to the crest of the hill, and it was as I approached the domus of Vespasian that my interest was piqued.

Two men were slipping in through the door of Vespasian's house, dressed in the tunics of slaves and carrying heavy burdens.

I knew the house's door was controlled by Quarto, Vespasian's huge African doorman – no one could enter without his permission – but something still felt off. There was something almost clandestine about the way the slaves moved. With absolutely no evidence to base my suspicions upon, I was immediately convinced that something was amiss.

Vespasian was still at the palace with his brother, and Titus was off in Germania. The house would be run by the slaves and by Vespasian's majordomo in their absence, for his wife was now bed-ridden most of the time, and the only other family members present would be Domitian, still only a boy, and Domitilla.

I considered my options as I walked, slowing a little. I could trust to the Fates and walk on to relax in my own home. I could hurry to the palace to confide in Vespasian, or I could take direct action myself. I had no authority in the Flavian household, of course, but I was well known there, having spent much of the past six years within the family's walls.

I could not ignore this, and if I returned to the palace, it might be too late. Beckoning to three of the meanest-looking guards, I crossed to Vespasian's door and rapped on it. There was a short medley of shuffling and thudding, then the door was pulled open by Quarto, who bowed his head in respect, recognising me immediately. I was struck with uncertainty in that moment. Now that I had knocked, what was I supposed to ask? I breathed in slowly.

'You just admitted a group of slaves.'

'Yes, Domine.'

Now I sounded, and felt, foolish. What could be wrong, if Quarto was so open about it?

'Is your mistress up to receiving guests?'

The doorman's brow wrinkled as he thought this through. It would be unseemly for Flavia Domitilla to receive guests in her bedroom, and I understood that she was now too weak to leave the chamber without the support of slaves. It was while the doorman was formulating a polite refusal that a fresh voice cut into the conversation.

'It's all right, Quarto. I'll speak to him.'

We both turned to see the figure of Domitian standing in the atrium, dressed in an elegant tunic, soft calfskin shoes making no sound on the marble. He was tall for his seven years, with dark, curly hair and a serious face. I looked back to Quarto, who was clearly struggling. The idea of dropping a guest into the hands of a seven-year-old did not sit well with the big doorman, but equally, when all was said and done, Quarto was still a slave, and Domitian the son of his master. The doorman bowed to the boy and stepped back towards the door. I thought to invite in my guards for a moment, but realised that this would not be particularly appropriate in another man's house, and so I told them to wait outside as Quarto closed the door on them, leaving me in the elegant but austere hall of Vespasian's domus.

In the atrium, Domitian beckoned, and then stepped away. Frowning, I followed, uncertain now of why I was truly here, and feeling a little trepidation for some reason. Two slaves hurried past with armfuls of linen, bowing to both of us as they did so.

'Why are you here?' Domitian said quietly. No preamble. No subtlety. A direct question.

'I saw slaves enter the house, young man, and their manner was rather suspicious.'

'Hmm.' The boy stepped one pace back and looked me up and down in the most disconcerting manner. I felt as though I had been instantly appraised, like a slave on the block. Whatever the boy saw in me, though, seemed to put him at ease.

'I like you.'

The evening was becoming distinctly odd. I gave Vespasian's son an uncertain smile. 'I like you, too, boy.' I did, in fact. He reminded me in many ways of Sabinus. Serious and straightforward.

'You hate the emperor's mother, don't you?'

That made me look about in alarm. I knew we were in the house of a friend, and I was speaking to a boy, but some things were dangerous to say even when alone in a cupboard. I gestured to the family's winter dining room, disused this past month and left half-furnished and untouched. Domitian gave me an oddly furtive look and slipped inside. I followed and closed the door.

'Be careful what you say, Domitian.'

'It's true, though. Father says so. He says you are probably the only man in Rome who hates Agrippina as much as him. You and Nero, anyway.'

He gave a light, humourless chuckle at that. I didn't.

'What has this got to do with clandestine slaves?'

'Everything,' said the boy, his face becoming all the more serious. 'I have a secret.'

Another strange assertion, and one that silenced me.

34

'What?'

'I have… there is something I know. I don't know what to do with what I know, though. You might?' he prompted helpfully.

'You're talking in riddles, Domitian,' I said.

'I've prayed to Minerva for wisdom, and you came. Can I trust you?'

'Of course.'

Domitian narrowed his eyes for a moment, then nodded, opened the doors and marched out. I followed, feeling distinctly uneasy. The young scion of the Flavii led me through parts of the house with which I was unfamiliar, parts where only slaves habitually went. He pulled open a heavy door with a little difficulty, though the hinges were good and the door well-balanced, so that even slave boys could manage. Inside lay a sizeable storeroom. Large amphorae marked with their source ports stood in purpose-made holes in the floor, stacked neatly to left and right. One side was clearly liquamen or garum, fermented fish sauce, judging by the acrid smell, while the other side, just discernible, was filled with wine.

'Where are we going?'

'To find my secret.'

'Have you been eavesdropping again?' I was, of course, fairly sure he'd never stopped.

'You remember how you told me it was rude to listen in on conversations?' I nodded. 'Yet when you're a boy,' he went on, 'and everyone overlooks you, how else are you supposed to learn the important things? Then I realised. Slaves. Slaves are there to do our will. So I stopped listening at doors and got slaves to do it for me.'

I pursed my lips, disapproving. 'That is not precisely what I meant. Spying by proxy is still spying, Domitian.'

'But how will I hear things any other way? And you cannot rely on grown-ups to be sensible, no matter what Dad says. Him and Uncle Sabinus almost hit each other one night over someone called Caenis. I listened – or rather Baulo listened *for* me – and I managed to get them talking again. Amazing, really. I didn't even really know what the argument was about, but just the right word here and the right word there, and it was all all right again.'

'So you legitimise bad behaviour with results. Does the end justify the means, Domitian?'

'Yes,' the boy replied with surprising confidence. I wasn't sure I liked the sound of that, and felt uncertainty as Domitian crossed to a door in the opposite wall and knocked, slowly, three times. The door was opened for him, and he slipped through into a room lit by only a low glow.

I felt my senses tingling with the unknown and what now felt like danger. What was I doing? I was in the house of a friend while he was out, playing some strange game of his son's devising and all because I'd seen two slaves looking suspicious.

If I'd felt nervous crossing that threshold, it was nothing compared to the shock that filled me as I followed the boy into the next chamber.

I stopped in the doorway, eyes wide. Domitian stood to one side of this second storeroom, three of its walls covered with wooden racks filled with salted meats and boxes of vegetables. Pride of place, in the centre of the room, though, was given to a grim tableau. A low chair was occupied by a man, naked but for his loincloth. He was battered and bruised, his flesh discoloured across his chest, pelvis and upper arms, blood crusting on him in places. I stared in horror. Three slaves stood around the chair; one gripped an ash club, the others were the pair I had seen slip into the house. I now realised where they had been, for they had two buckets of water with them. They had been to the local fountain for supplies, hoping to clean up the mess.

I recognised the slaves only vaguely, as one remembers noteworthy furniture. They were Vespasian's slaves whom I had encountered in the house over the years. The battered man I did not know. Oddly, one observation occurred to me even as I tried to find my voice.

The man had been badly beaten, but carefully so. I had come across this in the legions in Britannia. When a soldier had pissed off his fellows, sometimes they would give him a pasting, but they would always restrict it to the torso and upper arms, so that when the man was dressed and armoured, nothing would show to betray their condition to an officer. Such incidents were only uncovered with visits to bath houses and the like.

'What the fuck is this?' I said, finally, my head snapping round to the boy, who seemed oddly calm and rational, given what had been happening here.

'My secret.'

'You've been torturing people? *That's* your secret?'

The boy shrugged. 'It's more than that. No one pays any attention to me, d'you know? I bet I could walk straight into one of Nero's parties and no one would even look at me. I think it's because I'm seven,' he added sagely. 'I'm not old enough to be important.'

I tried to marshal my thoughts. This had all the makings of a disaster. First, though, who was this poor bastard? I glanced at the victim, who lolled, a balled-up rag in his mouth. He was wearing a thong around his neck with a tag on. A slave, then. At least that was something. Domitian could still get in trouble for this, but at least it was just a slave. I crossed to the man and lifted the tag to identify the man's owner. Gaius Rubellius Plautus.

I dropped the tag as though it burned and turned, eyes wide again.

'Do you have any idea who this slave's owner is?' I spluttered.

'Of course. That's why he's here.'

'What?'

The boy gestured to one of his own slaves, who closed the door to prevent this exchange being too audible across the house. 'I told you. No one pays attention to me. I'm just there while they talk. I hear things. Lots of things.'

'Like how pissed off the emperor's relatives are going to be when their slaves go missing? Rubellius Plautus is a great grandson of Tiberius, for the love of Jove! Gods, but you've made a mess, boy. Your father is going to be livid.'

'Father doesn't notice me any more than anyone else unless I jump up and down and wave my arms. Listen, this is important.'

My mind was still whirling, trying to work out what to do, but I stood, and I listened.

'Take out the gag,' the boy ordered his slaves, who complied immediately. Domitian turned to me. 'This is Phillipus. He's Rubellius Plautus' nomenclator.' He spun back to the battered slave. 'Tell him what you told me.'

The slave, his expression hopeless, looked for a moment as though he might resist, but as the Flavian slaves gripped their ash sticks meaningfully, he sagged.

'My master...' he paused, and I realised then just how terrified this man was, and not just of Domitian and his slaves. 'My master is in league with the empress.'

'Agrippina?' I turned to Domitian. 'In league?'

'Listen,' the boy insisted, then gestured to the slaves. One of his men put an ash club under Phillipus' chin in a threatening manner, and another torrent of words fell from his lips. 'The empress means to kill her son.'

I stared again, a shiver running through me. Agrippina and a man who had a legitimate place in the succession were planning to do away with Nero? It should have sounded ridiculous. Fantastical. I should have disbelieved it on principle. What I found, though, as I stared at the weeping slave, was that I absolutely believed it. I knew Agrippina, knew what she was capable of. She had killed more than once to secure her son on the throne, and now that he was turning against her, she was showing once more that she had the maternal loyalty of a scorpion.

'When?' was the question that slipped out. Phillipus was too busy weeping and shaking to answer, even when threatened with the stick again, but Domitian stepped forward.

'Saturnalia. I overheard something, and I tried to tell Father about it, and Uncle Sabinus, too, but neither would listen.'

Gods, but the boy had been ignored, so he had taken action himself.

'I told you,' Domitian repeated himself, 'I don't know what to do now. I could bring Father or my uncle here, but I think they might be angry.'

'I think you're right.'

'But what else can I do? I can't go to the emperor, and nobody listens to a seven-year-old. You could help. You're important. And you hate Agrippina, too.'

I shook my head. What a mess. Vespasian would understand, eventually, but he'd still be furious. And Sabinus was the head of the law-keeping force in the city. Bringing kidnapping and assault on another man's property to his attention was unlikely to prove a popular decision. Neither of the elder Flavii could know about this, it would go badly for all involved.

'Gods, but this is messy. You should have come to someone first, and not done this.'

'I tried,' he reminded me. 'No one listens to me.'

'Right.' I straightened. Something had to be done, and soon. This all needed to go away before the palace party ended and Vespasian returned, but Domitian was right that this information was critical. Something had to be done with it. I had the feeling that the palace would be a dead end. I was not important enough to secure a private meeting with the emperor, and I could hardly go shouting this news on the Palatine. I couldn't tell the Flavii about it, given how they were unwittingly involved. Domitian or his slaves had had the sense not to make their assault on any visible part of the man, but returning him to his house immediately risked much. If he ran to Rubellius Plautus and confessed, he might well die, but everything would be discovered. If the slave simply disappeared, it might be better for all, but right now he also represented the only evidence anyone had of a plot. We needed someone who would be sympathetic, who hated Agrippina but who was removed enough from the palace to be accessible.

As the slaves dressed Phillipus and returned him to a semblance of normality, I thought carefully, working through every name I could pluck from the air. The answer was so clear that when it struck me, I blinked.

Within the hour we were in the house of Junia Silana on the Esquiline. Once Agrippina's closest friend, the pair had become the vilest of enemies some years previously. Junia lived a somewhat lascivious lifestyle, a widow with a reputation for entertaining many of Rome's men. Whatever her reputation, though, she retained imperial connections, had a sharp mind, already had spies in place, and, best of all, she would give her own arm to see Agrippina fall.

We were shown in, the battered nomenclator escorted under guard to a room by our slaves, and once Junia had dismissed everyone barring myself, Domitian and two burly Iberian guardsmen so underdressed that little was left to the imagination, I explained it all.

The woman, once one of Rome's most powerful, shot a calculating look at Domitian, and then fixed me with something similar.

'My own popularity at court is shaky, Cocceius Nerva,' she said flatly.

'With respect, Domina, there is no one else in Rome who could stand up to the empress and survive. It has to be you. And you know what's at stake.'

'If this is not all lies.'

'I am confident it is the truth.'

She nodded slowly, and I tried a new tack. 'And think of the potential benefits if we can do this. If you can persuade the emperor? Not only the removal of your arch enemy, but also the favour of the emperor. Can you afford not to help us? Sooner or later, Agrippina will get to you the way she gets to everyone.'

'I think you underestimate me, Nerva. I have eyes and ears at every doorway from Gaul to Africa. Nothing happens in this city without my knowledge. Juno, man, but I'd even heard of Rubellius Plautus' slave going missing, though I am surprised who it is that took him.'

Something made me glance sidelong at Domitian. He was so entirely expressionless that I knew instantly he was absorbing everything she said. Gods, but *all* the boy needed was Junia's clandestine influence. I should have left him at home and come on my own.

'All right,' she said finally, 'but you are not talking about a game of stones in the forum. You are talking about taking on Rome's most powerful harpy. If I am to pitch my army into the battle I would know that I am fighting alongside a strategist of note. How would you proceed? Surely not with marching to the palace with no reserve force?'

I shook my head. The military analogy appealed to me. I am no lover of subterfuge, and the straightforward explanation made things much simpler.

'We have evidence, but it is just a little. One slave's testimony. That is a veteran front line in the attack. But a front line is of little use without the following ranks. We need other evidence, other testimonies.'

'And how do we get them?'

She was testing me, but my mind was already racing. 'Spies in the houses concerned.' I shivered. 'But I cannot do such a thing. I am tied to the Flavii, and if I am discovered, then I will bring disaster to their house.'

She gave me a wry smile. 'While I am disposable?'

'Hardly,' I replied hurriedly. 'But you just told us that you had eyes and ears at every doorway from Gaul to Africa. Including Agrippina's? Or Rubellius Plautus'?'

That raised a wry smile from her that came, I noted, with no denial.

The discussion went on for a while, but it was more a formality now. From the moment I had highlighted the chance of ruining Agrippina I knew I had her. By the time we departed her house, leaving the slave Phillipus in her care, and began to make our way back to the Quirinal, she had readily agreed to bring the matter to the emperor's attention. A little cleaning up by the slaves at home, and none of this might ever have happened.

As we walked away I could not help noticing the lad's calculating expression as he looked back at Junia's house. That presaged trouble.

We approached Vespasian's house once more, and as I prepared with heartfelt relief to amble off home and try to forget all about tonight, Domitian broke the silence.

'You don't approve.'

I sighed. 'This was dangerous and stupid, Domitian. Just be grateful that things seem to have worked out this time, and never speak of this to anyone. I hope your three slaves can keep their mouths shut, too.'

They would, of course. They were slaves, so they couldn't refuse Domitian's commands, but they would all be aware of what lay in store for them if they told their master what they had done.

'Teach me, then.'

'What?' I stopped outside the door.

'You say there are better ways. Teach me them.'

'No. This won't happen again.'

'I had a problem,' Domitian said quietly. 'Just like when my father and uncle were arguing, there was a problem, and I solved it. Now I've solved this one.'

'And we may have done the empire a service, but your little stunt could very easily have seen both our families fall from grace. Go back to being overlooked, Domitian. Believe me, it's a great deal safer.'

IV

Body after body

Rome, AD 59

Junia Silana gathered what evidence she could, which would certainly have been sufficient to condemn most people, and took it to the emperor. He had, apparently, been aghast, and yet had refused to believe it, even of Agrippina.

She had been summoned, arrived insolently late and arrayed as an empress, and simply brushed aside the entire allegation as a fabrication of her enemies, noting that a slave's word was suspect even under torture. She had been so forceful and direct that the emperor had crumbled in his resolve and abandoned pursuit of the trial.

Agrippina struggled on.

I had been to see Junia then, fretting over what we could do. There was no doubt in our minds that Agrippina was still capable of such a coup, and though Saturnalia passed without incident, it seemed likely that the conspirators' plans had been delayed rather than foiled. Many a man might have let go of the whole matter then. She was, after all, an almost unassailable target. But beyond the Flavii, I had more cause to want her to fall than most. I had enjoyed a comfortable upbringing with a loving family and had gone out into the world to make my name, only to come home to a butchered father, all on her command. I was beholden to no one but the gods, and the notion of letting that harpy get away with what she had done was too much for me.

Junia Silana had managed to slip two spies, her best people, into Agrippina's house, and one into that of Gaius Rubellius Plautus, explaining that the moment a move was made she would hear about it, and a fresh accusation could be levelled. Agrippina was sly, though, and still nothing seemed to happen.

And so the empress continued to try and inveigle her way back into the centre of power, attempting to assert her control over her son. Rubellius Plautus disappeared into careful obscurity for a while, and Nero continued to live the life of a rich playboy while his able administration ran the empire. The months passed with the rift between the emperor and his mother ever-present, sitting before us like a fault in the land.

Sabinus continued to acquit himself well as the prefect of the urban cohort, and slowly garnered a reputation as one of Rome's most honourable and trustworthy men. Flavius quietly and carefully lobbied for a minor governorship, though he remained unsatisfied. Vespasian continued to play the game of careful obscurity, staying away from Agrippina. His wife finally passed away that winter, with little fuss. The effect it had on young Domitian was deeper than any of us realised at the time, for even at eight years old, he was already a master of disguising his true feelings, and he seemed to greet her final, blessed passing with the same stoic calm as his father. After all, she had been on the verge of death for years. After an appropriate period of mourning, Domitian went very quiet, seemingly drawing into himself and concentrating on his studies. In retrospect, I should have realised that, with a boy as bright as him, apparent inactivity was extremely suspicious. Still, in light of what he'd done the previous spring, I heaved a sigh of relief that Domitian's adventure seemed to have been an isolated incident, and he had gone quiet now. Foolish.

Still, into this strange, strained world, I moved once more. The court was a place of extreme tension now, for every day we all wondered what fresh developments would arise in the relationship between the emperor and his mother. Nero seemed to have descended into childish games, sending messages summoning her and then feigning ignorance as to why and sending her home again, having her favourite slaves arrested on spurious charges, and parts of them returned to her in gift boxes, and generally making life stupidly unpleasant for her.

He must have assumed she was taking all this in her stride, though those of us who knew her better had formed other opinions. Junia Silana had received messages from her spies in the empress's villa of suspicious meetings. Nothing concrete that could be used as evidence, but highly suggestive that the empress was expanding her former plot to include more and more powerful persons in the city. Something was coming to a head, and we all knew it. The morning *salutatio*, where the emperor greeted his noble clients and heard petitions in the *aula regia*, was becoming sparsely attended. Few men were comfortable in the imperial presence, and those who were kept one eye on the exit at all times.

That was the atmosphere on the morning I stood in the ante-chamber of the emperor's reception hall with the small cluster of other senators waiting for our audience. A friendly face in the crowd both surprised and pleased me as we stood shivering, breath frosting, even the heavy wool togas doing little to warm us. Vespasian wandered over between the gathered nobility, that creased, pleasant face bearing an odd smile. It was rare in these days to see the younger Flavian brother at court where he might draw the eye of Agrippina, but I welcomed his presence as he approached and reached out to grasp my hand.

'Marcus Cocceius Nerva, well met. I have been meaning to speak to you for some time.'

'Oh? How can I help?' I answered, assuming he had some favour to ask.

He grasped me by the shoulder and steered me over towards a wall, a little away from the murmuring gaggle of senators. When we were in a more secluded place, he fixed me with an appraising look. 'I have been speaking with Epaphroditus.'

The emperor's secretary. I felt a shiver. 'Oh?' I said again.

'The sharp-minded Epaphroditus is attempting to divine the truth behind the accusations levelled against Agrippina. He is of the opinion that there is further evidence to be found, and he scratches at it like a terrier. He summoned me to answer questions about the matter, and I have been making my own enquiries, just for my personal peace of mind.'

I felt like a trapdoor was opening up beneath me. I tried to remain calm and measured as I nodded for him to continue.

'It seems that Phillipus, the slave whose evidence lay at the heart of this, was taken on a night both I and Rubellius Plautus were at the palace. My doorman tells me that you visited our house that night. He also notes some curious activity involving three of my slaves, coming and going in the presence of both you and my son.'

'I called in on my way home,' I said, a kernel of truth there. 'I noted your slaves carrying water to the house. There was something furtive about their manner and, given your absence, I thought I should check to be certain that nothing was amiss. Nothing was, of course.'

'Very neighbourly of you,' Vespasian said, his eyes narrow in suspicion. 'I spoke to the slaves involved. I have no intention of torturing them – good slaves are hard to come by – but the possibility of forced interrogation has occurred to me. I dislike being lied to by slaves, and they told me, barefaced, that they attended my son Domitian that night. I spoke to the boy, and he was adamant that nothing untoward had happened. That you visited and then left.'

He folded his arms. 'The problem is that I know Domitian, and I know when he's lying. I won't punish the slaves as they are acting on his orders, I'm certain. And somehow, whatever he and you cooked up that night, it appears to have left no evidence. Still, Epaphroditus seems to have pinpointed our family as somehow involved along with Junia Silana, who I know to have been a friend of your father's.'

I winced, then. Word of Flavian involvement reaching the palace could be trouble.

'If you will allow me to come and see you in a more private setting,' I muttered, 'I believe I can settle all these matters.'

'I doubt it,' Vespasian said, though an odd smile was creeping across his rough features now. 'I fear that one tug on the stitches of this particular blanket and the whole thing will unravel. Fear not, young Nerva. I came not to accuse you. I simply wished to reassure myself of what I already knew of you. I have more than an inkling of what happened that night. Domitian thinks I ignore him. I do not. And while Titus might be my glorious heir and beloved of the city, I am starkly aware that my younger son harbours an intelligence that could put us all to shame. No, nothing further will come of this. There is no trouble arising. In fact, Epaphroditus would prefer it if more citizens could provide evidence of such plots. It would make maintaining the imperial safety a great deal easier.'

He slapped me on the shoulder. 'In fact, Nero was pleased, apparently. That his loyal subjects would risk the empress's wrath to preserve his wellbeing impressed him greatly. I have been welcomed back into court circles, and the secretary has even made the suggestion that I might be offered the governorship of Africa. It would seem that your clandestine antics have had an unexpected effect on my career.'

He laughed, probably at my baffled expression. 'Still,' he said, 'it would not do to get involved in such things too often. I think that here Flavian involvement needs to end. Domitian needs to be taught a little more self-control, I think, And since I am fairly sure that it was you who took his mess and tied it up tightly, disposing of it, I am inclined to beg a favour of you.'

'A favour?'

'Domitian goes through tutors like a scythe through wheat. None of them can cope with him. With all my responsibilities I do not have time to take a paternal interest in his education, his mother is beyond the veil now, and his nurse does what she can, but she cannot replace a mother and a tutor. I wonder if you wouldn't mind taking the boy under your wing for a time. You are, I understand, between positions at the moment and simply taking part in court life. I suspect my clever but rash boy could learn much from your steady, thoughtful influence. What say you?'

Well, what choice did I have? I owed the Flavii for their support and hospitality when my father had fallen to the empress's blades, and they had guided and helped me ever since. To refuse would have been churlish to say the least. Besides, somewhere deep down, I felt a small thrill at the idea. Domitian was an interesting lad. He was too clever by half, and seemed to lack the social niceties drummed into the majority of our class. A bright boy given to speaking plainly regardless of consequence was fresh and welcome in imperial Rome.

As it happens, I never had the opportunity to accept that morning, for as I smiled, the door nearby burst open so suddenly and forcefully that it slammed back against the wall, sending dust and chips of painted plaster across the floor. The gathering of the rich and the great pulled back from the doorway, their conversation falling away into silence. Vespasian and I were already out of the way as the emperor swept in, garbed in a rich toga of purple and gold, scattered with stitched images of gods. He wore a radiate golden crown as though the sun burst from his head, but any magnificence his attire was intended to put forth was ruined by his face, which was screwed into a ball of fury. I had never seen him so angry, and resolved immediately to stay well out of his way. Vespasian clearly had the same idea, and we pulled off to the side. The emperor, hissing imprecations and curses like a fishwife, stormed off into the next room, Praetorians pulling open the doors for him. In his wake came half a dozen functionaries, including Epaphroditus and his own secretary, a dark-skinned youth with a worried expression, then a dozen Praetorians. Notably, though, two of his entourage represented the martial contingent of Rome. Sextus Afranius Burrus, the Praetorian prefect, strode side by side with Flavius Sabinus, commander of the urban cohort. To see the two almost rival officers together was unusual enough to draw comment. As they tramped into the room, Sabinus caught sight of the two of us and beckoned, exchanging a few words with Burrus and then veering off, heading for a door that led to one of the various administrative offices.

With a jerk of his thumb and a command, Sabinus ejected the scribe working there and, as soon as Vespasian and I were inside, shut the door.

'What has happened?' Vespasian asked quietly.

'Our beloved emperor actually lost the power of speech for a while,' Sabinus replied. 'It seems he has reached the end of his tether with his mother. Unbeknownst to us all, he has been working some ridiculous and convoluted plot to dispose of her quietly. She was supposed to drown this morning. The ship he sent to her to bring her to the palace was designed to sink on the jerk of a lever. It has taken a team of engineers and naval architects two months to build the vessel in secret at Ostia. Agrippina should have drowned, and all would have been well.'

'And?' I urged, marvelling at the lunatic genius of the plan.

'And the ship reached the city limits, obediently collapsed and sank. Forty-seven men died, but Agrippina somehow managed to get clear of the wreckage, swam ashore and arrived at her villa in the city dripping wet and not a little angry.'

'Gods,' Vespasian breathed. 'She will not take this lying down. The repercussions will be dreadful. We should perhaps leave the city until it blows over.'

Sabinus gave his younger sibling a flat look. 'This is not going to blow over, brother. You saw the emperor's face. He is one short step from having her crucified.'

'What do we do?' I asked.

'I am going to try and talk the emperor down before he does something he will regret. Disperse that crowd out there. There will be no morning salutatio today, and anyone within sight of the emperor might be in danger this morning.'

Vespasian nodded. 'Keep us informed,' he said, as we left the room once more into that open hallway where senators busily murmured their surprise and their theories. As Vespasian and I tried to draw their attention, Sabinus made for the door through which the emperor had passed, but before he could reach it, the door slammed open once more and Burrus and his Praetorians emerged, an entire squad of them with grim expressions, prepared for violence.

Sabinus intercepted his fellow prefect.

'What happens now?'

Burrus kept his voice low, but not low enough, thankfully. 'The empress is to be executed for treason. Now. By Praetorian blades.'

Sabinus simply stared in horror at Burrus, who shrugged his impotence in this and marched off with his men to murder an empress. I felt my pulse pick up, my mind racing. I turned to Vespasian, who had gone pale. 'What will they do with the rest of the household?'

He looked back to me. 'What else? All witnesses will die. The household is disposable.'

I had guessed as much, but to have it confirmed sent another thrill of panic through me. Vespasian had said only moments ago that Flavian involvement in all this needed to end. But Praetorians were making for Agrippina's house in Rome to do away with her and her household, among them two spies of Junia Silana's. It would not take a great deal to trace them to her and then, through her, to Vespasian and Domitian. Without explanation, I left Vespasian looking surprised and hurried to the door.

I had only moments. The Praetorians were already on the move. They would march at a steady military pace, but I needed to warn Hermes and Prima, the two Silanan spies, and get them away from the villa. As I emerged into the chilly morning air, I could already see the soldiers marching off down the slope of the Palatine towards the Via Sacra. My own entourage waited obediently as always. I hurried over to them, gesturing to the commander of my guards.

'I need to reach a villa on the far bank of the river with all haste. Send the slaves home and bring only men who can run.'

As he issued the commands, I ran over to my litter and spoke to the burly Gaul who led the carriers. 'Take Caligula's stairway and head for the Campus Martius. Cross the Neronian Bridge. We need to be fast.'

I regretted my words almost immediately as my litter bearers lifted the enclosed seat from the ground and hefted it, taking a deep breath. Then they broke into a jog, half a dozen of my guards keeping pace. We reached the top of the great staircase Caligula had constructed to connect the forum with his palace on the hill, and then began a terrifying, swaying and bumpy breakneck descent. I swear my teeth had loosened by the time we reached the level of the forum, and I had bitten my tongue twice. Then we were off again. No one gives much thought to the slaves who carry their litter, but it occurred to me on that uncomfortable journey just how strong and fit they need to be, surpassing any bulky gladiator.

We pounded through the streets of the Campus Martius and even through the curtains of my litter I could sense the change in the air as we passed from the crowded streets to the open bridge across the river. I twitched the curtain aside then, to see Agrippina's villa set in a swathe of manicured gardens stretching down to the water's edge. The villa itself was a grand affair, as befitted the sister, wife and mother of emperors. My own not-overly-modest home could have fit into one wing of this palace, with room to spare. My heart raced again, then. I had, apparently, underestimated the Praetorians. Somehow they had managed to get ahead of me, despite my speed, for I could see their gleaming shapes on the far side of the river already approaching the gate in the villa's boundary wall.

If I'd had any hope that this was going to be anything less than a bloodbath, I was disabused of that notion straight away. As we bounced and lurched across the bridge, I watched everything through the window of my litter. The Praetorians hammered on the gate, demanding admittance. When the doorkeeper refused and guards were summoned, the Praetorians did what they did best. They tore through the gatehouse as though assaulting a Gaulish *oppidum*, butchering with impunity. Bodies were dragged back and hurled into the street, where the ordinary folk of Rome melted away into doors and alleys to avoid being drawn into the chaos.

I knew then that I was too late and there was no hope of saving the two spies. I gave the order and, at the right bank we pulled over to the side and I left the vehicle, leaning on the bridge's rail and watching events unfold at Agrippina's villa.

Twenty Praetorians, led by a centurion, finished off any resistance at the gate. While four split off and scoured the grounds, putting a blade through anyone they found, the rest entered the villa proper. I could hear the screams and the shouting all the way from the bridge. I watched it all with mixed feelings. I was nervous that the two spies would somehow be connected distantly to myself and the Flavii, and I was disgusted at such wanton butchery within the very city of Rome. Yet a small and dark part of me revelled in the final fall of the woman who had been responsible for my own father's death, and because of whom the Flavii had lived for a decade in constant fear of accusation. Gods, but a few short years ago I would have paid all I had to be the man wielding that blade.

It did not take long. Body after body was brought out until the entire population of the villa lay in the cold morning air. Agrippina herself was still in her bath-house gown, the expensive pale blue garment so stained with crimson that it was visible even from such a distance.

So fell Agrippina, Rome's most wicked woman. In some small way, Domitian and myself had had a hand in her fall, and that felt both right and good, despite how sickening it might be to watch. As I saw it all happen, I had been thankful that the threat to the emperor had ended. Nero might have his faults, but he was a damn sight better than bitter old Claudius, and at least under Nero Rome felt positive.

I stood there for an hour, and then left and returned to my house. I did not want to see Vespasian, Flavius, Sabinus or even Domitian right then. I was struggling with how I'd felt watching the empress being heaped up with the dead.

I am somewhat pleased I did not stay. I understand from trustworthy sources that Nero attended shortly thereafter, intending to be certain that his mother was dead. He had her cut into pieces to be sure, then had eastern mystics carry out strange rituals to banish even her shade from the house and from Rome, desperate to see even the last shreds of her influence removed for all time. No proper burial was accorded to any victim of Nero's purge that morning.

Sadly, though undoubtedly Agrippina deserved her fate, that bloodthirsty morning was a blow to Nero's reputation. No matter how wicked the empress, the people of Rome frown upon matricide. Stories of rigged ceilings and collapsing ships made their way around the city, and the simple butchery of an empress by the Praetorians was seen as a crime the blame for which, though it might only be whispered in dark corners, was firmly at Nero's feet. It would take much work to recover.

The aftermath of the event was not as brutal as one might expect, though myself and the Flavii were lucky to escape it all with no stigma. The investigation at the villa that followed the deaths turned up two slaves known to have belonged to Junia Silana. She was exiled to the south that same month, and died in uncertain circumstances by the end of the summer. Even to her deathbed she kept any involvement of myself or the Flavii a secret. Gaius Rubellius Plautus, Agrippina's co-conspirator, was also exiled, in his case far away to family estates in Asia. He stayed there until an execution for treason several years later.

For us, at least, Rome had settled once more. The wicked empress was gone, the throne was secure, and at last there was no impediment to us taking our rightful place at court. Even Vespasian had now become one of Nero's favoured. I took on the responsibility of being Domitian's sometime tutor, sometime guide for Vespasian, and the boy seemed to have done with his clandestine antics, perhaps a little put off by the lack of recognition he received for his part in so aiding his father's rise. Things became normal, and we heaved a collective breath of relief.

There is always a calm before a great storm.

V

Spies

Rome, AD 63

For a while, it seemed that Rome was blossoming for the Cocceii and the Flavii. Despite the stigma that clung to Nero over his mother's murder, there were sufficient extenuating circumstances to offset the downside, notably that Agrippina remained a villain in the eyes of much of the empire, and Nero was, whatever his faults might be, a truly likeable and personable emperor. With Seneca and Epaphroditus working the rumour mill, matricide gradually came to be seen as a justifiable response to an attempted coup by a wicked mother. Nero enjoyed an almost unprecedented level of support from the general populace, which is not to say that certain sectors of society were not opposed to him.

His hedonism and carefree approach to life were reaching new heights, but the administration continued to work smoothly. As the details of Agrippina's plot and its unravelling became public, imperial gratitude for anyone who'd had a part in its discovery grew. Vespasian and his family became highly favoured at court, and while Sabinus continued to serve as the urban prefect, the younger brother was indeed given the lucrative governorship of Africa with an unwritten mandate to make himself rich. My part in proceedings was slightly overblown, and I was granted triumphal honours, a privilege usually reserved only for military success. My statue was placed in the palace alongside other such men, including the great generals Germanicus and Corbulo. I downplayed this, naturally.

I had agreed to keep an eye on the twelve-year-old Domitian, since Titus was still abroad until later in the year, and Vespasian now installed at Carthage. The young man's mother was now gone, and his sister had been married and moved out to the house of Cerialis. Domitian's education had already surpassed most children his age, and short of sending him to learn in Athens, for which he was still a little young, I just set him reading histories and military and social treatises. The boy was fast approaching adulthood, yet little about his nature seemed to have changed. He remained quiet, thoughtful, direct and sharp. He had begun to pay his personal devotions principally to Minerva, goddess of, among other things, wisdom, of tactics, and of justice, which already gave some indication of the direction in which his personality was developing. I had hoped to secure a position as praetor in that time, a precursor to provincial governorship, but it seemed that Nero liked to have me around and so I served in a series of lesser curatorships in the city. I was brought closer to imperial circles, spending much time with Seneca, advising the emperor.

I had begun, over those years after Agrippina's fall, to introduce Domitian to the palace, reasoning that he was only a few short years away from taking the adult's toga, and that with the family's increased court presence, he was likely to begin to move in imperial circles along with Vespasian, Sabinus and Titus. I had thought it important that Domitian learn how to act at court. The young man was always a little socially awkward, a problem born from his overly direct approach to all things, and I had assumed I would be able to ease him into a more comfortable attitude. I was wrong, of course. Where I had thought that Domitian, clever as he was, would take to the life and start to understand his place in it, what this exposure actually did was to put the young man more and more off such a social whirl.

I was foolish, for I was so involved with Seneca in keeping the emperor in the hearts of the people and making sure that his empire continued to function that I failed to notice the effect Domitian's exposure to the palace was having. It transpired that meeting more and more courtiers and senators settled in the young man's mind an unbendable impression that the majority of our class were little more than parasites, clinging to the body of the court and sucking gold and power from it. In truth he was probably a lot more shrewd in that observation than I have given him credit for. But generations of emperors have taught us that no matter how unimportant the senate might truly be, it is foolish and dangerous to ignore them.

There was an upside to this, though. While Domitian shied away from his 'parasites' and developed an almost prudish and sneering disapproval of the world of eunuchs, whores and catamites that graced the imperial chambers, he spent more and more time with the machinery of empire. In avoiding the rich, he came to know the freedmen and the low-born who carried out the actual work. Over the years his tutors had taught him all that a noble Roman should know, but now Seneca taught him the value of keeping an eye on the attitude and movements of those around us, and Epaphroditus taught him the importance of maintaining a working government, no matter what happens in the grand halls of the palace. He struck up an unexpected friendship with Epaphroditus' own secretary, a young Indian slave with a mind of order and intelligence to match Domitian's.

I dropped in one day on my way back from a meeting to find my young charge and one of the slaves of the treasury deep in conversation. Not having been noticed in the doorway, I listened with interest, which is ironic, given the role reversal with our earlier relationship.

'So the emperor's treasury is much larger than that of the empire?'

The slave nodded respectfully. 'Of all the provinces, the income of two thirds goes to the imperial fiscus, a third to the public aerarium, Domine.'

'Surely that's not right. I know the emperor likes his parties, but how much can they cost?'

The slave shrank back, aware that such pronouncements could bring about visits to the palace cellars for a beating, and that he was on dangerous ground now. 'Domine, the public chest has limited funds, but limited expenditure. The imperial chest pays for the army, the cities' infrastructure, the upkeep of temples and much more. The emperor receives the lion's share of the taxes, but his responsibilities are far greater than those of the senate.'

The slave suddenly noticed me in the doorway, a man of senatorial rank, and his face paled at his own words, which might have been perceived as a slight. For myself I didn't really care what a slave thought of imperial responsibilities, but I did wonder what Domitian thought, and so I beckoned to him. 'Time to leave.'

In short, I suspect that, while four years of exposure to the palace irreparably damaged his ability to smoothly integrate into the court and fuelled his old-fashioned and prim view of what was and what was not acceptable, it also taught the young man more about the actual functioning of empire.

I was becoming more impressed with this Flavian prodigy by the day. While he did not have his uncle Sabinus' way with court, he had the same devotion to duty and understanding of the importance of hard work. While he did not have Vespasian's easy humour and ability politick, he had every bit of his father's shrewdness and more. And while he did not have his brother's active and military energy, he was far more attentive than Titus, and was proving unexpectedly to be something of an archer in his spare time.

Domitian was growing into something that would surpass his own family.

I returned from the Palatine one September afternoon, planning to visit Domitian, who had taken the morning off in his home, and then to change in my own domus and spend an hour or two at the baths. I had planned to invite Domitian along with me, and at the social hub of the city, while we were fed and massaged, introduce him to a couple of the brighter senators in the hope that I could expand his net of contacts.

I reached the house of Vespasian and was led to the triclinium. Domitian was seated with a cup of watered wine and a small plate of pastries, his face thunderous and pale. I frowned. I had not seen him like this before. Domitian was usually too measured to let emotions seize him so. I crossed to the seat opposite and, without seeking permission, sank into it. I waited for a moment and, since the young man seemed to hardly notice me, his gaze locked on a letter lying before him on the table, I poured and watered a wine for myself and took a sip, patiently awaiting Domitian's attention.

Finally, he looked up.

'The whore has joined my father.'

I took another sip, placed my cup on the table, and took a breath, fixing him with a look of disapproval at his manner. 'You may have to explain that, Domitian.'

'Caenis. The whore.'

I cast back my mind. The name was familiar, and it took a while for me to connect it. Flavius had told me of Antonia Caenis back when we served together in Britannia, but it had been a long time since her name had arisen. She had been the private secretary of Antonia, daughter of the great Marcus Antonius. She and Vespasian had been close enough in his youth to draw a great deal of attention, only ending their relationship when he had married. I remembered Flavia Domitilla, in her grave this past three years, and had an inkling now of what she had meant to the boy.

'He still loves and respects your mother's memory.'

He looked at me and I did not like what I saw in his eyes. 'Caenis is a whore. That was all she ever was. My mother is barely cold, and how does my father respect her memory? He brings his favourite whore to share his bed in Africa.'

I did think that was a little unfair. Vespasian and his wife might have enjoyed a reasonable and respectful marriage, but like most of our class their match was made for financial and political advantage and had nothing to do with their hearts. Indeed, while Vespasian had likely always longed after Caenis, Flavius had once intimated that Vespasian's wife had also left a man she loved in Sabratha for the marriage. Such messy relationships are but one of the reasons I had always avoided them. The lack of a surviving father to push me into uncomfortable matches helped, of course.

'Whatever you think of Antonia Caenis,' I said, 'when they return to Rome remember to be polite and circumspect with her. She may not be your mother, but if she is your father's woman, no good will come of conflict.'

I thought it was good advice. I really did. Domitian did not look so convinced. As he had grown, his own moral code had become stricter and stricter. In fairness, spending time in the palace of Nero, where flesh was always pliable and available and where the eunuchs were trained to service the nobility, probably did little to ease his prudishness. There were times when I too winced at the things I witnessed in Nero's court, after all.

We lapsed into an uncomfortable silence as I tried to find a way to lighten the mood before inviting him to the baths. Domitian continued to sip his wine and read the letter again and again, his expression darkening gradually.

We both looked up sharply as a furious hammering noise arose somewhere across the house. A pause, and it began again. Someone was at the front door, and their call for attention sounded either urgent, or angry, or both. In a moment born of those days watching our backs in Agrippina's Rome, I immediately tried to run through what potential enemy could be coming for us, but those days were gone. The Flavii didn't have enemies in this new Rome. Still, Domitian shared my warning look. At a single call, while Quarto answered the door, Domitian had half a dozen of his burlier slaves attend in the triclinium.

I moved my chair closer to that of my young companion, facing the door, as the sound of angry voices by the front door culminated in a thud and a cry of pain. For a moment I assumed that Quarto had dealt with the new arrival in time-honoured fashion, but the sound of several fast, heavy, booted footsteps told me that it was, instead, Quarto who had been struck and knocked aside. I glanced to the slaves gathered around us, nerves beginning to pinch at me. How much use would they be against a house-breaking villain who had already floored a trained doorman?

My heart pounded as the boots approached, and I felt a moment of true panic as a figure appeared in the doorway, for he was wearing the uniform of a Praetorian officer. Visions flashed through my head of that day of horror when Praetorians heaped the bodies of my father and his household together unceremoniously in our atrium. The cold sweat trickled down my back even as I realised that I recognised this man. Flavius Scaevinus, a distant cousin of Vespasian's, and currently a Praetorian tribune.

He came to a halt in the atrium, standing straight, arms folded, as four heavy-set mercenaries dragged a man in a slave tunic into the open space before the door. The slave was unharmed, but his eyes were wild, and the wet of a fresh flood of urine stained his nethers. He was whimpering in panic.

Scaevinus' face was set in a granite expression, but despite the lack of visible emotion, it was clear to me immediately just how angry the man was. At that moment, a suspicion flickered through me, and I glanced sideways at Domitian. The young man was sitting calm, unblinking, though I could see the cords standing out in his neck, betraying his tension. He was like a cobra, still, but ready to strike. Unbidden, images of that cellar and the bloodied slave that had revealed Agrippina's plot leapt into my head.

I had assumed that Domitian had left such pursuits behind.

I had apparently been wrong.

The slave was thrown roughly to the ground where he grovelled, making desperate pleas. Scaevinus, arms still folded, took one step forward, holding the slave down with a hobnailed military boot pressed to his neck.

'It has always been the way,' the tribune said in a menacing tone, 'that the house of the Flavii look after one another. It is how we have risen from rural obscurity to positions of power in Rome. While the serpents of court writhe about one another, the Flavii remain united and strong.'

Domitian said nothing, coiled, ready to strike.

'Cousin or no cousin, son of Vespasian, I will not have spies in my house.'

My worst fears were confirmed. I shifted uneasily in my seat, wondering how best to attempt to calm the situation. Scaevinus was not finished, though.

'The next time I find one of your spies in my domus, I will bring the matter up with the emperor, but not before I have the spy peeled, salted and delivered to you in pieces.'

Still, Domitian did not react, his expression unreadable, his eyes unblinking. So cold was he, in fact, that I found myself wondering whether this was all a mistake, and whether the young man was not to blame.

No. I knew he was.

Two of the mercenaries stepped forward now. While the slave gasped and whimpered beneath the Praetorian's boot, his men produced a stout length of wood and took a position to each side of the prone prisoner. Their first blows broke both the man's legs, sending his whimpering into howls of agony as he writhed and thrashed, unable to escape the heavy pressure of the boot on his neck. The clubmen continued about their work, delivering blow after blow, a beating that could easily kill a man, and brought the slave right to the brink.

Still, Domitian did not move. Silently, he watched. I found that I had reached the edge of my seat, my fingers wrapped around the wooden chair arms, ready to rise. I watched the beating continue for just a moment, and finally pushed myself to my feet.

'Stop this at once,' I bellowed.

The two men with the clubs did so, surprised at the violence in my tone. I was angry now. I never angered easily, and men have often mistaken my calm and personable demeanour for a pacifistic nature. But I had served in campaigns in the bloody hills of Britannia, and I had seen my share of death and violence. I did not shirk from it. And this display had to end.

'Who is this?' Scaevinus spat, seemingly noticing me for the first time. His brow creased in thought, and he straightened a little, stepping back off the slave's neck. 'Cocceius Nerva. I've seen you in court, Sabinus' puppy. Who are you to give my men commands in a house of the Flavii?'

'In Vespasian's absence, I am the guardian appointed for his son here. As such I have considerably more authority in this house than you.' Scaevinus' eyes narrowed dangerously, but I had no intention of letting him take the initiative once more. 'You threaten a boy in the absence of his father with bringing to the emperor's attention some imagined misdemeanour that I am sure will be extremely difficult to prove? Let me retort with this, Flavius Scaevinus. While you might imagine you can threaten us with such a wrongdoing, I have half a mind to drag you through the courts with sufficient witnesses to the fact that you broke into a man's house, beat his doorman and then enacted a display of torture in front of an innocent boy. I wonder how well that will sit with your reputation, Tribune of the Guard?'

I stopped then, but I was trembling slightly with anger. I had hit home, though. It was hard to imagine the ruined shape on the atrium floor in a pool of his own gore would live through the night, and without the chance to interrogate him, Scaevinus would never prove his claim. However, there were more than adequate witnesses to his own crime.

The man stood, silent, glaring coldly at me. Finally, with a last look at Domitian, who still had not moved or opened his mouth, the tribune nodded to his men and the five of them stomped out of the house, their echoing footsteps diminishing with distance. I waited until there was absolute silence, and then gestured to the slaves standing around us.

'See if he can be saved. If not, send him on his way as peacefully as you can.'

Four of the Flavian slaves picked up the body and carried it away, while the other two hurried off to check on the doorman, who had been knocked unconscious. As they left, two slave girls appeared with a bucket and rags, and swiftly and efficiently cleared away the mess until the atrium was clean and neat and no evidence remained of what had happened.

Silence reigned once more, and I crossed to the door, pulling it closed, then returned to my seat, sank my wine and then poured myself another, with considerably less water in this one. Alone, silent, my angry trembling lessened by strong wine, I narrowed my eyes at the lad.

'Would you care to tell me about it?'

Domitian finally uncoiled, stretching out in a strangely languid manner. 'I had thought my man better than that. Scaevinus is hardly bright, and I really had not foreseen him catching on. I shall have to choose my spies considerably better.'

I stared at him then. 'Spies?'

'The notion came to me during our time with Agrippina's man.'

I shook my head, not following. 'What?'

'Junia Silana had two spies placed in Agrippina's house and one in that of Rubellius Plautus. It has become clear to me in recent years that a broad-striped tunic is but a badge of office, and a sword is only as good as the command that wields it, but what really matters, what is really important, is information.'

I stared. It was, of course, true. It was true then, is true now, and always will be. Wars are won and lost on the basis of information. So are thrones. To hear the sentiment tumble from the lips of a twelve-year-old, though, was somewhat disconcerting.

'Having spies in people's houses is extremely dangerous,' I found myself saying. 'Junia Silana had an ongoing feud and was one of the brightest women I have known.'

'I may have no feud, but I doubt you would label me dull-witted, Nerva?'

True. I nodded. 'How long have you had a man in Scaevinus' house? And why him?'

Again, that languid shrug. 'It began with the one in Plautus' house, Pharnaces. He's still there, you know? Since the master was exiled to Asia, he took most of his slaves with him, including Pharnaces, and I managed to speak with him before they left. Pharnaces has been sending me reports ever since. Plautus continues to work his foolish machinations, now with provincial powers, but I keep abreast of his plots, in case one of them involves Rome again.'

This truly surprised me. Oddly it had never occurred to me to check on the spy Junia put in place there, despite having rushed to save the ones in Agrippina's house. I wondered what incentive Domitian had supplied for the man to keep up his dangerous work. But I had the feeling, given what we had just witnessed in the atrium, that Scaevinus and Plautus might be just the tip of the iceberg.

'Why Scaevinus?' I asked again.

'My family has moved out of obscurity and into the public eye,' Domitian said easily. 'If we are to be on a pedestal there will be people wanting to knock us from it. That's how it works. Seneca told me that. So I made it my business to put a trusted man in any household that had a vested interest in my family. It started small, but I now have a small web of them.'

'Gods, boy. How many spies have you sent into people's houses?'

'Only ten. Scaevinus is the first to learn of it, though. He might be a Flavian, you see, but he has a lot of bad habits and he is something of an outcast in our clan. Even Sabinus doesn't particularly like or trust him, and Sabinus is a good judge of character.'

I deflated. Ten spies in households throughout Rome. *And Asia*, I added, rolling my eyes. I wondered what his father and his uncle would say if they knew. Sabinus would be aghast, I was sure, for the prefect had ever been strait-laced, and the most noble of Romans. He still gave me hard looks from time to time for our suspected involvement in Agrippina's fall. He would hate this. Vespasian, I think, would understand, for he was a much more political animal, but he would still fear for his boy's life and place the blame for this clandestine idiocy directly at my feet.

'No more,' I said firmly.

'What?'

'What you're doing could land your whole family, and me, in the cellars of the Palatine in the company of a very specialised unit of Praetorians. You're very clever. We all know it now, Domitian.

But you have started to play games with consequences, and the stakes are too high. What Scaevinus did? You're right that he's not too bright. If he had been, he would have taken your spy straight to Burrus, the Praetorian commander. Burrus would not have been at all pleased at having you spying on one of his tribunes. Then, between them, Burrus and Scaevinus would not have had a great deal of trouble persuading the emperor that you were involved in something dreadful. You are extremely fortunate that Scaevinus reacted foolishly, came here instead and beat the evidence to death. You will not be that lucky twice.'

Domitian nodded. 'As I said, I shall have to choose them better.'

'No,' I said in a flat voice. 'You need to not choose them at all.'

The young Flavian leaned back and laced his fingers together behind his head. 'If your only advice is to not act, then I begin to wonder what else you can teach me.'

I was starting to lose my temper. '*Not* acting is by far the best thing I can teach you right now. Domitian, just because you *can* do something does not mean you *should*. At least half of wisdom lies in knowing when *not* to do something. I will not bring this up with your father or your uncle, but you need to give me your word that this will stop. Let go your spies and involve no more.'

Domitian mused on this for a moment. 'A network of informants is neither new nor foolish, Nerva. It is an ancient move in the game of Roman politics. Seneca has enlightened me more than once. Augustus had them, Tiberius had them, Sejanus had them. Even Seneca has a few well-placed eyes and ears right now. I am not a boy any more, Nerva. I am ready to lose the bulla of childhood, and who looks after Flavian interests in Rome? My uncle, so noble and honest that he can't fart without taking the blame? My father, off in Africa rebuilding the family fortune from the provincial treasury? My brother, perhaps, chasing military glory off in the north? Maybe cousin Flavius, currently off in Moesia commanding the Seventh Claudia? Had I the luck to have been born one summer earlier, I would have taken the *toga virilis*

65

by now and would be officially a man in Rome with no need to answer to any guardian.'

I was taken aback by that. I had thought us friends enough not to be brushed off so easily. Perhaps he saw that he might have offended me, for he nodded, taking a slow breath.

'I am sometimes quick to anger, Nerva. This I know, and the letter about Caenis set me off on a bad path today. But I am under no illusions about who I am, and you need to be the same. I am quite capable of taking my place in the running of family matters in Rome. I still need your help, and sometimes your guidance, and will do even when I take the adult's toga, but I also know what is best for my family, and right now that is being aware of any move against us before it happens. I hear you. I will not seek to expand my informants. But similarly I will not abandon all for which I have worked so hard.'

I nodded. I understood. And while Domitian may have still been twelve in body, in mind he was already well beyond losing the bulla of childhood. He was the Flavian mind in Rome that year, and in the end, we would all be grateful for the spies he had put in place.

VI

A web of informants

Rome, AD 65

The summons had come early in the morning, when I was preparing for my own salutatio, greeting the growing web of clients and hopefuls who waited patiently outside my house. I would, as usual, have to rush them through in order to attend the imperial salutatio at the palace, where the increasingly erratic and tired-looking Nero would meet his own council and seemingly endless ranks of noble-if-grasping clients. The summons was to the palace, but not to the emperor. It was, instead, to attend upon Epaphroditus, the emperor's private secretary.

Many a senator or noble of Rome would baulk at the notion of being summoned by a freedman, a former slave so far down the social ladder he couldn't even see the soles of a patrician's feet, but *this* freedman was different. As Nero's right arm, go-to advisor, facilitator, and more or less the man who ran the machine of empire for him, Epaphroditus wielded a level of power even most consuls could only dream of. When this former slave called, even the most noble Roman came running, with his underwear around his ankles if necessary.

Indeed, Epaphroditus' position had become all the more important in this past year. During the previous July the usual summer fire had broken out in Rome, but this one had swiftly surpassed the destructive power of the many infernos that have ravaged the city over the centuries. The fire had broken out at the eastern end of the circus maximus and had burned for nine days, leaving little more than charred bones of buildings in ten of Rome's fourteen districts. Sabinus and his urban cohort had worked day and night alongside the *vigiles*, the sailors from Ostia, the Praetorians and every able-bodied man, woman and child, trying to contain and quench the inferno. Nero had been in Antium, and whatever you may read to the emperor's detriment, I will bear personal witness to Nero's heroism over those few days, throwing in his lot with the men of the city, helping to direct the work and even joining the lines of men with buckets of water. The aftermath was now threatening to break the imperial treasury, with the immense cost of rebuilding and helping those in need. Epaphroditus and his administrators had become a crucial linchpin in the machine of recovery.

The summons this morning was not connected to Rome's recent disaster, though, nor was it for me alone, as was clear from the wording. I had been granted the position of praetor designate, due to take on the full role soon, and it seemed that the message had been a form letter also sent to a number of my peers. I abandoned my salutatio and had my head slave send my clients away with a promise to see them again the next morning, and sent for my guest. Vespasian had not yet returned from Africa, utilising every month he could get to enhance the family's fortunes, and Titus had married and moved out to his own house close by. The house of Vespasian was therefore all but empty, and so, following the fire, which had miraculously left the Quirinal hill intact, I had moved the fourteen-year-old Domitian into my own house until his father returned. As I hurried to the Palatine that morning, I took the young Flavian prodigy with me.

Domitian was now old enough to take the toga virilis of manhood, though his direct manner often made people label him childish, and in some ways, I suppose, he was. I had considered putting him through his coming of age myself, but had decided to leave that to his father as more appropriate, when time allowed. I feared the delay in his change of status had done little to lift the young man's mood in the ongoing absence of family. Still, I did what I could.

We left the house with half a dozen guards and a scattering of slaves. Once I had fully taken on my praetorship I would have armed lictors to accompany me around the city, but as an administrator 'designate' I had yet to acquire them. We took a litter for speed and comfort, and kept the curtains closed throughout the journey – the charred corpse of the city was not palatable viewing.

Nero had moved his entire household into the old Tiberian palace, the newer, grander parts of the imperial residence having fallen to the fire along with the houses of rich and poor alike. As we arrived on the Palatine, it was hard not to look in the direction of the new construction, though, which heralded the next age of imperial residency. While the city rose from the ashes all around us, the greatest work was happening in the bowl formed by the hills at the eastern end of the Via Sacra, where Nero's new palace was being formed, a monument to vanity and hedonism that was already causing ill-feeling city wide and giving birth to rumours of Nero's personal involvement in the fire. I tore my gaze from that enormous complex with distaste, and we made our way into the oldest of the Palatine's imperial complexes.

Domitian was interested in our visit. He was, I suspect, hoping that he would be permitted to become involved in whatever had caused the summons. In reality I had only brought him because the fire of the previous year had brought home to everyone the need to keep their loved ones safe, and I could not leave Domitian at home on his own, for I would worry. He gave me a slightly aggrieved look as I instead directed him to the palace library and told him to keep himself busy while I hurried on to the office of Epaphroditus. As I moved through the palace, the corridors were flooded with far more Praetorians than one commonly saw; something important and possibly dreadful had happened.

I found several of my peers, including other praetors and an aedile, as well as half a dozen men I knew for their courtroom reputation, stood waiting outside the secretary's office, a sense of worried anticipation about them all. Clearly I was not alone in having noted the prevalence of Praetorians.

'What has happened?' I asked one of them as I fell in with the line. He shrugged and turned back to a conversation with a friend. I stood silent, tense, watching the secretary's door. I could hear the muffled murmur of voices from within. It sounded confrontational, but without the accompanying yelps and curses and thumps that would have signified Praetorian involvement. More a 'questioning' than an 'interrogation', then. Finally, the room fell silent, followed by a brief, low murmur, and then soft footsteps. Every pair of eyes in the corridor turned to the door, anticipating revelations.

When it opened, most of those waiting sagged with disappointment. We had all been expecting a furious Praetorian prefect, or Epaphroditus with sudden, empire-threatening news, or at least a half-beaten interviewee. What emerged from the door, in fact, was the imperial secretary's Indian under-secretary, an administrative slave boy with a serious face, dressed simply and with a pile of writing tablets beneath his arm.

I moved to ask a question even as the door shut behind him, but I was not the first. A pushy aedile, a snake-eyed man I had never liked, stepped in front of me and addressed the flustered young man.

'What is this all about?' he demanded.

The slave shot a panicked look at the official. He was clearly in a hurry and focused on his task. To delay in his duty and pause for gossip could cost a slave dearly, incurring even a harsh beating. But then, to refuse to answer a senior official in the Roman court could easily cause similar problems. Caught between a rock and a hard place, the slave answered in a torrent of educated speech, even as his eyes never left the corridor for which he was bound.

'The conspiracy seems to be a fiction, Domine,' the slave answered politely, making to move on. Other praetors now moved to hem him in, preventing him from leaving.

'Conspiracy? What conspiracy?'

The slave suddenly looked as though he might explode with nerves. Fortunately for him, another of the gathering made *understanding* noises. 'Ah,' the man said. 'I thought I recognised the voice in there. It's Scaevinus, is it not?'

The secretary nodded hurriedly, and the praetor gave a self-important little nod. 'The conspiracy that was unearthed a month or so ago down in Campania, I suppose?'

Again the slave nodded, and I cast my mind back. I had heard something about a conspiracy that had been unearthed and apparently overcome. I focused, interested.

'Scaevinus is in there?' the praetor prodded the boy. 'Being questioned?'

The door opened again, now, and the irritated face of the emperor's secretary emerged. 'Yes. Apologies, but it appears you were all summoned in error. You may go.'

The level of irritation in the corridor grew at the dismissal by a former slave, and those nearest the door pressed closer to the secretary.

'What's all this about?'

'It is the Epicharis debacle again?'

'Why call for us if we are not needed?'

Giving the gathered officials a look that carried both impatience and carefully applied politics, Epaphroditus nodded and explained, slowly, as though speaking to a child.

'Scaevinus' freedman had raised accusations against him, connected with the supposed conspiracy of Epicharis, yet Scaevinus has answered everything to an acceptable standard. It appears there is nothing to pursue, and these are the imaginings of a troubled servant. I am sorry for the inconvenience, gentlemen. I had called you all in preparation for the inevitable round of proscriptions and court cases that are the fate of such conspiracies, and in my attempt to be efficient, I fear I sent for you too soon. Please, accept my apologies.'

Grumbling their complaints, the various officials dispersed, and Epaphroditus arched an eyebrow at the slave boy, who jumped, startled, and ran off about his business.

I had almost forgotten I was standing there, for my own mind was making connections above and beyond those that were being spoken. The emperor's secretary turned to face me. 'Something I can help you with?'

'Flavius Scaevinus?' I asked him. My mind had been furnishing me with images of the angry Praetorian tribune who had dragged a slave into Vespasian's house and beaten him to near death in front of us. A nauseating feeling of recognition was stealing over me.

The secretary nodded. 'The very same. But he has an acceptable explanation for each of his freedman's arguments. It would appear, in the end, to be a case of a desperate servant hoping to topple his master.' Remaining in the corridor, he clicked the door closed behind him to deaden the conversation to those within. 'It seems,' he continued in a low tone, 'that Flavius Scaevinus' poor reputation includes excessive cruelty to his household. One can only blame a man so much for attempting to escape extreme violence.'

I brushed the explanation aside. I had other thoughts, other ideas. 'Who was this freedman?'

'His name is Milichus. I suspect he will not live to see the morning, now, having turned in his master.' Epaphroditus sighed. 'I have to admit to a wicked part of me that had hoped some truth might emerge among the man's accusations, for his master is hardly the most reliable of Praetorians. Certainly if Scaevinus *is* innocent of this, as he appears to be, it is only a matter of time before we unearth the foul deeds he is *really* up to.'

I fixed the secretary with a steady look. 'Don't release him yet.'
'Why?'

I pursed my lips, thinking back on how defensive and impulsive he had been when he had found Domitian's spy in his house. An overreaction if ever there was one, perhaps born of guilt? 'I think you're right,' I said. 'I think Scaevinus will be guilty of something, and something big. But if you let him go, the chances of finding out what it is will disappear like mist in the sunshine.'

Epaphroditus continued to frown at me, weighing things up. In the end, he nodded, I think swayed partially by the seriousness I continued to exude, partially by my growing reputation for being both clever and honourable, but mostly from an overwhelming desire to prove the unpleasant tribune guilty of some misdeed.

'I will hold him until nightfall. No longer.'

I nodded my thanks, and then turned and left. I walked at a steady, sedate pace at first, but as I passed along the corridors and my suspicions became more and more solid, my step increased until in the end I was almost jogging past slaves and freedmen, senators and Praetorians. Finally arriving at the library door, I pushed it open, then swiftly shut it behind me. My eyes strayed around the room and I was relieved to find that the only occupant seemed to be Domitian, seated on a couch with a book. He looked up.

'Did you know that Sisenna's history disagrees with Virgil in an extraordinary number of ways?'

I grunted a reply as I made sure we were alone, then stalked across to him.

'Flavius Scaevinus' servant turned his master in over connections to some plot against the emperor.'

Domitian gave me no answer, his expression unreadable as he looked back down at the book.

'I cannot decide whether Sisenna is at fault in his research or Virgil is to be accused of flagrant misrepresentation.'

'What have you been up to?' I asked, direct, pulling the book from his hands to draw his attention.

'What needed to be done,' the boy shrugged, examining his empty hands without looking up. 'Did Scaevinus confess?'

I pinched my nose, recognising the start of one of those afflictions I was coming to call *Domitian headaches*.

'No,' I said. 'He did not. In fact, he satisfactorily answered everything thrown at him, according to Epaphroditus, an outcome that surprises me, for Scaevinus is not famed for his quick thinking. It smacks of being prepared for the event. This stinks of your involvement, Domitian. I thought your man in Scaevinus' house was dead.'

Another shrug without looking, as he turned over his hands and examined the veins standing out on the back. 'He was. Is. But it was clear that there was something Scaevinus didn't want me to know. And if he doesn't want me to know it, then I *really* want to know it, so I managed to get someone else into his house. Someone better. When a spy dies, you don't give up, you find another spy. Do you think Junia Silana would just walk away after a single failure? A web of informants requires more than a single strand. Scaevinus is a black mark in our family, a problem waiting to happen, and if he is not actively plotting against us, you can be sure that he plots against *someone*.'

I squeezed my eyes shut, exasperated. Would the boy never learn?

'I didn't really expect him to confess,' Domitian said quietly. 'There was too little evidence and too much at risk. But there is more. I think he can still be caught out.' He gave me a glance now that startled me, for it seemed to be looking directly into my thoughts. 'We all want Scaevinus caught out, don't we?'

'I had a feeling you might know more. I felt sure this Milichus was something to do with you. Tell me what you know, and quickly. Time is short.'

The young man's expression became more serious, and he folded his arms. 'If nothing can be found from his own house, look elsewhere. Scaevinus has been having private meetings with people for months now. Munatius Gratus, Sulpicius Asper, Calpurnius Piso to name but a few. Only last night, though, he met with Antonius Natalis, their latest meeting of many, and with increasing regularity. Always somewhere quiet. Never in their houses. I suspect that if the secretary has Natalis brought in without a chance to consult Scaevinus, their stories will not match.'

Another suspicion struck me. 'Have you a man in Natalis' house?'

'He might soon discover his appointments secretary has gone missing.'

Again, I pictured that poor bastard in the storeroom that the young Domitian had set his slaves on.

'Stay here,' I said, wagging a finger at Domitian. 'Try not to hire, abduct or torture anyone until I get back.'

Fuming, I stalked from the room. The boy was walking a knife edge with everything he did. Sooner or later, he was going to get both himself, and me, arrested, or beaten to death in an alleyway. But this needed to be resolved. Imperial plot or no imperial plot, Scaevinus would know soon, if he didn't already, that Domitian had been involved. He would put two and two together, and then it would only be a matter of time before he came for us. I had absolutely no doubt that Domitian was right. He was clever, and he'd been careful. Scaevinus had to fall, because if he survived, he would be relentless in pursuing Domitian in revenge.

I was lucky, for as I made my way to the office of the one man I felt I could trust, I found it occupied. The commander of the urban cohort has his own complex in the city, but of necessity he also has an office in the palace, and I knew that Sabinus made a habit of spending most mornings there. I was admitted by the guard with little preamble, and as the door shut behind me, I carefully and cagily explained to Sabinus the details of Scaevinus and Natalis and the connection with the plot uncovered a few months ago, omitting any reference to Domitian's involvement. The elder Flavian looked at me as I rattled on, his gaze piercing. When I had finished, he straightened. 'There is clearly more to this, but I suspect I do not want to know any of it, am I right?'

I gave a nod, and the man wrestled with his conscience for only a moment before snapping shut the tablet he had been reading and reaching for his cloak. Whatever intrigues he suspected among his friends and family, a plot against the emperor took precedence.

We left the office and strode out of the palace to the open air of the Palatine, a fine misty rain now beginning to settle into the day from a pale sky the colour of Carrara marble. The urban cohort were chiefly quartered in a separate corner of the Praetorian fortress, but they also maintained a number of small watch houses around the city for rapid deployment in times of trouble. Most had burned the previous year, but the station on the Palatine had been one of the first rebuilds, and so Sabinus called in and collected a unit of his men before marching off in the direction of the house of Antonius Natalis on the Caelian Hill.

We arrived in record time, and the soldiers of the cohort immediately moved around the sizeable structure, checking the shops built into the front wall on either side of the house's door, scouring the alleys and streets around, and securing a position near a rear exit used by slaves and deliverymen. By the time I had regained my breath and adjusted my toga, the house's exterior was secured.

Sabinus, with a last calculating look at me, stepped forth and hammered on the door. The house's doorman opened up, a frown of concern passing across him at the sight of one of the city's most important legal and military officers. The prefect was moving instantly. Demanding entrance on imperial authority, he let four of his men barge the door back, pinning the slave against the wall. As two of them, nightsticks out, moved ahead to secure doorways, Sabinus followed. Another pair of soldiers came next and I slipped in after them. I'm not sure why I felt the need to be so personally involved, but there was, as usual in those days, a nagging fear that something would be said and Domitian's name would crop up unexpectedly. I felt I needed to be ready, just in case.

Natalis appeared in the atrium, dressed in a rich tunic, his expression furious and his voice powerful, demanding to know what this disruption was. If I had been in any doubt as to his guilt, it would have disappeared in that moment, and Sabinus was similarly left with cold certainty of the man's culpability. In a heartbeat, as Natalis saw Sabinus and the soldiers of the urban cohort moving through his household, his expression changed to one of horrified desperation. He knew what he had done, what was now happening, and his guilt was painted across his face like the red visage of a general at a triumph. He thrust out a finger and shouted for his guards, then turned and ran.

I watched as men of the cohort now pushed rudely past me in an effort to throw themselves into the fight. More and more soldiers in gleaming helms and chain mail, stout clubs in hand, flooded the nobleman's house, swarming into rooms and along corridors, pushing panicked slaves out of the way, and then overpowering and securing any figure who was armed or seemed inclined to resist. Through the strange domestic warfare Sabinus moved like a battlefield god, directing his men, striding implacable and noble, relentlessly following the desperate flight of Natalis.

I hurried at his heel, still struggling to keep my toga in position, stepping over slaves lying face down with their hands behind their heads, fingers interlaced on the orders of the soldiers. With only a few minor clashes visible where the more determined of Natalis' staff fought their corner, we reached that rear slaves' entrance to find it open. Natalis had attempted flight, but he had been outwitted by the urban prefect, whose men had been waiting for him outside. Natalis was being roughly handled by the soldiers, who were threatening to use extreme force if he did not comply.

'Gaius Antonius Natalis, you are under arrest on charges of suspected conspiracy against the emperor of Rome.'

'Wait,' Natalis said, desperation inflecting his tone, 'wait!'

'Go on?'

'I do not seek the emperor's fall,' the man said in a greasy, obsequious tone. 'But I was approached. I have been gathering evidence. I have it all. Names, places, dates. I can help bring it all down.'

I felt a wave of relief flow over me, and Sabinus and I watched as his men herded the entire household into the peristyle garden while the house's master was marched away to the Palatine to reveal all to Epaphroditus. I returned in their wake, at a much slower pace and, arriving at the palace, I was admitted and immediately went to the library. There was no sign of Domitian, and for a moment I felt concerned that something had happened to him. I spent a short while retracing my own steps in the palace, and found the young man exactly where I should have known to look. He was in the corridor outside Epaphroditus' office with several of the urban cohort, two Praetorians and a number of palace administrators.

'I thought I told you to stay in the library.'

'You said "Stay here." I took that to mean the palace,' Domitian said, his eyes unblinking, challenging. I swallowed my retort. Now was not the time for recriminations. I gave him a glance that suggested we would discuss this later, but there was time for nothing more. At that moment, the office opened, and a Praetorian centurion escorted Flavius Scaevinus from the room. The man looked defeated, yet still bitter and angry, but as he emerged into the corridor, his eyes fell upon Domitian and every emotion but fury fled from him.

In the blink of an eye he was out of the Praetorian's grip and lunging for his young cousin who had been at the very centre of his downfall. I saw it coming and leapt in the way. Some people will tell you that there is no armour like chain for dulling a blow, but I caught Scaevinus' powerful punch on my breastbone through what felt like half a mile of thick wool toga, and the attack was robbed of sufficient power to leave me merely breathless. As I staggered to right myself, and Domitian merely glared a challenge over my shoulder, both Praetorians and men of the cohorts in the corridor were on Scaevinus, grasping, punching, slapping, and pushing him to his knees.

The last I ever saw of Flavius Scaevinus was a beaten and defeated man being dragged half-conscious along the corridor of the palace. Domitian and I returned to the safety of my home, waiting for the plot to unravel and the inevitable consequences, hoping against hope never to hear either of our names mentioned in connection.

Natalis was as good as his word. He gave up everyone and their grandmother in a desperate attempt to save his own skin. It worked, for he was pardoned, though never attended court again, and was passed over for every position in the empire, ending his days in safety, but in quiet ignominy. The proscriptions that followed, though, were the worst seen in a generation. Epaphroditus, and through him Nero, oversaw the deaths of a swathe of senators and noble equites, even to include the noble Seneca on some tenuous connection. The web centred upon Calpurnius Piso who, it seemed, had been at the heart of it all from the beginning, even the foiled sub-plot a few months earlier. He, Scaevinus, and a score of others were brutally tortured in the cellars of the Palatine until they had sung every note they had to sing, following which each had been dragged to the Capitol, to the top of the Gemonian Stair, and there beheaded and cast down. The bodies of the conspirators had been torn to pieces by the howling mob in the forum below, entire limbs and bloodied bones taken away as souvenirs, while the heads adorned spears close to the senate house as a reminder and a warning.

The plot was over. The emperor lived, and we survived.

I think that was the moment my opinion changed, and I began to see the value of spies.

Twice now, Domitian, and to a lesser extent myself, had unpicked plots against Nero, and I had made sure, through Epaphroditus, that the emperor was aware of the Flavii' part in his continued security. It was the least I could do for all the help and support they had given me over the years. The emperor's gratitude towards myself and the Flavii was palpable. I accepted command of the Seventh Claudia at Viminiacum as a solid post on the ladder, and served a minimal single year before returning to Rome in glory. Sabinus maintained his prestigious position in the city, and took on Domitian's care while I was away, for Vespasian was busy moving ever closer into imperial circles. Sabinus' younger brother was invited as part of Nero's personal entourage for his tour of Greece, and such was his favour that even falling asleep during the emperor's recitals did not tarnish his shining reputation. Indeed, little more than a year after Piso's fall, I found myself back in Rome, once more being asked to keep an eye on Domitian while his father and brother accepted an imperial commission in the east, putting down a major revolt in Judea.

The youngest Flavian was fifteen now, and had taken the adult toga in the brief moment his father had been home, but he remained dangerously unpredictable and resistant to shrewd politicking. Without his father's influence, it was felt that he still needed a steady, guiding hand to steer him through the earliest days of his career.

Had I any idea what loomed in our near future, I would have politely declined, for new plots were forming against this emperor, this time on a grand scale and on the periphery of empire.

Nero's time was running out.

Part Two – Revolution

The secret of the Empire was laid bare: an Emperor could be created elsewhere than in Rome

–Tacitus: *Histories 1.4*

VII

Enemy of Rome

Rome, 8 June AD 68

I had thought we'd seen the treacherous underbelly of Rome, but nothing had prepared me for what was to come. Since the days of Caesar and Pompey nobody had thought to witness such a thing. It began in the March, and word filtered through into Rome as swiftly as one might expect. The governor of Gaul, Julius Vindex, openly declared that he would no longer be bound by his oath of allegiance to Nero.

The stories that were circulating, originating perhaps with Vindex, were of the most base, wicked, and extremely colourful sort, painting Nero as the worst imaginable incumbent upon the throne. Most of the accusations were clearly horse shit, but the problem is that the common man can be all too easily persuaded by horse shit and, with his recent behaviour fanning the flames, the emperor's name began to become a byword for seedy corruption.

The emperor and his efficient government immediately moved against the threat, the German legions marching to put an end to Vindex and his rebellion, but that was only the start. Before Vindex fell, the rot had spread. He had declared an allegiance with Galba, the governor of Hispania, proclaiming his support for the old senator as a replacement for Nero. The governor of Lusitania, Otho, a distant cousin of mine by marriage, threw in his support too. What had been a worrying but isolated incident quickly became a major threat to the security of the empire.

This was clearly the sort of plot against the emperor that was beyond being solved by a shrewd young man and a bunch of clever slaves, and so I made absolutely certain that Domitian, now a rangy seventeen, knew to keep his business within the house and to become involved in grander events in no way at all. The world was coming unstitched, and this was no time to be playing around with the threads. To my relief, Domitian was clever enough to see that non-involvement was the only safe path, and so both he and I attended court and undertook duties when required, and spent the rest of our time in family estates or at the houses on the Quirinal. The safest path, of course, would have been to have left Rome entirely for the coast, as was common practice in the hot, stinking summer months, but this was not a time to be seen abandoning the emperor. So we stayed, we did as we were bade, paid lip service to the court, and hid ourselves away.

Sabinus remained in his position as urban prefect, his forces stretched keeping a worried and edgy city under control. Flavius sat idling in his house. He was due a military command at any time, but now it was approaching, this seemed the worst possible time to be given a legion. He was grateful for every day that passed without the appointment coming. Vespasian was away in Judea, dealing with the war there, and Titus was commanding one of his legions; at least they were involved in an honourable conflict on the periphery of empire and far from this disaster. So long as we all kept our heads down, we felt safe.

The emperor, less so.

Nero threw everything he had at Galba and his allies, but it was battered aside as though it were nothing. Rome held its breath at the news that Galba was on the move, that he had raised a new legion in Hispania and was marching on Rome with them, that his allies were coming.

This was no plot against Nero that could be ended with a head rolling down the Gemonian Stair. This threatened to become civil war. And every day that Nero's armies failed, every day that Galba moved closer to Rome, support for the last emperor of the line of Julius Caesar ebbed and faded.

On that sunny June morning, I was going about my business hurriedly, itching to be back within the relative safety of my domus. I was serving as the Curator Aedium Sacrarum, overseeing the condition and contents of the temples of Rome. An easy job really, but with considerable authority and prestige. I had decided to visit the Capitoline temples that morning and was now, in the last hour or so before a planned visit to the baths, making hasty visits to each of the smaller temples and shrines. Domitian had urged me to devote my efforts to the grand Temple of Minerva on the Aventine, which was, I admit, becoming a little dilapidated. But for all the few notables who live there, the Aventine was still largely a plebeian region, and I had heard plenty of unsavoury stories about the place. Better to stay within the confines of the city centre while I could.

I had just completed a very satisfactory review of the Temple of Fides, and stepped out into the bright summer sun with my two lictors.

I only became aware of the trouble because of them. One turned and bellowed for me to move as he hefted his *fasces* and shifted his grip, changing its nature from symbol to weapon. I looked about in shock for a moment and realised where the danger was coming from.

A band of chanting Praetorians was pushing its way through the open spaces atop the Capitol. They had clubs and even blades out, shoving people out of their path, senators and beggars alike, even a priest with his covered head. They moved like a pack of predators, putting down anything in their way and they were headed straight for me. I dithered as my lictors formed a simple two-man cordon, braced to protect me from the rampaging soldiers.

On the cusp of disaster, I felt hands grasping at me, pulling, as I was jerked backwards away from them, panic filling me. The door behind me had not yet closed, and the attendant pulled me inside and pushed shut the heavy bronze door, dropping the bar to secure it.

I stared at the inside of the door in shock as I listened to what was going on outside. I heard the Praetorians reach the temple, heard the violence as they laid into the people there, including, I presumed, my two lictors. It was only then that I realised what I was hearing. The Praetorians were chanting, and the word they chanted sent a chill through me.

Galba. The usurping governor of Hispania.

That name, over and over again as they beat citizens and pushed them aside. Nero's own bodyguard had now changed sides?

I stood, shaking, until the noise died away. Only when there was the silence of a cemetery outside did the temple staff finally open the door. The Capitol was littered with battered and wounded citizens of all standings. One of my lictors, blood sheeting from a head wound, was helping up the other, who was unable to lift his scattered fasces thanks to a broken arm.

I cursed myself for not having brought a litter that day. Some prideful part of me liked to be seen in my expensive toga and with lictors preceding me, announcing my importance to all in view. As such I had walked today, showing off. That meant I needed to walk again, though now my lictors looked like the losers in a gladiatorial bout. I expressed my gratitude to the temple attendant, a man I would have cause to thank again that year, and moved off – not to the baths as planned, but home. My two lictors still led the way, but I was under no illusion that if we bumped into more Praetorians they would be little more than an obstacle.

We walked as fast as two injured men and an official burdened with twelve pounds of thick toga can walk. Every pace took us further from the centre of trouble and closer to the security of our own walls, until one of the lictors called out a warning. Some sort of growing scuffle was visible a little further up the hill, between us and my home. I had no wish to be involved in another such incident, and my worried gaze fell upon the house of Vespasian, closer at hand. I crossed to the Flavian house and hammered on the door.

Quarto opened it. His attention was immediately drawn to the trouble coming our way and he stepped aside to allow us entry. As he closed the door behind us, I heaved a sigh of relief and left my lictors to be looked after by Vespasian's slaves, while Quarto escorted me to the triclinium.

I was surprised to find that Domitian was not alone in the house. Flavius and Sabinus were both present, and I had apparently interrupted something important. To my relief, the prefect gestured to a seat and waved Quarto away.

'Good. That saves me finding you. There is dire news to share.'

I nodded. 'Galba is close, I suspect?'

Sabinus frowned, then nodded as he understood. 'The Praetorians? That is but part of it. Their prefect has declared for Galba and taken most of the Guard with him. They move through the city imposing their new master's control on Rome, even though he is some way off yet.'

'There is more?'

Sabinus nodded. 'The senate has done the unthinkable.'

There was a pause as Sabinus pinched the bridge of his nose. He looked tired. Finally he straightened with a deep breath. 'The senate has declared for Galba.'

'What?' Domitian sat forward, his face creased in consternation.

'They have declared Nero an enemy of Rome,' Sabinus continued. 'Any Roman found harbouring him or offering succour will be similarly considered an enemy of the state.'

'They can't do that,' Domitian snapped. '*He* is the emperor, not this Hispanic upstart. The emperor controls the senate, not the senate the emperor.'

'Would that were so, nephew, but whether there is precedent or legality to it or not, the fact remains that the senate of Rome, the Praetorian Guard, and at least three of the provinces have declared Galba the new rightful emperor of Rome.'

'You are faced with a difficult choice,' I noted.

'Oh? How so?'

I shrugged. 'The urban cohort will either have to declare for Galba or rally to Nero's side.'

Sabinus shook his head. He was ever the most noble of Romans, and I should have understood what he intended. 'Even if I wanted to rally to Nero, I could not. He has fled the palace with Epaphroditus and a few others. Nobody seems to know where he has gone, but he cannot run far enough. He is hunted now. I cannot legally declare the support of the cohorts for an official enemy of Rome, yet until Galba is in Rome and accepted universally, he remains a usurper in my eyes. I can no more stand for him yet than I can for Nero, for all that he might be what Rome needs. I am the urban prefect. It is my job to keep Rome safe and protect its people. I declare for no one. I shall do my job. The cohorts will declare for Rome itself and keep it safe.'

I shifted uneasily. 'Be careful, Sabinus. To keep the streets safe, you will have to protect people from the Praetorians. Do you really want to start a war between the cohorts and the Guard?'

'I will do what I must,' Sabinus said flatly, and then looked from son to nephew. 'Stay here, you two. Nerva, will you stay with them? I must attempt to bring order to the streets.'

I nodded. 'Of course.'

We watched the old man leave, sitting in stunned silence in the Flavian dining room. Only sometime after he'd gone did we speak again.

'Unacceptable,' Domitian said, suddenly.

'What?'

'The senate cannot declare the emperor *anything*. They have no authority. They are just a shell now. No one has maintained the fiction of their importance since Augustus.'

I sometimes forgot how well read and clever Domitian was, and he was no longer a boy, but a man now, inexperienced and awkward, but still a man. 'Regardless,' I said, 'it is done.'

'Besides,' Flavius put in, leaning to the table and pouring himself a wine, 'Nero has been erratic recently.' He noted the disapproval on his young cousin's face, but my old friend shrugged. 'We've all seen it. You're young, Domitian. You've only really known Nero. To you he's the embodiment of an emperor, but we've seen them come and go. Nerva and I remember Tiberius when we were boys. We watched Caligula rise and fall. We saw Claudius reign, and we saw him die, too. Nero was a little more fun than the others, but he's been getting unpredictable and dangerous.'

I nodded. 'That's true, Domitian. That idiocy in Greece, touring and reading poetry in the theatres? This huge ostentatious palace he's building in the heart of Rome? Making Corbulo fall on his sword? *Corbulo.* The greatest general since Caesar, killed because of a paranoid whim. And you haven't seen the parties he throws, either. Debauchery on a scale you wouldn't dream of.'

That caught his attention. Domitian had never liked, nor approved of, the sexual madness that reigned on the Palatine. Nero had even taken a eunuch lover and dressed the poor bastard as his dead wife. It was probably some awful joke, but the fact was that Nero *had* been getting worse this past couple of years.

'It matters not,' the young man snapped.

'Galba might actually be what Rome needs,' Flavius put in.

'What?'

'He's a respected senator, a successful commander, an old hand from a respected bloodline. Serious as a plague, they say. He'll be good for Rome, I think.'

'It doesn't matter,' Domitian persisted. '*Nero* is the emperor. Good or bad, *he's* the emperor. No one has the right to remove him, short of Minerva herself making an appearance.'

Flavius and I shared a look and made signs to ward off ill luck. It was never good to speak so lightly of gods.

'No gaggle of squawking senators, present company included, can make or break an emperor,' Domitian insisted. He rounded on me, wagging a finger. 'If you think Nero is such a fool and that Galba is so good, answer me this: why did we put ourselves through such danger to save him from plots? Why is this Galba more acceptable than Gaius Rubellius Plautus? Plautus would have taken the throne through Agrippina, and he bore the blood of Caesar just as much as Nero. Or why not Piso? He carried the blood of two of Rome's most distinguished houses, the Calpurnii and the Licinii. He was well liked, bright and noble, and we brought him down in favour of Nero. Why did we work so hard to protect an emperor only to abandon him now?'

It was a persuasive argument. 'Nero has changed, Domitian.'

'He is still the emperor,' the young man stated, reaching for his wine.

'No,' I replied. 'No, he isn't. Like it or not, he is gone. You need to accept that. No matter what you think, no one can save Nero now.'

Our conversation was interrupted by Quarto, who appeared in the doorway, wide-eyed and tense.

'What is it?'

'A visitor, Domine. Senator Manius Acilius Glabrio.'

I frowned at Flavius, who shrugged. Neither of us knew the man. Domitian was similarly unimpressed.

'He has Praetorians with him, Domine. He demands entry.'

Domitian rose from his seat now, wine cup still in his hand. 'Tell the man that we have no time for him today. He may call in the morning for my father's salutatio.'

'That will not be necessary,' announced a man in a toga, appearing in the atrium behind Quarto. Past the pair we could see men in Praetorian uniforms surging through the house. My heart leapt into my throat as the memory arose of my return to Rome and the destruction of my father's house.

'Cease this,' Domitian bellowed. 'Get out of my house.'

Glabrio threw a nasty sneer at Domitian. 'By order of the senate, all known supporters of the traitor Nero are to be invest-igated and their houses searched until the fugitive is located and brought to justice.'

'How fucking dare you,' Domitian snarled, taking a couple of steps forward. Flavius rose now, a hand closing on Domitian's shoulder, holding him back.

'You'll not find him hiding here,' I told Glabrio, my eyes narrowing. Sabinus had been gone half an hour, and I could only imagine what would have happened if he'd still been here. Or what would happen when he came home to learn of this, for that matter. For now, though, we had no choice but the path of obedience. I had watched a house's slaves try to stop the forces of Rome when we had gone to arrest Natalis, and I had seen the careless violence of the Praetorians that very morning on the Capitol. Even with my lictors, if we moved to defend the house, I could only imagine the Praetorians reacting with lethal force. To resist was to put everyone at risk. I moved to Domitian, protective, as Flavius held him tight.

'Let him search,' I hissed. 'He'll find nothing.'

'You have no right,' Domitian yelled as Glabrio, a slick smile crossing his lips, moved out into the atrium to begin his work. 'This is a private home.'

A Praetorian moved into the dining room, gave a quick look in every corner, and then left to stand outside as his fellows moved through Vespasian's house, searching for the missing emperor. I would learn later that day that half a hundred houses were hit the same as ours that afternoon, including Sabinus' and my own, despite our absence. The hunt for the fugitive emperor was on, and anyone who had enjoyed Nero's favour would remain under suspicion and observation until he was found.

The three of us stood in glowering, tense silence as the Praetorians searched Vespasian's house. Quarto returned to the door and his cubby hole, while two of the house's burlier slaves came to stand at the triclinium door protectively, as though they could do anything against a score of Praetorians. We waited an hour in there, in enraged, impotent silence as Glabrio's men searched the house. Inevitably, of course, they came up empty handed, having ransacked the domus and caused wholesale destruction. As they made to leave, Glabrio paused in the atrium and pointed at us.

'You are free to go, but remember that any man who harbours or aids the fugitive Nero will bring down upon themselves the wrath of the senate, the Guard and the new emperor of Rome.'

He turned to leave and I saw it happen too late to stop it. Domitian, a roar of sheer animal fury escaping him, threw his heavy, earthenware cup of expensive wine. It struck Glabrio between the shoulders, a hard, painful blow, and the thick crimson liquid splashed across his pristine white toga, running down the folds, staining it irreparably.

The senator turned, a look of absolute fury on his face. I think that for just a moment he almost ordered his Praetorians against us, but we were as yet innocent of all charges, and senators and officials of Rome ourselves. To attack us would be to open up a whole new Pandora's box. He shook with anger, but restrained himself with wagging a finger at Domitian.

'You, I shall remember,' he hissed, then turned and left with his men.

We stood in silence as the house emptied.

It seems to me that our lives were, in a way, defined by a series of enemies. First Agrippina, then Scaevinus, and now Glabrio had joined the line.

I never did go to the baths that day. It was a good thing. I hear fights broke out at our nearest public pool, each combatant favouring an old or new emperor. Seven men died there and the pool was pink for days. No search party found Nero in the end. He had fled to the villa of a friend outside Rome and there, knowing he was finished, had a knife pushed through his heart. Thus did the great dynasty of Julius Caesar end.

Rome had a new master now, and his name was Servius Sulpicius Galba.

VIII

The rule of Galba

Rome, 22 June AD 68

'He will be the man to set you on the first step of your career,' I noted, peering between the heads of two old senators who could not rustle up half a head of hair between them. *And perhaps to advance my own.* Nero had slowed my advance down, albeit with the best of intentions, and the consulship looked as far away as ever. Perhaps Galba would change that.

Domitian remained entirely unimpressed. We both wore our best togas and were accompanied by a small group of hired guards, as well as my two lictors, but there were so many people gathered on the city side of the Pons Neroniana that being crushed to death was still a real possibility.

Galba was almost here. He had moved at a stately pace from Hispania, allowing for a peaceful transition. It had been half a month since Nero's demise had become public knowledge, and already the people of Rome seemed to have forgotten him and were waiting with excitement for their new emperor. It would be no accident that the old man would enter his city across the bridge built by, and named for, his predecessor. It was akin to walking across Nero's body to sit on his throne.

'Trust my career to a usurper?' Domitian said with distaste.

'You've got to stop thinking of him as that. He is the emperor now, and nobody denies it.'

'Hmph. Then let's see how your new emperor deals with his city.'

I bit down on my retort. I was more than a little sick of hearing Domitian's opinion on the fall of Nero and the rise of his replacement. I looked out across the crowd. Apart from the two ageing senators doing their best to block my view, we had a good position. From the platform of the Temple of Dis Pater, we could see the crowds stretching all the way across the river to the road west. I fancied that in the still summer air I could already see the cloud of dust rising from the emperor's column.

There was a sense of anticipation, a question, in the air. Across the river, occupying wide pavements and parkland, and even flooding the grounds of what had been Agrippina's villa, stood serried ranks of soldiers, a strange collection of units. Thousands of former sailors in their blue tunics stood in rough ranks, two legions, in fact, that Nero had ordered raised in order to defend him from the very man who now approached, but who, though they had been partially equipped, had never had their status ratified or been given an eagle before the emperor died. They were no longer sailors, but until they received an eagle, neither were they legionaries. Their future hung on Galba.

Two cohorts of Praetorians stood nearby awaiting their new master, and close by them stood the German Guard, a loyal bodyguard of Batavians that had served the emperors alongside the Praetorians since the days of Augustus. Both units would need to swear allegiance to their new emperor.

It took more than half an hour before we caught our first sight of the imperial procession. The moment a small unit of dusty cavalry came into view, the crowds went berserk, cheering and waving, the new emperor's name bellowed by a thousand voices and more. It was hard not to be caught up in the excitement. Rome was to have a new age. Gone would be the corruption and debauchery of the Neronian court. Now would come a more austere and traditional empire. Now would be a time of *romanitas* and the *mos maiorum*.

'Look,' I said to Domitian, 'see how Rome clamours? What could be more glorious?'

A grunt was the only reply.

I tried to ignore him and watch the spectacle. Over the roar of the crowd I could just hear the officers as the approaching column moved and changed formation, fanning out, the infantry that followed the cavalry moving to line the sides of the road.

Finally the emperor came into view. He sat astride a magnificent white horse, a red cloak at his back, dressed in the armour of a conquering general, just like Caesar of old. The very sight of him made the crowd roar all the more.

As they approached the bridge something happened. From the borders of the approach, officers stepped out into the road in front of the imperial party. I had no idea what they were doing, and could only just make out who they were, but they were clearly officers, some in blue from the former marines, some in Praetorian white and some in the green and gold of the Germans.

The imperial party slowed their horses in front of the officers, their accompanying legionaries and horsemen continuing to file forward into ranks at the sides. Even though the watching crowds fell silent, trying to hear what was said on the far side of the bridge, the conversation did not make its way as far as our ears.

I know now, for I have spoken at length to men who were part of that exchange, what was said, though at the time all I saw was the response.

The sailors were first to greet the new emperor. They did so with respect and honour, addressing Galba as their imperator, honouring him and calling the blessing of gods upon him. They asked him a simple thing. They asked him to confirm their legions. They had been raised and promised. They had trained and armed. All they wanted was their documents, their eagles and their standards. It was not much to ask.

Before any answer was forthcoming, the Praetorians and the German Guard put in their requests. Galba's representatives in the city, including the Praetorian prefect himself, had offered a sizeable sum on behalf of the new emperor for them to turn against Nero. This they had done, and now they sought the payment promised. Blood money it might be, but ethics had never got too much in the way of the Praetorians when they sensed advantage. The German Guard wanted even less. All they wanted was an extension of their contract as all Galba's predecessors had done, confirming their place in Rome.

Galba's reply has become legendary in the years since that day.

'I am accustomed to levy soldiers, not to buy them,' the new emperor said.

Even across the river we could hear the outbursts of angry demands rising not only from the officers in the centre of the street but from their men to either side. They wanted so little, while they offered him a throne and its security. They argued, and the arguments became shouted demands. When these were met with irritated silence from the new emperor, they became threats. The sailors had been raised to defend Rome against Galba, after all. The Praetorians had supported him because of promises he had made. Shouts. Anger. Surging forward.

Someone made the mistake of drawing a sword and advancing on the imperial party, and in moments we watched the new emperor's legions move into action. The forces awaiting their emperor should have stood more of a chance – they were mostly armed and armoured, after all – but they could not believe what was happening as Galba's legions and cavalry burst into life. The veterans of the new emperor's army had honed their skills against Nero's forces all the way from Corduba to Italia, the fighting only ending with the emperor's deposition and suicide. They were fast, trained and prepared to kill.

The cavalry came first, ploughing into the waiting ranks of sailors and Praetorians, creating havoc. Swords rose and fell, spears stabbed out, butchering Romans within sight of the temples, eyes of the gods. The stunned defenders hardly had the chance to fight back before the Hispanic legionaries were among them as well.

The crowd screamed. Men, women and children fled the scene, and the rout of citizens created a fresh disaster as people were crushed in the press, trampled underfoot, injured in a hundred ways. Across the river the butchery seemed to go on and on, the newly arrived blades of the emperor creating a lake of blood that poured into the Tiber in such quantities that the river ran pink for hours. I saw it all. We had a good viewpoint for the destruction of Rome's forces by their own new commander.

Some reports put the death toll at 7,000. And beyond the killing, every unit met its own fate in the aftermath of that clash. The German Guard was disbanded, ordered to leave Rome and never return. The Praetorians were disarmed and forced to their knees, their officers dragged out front and clapped in chains, in which they would eventually lead the imperial procession into the city. They would accept their current pay and no more, or they could follow the example of the Germans.

My heart went out to the sailors most of all. Just two months before, they had been brought from their ships, given the pride of being legionaries, and promised their own eagles. They had taken oaths and, though their master had died before he could field the new legions, they had come to give that oath to another emperor. Instead, he had turned them down, shunned them, refused them. And not content with his cavalry butchering many of them where they stood, in return for their request, he ordered for them the worst of all fates: decimation.

A traditional punishment for legions that fled the field in cowardice, decimation had not been practised for a hundred years. It was, even to the bloodthirsty, a barbaric act. Every man waiting in a blue tunic was made to draw lots, dipping their hand into a bag full of black and white stones. Every tenth soul who drew the single black would never leave that riverbank, beaten to death with studded clubs by the other nine who'd drawn the whites.

The emperor waited with his column. Though the bulk of the people had fled, we stood and watched, bearing witness to the awful inauguration of our new leader. Galba sat expressionless astride his horse as one sailor in ten was pulverised into a bleeding lump of senseless meat. He waited patiently as Praetorians of rank and importance were stripped of their weapons and armour and chained together. He waited until the Germans had been escorted from the site.

And only when a tenth of the blue tunics had been soaked dark red, and the miserable clanking figures of the captive officers plodded forwards, did the new emperor ride on into Rome to take his place on the throne.

'Tell me now that Galba will be good for the empire,' Domitian said quietly at my side.

I had nothing to say to that.

–

The months that followed only proved the man's unworthiness for rule, and as winter rolled around, Saturnalia passed with a subdued atmosphere. Matters came to a head once more on the ides of Januarius at the Temple of Apollo on the Palatine. Galba was to make a sacrifice in the Palatine temple, seeking the god's favour with the ongoing restoration of the city following the disastrous fire of five years earlier.

As we gathered at the foot of the temple steps, listening intently – for it is always a good idea to pay attention when a god is invoked – my gaze strayed across the luminaries atop the stair with the emperor. Otho, the man who had supported Galba even before he left Hispania, was there, for rarely did the emperor go anywhere without his faithful ally close by. At his other shoulder stood Calpurnius Piso Licinianus, who he had made his heir over the disgruntled Otho. Then there were the generals Vinius and Laco, the latter now commander of the Praetorians, and the emperor's weird and disconcerting freedman Icelus. Those of us on a second tier of importance stood at the bottom of the stairs. Perhaps the least favoured here, though, was Sabinus, whose sterling efforts in keeping the peace in Rome during the disastrous day of the emperor's arrival had been rewarded with removal from the office he had served so well. With the change in power, the Flavii were once more out of favour.

But then, none of us were thriving under the rule of Galba. Even the palace staff whispered curses upon their new master, for his austere and plain lifestyle had rendered the jobs of many of them pointless after the frivolities and debaucheries of Nero. In short, Galba was less popular already than any man who had sat on the throne of the Caesars.

Moreover, Galba could hardly count himself secure. Word had arrived only two days ago that the legions on the Rhine, who had remained loyal to Nero, had refused to renew their oath to the new emperor at the turn of the year. Instead, they had proclaimed their own governor, Aulus Vitellius, the new Caesar, despite the fact that Galba's bony backside still graced the throne.

Despite our disfavour with Galba, Sabinus, a private citizen once more, had stated flatly that the Flavii would not support Vitellius' bid, though nor would they stand against him. Galba was horrible, but we all knew the fat old slug who now controlled Germania from his days in Nero's court. A more unpleasant, untrustworthy, gluttonous and vile human it would be hard to find, even in the seething cesspool of Roman politics. We could only speculate what Vespasian and Titus, still serving in the east, would think.

My eyes kept straying to Sabinus that morning as the droning voices lauded Apollo atop the stairs, the priests warbling in their cracked, ancient voices over the worried sound of a white goat being kept tethered nearby. He had been especially cagey and evasive that morning, something out of character enough for even me to pick up on. Domitian had too, I guessed, for the young man also watched his uncle across the gathering.

The goat began to bleat as it was brought forward, the sacrifice proceeding apace, but I had a feeling that something was going on. Sabinus had the air of a man waiting for a signal. As I shifted position to get a better view of the podium, I heard a crunch and looked down. I had trodden upon a snail, the shell shattered, the oozing creature within smeared across the sole of my boot. A chill ran through me. Omens come in this life in many forms and at many junctures, but rarely is one so clear and so timely. I stared at the poor thing.

A snail.

Galba truncatula – the common truncated snail.

Galba, smeared on the paving of the Palatine, its own little empire shattered.

As omens go, it was one of the worst. I knew in an instant that there was more to that feeling of tense anticipation than simple nerves. Something really was happening. I looked around, wits focused now. Sabinus was intent on what was happening atop the steps. I followed his gaze and realised something was different. I tried to work out what it was. As the incantations finished and the goat bleated in panic, the knife approaching, suddenly realisation dawned. Otho was gone.

With that revelation, my eyes darted this way and that. Otho had been one of Nero's close friends, a popular figure at court, a playboy noble and notorious gambler, but he had also been one of the pillars upon which Galba's power was raised. Where was he?

Everything happened at once.

Atop the steps, the sacrifice had borne fruit of the worst kind. The priest was holding aloft stringy, rubbery, dripping entrails with a deathly white face and wide eyes. Whatever he was telling Galba quietly up there was enough to make the emperor step back, shocked and shaking.

At the same moment, my gaze found Otho at last. The man was just beyond the gathering of nobles, his back to events as he moved away from the temple with a sense of urgency. That alone should have been enough, even without omens. Galba being warned of something dreadful by the priest and Otho abandoning him unexpectedly. But what really made my pulse race was the realisation that Galba's former aide was not alone. Sabinus had turned and slipped away, following. The very notion that the noble Sabinus might have been in collusion with a conspirator against the emperor was astonishing, but that conclusion was inescapable as Praetorians and soldiers of the urban cohort flocked to Sabinus and Otho, surrounding them as they slipped away.

I turned to warn Domitian, and the young man was not there. I blinked. Near panic was descending then, until I spotted the youngest Flavian through the crowd. He had somehow slipped through the assembly and was pounding across the flagstones, catching up with his uncle and the forces of what could only be an impending coup.

I started to pull at the men behind me, trying to heave my way through them into the open space where I could run. The emperor had his guard around, of course, Praetorians commanded by Hispanic officers, though they had done nothing to stop Otho and Sabinus and their group leaving. Of course, their orders would be to prevent anyone *approaching* the emperor unexpectedly, not *leaving*.

Now there was shouting from high on the temple steps. The priest was still looking in horror at the prophetic gore hanging from his fingers, and the emperor himself was staring in shock at whatever he'd been told.

I had to get away, but even as I pushed at the crowd they closed up, trying to get closer to the steps to find out what was happening. Laco, the Praetorian prefect, was on the top step now, bellowing orders. I turned at his words. The Palatine was to be sealed. Something about a usurper. Even as I realised what this meant, the Praetorians still loyal to Galba were securing the area, herding the civilians away into the palace itself. Here and there small knots of guards bellowed their defiance, but they were too few to help. The majority of the Praetorians may have turned on the emperor, but not those who were gathered here.

With a sinking feeling, I realised I was trapped. I had little choice but to allow myself to be herded with the others across the open space to the palace. Once, as we moved, I caught a brief, distant image of Sabinus, Domitian and Otho, with more Praetorians and soldiers around them now. Then I was manhandled into the doorway of the palace and escorted by the emperor's guard to the aula regia. In the imperial audience chamber all the civilians were gathered, soldiers on every door, presumably for our protection, though to me they were as good as prison guards.

We waited there for an hour or more.

I heard a dozen rumours circulating among the gathered nobles. Someone had heard the priest of Apollo pronouncing doom upon Galba, that his reign had ended. Someone had noted Otho's disappearance, and others that of Sabinus. In the end it was a low freedman administrator admitted to the room who told us what was happening. It seemed that a force of men had surrounded the palace and was laying siege to it. The gathered enemy outnumbered the defenders considerably, the attacking force comprised angry Praetorians, offended men of the urban cohort, disenfranchised marines, and even off-duty legionaries and auxiliaries who happened by chance to be in the city. We were urged by the freedman not to worry, for though the palace was guarded by a smaller number of men, they were comprised of loyal Praetorians and veteran legionaries from Hispania, and the building had been made secure. The emperor was content that the palace would hold, and the rest of his Hispanic legions were still quartered in the countryside outside Rome. By nightfall they would be aware of what had happened and would march to Galba's rescue.

Some were reassured by this, more were not. As the administrator left the room, senators flooded out with him, demanding to know more. The guards on the door tried to stop the exodus, but were overwhelmed, and I took the opportunity to leave, sweeping out with the chattering fools.

I was less than inclined to believe that everything was going to be all right. The palace was going to fall, Galba was going to die, and anyone who got caught up in the middle of it was putting their own life at risk. At least Domitian had had the good sense to run when he could, perceptive lad that he was. He would be with Otho and his uncle now, planning the next stage of empire, while I was trapped in a besieged palace. Slipping away from the senators, I thought through my options like an officer in the field. I would not get out of the complex, for the soldiers had sealed it tight against the besieging force. Even if I could get past the defenders, I would probably be killed by the outsiders before I could announce myself. But if I cowered in here with the others, I would risk being killed with them when the palace fell.

I was trapped, unarmed, and undefended, and sometimes there is no disgrace in avoiding conflict. Years earlier, under both Claudius and Nero, I had attended plenty of soirees in the palace, and I knew the public areas well. I knew where I needed to be, and made my way to the great dining room where I had watched Claudius expire at the hand of Agrippina. Nearby, along a couple of corridors, I found the balcony that had provided blessed relief at times from the tedium of court. It was high, with a long drop down the side of the Palatine to the Velabrum, looking across the valley to the Capitol. There was no way of escaping the palace from here, but similarly there was no way an attacking force would reach the balcony, and so no need for the defending soldiers to come here. As such, I closed the door to the balcony and waited there, alone and silent, far from events.

My gaze slid to the Capitol and I caught sight of that small Temple of Fides, where I had hidden with the attendant's help as Galba's supporters had raged across the hill, battering the life from the people. Would that I could be in *their* sacred company that morning.

I do not know how long I was on that balcony. It was only when I heard muffled cheering from within that I perked up. Acutely aware that cheering did not necessarily herald the end of the troubles, I stayed where I was.

What happened in the palace I know only through later conversations. After four hours of fighting, much bloodshed and considerable damage to the palace, it had been announced that Galba had been victorious. It seemed the enemy had been beaten back and reinforcements arrived to save him. It was, of course, a ruse. The emperor, lulled into a false sense of security, believing the trouble over and the coup crushed, took a small number of guards and attendants and left the palace, intending to go directly to the Temple of Jove on the Capitol and give thanks for his deliverance.

In truth, having left the temple at the start of all of this, Otho and Sabinus had ridden directly for the Praetorian fortress. There, with Sabinus' support, Otho had secured the loyalty of the Praetorians and the urban cohort. Tribunes and centurions had been sent to overwhelm the Palatine, along with the angry sailors of the fleet. Overtures had been made to Galba's legions outside the city, and they had been easily persuaded to come over to Otho for a little gold. Unable to take the palace without sacking it and risking a city-wide fire, the rebels had pulled back and allowed men of the Hispanic legions, freshly oath-bound to Otho, to step forward and announce that Galba was saved.

Such was the ruse that ended the siege and drew the emperor from his palace. I heard the commotion as he prepared to leave and visit the Temple of Jove. Making my way back inside, I found a tired-looking freedman and learned of the emperor's departure and plans. I had no time to follow, and little inclination, but I moved across two corridors to another balcony which would grant me an unopposed view of the forum and the road the emperor would travel from Palatine to Capitol.

From my lofty eyrie in the old palace I watched fall the second emperor of Rome within half a year.

Galba was allowed to reach the forum, far from any possible support in the palace, and the most open space available. He moved in a covered litter with purple drapes at the windows, accompanied by his council and a band of Praetorians under the command of a single centurion. Also in the litter rode his heir, Piso Licinianus, and the consul, his close ally, Titus Vinius.

They made it as far as the open square between the great basilicas of Caesar and of Aemilius before trouble descended upon them. A force of soldiers flooded from between every temple and basilica to surround the imperial procession. Galba's Praetorians realised all too late that the supposed end of the coup had been a lie. In time-honoured fashion, the men of the Guard took a look at one another and, to a man, bolted.

Some of them made it to safety, fleeing into the streets never to be seen again. Others were less fortunate, caught by Otho's attackers and cut down on the steps of temples and basilicas, blood running across elegant marble to pool amid the flagstones of the forum.

The litter bearers suddenly felt a shift in their loyalties and, beside the sacred shrine of the Lacus Curtius, they unceremoniously dumped the vehicle and ran away. They were unimportant, mere slaves, and the waiting forces ignored them, letting them go. The remaining four figures were less lucky. As the litter hit the ground Galba was thrown clear, rolling away from the broken vehicle into the open. Behind him, like the snake he was, Titus Vinius emerged, hands raised, distancing himself from Galba and seeking clemency.

Neither of them would be granted it.

Galba's Praetorian centurion, the only soldier to have stood by his emperor, bellowed defiance and drew his blade, charging to meet the rush of Otho's men. He was brave, but he was only one man. He dealt blows left and right like a champion gladiator, though in the end a blow to the groin floored him, and he was finished off swiftly, swords rising and falling, blood flying through the air in wide arcs.

Galba went the same way. Unable to rise, injured in his fall, he staggered and crawled away from the litter. I watched the soldiers crowd around him, heard his screams as their blades plunged down, and winced as one of the attackers rose, a head in his hand, struggling to hold his grisly prize with the lack of hair on the old man's head. Vinius made to run, and managed to reach the temple of the deified Caesar before the soldiers caught him. His flight ended with a sword blow to the back of his knee that cut the strings there and sent him screaming, flailing and tumbling to the ground, where he rolled, bellowing his agony until he managed to half-rise. He was almost to his feet when another attacker managed to plunge a blade into his back. The tip burst from his chest, grating between ribs, ending the consul swiftly.

I looked back from the fallen Vinius, across the body of the brave centurion, to Galba, where the soldiers had now moved away. The head had been taken, to Otho, I later learned, who had reacted with disgust, a sign of the man's laudable character. Galba's body had been mutilated. Long after the head had been taken the attackers had continued to rain down their hatred on the fallen emperor. He was a bloodied mess of chopped meat in stained purple rags.

I wondered for a moment where Piso Licinianus, the heir to the throne, had gone, and then I spotted him entering the Temple of the Vestals, a place of inviolable safety, in theory. Not today, though. Their blood up, the forces of Otho were not going to let mere propriety stand in their way. Though most would not enter such a place in violence, two men, one an auxiliary soldier, the other a Praetorian, disappeared inside. They reappeared in moments, dragging a shrieking Piso, and there, on the steps of the temple, they hacked him to pieces as they had done the emperor and the consul.

Thus ended the reign of Servius Sulpicius Galba.

I had watched it all from my lofty viewpoint. Somewhere in the north a usurper was still being hailed as emperor by his Germanic legions, but for now, here, Rome had passed from the foolish, vain grasp of Galba. Unable to support the old man, and unwilling to back Vitellius, the Flavii in the city had put their faith in an unexpected choice.

Marcus Salvius Otho had been the nearest thing to a natural heir for Nero, enough even to achieve the approval of the rigid-minded Domitian, and now he, the popular, likeable playboy, was emperor of Rome.

All that stood in the way of a new and peaceful empire was the governor of Germania: Vitellius.

IX

Galba's succession

Rome, 9 July AD 69

Marcus Salvius Otho was an emperor of promise. I had always considered my cousin Julia to be unfortunate in having married his nephew, given his reputation. Yet despite having been a notorious playboy, a gambler, a hedonist, and one of Nero's closest circle of debauchers, upon taking the purple in Rome he became surprisingly conscientious and attentive to business. Like Nero, he depended upon the more reliable freedmen in his administration while pursuing a careful policy of cultivating good relations with every important sector of Roman society. Indeed, for three months, Rome looked to be making a recovery. Perhaps most importantly, he reinstated Epaphroditus, who had been so important to Nero's administration, but had disappeared following that emperor's death and the arrival of Galba. The sigh of relief breathed by the palace staff was probably audible from Athens, for Galba's chosen administrators had been new to their work, inexperienced and generally failed to pull Rome back together. The moment Epaphroditus returned to his position, bringing with him carefully selected and chosen men, the wheels of state began to turn smoothly once more. Otho, of course, as a friend of Nero's, had seen how well that administration worked, and emulated the man.

Domitian was less enchanted. I found him in his favourite library one morning scribbling a list of names. I peered down it and recognised no one. Interested, I asked him who they were.

'People I would have chosen for my administration,' he replied. 'Some of them Otho picked. Others not. I am… concerned at his selection of Epaphroditus.'

That surprised me. Everyone else seemed to think it a good choice, and certainly it had worked well. 'Oh?'

'He is a more than competent administrator, but could an emperor trust such a man?'

Now I was baffled. 'Why?'

'You did not know? It was Epaphroditus who put the blade through Nero. Who killed the emperor. How could any emperor trust a man who had killed his predecessor?'

I blinked. This I had not heard. 'How did you hear such a thing? This is not common knowledge in the senate.'

'I have my sources, Nerva, you know that.'

'Anyway, in doing so he will have been following Nero's command. I had not known it was Epaphroditus who wielded the blade, but we all heard that Nero had been too frightened to do the deed and had to be helped. You cannot blame the man who did that.'

'An emperor's life is inviolable. The new emperor will have to make an end of all those who were responsible for the fall of Nero.'

'And what of those responsible for the death of Galba,' I asked pointedly, 'if an emperor's life is so inviolable?' I had not forgotten how both Sabinus and Domitian had hurried off that day in the wake of Otho.

'Galba was no emperor. He was a usurper, who stole the throne from a scion of Caesar's house.'

Cut and dried. Domitian knew the freedmen, had sources that I only suspected at that time, and had formed a very rigid perspective on the nature of imperium, perhaps influenced by his patron goddess Minerva. It could only be a good thing for the current administration that it was the amiable and forgiving Otho who now ruled and not the young man in the library with his list of names.

After the debacle that had been Galba's succession, marked by death and broken promises, the people felt that Nero's true heir had come, that Otho was the natural successor and that everything was right with Rome again. The army, or at least the part of it that Galba had controlled, took to Otho well, for he had travelled with them from Hispania. The Praetorians supported him, for he had lauded – and bribed – them. The urban cohort respected him, and the common people of Rome felt that he was the right man for the job. Even the senate had little bad to say about him.

Closer to home, the Flavii had returned to favour. Vespasian and Titus remained in Judea, their removal no longer a threat, and Sabinus had been reinstated as urban prefect, where he should be. My old army friend Flavius was given a full legionary command and sent north to protect the margins of Italia. Even Domitian, who remained adamant that Nero had been appointed by dynastic blood and the will of the gods and that his removal had been a crime against nature, seemed to favour Otho, the nearest thing to Nero's heir that could be found.

Everyone loved Otho...

Except Germania. Vitellius, the governor of that dangerous border province, maintained his claim to the throne, and he controlled four of the most powerful veteran legions in the empire. Supported, or more realistically *driven*, by his two generals, he had begun to move south. Fabius Valens and Aulus Caecina Alienus led a surprisingly successful campaign and by the end of March were threatening the borders of Italia. I worried for Flavius, who was there somewhere, campaigning and leading a legion against the threat of this fresh usurper.

All our hopes for a new, reasonable reign were threatened by the upstart Vitellius, a man whose wickedness had been legendary even in the debauched court of Nero. We spent those months waiting repeatedly for news of the war, praying that Vitellius and his generals would be destroyed far from Rome. The news that came was never good. Far from what we hoped, it seemed that Vitellius and his generals, in particular Caecina, were unstoppable. Just as Nero had thrown everything he could at Galba, so Otho ordered his own forces to engage the new threat. He surprised everyone, I think, by taking a personal role, riding north to take command. There, in northern Italia, at Bedriacum, the forces met for their greatest clash, and the result was the latest in a catalogue of disasters.

I received the news of the end of that promising reign with a sour expression one mid-April morning. Proving himself oddly noble at the very end, Otho had, by all accounts, looked out at the slaughter in Italia and decided that it was too much for the empire to bear, and that there would be no more deaths on his conscience. In the aftermath of that terrible day at Bedriacum, the emperor on whom we had all pinned our hopes walked away from his army, into his tent, bid farewell to the world and opened his own veins, leaving Vitellius undisputed emperor of Rome.

To say that we greeted these tidings with trepidation would be something of an understatement. Vitellius had an appalling reputation as a human being, had no experience of governance beyond his posting in Germania, was rumoured to have been pushed into his revolt by his two power-hungry generals, and rested his authority on the back of four legions who had spent the better part of a century learning barbarous ways on the edge of the empire. Omens were sought, entrails read, chickens watched, and none of it was promising. Once more, we had no idea how the Flavii and their allies would stand in a new Vitellian empire. Sabinus' position was once again at risk, we had no idea whether Vespasian and Titus, whose war was close to peaking, would be withdrawn, Flavius had actively led a legion against Vitellius, which would be unlikely to make him popular. Me? Otho had told me straight that I would be given the governorship of Cappadocia, but the command had never been confirmed, and with Vitellius now closing on Rome, it seemed unlikely he would grant favours to the chosen of his predecessor.

Later that month we had sat in the palace, awaiting the arrival of the new emperor to take his throne. Sabinus was busy with his men, and Flavius was supposedly still nominally in his command in the north, now travelling as part of the new emperor's force, his legion having taken a fresh oath. Domitian and I, then, stood on the balcony and watched with dismay as Vitellius began his hold on Rome.

It was not an encouraging sight. The emperor himself came in a carriage and, when he alighted on the Palatine, it transpired that he was so fat that it took three slaves to help extricate him from the vehicle, and they needed to support him to the palace doors. With him came his entourage, including his two infamous generals, who had won him an empire. Valens was a gaunt and miserable looking thing, to whom I took an instant dislike, almost as much as his master. Caecina was a different matter. I expected to hate him. He was an enemy who had cut his way to Rome through the bodies of other Romans. He was a power-hungry general who had pushed a governor into revolt. Oddly, though, Caecina was one of the most pleasant and personable characters I have ever met. He was handsome in the extreme, wore his armour as though born to it, had an engaging smile that drew a man in, and gods knew, women too. Most of all, he bowed his head respectfully to those he met on that day, while Vitellius and Valens simply marched through them without acknowledging them. Simply, there was something inescapably likeable about Caecina. I should have been on my guard from the start, given how in Rome no one smiles without concealing a dagger.

The Praetorians, who had supported Otho and had fought against Vitellius, were reorganised. Any man who couldn't be trusted – half of them – was reposted to some frontier legion, his position in the Guard taken by a rough, greedy legionary from the German forces. The new emperor gave his men licence to cause havoc. They did not sack Rome as they had other Roman cities on their journey south, but rape, theft and open murder in the streets became a common sight in the days and months following Vitellius' arrival.

That first day, as we watched the emperor's entourage reach the palace, while his German soldiers pushed, shoved, spat and beat their way through the forum below, Domitian shared with me thoughts that stayed, and still do.

Amid the chaos and the unpleasantness, we could see white-robed figures moving. Senators in their pristine togas. They drifted from the basilicas, palaces and temples as the new emperor arrived, and flocked to him and his cronies like iron nails to a lodestone, each trying to secure the favour of the new master of Rome before he could learn how untrustworthy they all were.

'Look at them,' Domitian sneered.

'It is a poor display,' I agreed.

'What, I ask you, Nerva, is the point of the senate?'

I frowned. It sounded like a disparaging comment, but I knew Domitian well enough to recognise a genuine question when I heard it. I worked my answer carefully before speaking. 'The senate is the lifeblood of Rome. The emperor may be its heart, but the power flows from him through the senate and out into the world.'

There was a short silence as the young Flavian mulled this over.

'You're wrong.'

'I am?'

'The senate is an impediment. An outdated institution. To use your analogy, the senate is the disease carried around the body by the blood. It is a parasitic thing.'

'The senate has plenty of authority,' I argued. 'The emperor cannot be expected to maintain control of every aspect of Roman rule. The senate is his right hand, enacting the detail based upon the emperor's grand plan.'

'Perhaps once upon a time,' Domitian said, gaze still fixed on the white shapes and their obsequious activity. 'Augustus played that game, maintaining the senate, but even Tiberius realised that it was just a sinecure. Caligula, whatever faults he may have had, recognised that the senate was an impediment to efficient rule. No one since Augustus has truly maintained the fiction that the senate is important. It is just a breeding ground for sedition and opposition.'

I shook my head. 'The senate provides governors for provinces. Your own father and uncle are of senatorial blood, as am I. And we play our part in the running of empire.'

Domitian snorted. 'Why, then, are you all shaking in your boots with the arrival of a new emperor? Why is my uncle afeared that his command will be swept from under him once more. Why will my father be expecting to be withdrawn? Because it is the senate's decree? Why are you no longer expecting to be sent to Cappadocia? Because the senate have other plans for you? No. It is the emperor's power to grant and to remove all these things. And if the senate claim any power, they do it because the emperor lets them.'

I tried to find a cogent argument in opposition, but every point I raised in my mind turned to ashes on my tongue as I watched the white-clad senators of Rome trying to grab what power and authority they could from their new master.

'The empire is still too big for the emperor to administer alone,' I concluded.

'And Nero's freedmen proved that time and again,' the young man replied, still watching the greed of Rome at work. 'The administration has kept the empire running even as emperors have come and gone, not *because* of the senators, but *in spite* of them.'

I had no answer to that. He was right. I was a senator myself, and until that day I had considered that a worthwhile thing.

April faded as Rome suffered under the cruel heel of the German legions and the new Vitellian Guard. May bled into summer, and once again the usual exodus from the city during the stinking dusty months failed to happen while every man of note and wealth remained as close to the new emperor's power as possible in the hope of securing some greater post.

General Valens proved to be every bit as sour as he had appeared, while his master, the new emperor, lived up to his reputation in every way. His reign, even in the first month, was marked by gluttony, greed, cruelty and leering wickedness. Flavius managed to avoid any fall from grace, though his military command was ended and he once more became a private citizen. Vespasian and Titus remained out east, crushing the Jews, and Sabinus, perhaps through his reputation for efficiency, retained command of the cohorts.

It was only later that we would learn of Caecina's part in this. Valens had been all for replacing every figure in power with pro-Vitellians, and the emperor seemingly cared little for the actual running of empire, leaving it to his underlings. It was Caecina who had secured Flavian continuation, and Cocceian, for that matter. I had not even known that Caecina was aware of us all until one day in early July.

I was returning from a meeting with a number of palace functionaries, my litter wobbling its way up the Quirinal towards my house. My retinue was larger than usual for, with the ever-present German legionaries in the streets of Rome, I had taken to doubling my private guard wherever I went. More than one nobleman had fallen foul of drunken Vitellians so far that year. I was passing Vespasian's house when I noticed a small gathering of Praetorians outside. I slowed just as the house's door opened, and Aulus Caecina, smiling as always, emerged. He mounted, turned and rode off, unaware of who was watching from the shelter of the litter across the street. I saw Domitian in the doorway, turning and making his way back into the house. His expression was troubled.

My interest piqued, I directed my men over to the door, exited the litter and knocked. The doorman made me wait, an unusual delay given my familiarity with the family. There was clearly some consultation, for it took a while for Quarto to return and admit me to the triclinium. There, I was surprised to find not only Domitian, but Sabinus and Flavius too, all three faces grave.

'What has happened?' I asked, stopping in the doorway. 'What did Caecina say?'

Sabinus frowned for a moment, then made the connection that I had arrived as the Vitellian general left. 'Caecina is concerned that not all the provinces have yet sent their full support for the new emperor. He wanted to know if we had heard anything from my brother.'

I crossed to a couch and sank to it. 'Judea is far from alone,' I said in a comforting manner. 'Fully half the empire is yet to declare for Vitellius. The man has been on the throne for a quarter of a year and even the senate have yet to fully ratify his reign.'

Something about Sabinus' expression was making me uneasy, though.

'What is it? Have you heard anything to the contrary?'

At a nod from his father, Flavius crossed to the door, looked out into the atrium and then shut it tight. A prickle crossed my skin. This felt more than a little conspiratorial.

'Sabinus?' I urged.

'You have ever been bound to the Flavii, Marcus, just as much as are the Petronii and the Plautii. I trust your alliance with us will hold your tongue in check, for what I have to say could be a death sentence for all.'

'What is it? I am your friend, Sabinus. Always.'

The elder Flavian leaned back in his seat. 'My brother has refused to swear his oath.'

That was not good. Not good at all. Vitellius was a horrible man, but he was also the unopposed emperor of Rome. A conscientious governor could not pick and choose a fresh candidate. 'What will he do?'

The answer that came had truly not occurred to me until it spilled from the lips of Sabinus.

'Vespasian will be hailed emperor.'

Eyes wide, I sank back into the seat. 'What?'

'It is not public knowledge as yet, but the governor of Syria, Mucianus, has been pressuring him to oppose Vitellius since the spring. And the governor of Aegyptus is with them. The entire east rallies behind Vespasian, but as yet they have made no move.'

I was stunned. I had seen Vindex and Galba rise to overthrow Nero, had watched Galba cut down in the forum, while Otho snuck away to steal a crown. I had read the report of Otho's honourable demise as the usurper Vitellius marched his legions against Rome. But they had all been other people's problems. We had, with some difficulty, guided our raft through the flow of events, but always a little removed from them, even when Sabinus and Domitian had run off in support of Otho.

This was different. This was the Flavii making a bid for power themselves, and any claim Vespasian made in Judea would have far-reaching effects. In Rome, his family and friends were within the grasp of his enemies.

'Surely not,' was all I could think to say.

Domitian leaned in now. 'Not just the east, either. On the Danubius, Antonius Primus and his legions will pledge their support. And support is not limited to the east. I have been made aware of a number of the wealthier and more influential families in Rome who would not quail at Father's investiture. Senators are fickle things, as you know.'

I nodded, troubled. Of course, Domitian would know more than most of us. The legions in Pannonia and Moesia were critical to any bid for the throne now, and support in the senate could make a huge difference in perceived legitimacy. Could this really be happening? If it was true, Vespasian would have an impressive force at his command, especially since he and Titus already commanded a powerful army gathered together to put down the Judean revolt.

'When will he move?'

Sabinus shrugged. 'He holds off as long as he can, though Mucianus and Primus are both pushing him to march already. Vespasian is hoping to force a change in rule without a war.'

I frowned. 'How?'

'If he can build a powerful enough opposition to Vitellius before the claim becomes official, perhaps Vitellius can be persuaded to step down. Otho took his own life when faced with an impossible war. Vespasian...' Sabinus sighed. 'It is my role to move things in the capital. To reach a point where Vitellius can be persuaded to step aside peacefully.'

I shook my head. 'Vitellius is not that kind of man.'

'We have to try,' Sabinus said. 'Rome has already been devastated by a year of conflict. If there is a chance we can resolve this without more, we have to try. And while I fear my brother has been more than a little rash, I am resolved that he is correct. Vitellius has to go.'

Domitian nodded eagerly. Vitellius was everything Domitian disliked. Gluttonous, twisted, sexually degrading, careless of the nuances of rule, ignoring everything but his belly and libido while leaving the empire to flail beneath him.

'What will we do?' I said quietly.

'I will maintain my role. I command the cohorts. It is my duty to keep Rome safe, and it is a full-time job with Valens and his legions in the city.'

'Valens will be an obstacle,' I noted.

'He will,' Domitian replied. 'But Caecina may yet be more of an ally than an opponent. I may be able to turn him to our cause.'

'You are risking much. The moment Vespasian claims the throne, the Praetorians will be at your door, cutting throats.'

'I don't think so,' Sabinus replied. 'As long as he holds back, Vespasian will be powerful enough to be a solid threat. Even if Vitellius cannot be persuaded to do the sensible thing, his generals are too shrewd to waste hostages. We are of value alive. Too much value to get rid of.'

Even then, sitting in that triclinium, I doubted the wisdom of everything I heard. Vespasian would rise in the east, threatening Rome until Vitellius either panicked and vacated the throne, or until the two forces met and one came out on top. But no matter what Sabinus thought, all I could see in the rest of us staying in Rome and trying to play power games was a death sentence.

We talked late into the night, making plans, creating lists of who could be relied upon and who must be marginalised. Like my own, some of Rome's most powerful families had been tied to the Flavii since the days of Tiberius. It was not far from dawn when I ambled home with my slaves and guards, my world turned upon its head, and even then I could not sleep.

The days that followed were much the same. We spent time in consultation, either at Vespasian's house, or that of Sabinus or myself. The conspiracy grew. In those earlier days when Domitian and I had unpicked similar plots by Agrippina and Piso, I had not realised just how much planning must go into a coup if it is to have any hope of success. Domitian and Caecina became semi-regular dining companions, and it was increasingly clear that Caecina and his fellow general, Valens, shared a far from cordial relationship. Domitian spent day after day widening the rift between the two in the hope that when the time came, Caecina could be brought into our plan.

It was two days after the Nones of July when everything changed.

We had been expecting a missive from Vespasian, warning us that the time was nigh. Instead, the warning came to the palace first. Vespasian had been proclaimed emperor by his troops in Judea, and Syria, Aegyptus and Pannonia had all declared their support. The news hit Rome like a tidal wave of panic. Vespasian remained in Judea, but Primus and Mucianus were both on the move already, from Pannonia and Syria respectively, marching their legions on Rome.

Everything we had put in place was rendered void by the sudden revolt with no warning.

Sabinus heard at the same time as everyone else, and the curses he heaped upon his brother for moving without notice were bitter. We had hoped for sufficient threat in the east to allow us to persuade Vitellius to step down, but now those hopes lay in ruins.

That morning, as one of Sabinus' clients, breathless and wide-eyed, relayed the news to us in the house of Vespasian, we feared that everything had come undone.

'What now?' I asked, quietly.

Sabinus ground his teeth. 'I must continue to do my job. The cohorts must police the streets with this news abroad, for there will be more disorder than ever now. I will attempt to speak to the emperor and push our agenda, suggesting there are non-military solutions. But the time has come. I had hoped that when this happened you would already all be on a ship for Campania, but events have overtaken us. I must get to work, but you three have to get out of here. I will not risk my son, Vespasian's boy cannot be put in such danger, and your name is tied to ours sufficiently to condemn you, Nerva. Now that Primus has marched, everything has changed. Get to Ostia and flee south until this is over.'

I nodded. My old friend and the young scion of the Flavian house hurried around for the next half hour, making everything ready to leave. Sabinus departed for the palace to do what he could. We had the chests packed and loaded on a carriage, the slaves ready, our travelling gear prepared, and two dozen strong guards to escort us through the city, in case we met resistance. We were done. We had just about made it.

Then we opened the gates at the side of the boundary wall, the driver preparing to break minor laws by driving a vehicle through the city streets during the hours of daylight.

Outside, in the street, stood two centuries of Praetorians, the new ones co-opted from the German legions. A horribly familiar figure in a toga stood at the centre of the line, arms folded. Manius Acilius Glabrio was the perfect ophidian senator. He had been a favourite of Nero, but had thrown in his lot with Galba the moment the wind changed. It had been he who had searched the house for Nero that day, and he who Domitian had insulted with a thrown wine cup. Glabrio had navigated Otho's reign and had been one of the first to flock to the side of Vitellius when he arrived. The sight of Glabrio was never welcome, and on this particular day even less so.

'Going somewhere?' the senator sneered, a horrible smile accompanying his words.

We did not reply. We stood still. If the Praetorians came for blood, our guards would fight to hold them off, but the battle would not last long, and the result would be inevitable.

'In the name of the emperor Aulus Vitellius Germanicus Imperator Augustus, you are hereby placed under house arrest for your association with the usurper Vespasian. Return to your rooms and surrender your guards.'

Domitian made to move, but Glabrio fixed the young man with a look, clearly remembering earlier insults. 'I have my orders. You are under house arrest. But if you resist, I am sure I will suffer no ill effects from ordering a number of deaths. Stand down.'

Close to me, Flavius murmured 'What now, Marcus?'

I shrugged. 'What else? We stand down.'

X

Weapons of war

Rome, 18 December AD 69

Five months we languished. Five months of house arrest. It sounds far worse than it was. In actual fact, when the dust had settled, it transpired that the order for the arrest had gone out only in the name of Domitian, being the son of the new usurper and therefore an important bargaining tool. Vitellius had been persuaded by his administrators, and by the silver-tongued Caecina, that Sabinus was the best urban prefect in the city's long history, and so an agreement had been struck that he remain in the role, on the condition he swear allegiance to Vitellius and never waver. This he did, for the sake of practicality and for the simple safety of Rome and his family. Flavius had not been included in the order, yet he had no official role in Rome under the current emperor, and so he spent his time with Domitian, keeping his spirits up and making sure nothing untoward happened to him. I did the same. The young man, being house-bound, had devoted his time to literature and poetry for which, it turned out, he had something of a talent. He had also taken to practising his archery daily until the Praetorians who watched the house every hour of the day took away the weaponry on principle.

Five months. Vespasian remained in the east, while Mucianus continued to move west, gathering support as he went. Antonius Primus, the headstrong commander from Pannonia who had moved too early and ruined our plans, seemed bent on hacking and slicing his way to Rome. He engaged in fighting every step of the way, though at least he racked up a record of continuous victories.

Vitellius did everything he could, both at home and abroad, to stop Primus and to bring the whole of Rome to his side. He spent a massive sum on handouts and games for the common people, bought senators whose honour was for sale, granted sums to any military unit who would take his oath, and threw every sword he could find in the way of Primus. Caecina was sent with an army of considerable size to head him off, but somewhere in the north the handsome young general, for months now a confidante of Domitian, changed sides and attempted to bring his legions into the service of Vespasian. Sadly, his smooth tongue was not enough, and he was overwhelmed and bound in chains by his officers, who remained steadfast in their loyalty to Vitellius. To replace him, Valens was then sent north, and every able hand was sent with him, including a legion formed, in a last desperate move, of gladiators. The two great armies met in late October at that same field near Bedriacum where Otho had lost his throne, and there Primus, a barbarous animal in a general's uniform, thrashed Valens and overcame the Vitellian forces. By the end of October, the emperor's last military hope was gone, and Primus was still marching on Rome.

November was a tense month as news of the continual approach made the populace nervous. Vitellius was rarely seen in public now, and Rome was under a strict curfew, maintained by both Praetorians and the urban cohort. It was just a matter of time. Vitellius had thrown at the approaching army everything he could find, even offering huge sums of money to any citizen who could wield a stick if they would march north. Few did.

Primus moved methodically, removing every obstacle as he went. Mucianus, reputedly, was also closing and hoped to arrive in Rome at roughly the same time. Caecina had been released from his chains after Bedriacum, and was now commanding part of Primus' army. Caecina was ever a survivor, and he played the game well.

At the start of December we had a visitor at the Flavian house. The unpleasant Acilius Glabrio strode in as though he owned the place. Full of self-importance despite the growing danger he and his sort were in, he ordered Domitian to pen a letter to Primus and Mucianus demanding that they withdraw from their advance and advising them that the Flavian family and their various supporters in the city could be executed if this uprising continued unabated.

I had expected Domitian to refuse with a certain acidity, especially given his personal history with Glabrio. In fact, even the senator was taken aback when Domitian rose from his seat, dropping the poem he had been composing. In a heartbeat he was beside Glabrio, his needle-pointed bronze stilus at the senator's throat.

'Do you feel secure, Glabrio?' he asked in a most unpleasant tone. Behind the senator, two of the Praetorians who had accompanied him inside put their hands on their sword hilts and made to move, but Domitian looked at them over Glabrio's shoulder and shook his head until they stepped back.

'Don't be a fool, son of Vespasian.' But Glabrio was sweating.

'Vitellius controls the city, Glabrio, but inside these walls, this is Flavian land, and I am the master. Never forget that. I will never, *never*, bow down to the obsequious pressure of untrustworthy senators. I will write no letter for you. You will turn round with your guards and leave my house. I will give orders to the doorman that you are no longer to be admitted. I may be under house arrest, but on this side of the door you have no authority, and if I decide to pluck out your eye for your insolence, I will do so unchallenged. Now fuck off.'

With that, he removed the pen and Glabrio staggered away, white as his toga and pouring with sweat. He and his Praetorians left without a further word. I watched Domitian carefully. It would be easy to put his reaction down to the history between the two men, exacerbated by Domitian's half-year incarceration. But it was not just that. It was, that morning, as though something had been triggered inside him. I had known him to be exceedingly clever and quick to anger, but that morning, I knew beyond the shadow of a doubt that he could kill, and would have done so had Glabrio made the wrong move.

That was the last time Glabrio even tried to enter the house.

–

The ides came and went. The city was moving into what should have been the most joyous and festive time of the year, with Saturnalia and then the new year. In fact, festivities were minimal at best, the atmosphere in the city tense and nervous. Stories were circulating of horrors inflicted on captured towns and units by the armies of Antonius Primus, and there was a general worry that the same was coming to Rome unless the more moderate Mucianus could reach the city first and keep Primus in order.

That first night of Saturnalia little happened, the streets almost empty, still under imperial curfew, small gangs of German legionaries, disgruntled Praetorians and careful men of the cohorts all moving about the city, keeping order.

The next day Sabinus called in during the morning. The time had come, he announced. Despite everything, the plans we had laid months earlier were going to be put into action. Now that Primus was but a few days from Rome with his armies, the bulk of the provinces were favouring Vespasian, and Rome was all but defenceless, Sabinus was going to persuade Vitellius to abdicate and avoid carnage in the streets of the city.

The prefect had gathered a small party of important persons to present the offer to the emperor. Both consuls, some of the more renowned senators, even the head of the Vestals. I offered my support, but Sabinus shook his head. This, he said, needed to come clearly from the wider heart of Rome and not from a distinctly Flavian group. Vitellius had to know that this was a proposition for the good of the empire, and not an ultimatum from Vespasian's family. Sabinus, ever the most noble of men. Even in this he was determined to do it right. I agreed, and would stay with Domitian and Flavius while the offer was made.

I heard what had happened that next day from those who were with him. In the company of some of the most distinguished names in Rome, Sabinus made his way to the palace. He was admitted to Vitellius' presence and there laid out an offer. Vitellius would be paid a large sum and granted a palatial seaside villa. He and his family would have their lives guaranteed, his son continuing to inherit, all the family's holdings intact. All he had to do was make a public announcement of his abdication. After all, the senate had never ratified his reign, and so he could leave the throne without any real stigma, the power passing to Vespasian without issue. It was generous, sensible and well laid out.

Vitellius had no choice, and he knew it. His army was gone. Primus was days or even hours from the city, Mucianus on his heels. The empire had gone over to Vespasian, and if Vitellius decided to fight, he would be dead within days, and his family with him. The only forces he could still count on were a few centuries of German legionaries that remained in the city and a part of the Praetorian Guard who had been well and truly bought by him, the rest dead on the battlefields of the north. There was really no alternative. Vitellius agreed to Sabinus' proposal, and there it should have ended, and everything should have been peace and relief.

Then Vitellius blew it. He stepped out of the palace that bitterly cold afternoon clad in very theatrical funeral garb, his family at his side similarly dressed. It was showy and brought out the worst thing possible among the watchers: sympathy.

In the forum below the Palatine, Sabinus and his party in attendance as well as many of Rome's populace, Vitellius stated his intention to abdicate. The fool could not, however, resist a little drama. Not satisfied with being offered a future, he wanted the world to know how gracious he was and how Vespasian had brought him to this like the martial dog *he* was. His speech was a lament, rather than a statement. Sabinus had watched with growing unease, and had realised that things had gone wrong as those gathered around had begun to shout Vitellius' name and demand that he retract his announcement. Before the emperor could do anything, his loyal Germans and Praetorians had flocked to him, refusing to accept his abdication. Vitellius and his family were huddled back into the palace by his men, and Sabinus and that small party of notables found themselves suddenly facing angry Praetorians and legionaries in the forum.

As their blades were bared, Sabinus did the only thing he could do. He ran.

With two consuls, togas slipping from them, a dozen senators in a panic, half a dozen noblewomen and a small gaggle of citizens, the urban prefect fled for his life as the Vitellian soldiers bellowed their defiance and brandished their swords. Fortunately for the older Flavian, he had a small party of men from his faithful urban cohort with him, and they held off the more rabid Praetorians long enough for the fugitives to run to the nearest defensible place, the Capitol. There, the steep inclines and massive retaining walls of temples left only a few narrow approaches that could be guarded and held.

Of all this, at the time, I was unaware. All I knew was what we heard in our house on the Quirinal. A messenger from Sabinus reached us early in the afternoon, confirming that Vitellius had accepted the offer, and that he would announce his abdication that afternoon.

We waited, tense, expecting the next letter. Nothing happened.

As the hours wore on and the light began to dim, Quarto the doorman finally informed us that something was happening in the street. By the time we reached the front door, the street was empty. For the first time in five months, there were no Praetorian eyes watching the Flavian house.

I frowned, peering up and down the street.

'Perhaps as part of his speech, Vitellius has ordered the guard to stand down?' Flavius murmured, looking this way and that.

I was struck with an ominous feeling. Something was wrong. I shook my head. 'If everything was proceeding as expected, the Praetorians would have told us they were off, but they left unexpectedly with no announcement. Something has happened.'

Domitian was there with us now, his gaze raking the house's surroundings. We caught sight of a pair of figures in the distance, running. Uniformed figures with nightsticks, men of the urban cohort, pounding along the road fast, heading for the centre of the city. If we'd needed any further hint that all was not well, that was it.

Flavius and I watched for a few moments, exchanging theories, and we only realised Domitian was not with us when we heard a commotion back in the atrium. Turning, I saw the youngest Flavian had thrown a cloak around his shoulders and exchanged his house sandals for a pair of hard-wearing calfskin boots. He was prepared for the outdoors, somewhere he had not been since July.

'Wait,' I said, holding up my hands.

'No. Sabinus is out there and something is wrong.'

'He would want you safe.'

'You think this place is safe?' Domitian asked, throwing out his arms. 'If Vitellius is still in command, and Sabinus has stood against him, how long do you think it will be before the emperor's Praetorians are back, and this time with their blades drawn. Arrest will no longer be enough. We need to find my uncle.'

He was right. The Praetorians had left, but if Vitellius had refused to step down and had gathered his forces to him, Sabinus, Domitian and Flavius were only of use to him now in chains and in the palace. The Praetorians would be back. In moments, Flavius and I had similarly changed. Domitian gathered the guards that remained in the domus, most of them having been dismissed on the day of his arrest, and we left the house on Pomegranate Street with a sense of desperate purpose. We broke one of Rome's oldest laws that day, taking blades into the sacred heart of the city. Domitian wielded a sword taken from his father's office, and Flavius and I carried the blades we had brandished against the tribes of Britannia. Weapons of war bared and with intent to kill within the city, in defiance of most ancient laws, we marched towards the Palatine.

I had argued for a circuitous route, minimising the chances of running into marauding Praetorians, but neither of the Flavii were in the mood to listen, and Domitian simply strode out ahead, sword bared, waving the guards on and down the great Vicus Longus towards the heart of Rome.

It was quite by chance that we ran into friends before foes.

Rome had erupted into violent chaos. Vitellius' men were seemingly everywhere, and I caught distant sight of packs of Praetorians and legionaries here and there down side streets as we jogged. We moved into the triangular space where Lantern Street peeled off, and there, to our relief, we spotted a small group of men from the urban cohort of Sabinus marching in our direction, armed for war.

'What are you doing out?' demanded a centurion, wide-eyed with surprise.

'What's happened?' Domitian asked him, ignoring the question.

'The prefect is trapped on the Capitol. The Praetorians refused to let the emperor abdicate and they've got him sealed up in the palace. Sabinus sent us to find you. We're to escort you to the Capitol.'

I shook my head. 'Sabinus is trapped on a hill and he wants us to be trapped with him? That's hardly strategically sound.'

Flavius nodded. 'We need to break him out and get out of the city. Primus is close.'

The centurion pointed back towards the forum with his sword. 'The city is being closed, and you'll not leave Rome in one piece. Right now the Praetorians are still sealing the Capitol in, though, and we can join Sabinus. In half an hour the hill will be under siege and we'll not get through. My orders are to take you there now, while we can.'

I was still prepared to argue, as was Flavius, but our reservations were made moot in an instant as Domitian gestured to the centurion and strode off in the direction of the Capitol. Exchanging a look, Flavius and I hurried after him, the soldiers gathering protectively around us. We moved into the Clivus Argentarius as we neared the slopes of the Capitol, and as we crested the rise with a good view of the forum, my heart pounded with shock at what I saw.

Rome was at war.

The forum had emptied of the throngs of ordinary folk and was rapidly becoming a military camp. Praetorians and legionaries from Vitellius' German army were gathered in groups, not organised or lined up with military precision, but more like marauding bandits. Weapons were being distributed and already a small collection of bodies lay at the near end of the forum. No one was going to approach the Capitol from the forum without landing themselves in the middle of an ongoing clash. I realised then how accurate the centurion had been. Within a short space of time, the Capitol was going to be completely surrounded and sealed off. Glancing between the columns on our left, I could see more units circling the hill, preparing to blockade other approaches.

In response, the centurion stopped us, turned, and left the forum, making for another approach. We ran now, all thoughts of subtlety gone. Praetorians had seen us, and men were bellowing, racing to stop us. We hurtled along the hillside beneath the great retaining walls of Juno's temple, which towered above us. We reached the narrow way that led up through the Lucus Asyli and on to the Capitol. Turning the corner to the climb, we realised how close we had come to disaster, for Praetorians were arriving from the far side, having skirted the hill from the Palatine.

The centurion bellowed a warning, and it was the last thing he ever said, a thrown pilum slamming through his middle and impaling him. The brave officer fell there, shaking, on the stony ground. I felt the urgency of battle for the first time since those days Flavius and I had stomped around Britannia and, as Domitian pounded up the steps to the hill where his uncle was besieged, Flavius and I joined the brave men of the cohorts.

There were only a couple of contubernia of Praetorians yet, though we could hear the sounds of more on the way, from every approach. If we let them be and just ran, they would be on our heels all the way up the stairs to the Capitol and men would fall in flight. Instead, weapons ready, Flavius and I stood side by side and fought for our lives.

I was no longer a young man, and had never been an unparalleled swordsman, but no scion of an old house in Rome passes through his education without being taught a thing or two about the use of a sword. I think the Praetorians were a little taken aback by our resistance, expecting to easily overwhelm half a dozen policemen and a couple of middle-aged senators. Instead we gave as good as we got, or better. Side by side, Flavius and I stabbed and slashed, blocking blows and delivering them. The metallic smell of blood filled the late afternoon air.

There is a certain odd joy to be found in the simplicity of battle. Life may be full of difficult decisions and troublesome paths, but in a fight to the death, once the bowel-loosening anticipation is past and it becomes simply a test of resolve and strength, you against them, all indecision and worry is gone, and instinct and desperation take over. It truly is the freest moment in life. I fought like a hero of old, or so the men of the cohorts told me afterwards. In the space of thirty heartbeats we had bested the Praetorians. I drove my blade home into the unprotected gut of one of the last, his white tunic puckering around the wound and then flooding crimson. I yanked the sword free and stepped back, panting, as the mortally wounded man dropped his blade and looked down at his own demise with shock and panic. He fell to his knees, keening like a lost infant.

I would probably have stood there for hours, shaking in the aftermath, had not one of Sabinus' men grabbed me by the shoulder, shouting something urgent and gesturing up the slope. More of the cohort's men were stepping out from the sides now and taking up defensive positions on the climb. I came to my senses swiftly, looking about. More Praetorians were arriving already, pounding towards the slope, hoping to catch us before we could retreat to safety.

We ran, heedless of the strain on our muscles, climbing the slope to our place of refuge. The Capitol was surrounded now.

The Praetorians who'd come behind us were approaching carefully, but the men of the cohorts were gathered with rocks and tiles, hurling them down the slope, holding the enemy at bay. The way was blocked both in and out. The Capitol was under siege.

Flavius and I reached the top and found Domitian with his uncle in the wide Asylum space between the great temples. Sabinus hurried over to greet us, his face grave as he clasped our hands and shook them with relief.

'You're wounded?' he noted with concern, pointing at me. I looked down to see a red line across my chest and shoulder, gently leaking into my tunic. I had not even noticed. I shook it off. It was little more than a scratch.

'What now?' I asked.

Sabinus took a deep breath. 'We hold. We are in the most defendable place in Rome. We hold it against everything Vitellius can throw at us. Primus is a day away at most and I have sent men to warn him to hurry. This place might not hold forever, but it can hold until Primus arrives.'

I nodded.

By the gods, I hoped he was right.

XI

The Capitol

Of all the hills of Rome, the Capitol is the one that might have been designed for defence, high and with steep sides, precipitous in places. Since the time of the kings, it has been home to Rome's most sacred temples, carved away in places and fortified with great stone cliffs to hold the weight of Rome's piety. It is a citadel of the gods. In truth, it is actually two hills, the Capitoline and the Arx, joined by the narrow saddle of the Asylum, together comprising the Capitol.

Because of the Capitol's sacred nature, it is carefully controlled. Access is only possible along four routes. The main approach climbs from the forum, curving around the Temple of Saturn. A secondary route crests through a monumental gate before the Temple of Jupiter. The dreaded Gemonian Stair ascends and opens out before the Temple of Juno on the Arx, and the only other feasible approach is the narrow stair that emerges into the sacred grove of the Lucus Asyli, the one we fought our way up on our arrival. Four approaches, three facing the forum and one to the rear.

We watched, that dreadful evening, as the forces of Vitellius laid siege to the most sacred heart of Rome. This was no ordered assault, though, no Alesia or Avaricum, for the enemy were commanded by no great general, but led by a cluster of officers giving conflicting commands. That played to our advantage. They came at every one of the four routes as the sun slid from the sky and the evening drew in.

The Capitol was defended that night by an odd and motley collection. Sabinus took charge, naturally, and at his side were myself, Flavius, and an officer of the urban cohort. Beyond that we had perhaps two hundred men under arms. Oh, and five women led by a matron named Verulana Gratilla, each of whom refused to stand back and hide. Initially, Sabinus had refused to let Domitian take a part in the proceedings, but with a little persuasion, the youngest of the defenders was permitted to put himself in harm's way, as long as he stayed near one of us. He was, after all, the most important person on the hill that night, as the son of the would-be emperor.

Squads of men came up the slopes again and again. Flavius took command of the Jovian approach, Sabinus of the main approach from the forum, his tribune the treacherous Asylum climb, and I the Gemonian Stair. Domitian, like many of those on the hill that night, moved about as the need arose, answering the calls of whoever was hardest pressed. The defending force reacted impressively, always supporting whatever approach was under the heaviest assault. With my meagre force of soldiers and citizens, we swiftly blocked the stair. There was no gate at the top, and I sent a thousand apologies up to the gods and the spirits of Rome's illustrious ancestors as we toppled statues and their bases and heaved them onto the stair to form a makeshift barricade, adding to it furnishings, timbers, even an honorific column that we managed to fell. It would not hold forever, but to anyone climbing the stairs under attack, it presented sufficient obstacle to keep them back. A few of us had swords, more had nightsticks, and the rest had fashioned clubs from whatever could be found. None of us had any form of missile weapon, of course, and we had cause that night to lament that Domitian, by now an accomplished archer, had no access to a bow.

Instead, we did what we could. We pulled down low walls and lesser roofs, and used the bricks and tiles as weapons, hurling them at the attackers. It may not sound effective, but I once saw a man struck by a falling tile as he walked along the street. He was dead before his wife could cradle his body, his head caved in.

Thus with just bricks and tiles and fallen statues, a small force continued to hold off the elite guard of the emperor for hour upon hour. The attacks came in waves, ebbing and flowing, and in each lull, as the night became ever darker, we tended to our wounds. We lost men in a steady trickle, and in addition to the brave fallen that night, we watched the small knot of our badly wounded men growing and growing.

Domitian joined me in my fight from time to time, his face always serious, never taking joy in his first martial experience as many young men might. Though he had no bow to hand, his skill at archery made him a formidable warrior with a rock, too, as many found out that night. I found that when the women occasionally joined me, their spite and anger outstripped any of the men, and I almost felt sorry for the poor bastards on the receiving end of their missiles and barbed insults.

It was as night was becoming truly black that the first disaster befell us. Unable to break any of the defences, and hampered by the lack of light, the attackers had become frustrated and resorted to fire. Burning brands were cast up from below and soon fire raged on the Capitol. Sabinus and Flavius were having similar troubles, and the gate before the Temple of Jupiter was smoking now, sending roiling black up into the sky.

An hour later, on the far slopes, wily Praetorians and legionaries had realised that the private housing to either side of the narrow stair reached up to almost the height of the hill. They began to invade the residential blocks, emerging onto the roofs and jumping to the Capitol. Some fell to their deaths, but some succeeded and small skirmishes broke out where they managed to gain a foothold.

Though we had fought like lions far into the night, the heart was going out of the defenders and I could see it in their eyes. Then, when the encroaching flames from the forum side and the inferno from the burning buildings on the far slope finally took a true hold on the hill, we all realised that the end was near. Every face turned to the Temple of Jupiter, Rome's most holy place, as it erupted into a golden ball of fire.

We had only needed to hold out until Primus and his army reached Rome, yet within five hours our numbers had halved, our ammunition was depleted, and the hill was aflame. Every soul on the Capitol that night knew in their heart that when Primus arrived, the Capitol would be naught but an ash-clogged cemetery.

We were all relieved when the enemy pulled back to regroup. Along with several senators and centurions I joined the consuls and my friends as we debated with Sabinus.

'The Capitol is falling,' one of the consuls sighed. 'We have to leave.'

'How?' Flavius spat. 'The enemy have us besieged.'

'If we make a concerted push, we might break their lines and escape into the city,' the centurion Casperius Niger put in.

'No, if we flood the hill, escaping in every direction,' a senator suggested, 'some of us will get through.'

'And many will die,' Domitian retorted. 'Better to die fighting for what we believe in than as cowards with Praetorian swords in our backs.'

'Quite right,' Sabinus said, his face grave. 'No running. We have to hold, for it is all we can do. There is no refuge out there. The city is for Vitellius, and will be so until Primus floods it with men. There is little chance of escape. Like Vercingetorix against mighty Caesar, we must hold. We must trust the gods and hold. Our allies are close.'

No decision could be reached, though, for at that moment we heard the next charge, and looked down to see men racing for the hill in a massive, concerted assault from all sides at once.

We ran back to our places, preparing for a last defence. I had cause then to appreciate once more Domitian's condemning of the senatorial class. It did not escape my notice that while soldiers and freedmen, slaves and women, gathered at the barricades, armed with whatever they could find, the bulk of the senators who had become trapped with us were gone, attempting to find a way off the hill.

This time there was no attempt by the Vitellians to pull back. They were determined to finish it. Many attackers fell to the last volleys of our rubble, and then finally, inevitably, we found ourselves fighting across the barricades with swords and clubs. Casperius Niger and Didius Scaeva, two of the veteran centurions of the cohorts, were at my shoulders as we stabbed and hacked, feeling the ashes of Rome's temples settling on our cheeks, the heat of the burning hill searing our skin. I took a wound to my arm finally, which robbed me of sufficient strength to wield my sword. I tried to fight left-handed, but there was no hope, and I knew I was done for. I watched Scaeva felled with a blow to his neck, his blood washing over me in a hot wave, and suddenly Niger had me by the shoulder. He turned me and looked me in the eye, the way soldiers do in times of crisis, when rank is irrelevant.

'We're lost,' he said, flatly. 'Go. Save Sabinus.'

I almost argued, but as I looked around, I realised there was now a grand total of five of us holding the Gemonian Stair against more than a hundred, with more of the enemy arriving all the time. We were doomed. I nodded to the officer and ran.

It was not panic. I was not looking for a way out. I was prepared to die nobly for the cause, but I was faithful to the Flavii as always, and it was my duty to fight for them to the end. Not for Sabinus as such, that night, but now for Domitian, son of an imperial claimant. I ran, for the centre of the defences at the top of the Clivus Capitolinus.

There, a similar story was playing out. Sabinus and one of the consuls led a last desperate fight of fewer than a dozen men holding a wide road against hundreds. Sabinus was wounded, and coated with grime and soot. He turned as I ran to him, and I could see in his eyes that he, too, knew we were lost. We had held as long as we could, and Primus had not come. He looked about, then pointed at me.

'Save the boys. Get them out of here somehow.'

I blinked. We were besieged. There was no way out, and we'd come to that conclusion some time ago.

'How?' I barked, desperate.

'I don't know, and I don't care, but for everything the Flavii have ever done for you, that *I* have ever done for you, find a way. Save my son and my nephew.' He pointed off to the far side of the hill, and for a moment I caught a glimpse of both Flavius and Domitian desperately throwing rubble through the burnt-out gate before the temple.

I nodded my understanding and turned and ran again.

As I closed on the ruined gateway, an idea forming in my mind at the sight of the burning buildings, I half expected my old friend, or at least Domitian, to argue with me, to display the stubbornness endemic in the Flavii. They did not.

'Come with me,' was all I said, gesturing to them.

As I marched away, leaving the other consul, a centurion, two women and half a dozen soldiers of the cohort to hold the last barricade, Flavius and Domitian both broke off the fighting and hurried after me.

'Where are we going?' Domitian demanded as they caught up, breathing heavily.

'We're trapped,' Flavius noted. 'We'll end here, Marcus. We should stand with my father and die with him.'

'No, we shouldn't.'

It was only as I had arrived at this highest place, where the magnificent Temple of Jupiter blazed and crackled, falling in on itself, that I had decided on the only possible course of action. There was no way off this hill, unless we wished to throw ourselves from the cliffs. If we could no longer hold, and we couldn't escape, then all there was left to do was hide.

Many of the temples and shrines and buildings at this end of the Capitol were either burning, or had been partially destroyed in the search for rubble to throw at the attackers. My eyes, though, were on one in particular. The Temple of Fides, near to the Tarpeian Rock, was already badly burned, and the house of the temple attendant that was attached to the north side was scorched and blackened, missing a corner and its door, but was more or less structurally intact.

'We hide,' I said.

'What? Where?'

I remembered the day Galba had been proclaimed, and Nero fled. The day Praetorians had rampaged across these heights and I had been saved a beating by the temple attendant and his staff. The goddess of good faith had saved me that day through the ministry of her priests, and if there was one place in Rome we could be safe now, I felt that had to be it. We rounded the corner of the temple and there I found the bodies of the attendant and one of his slaves, crushed by falling masonry as the pediment of the temple had fallen. The other slave was nearby, cruelly burned to death. We hurried to the half-ruined house and, heedless of the danger of falling rubble, I forced my way inside. The interior was ruinous, filled with fallen beams and parts of the roof, an interior wall collapsed.

'When the hill falls,' Domitian said, 'they will search everywhere.'

'I think they will miss us. I have faith in Fides,' I said, and pushed through into a back room. There I found the attendant's freedman, cowering. He yelped in panic as we entered, but we managed to calm him and explain. We would all hide here and pray to the goddess for aid. He agreed emphatically.

We cringed there for what seemed an eternity, my arm still throbbing, the blood flow slowed to a drip. I heard the clashes of fighting again and again, gradually coming closer as the barricades fell and the defenders were pushed back. It was not long before the sounds of battle ebbed, though, and the silence they left was soon replaced with the chanting of Vitellius' name. The Capitol had fallen.

I think it was morbid curiosity that led me to move. Telling Flavius to keep his cousin safe, I picked my way out of the rubble. The heights of the hill were as bright as midday with the flames all around, and I could see that all activity seemed to be focused at the far side of the hill. I stood there, pressed against the wall to be less noticeable, and squinted into the golden darkness.

Vitellians controlled the hill, and they were almost all I could see. Almost.

Two men remained from our valiant defence, both wounded, disarmed, and captive in a circle of Praetorians. A chill ran through me, not at the sight of Quintus Atticus, the consul, but at his companion in wretchedness, Flavius Sabinus. I watched, cold and furious and impotent as the animals that served Vitellius hacked off the head of Sabinus and kicked his body down the stair, followed by the same treatment for the consul. Thus in horrible ignominy ended the life of the most noble man I had ever known. I bit down on my fury. I would remember this. There would be a reckoning someday.

I turned to see that Flavius and Domitian had ignored my words and were standing in the doorway behind me, ashen faced, both watching the grisly display. I grunted and gestured for them to move back inside. Already, their prisoners murdered, the Praetorians were beginning to search for survivors. They would be looking, in particular, for the sons of Sabinus and Vespasian.

We hid for hours in the corner of a ruined building, covered with a scorched blanket. At least twice the building was given a cursory once-over by the victorious Vitellians. None of them believed the house sufficient cover for two men, let alone four, and none of them bothered reaching the rear corner where we hid. It was only as the dawn light invaded the ruins and all was quiet that we finally lowered the blanket and rose, stretching stiff muscles and joints.

We emerged from the building gingerly. Rubble was everywhere and several temples, including that of great Jupiter, were little more than burnt-out ruins. Smoke hung above the hill in a threatening haze. My heart jumped as I saw the figures of armed soldiers at the periphery, and we retreated inside again for a while. Curiously, perhaps an hour later, our attention was drawn by singing, which seemed terribly incongruous. We glanced out and I was surprised to see a small column of priests of Isis, their bald heads bared, their white robes pristine, swaying in time as they walked amid the ruins, a gathering of their faithful following on.

The Isaic priests are a weird lot, and it says something about them that even the burning and violence the hill had seen that night could not put them off their rituals. On certain days, they tracked a snaking route from their temple in the Campus Martius, across the Capitol with a nod to Rome's leading divine triumvirate, and down to the Tiber behind the Temple of Spes, where they involved themselves in some strange ritual of washing. They were not about to let a mere civil war get in the way of their devotions. I shook my head in wonder, and then turned at the sound of a cleared throat. The freedman of Fides who had taken refuge with us through the night was holding up a white linen robe and pointing to a chest in the corner which held a number of similar garments, washed and carefully folded.

I looked back at the column. There was enough similarity between the get-up of the Isis followers and the robes of the Fides priests that only someone looking very carefully would spot the difference. Thanking the freedman for his quick thinking, we all took a robe and shrugged into it.

We waited just inside the doorway as the singing came closer and closer and then, finally, slipped out of the ruined building and fell in with the column of Isaic fanatics, who looked surprised for only a moment and then accepted our appearance without question. We crossed the hillside, hearts in our mouths as we passed pairs of angry-looking Praetorians here and there. We made our careful way in swaying procession through the burnt-out arch and down the hill, past the night's barricades that had since been moved aside. We sighed with relief as we reached the forum level and turned, making for the Velabrum, every step taking us further and further from the enemy.

We left the column a short while later, when Domitian noted that we were passing a house of the Cornelii, where one of Vespasian's friends lived. Still nervous, we begged his aid, and he took us in. We bathed, ate and dressed in fresh tunics before being tended by a physician. Once more feeling human, we waited in the house of the Cornelii for the world to change.

And change it did. That very afternoon, Antonius Primus and his victorious legions reached Rome. The Praetorians were stood down, the offenders removed. Primus set about securing the city, though a few days later Mucianus arrived and took over the job, much to Primus' disgruntlement. I never saw Vitellius' end, for we were still hiding when it happened, unaware as yet of our safety.

The huge, sick and twisted fallen emperor was dragged from the palace – it must have taken some doing, for he weighed the same as four men – to the Gemonian Stair where Sabinus had been killed. There he was hacked to pieces. There were still rumours circulating that Nero lived, and since no one wanted that to happen with Vitellius, his head was skewered and left on the Capitol as proof of his end. His body was cast into the Tiber to float away with the refuse, and his family put to death the same day.

Thus ended the civil war. A year of fighting, of terror, of emperors rising and falling, a year of four emperors. Domitian, Flavius and I had watched them all from the very heart of matters, and we had survived.

Vespasian was now the undisputed emperor of Rome, and, accordingly, Domitian was given the title of Caesar.

The Flavii had arrived.

XII

Politicking

With the new emperor still in the east, and Titus still involved in the Jewish war, Rome's governance fell to those who felt they had the right and the ability, whether they were correct or not. A number of generals and governors who had been instrumental in Vespasian's rise took the reins of state, though over those troublesome months, the pack was continually thinned until one man rose above them all, his control in the name of Vespasian all but absolute. That man was Mucianus. And even as the powerful military men vied and fell or rose, the senate continued in its attempts to be recognised as Rome's governing body, only to find themselves as powerless and ignored as ever.

Second in power after Mucianus, a surprise to many, came Caecina. Though a former confederate of both Galba and Vitellius, the wily Caecina had turned on his master in favour of Vespasian, and had consequently secured a solid place alongside the Flavii.

The third figure of note, power, and influence in Rome for those months was perhaps more surprising, and often overlooked and unnoticed despite all his work. Domitian, now eighteen, and with the official title of Caesar, and the rank of praetor, began to make his presence felt. One thing that quickly became obvious to me was that Domitian disliked Mucianus. I watched as the emperor's son began to display an unexpected mastery of Rome's politics in thwarting the aims of Mucianus.

The powerful governor levied harsh taxes, making the populace grumble about Flavian avarice, and Domitian immediately called private meetings of the *a rationibus* and the *magister rei privatae* and their staff, all those administrators whose responsibility was imperial finances. Mucianus was too powerful now to be simply gainsaid, but between Domitian and his freedmen they managed to curtail and bypass the worst of the man's edicts, preserving what they could of Vespasian's popularity among the masses.

As the days went on, it became almost a game; Mucianus issuing edicts, Domitian countering him with masterful skill. I almost laughed out loud on the day Mucianus took it upon himself to appoint to the governorship of Hispania Baetica his cousin Publius, securing a family powerbase there. Before the ink had even dried on his order, while Mucianus was still preparing to send it to the senate for ratification, Domitian called an assembly of that august body without Mucianus' knowledge and had them ratify Lucullus in that governorship. I gather Mucianus raged late into the night over that particular event.

And so it went on, the two men, the emperor's right-hand man and his own son vying for control of the state, Caecina now becoming more and more allied to Domitian and standing against Mucianus. While I did not particularly trust Caecina, I could see something dangerous in Mucianus, and perhaps the silver-tongued young man seemed a healthier alternative.

I called in at Domitian's house one morning to find Caecina there. It was as I watched the look that passed between the two that I realised what had been happening behind the scenes over those months. The former Vitellian, Domitian's confidante, who the young prince thought he had dancing to his tune, had somehow turned the tables. Now, it seemed Caecina had Domitian's ear. I cannot be certain even to this day, but I strongly suspect Caecina of being the driving force behind Domitian's rise to prominence over those months. The man who pushed Domitian into his opposition with Mucianus.

That morning I found the pair laughing raucously, though as I stepped into the room, that knowing look passed between them and they subsided. One of the threads that bound Domitian and

I together had been cut with the politicking of Caecina. I could feel it in the atmosphere.

'Marcus,' the young Caesar said with a smile. 'Come, sit.'

I did so, accepting wine from a slave, and remained silent, eyebrow arched until Domitian burst out laughing once more and swept up a scroll from the table, passing it to me.

'Read it,' he grinned.

I did so. For a while, as I read, I was not sure why. It was a private letter from his father and all the information in it was rather banal and personal, with the exception of an urging to work alongside Mucianus. It was only as I neared the end that I realised why they were laughing.

Vespasian always had a ready wit, even if some say it was a rather rural and lower-class one. In the last line, before signing off the letter, Vespasian had said to Domitian:

I thank you, my son, for permitting me to hold office and not yet dethroning me.

I spent a while that day with the two of them, and became somewhat uneasy at the influence I could see Caecina exerting. The problem was that he was so damned likeable and friendly that it was hard to do anything about it. Had he been a thief, you would have found yourself handing him your purse and only realised you'd done it an hour after he left.

—

The winter rolled into spring, and matters only became more difficult. There had been some sort of revolt against the new regime in Aegyptus, and Vespasian moved there to settle matters with his usual no-nonsense attitude, leaving Titus to finish up in Judea. In Germania, ever the source of imperial trouble, a new revolt arose under some fellow by the name of Julius Civilis, threatening the peace, and Petilius Cerialis, already in the region with a force, was dispatched to deal with it. In Rome, the power players had gradually diminished through Mucianus' machinations until only really he and Domitian remained, with Caecina ever whispering notions into the young man's ear.

Matters between the two powers became more and more strained each day. Mucianus used every ounce of his power to limit that of Domitian, preventing the young man from securing a position with the *vigintiviri* in which he would have gained control of criminal sentencing in the city. Conversely, while he cared not a jot for the senate, Domitian employed them readily in overturning anything Mucianus put in place that he did not like.

It was a war, of sorts. An uncivil war, I might call it. One thing that truly surprised me was just how in-depth Domitian's knowledge of the administration had become. Mucianus would make grand pronouncements with aplomb, and Domitian would enact seemingly innocuous minor laws and cite precedents that overturned much of what the former governor tried to do. I realised in those months just how much attention Domitian had paid to the work of the freedmen in the palace during those later years of Nero's reign. Indeed, more than once that winter and early spring, I called on Domitian to find that Philo, the young secretary from the palace, was there, answering questions on the minutiae of imperial administration, arming the young Caesar for his next bout against Mucianus.

When the civil war had kicked off a little more than a year ago, Domitian had been an awkward boy in a young man's body. Now, somehow, he had become an accomplished politician, an orator and a clever administrator.

Spring pressed on, and news came from both ends of the empire. Aegyptus was settled and Vespasian expected to return to Rome during the summer. Titus had all but crushed the remaining rebellion in Judea, and now had the majority of the troublemakers sealed up in Jerusalem, under siege. Once the city was broken, the war would be over, and Domitian's brother, too, hoped to be home before winter. Less happy was the news from the north. Cerialis was still organising his forces in Gaul and Upper Germania, but further down the Rhenus what had looked like a small-scale revolt was starting to look like a major uprising. Legions had been under siege, towns burned and all manner of trouble reported. There were even rumours of another emperor being raised there, and none of us wanted to contemplate the possibility that the civil war had not ended at all, but rather hit a temporary lull.

Mucianus, concerned by the news, decided to attend to the troubles in person. He spent half a month securing the support of the Praetorian commanders, the urban prefect and a number of ex-consuls in an effort to make sure his power remained viable while he was absent from Rome, and then sent orders for the gathering of a force in Gaul, marching to meet them.

'You realise,' I noted one afternoon over wine, 'that with Mucianus gone, you will be the Flavian power in Rome.'

Domitian nodded, though there was uncertainty in his expression, and I noted with a sense of foreboding how his eyes darted momentarily to the ever-present Aulus Caecina, who poured another glass for everyone, despite slaves being present and able to do so.

'Possibly,' the young Caesar answered.

'Oh?'

Again those eyes darted back and forth, then settled on me. 'I worry about Mucianus unopposed, commanding an army. I fear he intends to remove Cerialis, my brother-in-law, and take full control of the north.'

I shrugged. 'It's one small war. Nothing compared to what your brother's been doing in Judea. Let Mucianus have it if he wants it. The real prize is always Rome. You can be the one to hand it to your father when he arrives.'

Caecina leaned forward at that. 'Mucianus was not always the emperor's friend. In fact, it's said they used to hate each other. I wonder if Mucianus ever intended Vespasian to rule, or whether he was using Domitian's father to secure the east while he took Rome. And now he'll be in Germania with the largest army in the empire... eight legions, if they can all be trusted.' Caecina leaned back, twisting his wine glass back and forth, looking into it as he spoke. 'I suspect I don't need to remind you how emperors can be made in such places.'

The shadow of Vitellius still hung over Rome for us all, his victims, especially Sabinus, barely cold in the ground.

'So you would rein him in?'

Domitian answered this time. It was like being teamed up on, each loosing his verbal arrow as my attention was on the other. 'I want command of the army.'

'What?' I turned back to him and, predictably, Caecina spoke now.

'Is it so surprising? His father led a legion invading Britannia. His brother led a legion against the Jews. Domitian is on the cursus honorum now. He is due a command of his own.'

'I agree,' I said, not taking my eyes from Domitian. 'But not at the cost of Rome.'

In the silence that followed I knew defeat. I could see in Domitian's eyes that he had fallen entirely for Caecina's argument.

XIII

A scorpion

Lugdunum, May, AD 70

'Good to be away from the city and its predators, eh, Marcus?'

I nodded, though in the privacy of my head I noted how we seemed to have brought the predators with us.

Mucianus had struggled with Domitian's demand to be part of this for a time. He really didn't want Domitian in the army, but leaving the lad alone in Rome troubled him even more, and so finally Domitian was given command of a legion. Thankfully, I was innocuous enough to be granted a similar commission, and so Domitian and I both rode out at the head of legions as part of Mucianus' force. Caecina was given no command, but if I had thought us free of his interference, I was wrong. With the power to grant ranks within his own force, Domitian appointed Caecina as his second in the legion, and so the damned man came with us anyway.

Even with Domitian's newfound confidence and skill, he could still do with steering from time to time, and Caecina, I was sure, was steering him with thought only for his own course. I started a campaign, therefore, as we travelled north, to turn Mucianus against Caecina. I didn't like either of them particularly, but Mucianus, dangerous as he was, was easier to deal with. With Caecina, any attempt to control him was like trying to nail fog to a door. I spent every possible opportunity influencing the overall commander against him, and similarly took the subtlest of opportunities to make Caecina look bad.

'Caesar's legion has camped in the wrong place,' Mucianus said as the army set up camp one night, indicating Domitian's legion's position closer to the river than the commander had suggested.

'His second, Caecina, preferred the location,' I commented innocently, driving a nail in that particular crucifix.

Another morning: 'Why have the scouts not returned? I am waiting to move, but with no knowledge of what lies ahead, we can hardly commit.' Mucianus was twitching and irritated. I knew damn well that the scouts had been told to range twice their usual distance that morning, for it had been I that had nudged Caecina into giving the order. My part remained overlooked, of course, as I replied to the commander.

'Caecina thought it better to drive them further ahead.'

I flatter myself that I had almost succeeded in blackening Caecina's name by the time we reached Lugdunum. I swear that Mucianus was a hair's breadth from signing the order to send Caecina back to Rome. Then, one morning, not long after we arrived in Lugdunum, where the forces were gathering to support Cerialis, an incident occurred. The general was marching from camp back to his headquarters in the city, and we happened to pass the artillery practice ranges. Sometimes events are just too convenient to be accidents.

'We seem to be lacking in weapons,' Mucianus noted, casting a brief eye over the work.

'Not all the artillery vehicles have arrived yet,' Caecina replied, walking nearby with us. 'Ours only began unpacking this morning, and at least one legion's are still on the road with the wagon train. The cavalry rearguard have reported in, though, and we expect everything to be on site by nightfall.

Mucianus simply grunted a response. He would not lower himself to wasting words on the man, a direct result of my campaign.

I felt the silence growing lead heavy and tried to think of something I could say that would make the late arrival of the wagons Caecina's fault. Hitting on a possibility, I opened my mouth to let loose when Caecina suddenly gave a shout of alarm, just as a cacophony broke out across the nearest range.

With a horrible splintering sound and a crack, the arm of a scorpion bolt thrower snapped, and the mis-shot bolt whipped through the air on a direct line for Mucianus. I barely had time to turn my head to see the shot before the incident was over. I spun around in shock, expecting to find Mucianus pinned to a wall. Instead, I found the commander standing with a wide-eyed look of surprise as Caecina lowered a shield, the groove carved across it by the bolt he'd turned aside having cut a short furrow in his upper arm in its passage.

Mucianus was stunned, staring at the man he'd been growing to despise thanks to me, and who had just saved his life. All around, machines fell silent as men praised the gods and the young officer for having saved their general. All around was a sense of relief and amazement.

Except in me. I found myself wondering where Caecina had happened to find a shield he had not been carrying earlier just in time to save Mucianus from an accident.

The artillerists were punished, though only lightly. Such accidents happen with bolt throwers from time to time, and it is rarely the fault of the crew. Mucianus warmed to Caecina in the aftermath, and from that moment on there was no hope of the former Vitellian being sent home. My campaign had failed.

A few days later, I walked in on the tent of Domitian, announced by the guard, to find Caecina there, wearing a satisfied smile, which always made me wary.

Domitian threw me a grin, leaned back and stretched his arms.

'The time has come for a show of arms,' the young Caesar said.

'Oh?' Trepidation flooded me suddenly. I did not like this.

'I need to show Father my martial worth. I shall end this revolt and see this Civilis man dragged to Rome in chains for Father to scold.'

I shook my head. 'Cerialis, your brother-in-law, is putting down the revolt. And if he fails, Mucianus will slip in and finish it, taking the glory.'

Caecina snorted. 'Don't overestimate Cerialis. I served with him in Britannia as a tribune in the Ninth. I was one of the riders who fled the Iceni when he walked straight into their trap. He made the same blunder marching on Rome last year. I watched it happen. He's a headstrong fool, and he'll cock up Germania just the same. And do we really want Mucianus in control of eight legions and the most troublesome province in the empire?'

Domitian nodded. 'I have no wish to witness the rise of a new Vitellius, Marcus.'

'Think about this,' I urged him. 'Consult your father first.'

Domitian shook his head. 'It will take months for a reply to reach me. By then the revolt will be over, and if the worst of my fears come to pass, Mucianus will be in Rome, wearing purple and sitting on a throne. It is too late. The cart is in motion, Marcus.'

I felt a chill. 'What have you done?'

'Only what he must,' Caecina said.

I turned on the infuriating man, thrusting out an angry finger. 'I am not talking to *you*. I am talking to *Caesar*.' Back to Domitian. 'What have you done?'

The answer came not from Domitian, but from a sudden intrusion. Domitian's guard hurried in, gabbling. He barely had time to announce Mucianus before the general was past him, storming into the tent, his face pale. The commander had a scroll case in his hand, which he waved at Domitian.

'You think you can command here, boy? You think you are emperor because your father lets you waffle at the senate?'

Domitian was on his feet. 'You have no right to take that.'

'I make it my business to know what information goes in and out of my camp, *Caesar*,' Mucianus snarled. 'You have a little authority because of who your father is, but I put him there. *I* have the authority here. If anyone removes Cerialis from command it will be me, and it most certainly will not be you who replaces him.'

Domitian stepped uncomfortably close to Mucianus. 'You have only the authority my father grants you. You are a senator and former governor of Syria with no actual current role. No more than that. Perhaps you should remember as much when you address the emperor's son.'

I watched Mucianus' eyes narrow dangerously. The two men had never been closer than this to coming to blows. The governor took a deep breath, girded himself, and then spoke in quiet, calm tones.

'I have intercepted, read, and prevented your foolish demand of Cerialis. The latest reports from the north suggest that your noble brother-in-law has all but ended the revolt and that with the additional troops I am sending him, he will return Germania to the fold in little more than a month. It seems we will not be needed in the north after all.' He gave the emperor's son a truly unpleasant smile. 'We are therefore free to return to Rome forthwith. A good thing for you, young Caesar, because you may be the emperor's son, but this is my army, and you are just a legionary legate in it. It would be embarrassing for both of us if I were forced to strip you of your command and send you home in ignominy.'

He cast the young Caesar's letter to the ground, where the case popped open, the seal already broken, and the letter rolled out onto the carpet. Domitian glared at it as Mucianus turned and left with no word of farewell.

As I pondered on these alarming developments, it was Caecina that broke the uncomfortable silence. I remember his words to this day, right down to every inflection within them.

'He will have to go,' he murmured.

Part Three – Succession

Time will bring to light whatever is hidden

–Horace: *Epistle IV to Numicius*

XIV

Dabbling

Rome, March, AD 71

It came as a great relief to those of us watching the uneasy power struggles within the new emperor's Rome when Vespasian finally returned from his sojourn settling Aegyptus, late in the summer. That next winter Mucianus continued to try and exert the same power he had in the emperor's absence, but Vespasian was having none of that, and quickly curtailed the governor's activities. Still, the unpopular fiscal policies of Mucianus were continued by the emperor, for Rome needed its treasury rebuilding after the costly later days of Nero and the ensuing civil war. Vespasian's name quickly went from being a byword for saviour to a curse word for tax collectors over the colder months, and the strain on the usually jovial emperor began to show. Men who said the wrong thing often found themselves in exile and regretting their choices, while Vespasian and his administration worked hard to paint a beneficial sheen across the emperor's face even as he signed the exile orders.

In the February, Titus also returned from the east. Jerusalem had fallen, and the Jewish war was finished at last, after five years of fighting. A few stragglers held out at Masada, a fortress of Jewish zealotry in the desert where Flavius Silva, a distant cousin of Vespasian's, was besieging the place, but the crisis was over. A triumph was announced for the victorious general as well as his father, who had been the driving force of the war, and his younger brother, in a display of Flavian solidarity.

I was granted the consulship in that new year, the apex of a political career that I had been seeking in a roundabout way since the days of Claudius, made finally possible by my ties to the reigning emperor. It was an honour, for certain, and one that showed how valued I was by the family, although it did lead me to wonder to what men usually aspired once they had crested the summit of the cursus honorum. You could be consul twice, of course, but the only higher step was the throne. Still, as consul my attention was highly sought that winter and spring, more as an extension of the emperor's ear than for any real power I could wield myself. Even the two highest posts in Rome's government had their power handed to them by the emperor, after all. I was kept busy, though, and only saw my friends periodically, usually at official engagements.

Sometimes taking a step back allows you to see the whole picture. A parent watching a child grow notices much less change than a periodic visitor, and such was my view of the Flavii that winter. I watched them all in snippets, and saw the changes. Vespasian became more care-worn each time I saw him, and only that year did I realise that the emperor was no longer a young man. I suppose none of us were, really. Even I had now passed my fortieth summer, and Vespasian was sixty-two. He and Mucianus were at odds almost every time I saw them, and I watched a strange arc in the governor, as he moved from the expectation of power, through desperation in struggling to achieve any position of influence, to despair at increasing limitations. It appeared he would never hold the favour of Vespasian again.

Titus was full of himself. I'd never really known the older brother as I had the younger, but I could see a lot of the Flavian blood in him. He was bright and had a ready wit. He had already married twice and had a daughter, and was rumoured to have a mistress still out in Judea, but the emperor's heir was officially single, and the ladies of Rome swooned over him constantly, the war hero returned from the east. I think his popularity grated on Domitian at that time.

Caecina moved in the background like a puppeteer, pulling strings, each time setting Mucianus and the emperor against one another. I was not sure what he was up to, but as long as he was stirring that pot, which was already boiling, he was not causing trouble for Domitian or myself, so I largely ignored his machinations. Of course, I missed a lot, attending to my own busy life, as I would learn.

As for Domitian, his was the most fascinating winter to watch. The youngest Flavian had, despite being held back by Mucianus, exerted a surprising influence in his father's name in Rome. Then Vespasian had returned, and then Titus, and swiftly Domitian found himself with nothing to do. The emperor no longer needed him in the senate, and there was an older prince in Rome. Domitian turned to his books and, like me, only really put in a public appearance at events. But it was at those events that I saw his life change.

He had grown into a thoughtful, quiet and academic twenty-year-old, and it was at one of his father's reputation-building dinners that we began to see how different Domitian and his recently returned much older brother were. One of the many sycophants had been marvelling over Titus' accomplishments in the east, and the older Flavian had taken it all in his stride with appreciative nods. After a time, he noticed that Domitian was watching him, stony-eyed. 'There is a problem, brother?'

Domitian shook his head. 'No. Every man is different, and so is every war.'

'And what would you know about war, Domitian?'

The younger brother bridled at that. 'Those of us who were busy absent in distant conflicts might want to adopt a less hostile approach to we who fought a defence of the Capitol against the army of the usurper.'

Titus snorted, and this just set Domitian off further. 'Besides, Titus, there is more to command, to rule, and even to city life than baring a blade.'

'Yes,' Titus said. 'I understand you have been dabbling in poetry.'

I could not be sure whether that was meant as an innocent comment or a jibe, for Titus was surprisingly straight-faced. Domitian clearly took it as the latter.

'Those who can barely string together two sentences should perhaps not mock the learned, eh brother?'

I could see Titus subsiding now. He'd just not liked the look Domitian was giving him and had decided to rib him over it, to goad him for a while, and now he was done. This was a party, after all. He sat back with a smile, holding out his hands in a peaceable gesture.

'Wine-sot,' Domitian hissed as he leaned back. He'd meant to say it under his breath, but I watched Titus' face and he had clearly heard.

'Why do you not regale us with a poem, then?' the older brother said savagely.

'I have no composition with me.'

'Or perhaps you too are a wine-sot and the right words have fled your lips?'

With a growl, Domitian rose to his feet now, pointing at the lyre player, who stopped plucking his refrain. He threw a hand to his breast and swept the other out oratorically around the crowd.

'As snowy peaks grace the sky,
So must winter petals die,
As Ceres comes with harvest rich...'

He paused, and suddenly his face creased into a grin.

'For spring can be a heartless bitch.'

I blinked. We had all been expecting something erudite and delicate, a beautiful, if tedious and lengthy, composition. But Domitian had read his audience. He'd known that the tension was building, that how Titus walked away that night would depend on what he said, and he'd decided in an instant to give us all an impromptu comedy.

He had read the room right. The entire gathering exploded in raucous laughter. I myself was chuckling, and my eyes sought out the two men at the centre of the little exchange. Domitian and Titus were grinning, both of them. I had wondered to some extent how the brothers' relationship would grow with Titus' return, for they were almost of different generations. I saw in that party that the two brothers could argue and fight, and I was sure there would be more of that, but I also saw that at the bones of it all, they were still brothers.

When he had finished, to thunderous applause, even from the known court poets present, I noticed one set of eyes that seemed lost in Domitian's words, and the girl's gaze never stopped alighting on him for the rest of the evening.

By the end of the soiree, I noted that Domitian had caught sight of the girl, and was returning those looks with similar of his own. He was smitten. Neither his father nor his brother seemed to notice, nor, apparently, did the girl's husband, who busily involved himself with his peers throughout, laughing often.

Over the next two months, the silent relationship between the pair of them only seemed to grow. I learned who the girl was: Domitia Longina, daughter of Corbulo, the greatest general since Caesar, who had died in connection with the Piso plot Domitian and I had uncovered. It made my teeth itch to watch the pair of them, for Domitia was never present without her husband, who remained seemingly oblivious, and Domitian mooned over her without making any move, for fear of causing trouble. Domitian may have had his faults, but in matters sexual and romantic, he was ever a student of propriety, almost to a prudish level.

–

The triumph for the Judean War was almost as epic in scale as the war had been, or so the poet Statius joked in the days that followed.

The people marvelled at the sheer quantity of treasure that passed them by, always under the watchful eye of armed Praetorians, a river of silver and gold that wound through the city, surpassing the Tiber. Drapes and bolts of silk with rich purple dye from the murex fields of Judea's coast, jewel-encrusted crowns of Jewish kings on purple cushions, the sacred candlestick of the Jews from their ravaged temple, exotic animals found only in those eastern lands, and chained rows of captured zealots, waiting to populate the city's slave markets.

The trophies that went past were sometimes as tall as houses, with kneeling naked princesses chained in humble position on gold-carpeted wagons, scenes of the war in impressive scale, soldiers in gleaming armour in serried ranks, and finally, when the people were left with little breath with which to gasp at wonders, the statue of victory borne aloft, and then, in a gleaming chariot, the emperor himself, with both his sons at his sides.

I watched the triumph, and I watched the younger brother spend the following evening at the party lost in the eyes of Corbulo's daughter.

Vespasian and Titus were deep in conversation and, as consul and a close family friend, I was nearby, close enough to hear the pair.

'It is time you took a wife again.'

'Father, I don't need a wife.'

The emperor tutted. 'You have only a daughter. If we are to found a dynasty and prevent another civil war, you need a son. I am not young, Titus, and it will not be many years before this place is yours.'

'Father…'

'I know. You want Berenice of Cilicia in your bed. Have her. The gods know it won't be the first time you did. But she is a bed-warmer, and not a wife. You need a good Roman wife to have good Roman sons, and preferably before I cross the final river.'

Titus sighed. 'I am young, Father. There is plenty of time.'

'Life passes quicker than you think, my son. Make sure you use your years well. Think on wives. And while you're at it, we need to start looking at suitors for your own daughter.'

Titus levelled a frown at the emperor. 'Father, she's seven. It's far too early to start looking for a husband.'

'It is never too early,' Vespasian retorted. 'I had your first wife lined up for you while she was still playing with dolls.'

'And look how that turned out.'

Vespasian's gaze rose from the table and settled upon Domitian, who was busy obliviously gazing at Domitia Longina across the room. 'Perhaps we could secure the dynasty further,' he mused.

'Father?'

'Marry her to your brother. He's young and unattached. Shall I make the arrangements?'

To Titus' credit, I saw him look across at Domitian, his expression wracked with doubt. 'I'm not sure that's a good idea, Father.'

'Nonsense. And with six years till she's of age he has plenty of time to get used to the idea.'

I spent the rest of that evening wondering what I could possibly do about this. The answer was, of course, nothing.

It was several days later that the situation took a turn for the worse. I had a meeting with the emperor to hammer out a plan to deal with a wave of graffiti that was sweeping the city, painting Vespasian as a lower-class country bumpkin despot. I arrived at the palace a little early. These days, one had to be especially careful in an imperial audience, for Vespasian tended to vary locations. Sometimes he used the palace of Tiberius and Caligula on the Palatine. Sometimes he used parts of Nero's unfinished great Golden House, though that remained unpopular with people. Sometimes he preferred to meet in the more downplayed house of the Flavii on the Quirinal.

I arrived to find two Praetorians on guard outside the door. The pair were smirking at one another until I appeared, whereupon their grins vanished and the two men straightened. I quickly realised why as I listened. The argument raging behind the door was clear as a bell in the corridor.

'I am the emperor of Rome,' barked Vespasian, 'not some freedman you can choose whether to obey or not.'

'And I am Caesar,' Domitian snapped in reply. '*Caesar.* Or does that mean nothing now that you and Titus are home? Is it just a sinecure? An empty title?'

There was an unpleasant silence and the emperor's tone lowered dangerously. 'I am also your father. You will heed my decisions, boy.'

'I'm not a fucking *boy*, Father. I haven't been a boy since you left me to go rampaging around the east with your whore. I am a grown man, a prince, and you may think I am just a pale academic, but I held Rome together for you while you claimed the throne *in absentia*. I fought with Uncle side by side on the Palatine and watched him die for your purple cloak. I am not some child to be commanded. And I *categorically* will not marry my niece. Even were she of the age and handsome as Venus herself, I would not.'

'You will do as you are *told*,' bellowed the emperor.

'Fuck off,' was all Domitian said in reply, and as his footsteps approached the door while his father went into a fit of apoplectic rage behind him, I stepped away along the corridor, the two soldiers trying to melt into the wall and become invisible. Domitian stormed from the room, narrowed his eyes at the Praetorians, then looked at me.

'Good luck,' was his only comment before he stomped off.

The following hour was filled with an extremely uncomfortable meeting, and I was grateful to leave the angry emperor's study. There was a conflict building within the family, but I assumed it would not be my place to be part of it. Unfortunately, one downside of being closely tied to a family is that you get to experience the ups and downs indiscriminately, and there was no chance I was going to be able to avoid this.

—

I had arranged to meet Domitian at the baths in the Campus Martius, a grand place of marble, statues, steamy pools and very helpful young slaves. I had a few ideas I wanted to put to the emperor, and thought I would run them by the cleverest member of the family first to see what his thoughts were. It irked me when he turned up as expected, but with Caecina in tow. I had thought the man moved on to higher game, but it seemed that he had merely broadened his scope and was now playing with the entire family. As we all lay on couches side by side, nubile African girls pounding the knots out of our oiled muscles, I threw my ideas at Domitian. It set my teeth on edge and ruined any relaxation when half the time it was Caecina who came back with an opinion. In truth they were valuable thoughts, but it irked me in that I had not asked *him* for them.

I was coming quite close to telling Caecina precisely what I thought of him when two shadows fell across us. I looked up to see a pair of unexpected figures standing in the doorway to the massage suite. Titus alone would have been a surprise, but his being in the company of Mucianus made me frown.

'I need you to reconsider your stance on Julia,' Titus said quietly.

Domitian waved at the slaves and pointed to the door. The room emptied of everyone but us in moments, the Praetorians on guard shuffling them away and then making sure no one came within earshot.

'I have said all there is to say,' Domitian replied.

Titus sighed. 'I know you don't want her. I know you moon over Corbulo's girl, even though she has a husband. And I sympathise, Domitian. You might not think so, but I do. Father wants me to take another wife, and I've just been waiting for the chance to bring Berenice over from Judea. She is the only one for me, Domitian, but she could never be an empress.'

'So you'll just keep her as a whore, like Father with that Caenis woman.'

Titus bridled for a moment, keeping a rein on his temper with difficulty, then began again in measured tones. 'It is for the family. It is *always* for the family. I cannot marry Berenice, and you cannot marry Domitia. Marrying my daughter will tie the family bonds ever tighter. I know she is your niece, but it is the done thing. The Julians all did it.'

'And look how *they* ended up,' Domitian spat. 'Father doesn't need to marry me to gain power or wealth like the family used to do when we were nobodies. He's emperor now. You don't need me for legitimacy, and no one cares whether I have a son. That's *your* priority. *You're* the heir. I'm just the second son.'

'There is no need for that bitterness, Domitian,' Mucianus put in.

'This is none of your business,' Domitian snapped at the governor, then turned to Titus again. 'And I'm not being bitter. You are the heir. You get the glory, the power, the wealth. But you also get the responsibility and the strain. I am the second son. I get nothing but empty titles and a fat purse, but the advantage of that is that nothing is desired or expected of me. I am happy with that. Let me be.'

'I wish I could,' Titus sighed, and sagged a little. 'I don't want to do this. Julia probably wouldn't want you either. But this is Father's wish, and I will not stand against him.'

I realised then why Mucianus was here. He was pushing to solve Vespasian's problem for him in the hope that it would heal some of the rift between the emperor and himself. Indeed, before Domitian could speak, it was Mucianus who butted in once more.

'You are Caesar,' he said. 'You may be the second son, but in the eyes of Rome you are still of the imperial family. You are important by the very nature of your blood. That means you have responsibility. You cannot marry for love. You must marry for duty.'

'Oh?' added a fresh voice.

I pinched the bridge of my nose in irritation as Caecina now shoved his nose into the conversation. 'And why is that, Mucianus? Of what value is a marriage of duty? Look to the prince there. Married twice, both by his father's arrangement. And where are they? Both divorced. The first was no longer needed once her family had paid the emperor's debts. And the second connected to the Piso plot and hurriedly got rid of in case the bad name somehow stuck to her husband.'

I saw Titus beginning to get angry. He didn't anger often, or easily, but when it happened, he could be dangerous. Fortunately for Caecina, Mucianus turned on him before Titus could vocally take offence.

'And that is the point of wives. They bring power, or wealth, or higher position. Otherwise you might as well stick with a whore. Look at Nerva there. Forty years old and never married. And he just drifts around the court clinging to your toga hems. No real power.'

I might have taken offence at that but, like Titus, I didn't get the chance because Caecina was there again now, rising from his massage couch. 'And your own wife, Mucianus? From a lesser line, and fairly impoverished, I think. What did you get from her? Not money or position, for certain. But I hear she has pendulous breasts. I think I know what you got from her. I love a little hypocrisy, don't you?'

Mucianus suddenly lunged for Caecina, his face darkening, and it was Titus who thrust out an arm to hold him back. It was odd to watch. The argument had started between Titus and Domitian, but had somehow shifted until it was Caecina and Mucianus snapping insults at each other, while the rest of us watched. Of course, Caecina already hated Mucianus, but now it was clear that the feelings were reciprocated.

'This is not productive,' Titus sighed, then looked across at Domitian. 'Father's mind is made up. You will have to accept it anyway. I thought perhaps we could come to a friendly agreement first, but since you are adamant, I will leave you to fight Father over it.'

He turned to the other two, who were four paces apart and glaring daggers at once another, facing off like gladiators waiting for the match signal. 'And you two. Mucianus, you should know better than to spar with men like that. Caecina, I know what you are. You are a serpent who coils himself around whatever looks most solid. You cling to Domitian because he's your access to power and authority. But I know you for the slimy survivor that you are. Be very careful. I begin to anger.'

With that he was gone. He walked calmly from the room, Mucianus stomping away after him, throwing barbed glances back at Caecina as he went. The Praetorians escorted them from the baths, and the slaves returned gingerly. We lay for a while longer under their ministrations, though we were silent now, and the mood had turned sour.

Another day passed, and the one after that, a little after noon, I had a visitor. Domitian, with his escort, came to my house, blessedly without Caecina this time. He looked content and even oddly excited. I invited him into my triclinium and had wine poured. As he tasted it, he looked up across at me.

'You have known me most of my life.'

I nodded.

'I learned many things from you. And through you from men like Epaphroditus. Titus had a court education, and he is driven by it, but I learned more than a prince learns. I have the added benefit of being able to think for myself.' He smiled at that.

I simply waited for the point.

'I have spoken to my father. But unlike last time, this time I treated it as an oration. I planned my strategy as I would with the senate, and I marshalled all my arguments.' He laughed suddenly. 'I won him over, Marcus. He has withdrawn his demand that I marry Julia. He has even given me his blessing to marry who I like, on the condition that she fits within the mould of an empress.'

I exhaled slowly. 'Domitia Longina has an excellent pedigree.'

'She does,' Domitian smiled, but his face slid quickly into seriousness. 'The problem is that I cannot approach the matter directly. The Flavii and the Plautii have alliances that go back as far as both families remember.'

'And her husband is a Plautius,' I finished for him.

'Quite. I need an intermediary. Caecina has the way of persuasion, but his history is a little chequered. You have an immaculate record, and the Cocceii have a history with both families. Will you approach Plautius Aelianus for me, with the notion of divorce?'

I nodded. I had no idea how the notion would be received, but what choice had I? Domitian smiled again and stayed an hour with me, drinking wine and talking of mundane matters.

It was evening before I found myself in Plautius' company, having sent a messenger and arranged a meeting, again at the baths. Like most of our class, I find that business is always easier to arrange in the informal atmosphere of the baths. We sat in the hot water, my status as a consul enough to keep the bulk of the patrons at the far end of the pool, especially with my armed lictors standing close enough to beat seven shades of shit out of anyone who dared trouble me.

I had never met Lucius Aelius Lamia Plautius Aelianus, though he was of a noble family, his reputation in the city and at court was flawless, and he was known to be an intelligent man. He was also clearly fearless, having chosen as a wife the daughter of a man condemned as part of Piso's treasonous plot. Oh, we all knew Corbulo to be innocent, but it takes a brave man to accept the stigma of treasonous connections even if they are ephemeral.

What I did not expect was his wit.

'Good evening,' I greeted him, still trying to work out what I was going to say. 'Odd that we both show our faces at court, and yet I have never had the pleasure of speaking to you personally.'

Plautius chuckled lightly. 'And were it not for the love-struck young Caesar, that would still be the case.' I frowned at that. 'Let me save you some time,' Plautius said, leaning back against the bath side. 'You want me to divorce Domitia because the young Caesar is infatuated with her, and despite his initial arguments, the emperor has given his consent. Domitian feels he cannot approach me without endangering our family ties. Is my arrow close to the mark, Marcus Cocceius Nerva?'

I laughed, a little uncomfortably. 'A shot to the centre of the target, senator.'

'A man would have to have been blind this past winter to miss the looks the young Caesar has been throwing her. And he seems to be a bit of a marksman himself.'

'It is an uncomfortable thing to ask.'

Plautius shrugged. 'I am honoured to be asked. When Caligula and Claudius wanted a woman they just took her.'

Now, I laughed. The man seemed unguarded and easy. 'I take it you are not adamantly opposed?'

He sighed and kicked his legs in the warm water. 'I have always been fond of Domitia, you know? She has given me a son and two daughters. Our marriage was agreed by her father before his unfortunate demise, and though many tried to persuade me to drop it, I married her anyway. But it was only ever an arrangement of choice for me. She never loved me. Never will. Perhaps it is the will of the gods that I have kept her safe when her family fell from grace.' He gave me a grin. 'I presume the young Caesar will lavish me with riches and estates for letting her go?'

I chuckled. 'I imagine he would give you a country of your own.'

'Ha. That would be nice. Maybe I would be a king.' His face became serious once more. 'I don't want riches. I don't want land. But I do want Domitia to be happy, and she has done nothing but moon over him in return since the winter. I shall arrange the divorce promptly, and perhaps you will remind the young Caesar from time to time how accommodating I was. Sometimes it is nice to be owed a favour by the imperial family.'

I laughed again. In fact I laughed a lot that day. Plautius divorced Domitia straight away, and her marriage to Domitian was announced within the month. I knew she would be valued, and that she was safe with her new husband, for whatever a man might say of Domitian, he was ever respectful of the delicate sex. With Domitian's rejection of his niece, Vespasian turned his family ties in another direction, persuading my old friend Flavius to marry his own son to Julia. Things seemed to be working out.

But in all of this, there was one sour note that had arisen. Amid the joy of Domitian and his new wife, I had watched two camps forming on opposite sides of a field of battle. Titus and Mucianus at one end, and Domitian and Caecina at the other. It was only a matter of time until war broke out.

XV

Not a statesman

Rome, February, AD 73

I was beginning to see Mucianus as every bit as much of a threat to Rome's stability as Caecina. The latter manoeuvred where he could from behind the scenes and stirred constantly, but the effects were not immediately noticeable. That being said, sometimes a small ripple denotes a damn big fish beneath the surface, and with hindsight I should have worried less about those I could see causing trouble and more about Caecina's apparent passivity.

Mucianus remained out of favour with the emperor, and Vespasian was not a man to change his mind easily. Thus the former governor, rather bitter over how much effort he had put into setting Vespasian on the throne and with only enforced retirement to show for it, cleaved ever closer to Titus as his potential route to influence, just as Caecina had done to Domitian.

Titus was worrying me a little, too, for that matter.

The emperor's heir had been granted truly astonishing power. He all but ruled now alongside his father. He had been made consul the year after me alongside Vespasian, enacted laws on his behalf, addressed the senate for him, held a variety of political and religious offices, but most powerful of all, he was made the sole Praetorian prefect. As Vespasian's grip on the empire tightened, squeezing much needed gold out of the rich, and even charging the poor to piss in street pots, passive resistance rose endlessly in the form of graffiti, rumour and acerbic poetry. Vespasian was careful to seem benevolent where possible and pardoned many people caught defaming the emperor's name, but every now and then someone would push it too far and find his name on a list. That then became Titus' problem. The names on those lists inevitably found themselves dragged out of bed by Praetorians and dealt with harshly, sometimes fatally, by the seemingly jovial heir to the empire.

The picture I paint of Vespasian is perhaps not the one history preserves, but while it may sound harsh, money has to come from somewhere, and an emperor must maintain his Romanitas. What was done by him and Titus was nothing new. Since the days of Augustus, it has always been necessary for an emperor to keep a tight hold on things and to deal directly with unpleasant matters. Indeed, Vespasian was perhaps unusual in how many of his detractors he let get away with their crimes. Still, Titus was becoming very powerful and gaining a dangerous reputation for his work, Mucianus, of course, his companion throughout.

And while the two of them cut a bloody path through Rome, Caecina and Domitian similarly remained close – the two command corps facing one another across the field of battle. The consulship passed the next new year into the hands of Domitian, a sign of favour from his father. And over the first month, the younger Flavian was so beset with requests and pleas from senators that he took half a month away from his duties, leaving the work in the hands of Messalinus, his co-consul. He left Rome for a short break in one of the imperial villas in the Alban hills, one once favoured by Caligula, and with him, he took his wife, myself, Caecina and a number of less-favoured friends.

I was enduring the chilly February air in the villa's garden one morning, avoiding the triclinium where Caecina was holding forth on some irritating subject or other, when I saw the column of horses winding their way down the track to the villa. The guard on the gate hurried out to see who it was, and the fact that they were admitted without even a request or message sent to Domitian told me everything I needed to know. The visitor was clearly more important than Domitian, and so could only be

Vespasian or Titus. Vespasian was suffering with gout, and so if it had been he arriving, he would have been in a carriage. Two figures led the column on horseback, which made it clear that Titus and Mucianus were paying a call.

Noting that I had a while before they were admitted, I hurried back into the warm villa and found the others, still arguing over minutiae in the triclinium. They looked up as I entered.

'I'd wondered where you'd got to,' Domitian smiled. 'Caecina was telling me tall tales about some magic cure for baldness. Apparently it involves rubbing myrrh into the scalp. I've used myrrh in temples, and I favour rubbing neither the sticky sap nor the hard resin into my skin. Pliny, who we all know to be accurate, says one should use a paste made from the ashes of dead flies. Unpleasant, but at least it washes off again. You're starting to recede a little, Marcus,' he said to me with an impish grin. 'Where do you stand on the subject?'

I managed to resist pointing out that baldness is often hereditary, and that Domitian's father could hide in a basket of eggs. I had more on my mind at the time. I noted that Domitia Longina, close by on the couch, had a barely hidden smile, perhaps having come to the same conclusion.

'You have visitors,' I noted. 'Titus and his pet ape.'

The smile slid from Domitian's face. His relationship with his brother was an odd one. They remained on reasonable terms, considering that they did not know one another that well, having spent most of their life apart and with an age difference of twelve years. And they were both bright enough to recognise the importance of Flavian solidarity, often overlooking their differences to present a combined front. The past year or two, though, had placed increasing strains on the ties that bound them, and it was showing when they met in person. The presence of Caecina or Mucianus, or, gods help us all, both of them, only made it worse.

Domitian waved his arm at the various nobles and the slaves. 'Everyone out.' Then to a few of us: 'Not you, Caecina, nor you, Nerva, or my love Domitia. Stephanus, show my brother and his friend in when they arrive.'

We sat, tense, silent, wondering what had brought the older brother from Rome, until finally he was announced with brief pomp, and strode into the room, unclasping his cloak and letting it fall, to be caught and gathered up by a slave that followed on. Mucianus remained cloaked, similarly dressed in military uniform.

'Brother,' Titus said, by terse way of greeting. Domitian answered with just a nod.

As Titus' slaves finished dusting off a seat and stepped back, the emperor's heir gestured for them to leave, and he waited until the door shut. Then he took a breath, as though preparing for a contest.

'You are aware of the Priscus situation?' Titus said.

Domitian shook his head. 'I know him is all. Helvidius Priscus, yes? Witty fellow. Philosopher of a sort.'

Titus chewed his lip. 'That would be him. There has been… trouble with him.'

'Pissed off Father, has he?'

'Quite. He said some rather unforgivable things, and the warrant was written and delivered before the ink was dry. I had to send my men. There was no need for an interrogation, though. The case was clear. He does not deny what he said. In fact, he makes light of it. He jokes that Father was always a good friend, and the Vespasian he knows would never take offence at a few jests.'

'He clearly is not aware that an emperor cannot be as forgiving as a nobody,' Domitian replied.

'Again, quite. At least Helvidius Priscus has not been given over to my tender ministrations. It was a sentence of exile.'

'Good,' Domitian said. 'There will be time for him to ponder on his mistakes.'

'Not a lot of time. Unfortunately it was reported that as he departed, Priscus said something rather prickly, which has now become a slogan daubed on the walls of the city. Before I knew it, the order for his execution was handed out.'

Domitian leaned back. 'Sad. Although he has only himself to blame. A man needs to be careful how he addresses the most powerful figure in the world, don't you think?'

Titus steepled his fingers. 'This is a mistake. Helvidius Priscus is a good man. He has always been a friend of the Flavii, and he is extremely popular among the senate.'

'As if that collection of yawning shits is worth consideration,' Domitian replied archly, with an unpleasant smile thrown in the direction of Mucianus, who with me sat as part of that ancient body. I had long since learned not to take offence at Domitian's senatorial jibes, but Mucianus' face reddened with anger. Titus noted this and held up a warning hand to his companion before addressing his brother again.

'It is a mistake, but Father is angry, and adamant that Priscus will meet his end. His death will turn many in Rome away from us. Epaphroditus and his people work every hour to build up Father's reputation even as he himself seemingly does what he can to ruin it. Even Epaphroditus may not be able to put a good face on this one.'

'And you come to me because?'

Titus sighed. 'I have argued with Father over this until my face went blue, but he will not hear me. I think the matter has to come from a different direction for him to consider it. As consul, you have the authority to intervene in legal matters. You can overturn the sentence.'

Caecina stirred. He knew Titus disliked him, and had kept quiet thus far to be safe, but now he spoke. 'There are two consuls, and Messalinus is still in the city. Why not go to him?'

Titus shot the man a steely look, and then turned back to his brother, directing his response to Domitian. 'Messalinus is a coward. He would never stand up against the emperor.'

'Of course he wouldn't,' Caecina laughed. 'After all, look what happened to Helvidius Priscus.'

'Quiet,' snapped Titus, with a finger jabbed at Caecina. Then he turned to Domitian again. 'You are clever, brother. We all know it. And you've an orator's tongue, as we saw by how you talked Father round to your choice of wife.' At this point he gave a respectful bow of the head to Domitia Longina, who reclined nearby, taking all of this in. 'Messalinus would just get himself on a list. *You*, though, could persuade Father.'

Domitian shook his head. 'You're wrong about the authority I wield. A consul is not a statesman, Titus. He is not a shark in the pool of Rome. You know what he is? He is an empty crustacean. A shell. He has no real power. All he does is enact the will of the emperor. Long gone are the days when the consulship meant anything. Now it is a burden, not an honour. It carries no authority, but attracts beggars and sycophants who think a consul can make them rich. Yes, I can use my authority to overturn the sentence, but Father can veto that in a heartbeat. Then, instead of watching Priscus talk himself into a death sentence, I will have angered the emperor myself, and still have to watch Priscus die. No, Titus. I can do nothing. I *will* do nothing.'

Something about that felt like a knife in the back. I had sought the consulship all my life, and it had been Domitian's father who had honoured me with it. For his son to tell me the honour was worthless was something of a kick in the teeth. I rallied, though. This was not the time for taking offence.

It was Mucianus who stepped forward, then. I prepared myself to rise and intervene, but only as a last resort. Stepping between arguing princes can be a dangerous pastime.

'The consulship is not empty,' the former governor insisted. 'In the right hands, at least. Don't forget that I remember you in that year after the civil war. I watched you twist the senate against me. I know what you're capable of, and your brother here made a proud and powerful consul. You? You are but his shadow. If you will not use your consular powers to help those in need, then what use are you?'

Domitian's eyes became flinty as he fixed Mucianus with a look. 'The same as any other consul or senator of Rome: none at all. You all persist in this antiquated notion that the senate and the consuls have some sort of meaning. The only point to the whole charade is to give greedy and arrogant noblemen something to fight over. The real power lies with the emperor. Look at Father. The common folk of Rome see him as a smiling man, as he is on all his statues. And when someone decides that maybe the emperor isn't helping him after all, he appears on a list, Titus whisks him away, and the problem is no more. Where in this process of rule does the senate appear?'

'I argued against your consulship,' Mucianus grunted. 'I knew you'd be trouble.'

'You may be dancing on the end of Titus' leash at the moment, Mucianus, but you are still nothing, and I advise you to remember to whom you speak.'

Titus took a step forward. 'I ask you to do this for me, brother. Since my return from the east I have stood up for you. You and I, we do not know each other all that well, but you are my brother. There were murmurs that first year that you should not carry the title of Caesar, that I should be the only one. Yet I stood firm in the senate and defended you. The Judean triumph was granted to Father and I, for we were the generals who brought the Jews to account, and yet it was I who lobbied Father that you be included in the chariot. Gods, Domitian, but it was me who persuaded Father to make you consul this year. All I ask is that you try.'

It was well said, and a persuasive argument. I could see Domitian faltering. He was debating inside as to how to proceed, and I very much suspect that he would have agreed, had not Caecina seen the same thing and chosen that moment to interfere once more. 'Caesar has made his decision,' the serpentine bastard said. 'He gave you his answer.'

Before Titus could respond, Mucianus was stepping forward. As the former governor made a number of crude and anatomically unlikely suggestions about Caecina's parentage, Titus began to snap at Domitian. The younger brother flared up and argued back as Caecina rose from his seat, shaking a fist at Mucianus. I watched in despair as the room erupted into furious argument with an increasing edge of physical violence, and my gaze slipped to the room's other occupant. Domitia Longina was frowning at all this.

I looked at her and realised in that moment that she represented imperial redemption in herself. Her father had died accused of treason, yet she had prospered and was now a prince's wife.

In a heartbeat I was on my feet and stepping between the shouting, almost brawling, pairs, waving my hands.

'Listen!'

It took a moment for the arguments to subside. All eyes turned to me.

'You're arguing over how to overturn the emperor's decision, but from what I can see nobody here argues with the fact that the fault in all this lies squarely with Helvidius Priscus himself. His all-too-sharp wit has landed him on the wrong side of the emperor, but we all know Vespasian well enough to know that he can be brought around. The problem is that Priscus, knowing what he'd done and how it could be repaired, instead compounded his foolishness by doing it again and further angering the emperor.'

There was a small chorus of nods. This much was clearly true. Priscus was a clever man, but in his response he had been more than a little imprudent.

'It is not the place of the emperor's sons to defy their father, and not the place of consuls or senators to argue with the emperor to save a man who clearly cannot save himself.'

This was also a matter of general agreement, though I could see Mucianus frowning. I continued swiftly. 'The answer is clear that it is Helvidius Priscus' responsibility to solve his own problem, and I believe it can be done. All he needs to do is publicly retract his words and perhaps pen a glowing panegyric to the benevolence of the emperor. People will soon forget his earlier words and hear only his praise. And Vespasian is not a man to hold a grudge when common sense could prevail. With sufficient contrition on the part of Priscus, Vespasian will be won over before the sentence is enacted. He might even have his exile overturned and be welcomed back to court.'

'If he can be persuaded,' Titus said quietly.

'No.'

We all turned to see Mucianus folding his arms.

'What?'

'In what ideal of Rome is it acceptable that a man must sell out the freedoms given to him by half a millennium of tradition to save his skin? That is not Rome. Selling your freedom for favour? That sounds like the court of Sejanus: a place of fear and corruption. Do you want the Flavian court to be such a thing?'

'Better to sell our freedom for favour than to be free and dead,' said Caecina flatly.

Mucianus narrowed his eyes at the man, but then turned back to the two Caesars. 'The emperor should be persuaded to overturn the sentence without Priscus being made to take back his words and pour honeyed praise he doesn't mean.'

I could see my work being undone as the four men started to bristle once more. Caecina took a pace forward, finger coming up to wag at Titus and Mucianus. 'I find it darkly humorous that of all people you two should take a stand for the freedoms of a man to defame the emperor, when you have made it your business for a year now to pull the fingernails off men who have done just that. Hypocrisy reigns in Rome, it seems.'

'You rodent,' snapped Mucianus, lunging, only to be caught by Titus.

'I think you'd best take him away,' Domitian advised his brother, nodding at Mucianus.

Titus took a deep breath. 'Do not seek me out for favours in future, brother,' he said, 'if you will not grant such a small one for me.'

Domitian straightened. 'Go in peace, Titus, but I would ask that you keep your dog on a leash in future.'

Mucianus made furious noises, but again Titus silenced him with a look, then pointed at Caecina. 'Say what you will about the company I keep, but remember that your own familia harbours poisonous reptiles. That one there is as trustworthy as a Dacian wine merchant. All he ever does is use people to secure his own position.' He turned his glare on Caecina. 'Father is old. Soon, there will be a new emperor. A word of advice, Caecina Alienus: find a big rock somewhere and hide under it when that day comes.'

With that, Titus turned, gesturing to Mucianus, and the two men strode from the room. The door clicked shut behind him. There was a long, strained silence, and then Domitian breathed slowly and deeply, and rolled his shoulders. 'I think I will go to the gardens and watch them leave. I will be happier when I know that man is not on the estate.' He left in the wake of his brother, and like a faithful hound – ironic, really – Caecina hurried away at his heel. As the door swung shut once more I realised I had been all but ignored and left alone with Domitia Longina.

'It is like one of Nero's dinners,' she said with an odd smile.

I frowned. 'Oh?'

'Perhaps not for the menfolk,' she chuckled. 'Men are always so forthright, I find. Most say whatever comes into their mind without bothering to filter it in any way. They snap and bark and argue. But the women of the court, especially in the old days... ah, Nerva, if you only knew. They gathered into warbands at any given opportunity. The politicking of Rome's matrons would put any imperial struggle to shame. The princes and their pets are so similar. The question is whether they are a gaggle of arguing hens, or sparrowhawks, waiting to swoop.'

I shook my head at her dizzying flood of analogies. 'Explain, good lady?'

'Most of the time, matrons will spend so much time planning, intriguing and politicking that they have no actual time to cause trouble. But here and there you will come across a clique that has focus. There you will find an Agrippina or a Messalina. Then you're in trouble.'

I shivered at those names, especially Agrippina. Gods, but that woman had been dangerous.

'Watch them all,' she said, 'my dear husband included, for all his devotion to the goddess of wisdom. Watch them all and decide whether they are hens or hawks. Are they all bluster and argument, or is something more dangerous going on?'

I nodded slowly. It was sound advice, and I had a horrible inkling that something was coming. With luck, it would be a war of mutual extinction between Mucianus and Caecina. I had a pleasant mental image of the two men dead on each other's swords, like Petreius and Juba of old. It was a nice thought, but the problem was that I could see neither man dying without taking half of Rome with them.

In some ways I was saved from my worries for a while, for the emperor allotted me the coveted governorship of Africa, replacing Rutilius Gallus. I left Rome within a month of that argument between the brothers, and spent three years in my posting, not making even half the fortune Vespasian had done when he had occupied the position. During my sunny, busy days I all but forgot about the machinations and potential disasters happening back in Rome.

XVI

Somewhere to be

Rome, August, AD 76

My tenure in Africa had been peaceful and pleasant, and I returned to Rome with some trepidation. Many governors return in a grand *adventus* with a huge entourage, throwing money to the poor, rose petals abounding and dancers in the street, drawing the adoration and cheers of the crowd. Some prefer to sneak back into the city like the thieves they undoubtedly are. I chose the latter, not through humility or embarrassment, but because I really did not know what to expect, especially given the rumours I had heard that the emperor's sons were no longer on speaking terms. In the absence of my steadying influence, and there is no false pride there, for I know that had been my role, the two camps had all but gone to war, Mucianus and Titus, Caecina and Domitian.

The city was still standing, which was a relief. Actually, given the regularity of destructive fires in Rome, even that was never a given after a prolonged absence. But Rome seemed settled, and there were no riots, unhappy citizens or gangs of marauding Praetorians. Just the vigiles going about their business beating up criminals, and disgruntled painters daubing slogans on the walls, for which they too would get a beating when the emperor found out.

I planned to check in at the palace. It was always the done thing for a governor to present himself upon his return and receive the emperor's praise or wrath appropriately, and to hand over a nice gift to show your gratitude and loyalty. I had decided to delay my visit for a day, though. My gift was following on and would arrive during the night when vehicles were permitted in the city streets, since four great lions, destined for the new amphitheatre the emperor was building, were better kept in their wheeled cages than on a leash. I planned to spend a few days in the city before disappearing to the coast for the summer in the usual fashion.

I had been in my domus at the upper end of Pomegranate Street for just a few hours when the visitors arrived. I'd barely taken off my shoes.

Domitian had changed slightly in my absence. He was in his mid-twenties now, and fully grown, but his hairline had begun to recede. I smiled as I realised his ornatrix had carefully styled his hair to a lavish curl that now crept forward to hide some of the increased forehead in the same manner as Caesar's coiffure in his day. He was impeccably dressed and quite regal. Behind him came the figure that had brought the sinking feeling. Domitian was welcome. Caecina was not. But one does not refuse entrance to a prince's companion.

'We have been discussing Britannia,' Domitian said conversationally as he sat and accepted a glass of wine.

'Oh?' was all I could think of to say to this.

'The emperor is usually very shrewd in his choice of governors,' he continued.

I noted a new change, there. Gone was *Father*, replaced with *the emperor*. What else had changed in my absence, I wondered.

'All governors are either extended family members, of course,' he went on, 'or drawn from families like your own, tied to ours for generations. But he usually selects men perfect for the job. Men with a proven record and often with a prior knowledge of the place they are being sent to govern.'

'Where is this going, Domitian?' It still seemed a baffling matter to bring to my door, especially now. I really couldn't care less who was put in charge of that soggy northern island.

'You know who was sent there when you went to Africa, of course?'

I nodded. 'Cerialis.' Domitian's brother-in-law, the hot-headed general I had known for years.

'Yes. Petilius Cerialis.' He turned at a darkening of Caecina's face. 'I know you don't like him, but he's family. And he has a record.'

'He has a record of failures and dangerous mistakes,' the other man noted.

'I cannot fault you on that,' I said, in a rare moment of concurrence with Caecina. 'Cerialis has only escaped abject humiliation several times by way of his connections.'

'True,' Domitian conceded, 'but his successes outweigh his failures, and when he succeeds he does so impressively. The Civilis revolt in Germania: extinguished. And then this warring Brigantes lot in Britannia. They've been causing trouble since the days of Claudius, and Cerialis brought them under control. But Cerialis is back in Rome now, like you, Nerva, and the emperor has appointed Frontinus in his place.'

I knew the name, but had to think for a while to place it. 'Ah, Frontinus. What's wrong with that choice? He's an ex-consul, and if I remember rightly he was with Cerialis in Germania. Didn't I hear something about him making a name for himself on the battlefield against some Belgic tribe?'

'He put down the Lingones and their allies following the revolt,' Domitian agreed. 'But his only military commands have been in support of Cerialis. He's never had a full army at his fingertips. In Britannia he has four legions and a collection of unsettled tribes around the borders. He's been there for two years already and so far all he's done is conquer a tribe that was supposedly already settled and within the Pax Romana. Not a good start. In two years Cerialis had the north in a stranglehold. In my opinion Frontinus is not the man for the job.'

I still had absolutely no idea why all this was being discussed. I noted in the pause that followed Domitian's gaze slide past me and settle on something. As he straightened once more and brought his eyes back to me, I turned. He had been looking at my water clock, which gently trickled away in the corner of the room, telling me that the hour was just coming up to *antemeridianum tempus*, that the midday meal would be a little over an hour away. Was he hungry? If so, he did not show it, for he had not touched the plates of food, limiting himself to a little wine.

'You have somewhere to be?' I asked.

Domitian frowned. 'No. Not yet. Anyway, what was I saying? Yes, Frontinus. Well, he's due for recall next year, but I have petitioned the emperor to call him back early. The question is who would replace him. The emperor is currently favouring Agricola. You know him?'

It was a name I'd heard. He had some ties to the family, like me, but our paths had never crossed in more than a peripheral manner. 'From what I've heard he was a capable governor in Gaul. Honest. And he's got a good war record, hasn't he?'

'I've nothing against the man, but like Frontinus, Agricola's only military successes have been serving under Cerialis and Plautius. He's never had a command of his own. We need a proven general on the island. Britannia is important.'

'It is?' I couldn't imagine why. It had only ever provided a bit of lead, some pale and soggy slaves and a series of troublesome rebels, as far as I knew.

'It is important to the emperor. He was one of the generals who began the conquest back under Claudius. It's not a big island and here we are five emperors later and still fighting to take the place. It needs to be brought inside the empire and settled so that we can transfer the legions to other trouble spots like the Danubius.'

I couldn't argue with his logic. He had ever been a clever student and a voracious reader. I hadn't previously seen him as a tactician, mind.

'I take it there is a point to all of this?' I put in, finally.

Domitian nodded. 'I suspect you can guess who Titus is pushing for the position.'

I sighed. 'Mucianus, yes?'

'Precisely.'

I shrugged. 'He has a good military record, and was an efficient governor. He fits the profile you mentioned. And having him so far from Rome would certainly please some people,' I added, my gaze turning sour as it slipped to Caecina.

'If I were on better terms with my dear brother, I might be able to persuade him to Agricola. The two are friends and have been for years. But I have an idea of my own. Rather than Mucianus, who we cannot trust, or Agricola, who remains largely untested, I would send Antonius Primus.'

I frowned and mused on this. As an idea it had merit. Primus was an absolute animal, of course – his activity during his march on Rome to take down Vitellius was appalling, he had virtually depopulated whole Roman cities in the process – but there was no denying that he had cut a path to Rome through everything Vitellius could raise. He was a hot knife in butter. If the emperor really wanted Britannia conquered, and fast, Primus might well be able to do it. It would not be pretty, but it would be done.

'I don't disagree with your choice,' I replied carefully, 'though I'm not sure what my place is in this.'

'The emperor trusts your judgement. Every voice raised in support of Primus would be helpful. The gods know that Mucianus and therefore Titus will argue against him. Your backing might make all the difference.'

I caught him looking past me again. What was it with the water clock? As he went on, rattling out a list of Primus' appropriate qualities, I took the opportunity to turn again. The water level was fast approaching the line for antemeridianum tempus.

Caecina then began to barrage me with a list of faults in any other choice of governor. It made sense that they had come to me for support of their choice in candidate, but it surprised me how vehement they were over this. After all, Domitian's involvement in the running of empire was limited to being a show prince, really, with his brother groomed for the succession as their father shuffled slowly towards his seventies.

I let the man rattle on, the bile flowing over me. What had happened to the silver tongue the man had showed half a decade ago? Now he was simply irritating. Of course, that was because half a decade ago he had been a traitor who had managed to survive a war and was trying to worm his way into the circles of power. These days he was close to Domitian, and that was as high as he was going to get, so he had no need to flatter and charm.

Every now and then during the monologue, Domitian would surreptitiously glance at my clock, and it came as absolutely no surprise to me when he finally held out a hand to Caecina.

'Enough. We have taken up far too much of Marcus' time, and he's barely unpacked from Africa. We should leave him for now.' He rose, and as he did, I glanced at the clock. Absolutely on the hour.

As I walked them to the door and slaves brought their cloaks, I wondered what appointment they had that required such time-keeping. Their own slaves were gathered in one of my antechambers, along with Domitian's lictors. The entire crowd joined us, preparing to leave and make their way to their next appointment. I was with the pair when the front door was opened and so I had an excellent view of the street.

For a moment, I simply marvelled at the miraculous timing. Mucianus was riding a horse up the street, slowly, with a gathering of his private guards and slaves around him. Then the reality of it struck me. To be there exactly as my door was opened could hardly be an accident, and this far up Pomegranate Street there was nothing that could interest a man like him. Suddenly all the glances at the water clock made sense. Had the whole matter of Britannia merely been an excuse to be in my house at this moment? My gaze slipped to the two men beside me. Domitian's face was so expressionless it could only be the result of a careful response. Caecina was less controlled. He was smiling in a horrible, oily manner.

I felt that sinking feeling I'd had earlier return, bringing a chill along my spine. What was all this about?

The answer came in moments.

Mucianus turned to the open door, and from the surprise I saw register on his face he'd not been expecting me, Domitian or Caecina. He was simply riding past, or he *thought* that was the case, at least. In the frown that quickly slid across his face I saw it all. I saw him work out that it had somehow been these two that had been behind whatever errand he was on that had brought him here. That was the only conclusion.

Then the attack came. I jumped at the suddenness of it. One moment, Mucianus was frowning at us from horseback, his guards and slaves around him and trailing along behind. The next, thugs were pouring from alleys and doorways, flooding the street. With screams of panic, the ordinary folk of Rome fled, scattering up and down the street, running for any perceived safety. Several ran toward my door, though the gathered muscle of Domitian and my own household spread out in front of us, preventing them from approaching. They turned and fled one way or the other, trying to escape the trouble.

But the trouble was not coming for the people of Rome. It had a different target. Mucianus was well protected, but this wasn't just a few opportunistic thieves. This was a deliberate and calculated assault. The men were attacking with good military blades, and they were trained killers. The attackers leapt at Mucianus' guards, and even had they not had the advantage of numbers, it would have been a foregone conclusion. Obeying Rome's rules, Mucianus' men carried only clubs within the city limits, while the criminals had no such qualms. As the guards swung their stout batons, breaking bones and bruising flesh, the attackers slashed and stabbed, a blood mizzle rising in the warm air amid the screams. Thugs were felled here and there, groaning and clutching limbs, but with every passing heartbeat Mucianus was less and less protected, his soldiers falling to the filthy cobbles with great bloody rents in them, necks torn and hamstrings cut. Blood ran in rivers along the sloping street.

Mucianus was stunned with the attack's unexpectedness. He spent precious moments dancing his horse this way and that, jabbing out a finger and shouting pointless commands at his men, who had no chance to do anything about them, struggling for survival as they were. Finally, he seemed to realise the very real danger he was in, and that his men had no chance. With a last look around, he slapped the reins of his horse and urged the animal to move. He had to escape, else he was a dead man.

Even as the horse whinnied and began to move, the attackers realised their prey was making to flee, and four of them ran at the beast and its rider. Before Mucianus could escape the closing noose of killers, men were leaping at him, grabbing the reins and the horns of the saddle, gripping his legs. I missed precisely what happened during the struggle, for Caecina barked a harsh laugh, and I turned to give him an angry glare. By the time I turned back, the horse was pelting off up the street, its saddle empty, and Mucianus was struggling to his feet in the middle of the mucky roadway, covered in ordure, face flashing between fury and desperation.

Around him, the last of his guards were overcome and put down as street killers moved among them, finishing them off, putting a blade into the throat of any man still moving. As Mucianus was systematically stripped of the last of his defence, he looked this way and that, seeking any solution, any way out. Close to a dozen of the killers were in a ring around him and closing in. Despite the law-abiding nature of his guards, there was still enough of the soldier about Mucianus that he bore a sheathed sword at his side, and he drew it now, wiping the crud from his face with his other forearm.

His gaze fell upon my door.

'Why do you do nothing? Help me!'

I took a step forward, hand coming up to order my slaves to run in and aid the man, but Caecina suddenly gripped me and pulled me back, shaking his head. As he did so, Domitian swept a finger round at the gathered staff of my house and his own guards, ordering them to stand fast. The young Caesar cleared his throat.

'I would love to help you, Mucianus, but we are stricken with colds and sore throats, and the physician tells us to avoid chilly air and stay indoors.'

188

Mucianus stared at us. He could not believe the brazen refusal. Either he had not realised until that moment that this entire thing had been engineered, right down to the selected attackers, or he still felt that I would help him in defiance of the young Caesar. I felt the distaste rising in me as I watched, helpless. I even struggled briefly, trying to step forward out of Caecina's grip, which was surprisingly strong, but as I moved, Domitian's lictors were there, penning me in. There was nothing I could do.

I watched, sickened.

The thugs closed in, blades flashing. Mucianus was brave and strong. He caught three blows in quick succession, parrying them, and turning them aside. He even managed to cut a deep slash across one of the attackers' chests, the man falling back out of the fight, howling and clutching at a deadly wound. But he was outnumbered and there was no hope. The first blow caught Mucianus on his left arm, cutting deep just above the elbow, scything to the bone. The man bellowed in pain, still managing to master himself enough to swing with his other hand.

I felt queasy. I had no love of Mucianus. Indeed, I disliked him intensely, and did not particularly trust him, but this was appalling. No Roman nobleman should be so brutally murdered in cold blood in the streets of Rome, no matter how wicked they might be. A second blow struck him, this time in his shoulder, sending him staggering forward into his attackers.

He managed one more lunge, and then a flurry of blades struck at him from all sides. As the flashing swords and daggers came back up into the warm summer sunlight, they were painted crimson. Another flood of blows. I threw up into my mouth as the crowd parted and what looked like chopped meat in a butcher's shop turned and opened its one remaining eye to glare accusingly at us.

'Help me,' it mouthed, little more than a croak emerging.

This was a killing. It was Clodius Pulcher butchered on the Appian Way on the order of Milo. It was Julius Caesar, stabbed mercilessly on the steps of Pompey's theatre. It was Galba, hacked to pieces and beheaded in the forum. I watched, disgusted by the whole scene, as the shattered mess that had been Mucianus reached out imploringly one last time before the blades came in again, tearing, stabbing, slashing, cutting.

All that remained of the man who had all but ruled Rome for months was a twitching heap in the middle of the street. Blood ran in torrents down the slope towards the heart of the city, carrying tidings of gruesome death towards the palace.

The attackers melted away, then. If anyone had needed confirmation that this was a political killing and not a simple criminal act, it was the fact that the attackers gathered up their fallen and any scattered weapons before they disappeared into alleys and side streets. No evidence would be left to link them to the man who had ordered the attack.

The *men* who had ordered the attack.

It anything could have lowered my opinion of Caecina it was the grin plastered across his face as he looked out at the grisly scene in the street. I expected such unpleasantness from him. But what had happened to Domitian in these past few years that he found such a thing acceptable? I had been in Africa, of course. Until my posting, I had been a close part of Domitian's circle of friends and advisors. When I left, he undoubtedly fell back more and more on Caecina, and the bastard would hardly let anyone else gain any influence. I vowed silently in that moment to make sure I was around in future to counteract the poison of Caecina. After all, what need had I of a political career now, when I had already achieved that empty title at the top of the ladder? Even if Vespasian offered me something astounding, I would politely decline and stand by the prince. After all, had I not agreed a decade ago to keep an eye on him for his father? He needed that guidance and care now.

'The streets are so unsafe these days,' Caecina chuckled.

At least Domitian did not seem to find it humorous. The young Caesar turned to me. 'I will have my men notify the nearest station of the vigiles, so they can come and clear up. I trust you will not mind if we stay here until the matter is dealt with?' he asked.

I simply nodded. What else could I do? I could see what would play out over the next few days. Mucianus' death would be reported. There would be a high-profile, well-attended funeral, and once that was out of the way, the recriminations would begin. Titus, Mucianus being his pet project, would be furious. He would lay the blame squarely, and correctly, at the feet of Caecina. Maybe even involve his brother.

Questions would have to be asked, given the known feud between the two men. Caecina would deny any involvement. So would Domitian, if anyone dared to accuse him, though I doubted anyone would. A few enquiries would place them at my house, conveniently at the scene, and I would be the one noble voice in Rome that could categorically say, with my hand on the altar of Apollo, that Caecina and Domitian and their men were in my domus the entire time and had no involvement in the killing. My name was good enough to carry finality to the case, and in the end it would be recorded that Mucianus was attacked in the street and killed by opportunistic criminals. There would be no comeback. Likely my relationship with Titus was about to take a beating, but that would be the end of it. Mucianus would be gone and his unhealthy influence removed from Rome.

Only one treacherous serpent remained, but I couldn't see how Caecina could be peeled from Domitian's side.

The gods have a funny way of playing with men's lives, though. Even as we watched Mucianus fall in the street they were already rolling their dice and observing the rest of us.

XVII

The Capuan

Rome, February, AD 79

The aftermath of that killing was somewhat predictable. For the better part of a year, Titus had railed and snarled at Domitian every time they crossed paths. The older brother knew what had happened as much as any of us, but, just like everyone else, he had no proof. He'd even gone as far as to demand Caecina's arrest, but his father had refused him and told him to drop the matter.

That had only changed things a little. With Vespasian's refusal to pursue any response, Titus was impotent to act, and what developed between the brothers could only be described as an icy distance. Twice, Domitian uncovered agents of Titus in his house, seeking anything he could use to bring Caecina down, but to no avail.

I did begin to notice as the months came and went that Caecina began once more to involve himself in politics, though carefully and subtly. I could never quite be sure of what he was up to with his alliances and machinations, though I felt certain it would be aimed at Titus.

I privately formed the opinion that Caecina was doing everything he could to keep Domitian and Titus at each other's throats, to what end I could not say. I think that even with Mucianus dead, Caecina saw Domitian as his doorway to power, and Titus as a roadblock. But, to Domitian's credit, he continually kept Caecina's plans in check, and actually attempted to heal the rift with his brother as far as he could, though that was not far. Those spies who were found were given nothing more than a slap on the backside and sent back to Titus.

As we rolled on into the next year, things became a little easier, though with the brothers continuing to endure an ever-frosty relationship. Finally, the city settled once more. The emperor's sons were rarely to be found in one another's presence, but both were avidly loyal to their father.

In fact, with little of note in either trouble or success, three years passed, a rare occurrence these days. Then, on one seemingly innocuous morning, I was summoned by the emperor's younger son.

'This seems oddly familiar,' I murmured as we moved through the Flavian house. Domitian led, and apart from he and I, the only other person present was one of his slaves, a burly fellow with a mean-looking scar on his forehead.

The house was eerie in its deserted echoing halls. Gradually, over the decade Vespasian had ruled Rome, he and his family had spent less and less time at the old family domus in Pomegranate Street. Flavius still lived nearby in his father's old house with a family of his own, but Vespasian's house had now lain empty, cold and dark for several years, visited only by slaves on errands, while the imperial family resided on the Palatine.

I couldn't really remember the last time I had been in the place, but I could very well remember the last time I had come through these particular rooms. Domitian had been but a boy then, albeit a very clever and slightly odd one. That day we had found a slave there, half beaten to death, and used him to unravel all Agrippina's plotting. It seemed extremely odd that we were here now, and it sent shivers up my spine, remembering those dreadful days.

'I... I wasn't sure what to do,' Domitian replied, in an odd echo of that day.

'What have you done?'

As we passed through the storerooms towards that one where we had found a conspiracy, unlocking doors as we went, Domitian murmured quietly, 'I never really stopped, you know.'

'What?'

'After those days. The more Rome changed, the more important it became to be aware of everything before it happened. Oh, there was a brief time when I retreated and did nothing, when Nero fell and the usurpers came in droves.'

'You're talking about spies, aren't you?'

By way of answer, he just continued quietly. 'It was partially that there really wasn't time to acquire the right people and slip them into position before the target was dead and the whole thing became redundant. But there was also the increased danger. With emperors coming and going, soldiers on the streets and the like, any information I gathered would be hard to put to good use. But once the war was over and Father was on the throne, I began again. It seemed prudent.'

As he produced a ring key and unlocked the last door, I noted oddly the shift in terms once more. It had been years since I'd heard Vespasian called 'Father' and not 'the emperor' and something must have happened to bring him back a little closer. We moved into that final room, and I blinked in surprise.

There was no bloodied prisoner here this time, no band of slaves, no chair and ropes. The storage room had changed beyond recognition. It was still storage, but now the walls were filled with shelving stacked with writing tablets and scroll cases. It was a room of information, pure and simple. In the centre sat a table covered in documents, with a single chair.

'No one knows about this place,' he said as he crossed to the table. 'I come here alone. Neither Father nor Titus ever visit the house, and even the slaves only come to collect things for them. The house is mine. Mine and the rats', anyway.'

'You've been busy,' I said, breathing shallowly and looking around the shelves. Just how had he managed this without anyone realising? How many spies did he have? There had been nothing like this in Rome since the days of Tiberius.

'I have managed to keep track of the movements of any number of influential men this past decade, Marcus. The freedmen I watch and engage with myself, but the wealthy and the powerful are outside that sphere. And I had intended to keep this entirely secret, but I find that I am in two minds as to how to proceed on a certain matter. I have a number of friends, of course, some even quite close, but only you outside my family have been reliable and true since the beginning. We share a certain history, you and I, and despite your age, I feel we are spirits alike.'

I nodded, slightly distracted. Where in all this documentation, I wondered, was the information on me? Who was Domitian's spy in my house? I felt sure there would be one. I had ever been reliable and true, but he would know that because he would have been watching my household from within.

'What have you found?'

Domitian turned, and I could see conflict in his expression. He had a piece of vellum in his hand, a single sheet that was stained with scorch marks and burned around two edges. A document that someone had tried to dispose of. He held it out, wordlessly.

I crossed the room, a sense of strange and dreadful anticipation filling me as I reached out and took the page, turning it and lifting it, my eyes picking out the spidery handwriting. It was penned in short form, with a number of unknown abbreviations, and in a hurry by the looks of it, not meant to be sent to anyone, but a personal document for the use of the author itself. The writing was hard to follow, especially with the abbreviations. I read it through twice, and frowned. 'I can't really make it out. It has the feel of a military speech, like a general about to lead an army to war.'

Domitian nodded. 'Perhaps it will help if you realise that SC is an abbreviation for scorpions, and is a reference to the Praetorians, while CU is the urban cohort. THE EGG is a nickname for my father. Now read it again.'

I did. And now that I had a handle on parts of it, and how the author had slipped such abbreviations in, I could also unravel other more arcane parts of the text. I stopped breathing as I read down and the nature of the document became clear. My eyes widened. I hissed out and drew breath, then read it again, just in case.

'Quite,' Domitian said. 'I had a similar reaction.'

I stared. Whoever penned this document was preparing to harangue the military forces in the city and raise them against the emperor. This was a usurpation plan. My eyes slid up to the man who had uncovered it.

'Someone means to depose your father? Who is it? Where did you get it?'

Domitian shook his head. 'Read it again. I grant you it could be read thusly, but I see it a different way. To me, it seems the writer is expecting the emperor to be gone soon, and this is a plan to seize the throne when he goes. To interrupt the dynasty and crown himself.'

I did read it again, and it did make sense. It could be either. And Vespasian was seventy now, so the throne would not be his for much longer. Critical parts of the message had been burned and were illegible. There was certainly no date and no names were mentioned other than the emperor and someone known only as 'the Capuan'.

'Whose is this?'

Domitian sagged back against the table. 'Aulus Caecina Alienus.'

I closed my eyes for a moment. I had always known the slimy bastard was trouble, but I had assumed him at least loyal to Domitian. It seemed that in the end, Caecina was loyal to only one man: himself. 'You got this from a spy in his house?'

Domitian nodded. 'And I can tell you with all certainty that it is his writing. I know his script. Also, the scorpions is a term he uses, as is the egg, in reference to my father's head.' His hand unconsciously went up to the receding line of curls above his own tall forehead.

'This Capuan seems to be in on it.'

Again, he nodded. 'The Capuan is most certainly Eprius Marcellus.'

Gods, one of the emperor's own circle. Marcellus was a close advisor of Vespasian. Only two names were mentioned on this page, but there could be more, of course. Something clicked into place. 'That's why you think it's aimed at succeeding your father rather than removing him, isn't it? It's the enmity between Caecina and your brother.'

'Titus has made no secret of the fact that when he sits on the throne, Caecina will fall. I think this is more self-defence than anything. A coup through desperation. But what do I do, Marcus?'

I shook my head in surprise. 'You bring the plot to light and let the culprits take what's coming to them. You know that. We've been through this before, and that was for an emperor we didn't even care about. This is your family. You've always told me straight that the emperor is sacrosanct. It is a belief I have come to share, but one you propounded often. You cannot let your friendship with Caecina stop you.'

Domitian looked confused for a moment, then something dawned on him. 'You think I am uncertain because I favour Caecina? Marcus Cocceius Nerva, be reasonable. I have been a friend of the man, but I would gut him myself for such a thing.'

'Then what is the problem?'

'Marcus, I have never been on the best of terms with Titus. He is my brother, but I hardly know him, even given this past ten years. He is my father's heir and a co-emperor of Rome, while I have been little more than a courtier. I have tied myself to Caecina over the years. I know it was foolish, and I think I always knew, but sometimes, when you are an outsider, it is nice when anyone takes an interest. Titus hardly knows me, and only then as a consort of his enemy. And he remains angry. He still harbours a suspicion that I was complicit in the murder of his friend Mucianus.'

'Which you were.'

'Which I was. Between that and the connection to Caecina, there is a very good chance that Titus will not believe me, or perhaps even accuse me of complicity. I allowed a gulf to open up between us, which I am no longer sure I can safely cross. Marcus, dare I take this to Titus? Or worse, even, to Father?'

I shook my head. 'Not to your father. He would deal with it well, but if Titus learns there was a plot against him and you took it instead to your father, how do you think he will react?'

He sagged a little more. 'It would surely widen that gulf.'

'It would. You have to trust your family. Trust your brother.'

He nodded weakly. 'You're right, of course. But I... I think I needed that reassurance. The very idea of a plot to raise the Praetorians against him when he is their commander...'

I pushed the document back into his hands. 'We should go now.'

And we did. In moments we were out of the house and back on Pomegranate Street. We did not wait for the litter to be made ready. There was no clear timescale on this plot. The suggestion was that we had time and that it was planned for the day Vespasian passed away, but we could not guarantee that. If things had changed, and Caecina planned to move soon, we needed to hurry.

We clattered down the street towards the heart of the city in just tunics and with cloaks pulled tight around us against the winter chill. We had not been toga clad, and it takes some time to settle the garment correctly, even with an experienced slave on hand, so we'd left as we were, poorly prepared for either weather or palace life. People scurried out of our way, partly because of our clear eminence, partly perhaps because of our urgency and our expressions, but mostly because of the small army of slaves and guards that accompanied us.

As we neared the Subura, our men slightly more on their guard in that dangerous region, a thought occurred to me. 'Titus will be at your father's dinner at the palace. I should have been there, really. Where is Caecina now?'

Domitian's face paled. 'He could not join me today because of a prior engagement. You don't suppose...?'

Sharing a look, we started to move faster, puffing and panting as we crossed the forum and approached the stair of Caligula which led up to the old palace where Vespasian was holding court. At the stair, the two Praetorians on guard, who prevented the general populace approaching the palace, took a look at the small gathering, registered surprise at the sight of two such important persons in such a state, sweating and panting, and stepped neatly aside.

That climb on that day was yet another reminder that I was no longer the hungry young tribune I had been when my career began. I was closing on my fiftieth year, and had spent much of the past twenty sitting down. I could do with being fitter.

Again, at the top of the stair, and then at the palace doors, Praetorians stepped aside with expressions of surprise. As we hurried through the palace towards the hum of conversation that clearly marked the dinner of the emperor and his friends, I found myself verging on having second thoughts. In my head I kept seeing the arguments I'd witnessed between the two brothers when Mucianus and Caecina had been there. Despite my reassurances to Domitian, there was every chance that Titus would react badly to this, and with the emperor and Caecina in the room, and possibly Marcellus too, I could not guarantee that this was the best idea. Still, we were settled upon a course now.

Had I been thinking more clearly, I would have come up with a plan with Domitian as we approached. As it was, we were both wrapped up in our doubts and fears and it was only as we entered the great winter triclinium with its festoons and gilded décor that I realised we'd not actually discussed what would happen next. Thus as Domitian hurried towards his brother, Praetorians dithering, uncertain what they should be doing – for this was an unexpected intrusion, but by the emperor's son and one of his close friends – I paused and looked around. Marcellus was not here, which was good, but I could see Caecina in all his oily glory, handsome and dangerous, sitting almost directly opposite Titus. With a bow to the emperor, who had looked up in surprise at the sudden arrivals, I scurried around the table towards the traitor.

I stood some distance from the man, just in case, but was prepared to move. Praetorians were closing in groups, several to protect the emperor from any threat this might represent, others the same with Titus, more moving to keep me surrounded if necessary.

As I kept still, close to Caecina, and Praetorians kept still, close to me, I watched the activity across the room. Domitian crossed to Titus, who sat upright on his couch as his brother approached. The younger hissed something quietly, and then Titus rose and the pair went into a huddle. I saw the piece of vellum change hands and then a short, murmured but very urgent conversation. Relief flooded through me as Titus passed the document back and then reached out and gripped his brother on both arms, leaned in and gave him a kiss on the cheek.

All would be good between them. My eyes slid momentarily to Vespasian, whose aged and lined expression was darting through a series of emotions. He had been surprised at the interruption, then suspicious as the huddle occurred, then proud as his sons displayed such affection, but now he slid into suspicion again.

Titus turned.

Had I been Caecina, I suspect my bowels would have loosened in that moment. There could be no doubt who the emperor's heir was looking at when he turned, and those who had witnessed the expression that crossed his face had usually been in a cellar surrounded by Praetorians with very specialised skills, and did not live to tell a soul what they saw.

Caecina rose suddenly from his couch. His hands came up, spread-palmed in a gesture of conciliation and surrender. 'Do not listen to untruths,' he advised Titus in his most silvery, persuasive tone. If he had hoped his wiles would work on the prince who had hated him for years he was entirely mistaken. Titus' gimlet eyes narrowed.

'I am a loyal servant of the house of the Flavii,' Caecina said, backing away from the table.

'You are loyal to no one but Aulus Caecina Alienus,' Domitian announced, stepping shoulder to shoulder with his older brother. Side by side there could be no denying the family blood.

Domitian was slighter than his stocky, muscular older brother, but a little taller, and their features were almost close enough to suggest twinhood.

'When have I stood against you?' Caecina demanded. 'Even when you marched on Rome as little more than usurpers, I tried to bring the army over to you.'

'When you knew Vitellius was done for,' added Titus. 'You turned on him, just as you'd turned on Galba when you saw your opportunity.'

'I am…' Caecina began, but that was all he managed.

Titus had finished his sentence with a single gesture, and I was crudely nudged aside as four Praetorians passed me and reached Caecina.

'There is no plot against you,' Caecina managed, turning his face to the emperor as the four guards grabbed and held him, dragging him back away from the table. The astonished faces of a score of Rome's most eminent noblemen around the table moved from him then to Titus. I caught the emperor's face once more. Vespasian looked angry. As he had aged – and he really had aged these past few years – the once smiling countenance that had become his public image had turned a little dour. Now he looked ancient and furious. It was Titus, though, who moved next. The heir clapped one hand on his brother's shoulder and then marched around the room.

He passed his father and stopped some ten feet from the restrained man.

'I warned you twice that you would regret crossing me, Caecina Alienus. Had you managed to restrain your treacherous nature until the day I succeeded my father, I might have been persuaded to grant you a comfortable, if very distant, exile. But your treasonous nature cannot be contained, can it?'

Caecina opened his mouth to reply, perhaps to argue, or beg, but instead he looked down in shock to see the sword in his gut. At a flick of a finger from Titus, one of the Praetorians had buried his blade in Caecina's belly and left it there, stepping back.

'Take him somewhere to die,' Titus said in a quiet, callous tone.

The Praetorian grasped his blade once more and pulled it free with a very unpleasant sucking sound. I had been in battle a couple of times in Britannia in my youth, and I had seen death aplenty there and that day on the Capitol. I knew the wound I was seeing now, and knew what it meant. The blood that flowed out came slowly, and was accompanied by an acrid smell of faeces. The blow had been deliberately aimed to be fatal, but slow and very painful. No main blood vessel had been cut, nor the man's liver, from the colour of the flow. But the smell made it clear that the sword had cut through his bowel, and the contents were now leaking into his belly.

Soldiers who took that wound were routinely killed cleanly by their mates, and were grateful for it. The agony of slowly rotting innards and the disease that would come and eat away the flesh if he lived long enough was just not worth thinking about. And it was a guaranteed death. Even if there was a physician who could save him, within the hour the news of what had happened would be all over Rome, and no man who could save him would dare to do so.

Caecina's future would be measured in hours or days at most, and every passing moment would bring increasing pain and despair. As he gasped, face pale, still staring down at the crimson blossom around the slash in his tunic, the soldiers dragged him away, out of one of the room's many doors.

Silence descended, broken finally by the emperor. His ageing wrinkled face formed into a smile. 'Always thought he was a bit of a shit,' he chuckled, pinching his nose. The room erupted into laughter at this dark wit, all except Domitian, Titus and myself. We looked at one another. Whatever had happened over these past years that had come between the brothers, it was over, and they were truly siblings again, and I, as ever, was a loyal friend of the family.

One matter remained to be dealt with.

I was with the brothers, both of them, when we went for Marcellus. There was no suggestion that we worry about the nuances of law that day. With half a century of Titus' Praetorians, we left the palace, each of us armed for war. We took a carriage from the palace stable. Wheeled vehicles are forbidden in the streets of Rome during daylight hours, but the light was already fading in the wintry afternoon sky, and besides, who was going to stop the carriage and arrest the sons of the emperor? The three of us rode in the vehicle, the Praetorians on horseback, and we moved at speed. For reference, over a flagged road, it is much more comfortable to ride a horse than resort to a cart, but still, we bounced, lurched, and teeth-clattered our way across the city at a pace that would impress Pheidippides.

We arrived at the house of Titus Clodius Eprius Marcellus on the Esquiline while the sun was still up, a light cold rain beginning to mist the air. Marcellus had been one of Vespasian's closest companions at times, and was one of the pre-eminent men of Rome. His fall would be a lofty one, and would be fodder for gossip in the city for some time. But there was something we needed here, more than just his death.

'Remember,' Titus said to the centurion as his men dismounted and hammered on the door, 'that I want him alive. We don't know if this was just the two of them, or whether there were others. He must be interrogated.'

The centurion saluted, and then we were moving. The princes had acted a little rashly on the Palatine, impaling Caecina before trying to interrogate him. It might still be possible to do so as he lay, dying of rot in a corner, but there would be no saving him now, and therefore little incentive for Caecina to tell the truth. Marcellus, on the other hand, still had everything to lose.

We were admitted to the house and stomped through it with the Praetorians, our attention attracted by a commotion ahead. We passed through a peristyle garden and approached a doorway where two of the Praetorians stood, swords drawn. As they stepped aside, we witnessed what had happened.

Marcellus lay in the centre of his room, on his back. He was still twitching, and the shaving razor fell from his jerking fingers even as we arrived. He had drawn the blade across his throat from ear to ear, and the blood was sheeting from the wound still, forming a huge dark lake around him. He was dead already, and with him had died any hope of identifying other plotters.

In an attempt to divine further truths, Caecina was found and tortured even as he died, but even coward that he was, he took any other names to his unmarked grave.

For now all I knew was that the next villain in our chain had come and gone. First Agrippina with her hatred of the Flavii, then Scaevinus and his plotting, then Glabrio, the senator who had stood against us, and now Caecina. Who would be next, I wondered as I watched that day end in bloodshed.

But the gods had other plans for the coming days, and villainy would have to wait.

Part Four – Imperium

*Let Caesar, decked with abundance of gold, sacrifice to
Minerva on the Alban mount, and let many an
oak-garland pass through his imperial hands*

–Martial: *Epigrams 4.1*

XVIII

The heir to Rome

Reate, 24 June AD 79

'How is he?'

The strain was showing in Titus' face as he stopped his pacing and looked up, worried.

Andromachus the physician stood in the doorway, his expression suggesting little positive to come. 'The illness continues to progress and there is little we can do to help now, Domine.'

Titus grunted. 'Then what use are physicians?'

Domitian reached out and grasped his brother by the shoulder. I watched from my place across the room, seated comfortably next to my old friend Flavius. 'Don't take it out on the surgeon,' the younger brother said quietly. 'You know it's not his fault.'

Titus sighed. 'I know.' And turning to Andromachus: 'My apologies. Go on.'

The second-generation Greek, court physician to Vespasian as his father had been to Nero in his time, shrugged. 'It is not a deadly illness. It is the sort of common illness that does the rounds each year. Had it been any of us in this room who caught it, we would have fought back and shaken it off in half a month or so. But the sad fact is that the emperor is not a young man. At seventy, the body no longer has the resistance and strength to fight illness the way a young man does. What might confine you to your bed for a week is a threat to his very life.'

'He is strong,' Titus said defiantly. 'He is the conqueror of Britannia, the man who brought peace to Rome, the scourge of the Jews. He has a strength few men can claim.'

Andromachus nodded. 'And that is why he has lasted this long, Domine. Many his age would never have made it back to Rome, let alone up here.'

I nodded quietly to myself. Vespasian had left Rome in the spring, his usual self, and the majority of the court had followed him on his tour. He was feeling a little low in energy, he had said, and so we would visit the great spa, baths and temples of Baia. It would be a social affair. While the emperor was recovering his vim, he would entertain the locals; we would have festivals, games, dinners and parties. We spent time at Pompeii, always a hive of excitement. It was almost a month of good-natured fun, and the emperor seemed to be regaining his self, returning to old form. Then one morning he had woken with a cough.

The illness had worsened over a few days, and he was attended by some of the best physicians and priests in the world at Baia, each of whom tried their own, often bizarre, solution, none of which seemed to make any real difference. In the end, the travels were cut short and the entire court, with all its attendants, returned to Rome. Vespasian continued to decline there, much to the concern of his two sons. He made the decision only a few days later to return to his home. The Flavii had originally come from Reate in the north of Italia, and still had estates there. The emperor stood by the efficacy of the healing springs at his local spa town of Aquae Cutiliae, and so he would go there to see if it would ease his condition.

Most of the court was left at Rome, only those of us close to the family were invited to travel with them. This was no longer a social whirl, but a private family matter. The emperor was clearly gravely ill now, and in decline, and we were trying what we could to arrest that. The journey was slow and difficult, even in the summer months, and we had to stop often, for Vespasian did not have the strength for long hauls, even bed-bound in his carriage.

For the first five days in the north, the emperor had spent much of each morning and afternoon at the baths complex, helped there in his weakened condition by many attendants, and briefly we wondered if he was recovering, for his spirits seemed to have risen. The sad fact was that this was merely a symptom of having left behind the cares and difficulties of rule in Rome and enjoying a relaxing time in the land of his fathers. The illness was not receding.

Andromachus the Cretan had come with us from Rome, and had attended the emperor every day. He was, beyond a doubt, the most capable and pragmatic physician of our time, and the emperor could not have been cared for by anyone better. Even he knew that, which is why Vespasian's ongoing decline was accepted now as a sad inevitability by all except Titus, who railed against the Fates, challenging the gods to try and take his father. Not that it made any difference apart, perhaps, from making the gods angry with Titus.

'You have an unpleasant decision to make, Domine,' the physician said, addressing Titus directly.

The heir to Rome frowned, wringing his hands. 'What?'

Andromachus braced himself, and I winced. No physician did that with anything but bleak news. 'Your father is near the end of his ability to fight. He will not go to the baths tomorrow, for he can no longer rise from his bed. The illness has robbed every muscle of tone and strength. I am sorry, Titus, son of Vespasian, but your father will never leave that bed.'

I heard a hiss of despair from the young heir then, and was once more impressed at Domitian, who remained by his brother's side, squeezing his arm, murmuring words of support. Of course, Titus had spent his life marching across the empire with his father, and the pair had ever been close. Vespasian had been absent for much of Domitian's life, and that, along with his natural tendency to logical approaches, had left the younger brother with a more objective, less emotional response to their father's decline.

'What are you saying?' Titus muttered.

'Your father is dying,' Andromachus said as kindly as he could. 'There are treatments I can give him still.'

'Then you should be doing that, not standing here.'

The physician nodded slowly, arms folded. 'But you must understand that any treatment I apply now is not with intent to heal.'

'What?'

'Titus, your father will die, and soon. Anything I do will prolong his life, but it will not save it, nor allow him the strength to leave his room, or even his bed. I will be dragging out the inevitable.'

'But you can extend his life?'

'At the expense of his comfort. Titus, while it might give him a few more days, anything I do will cause him pain and difficulty now. In my medical opinion, it would be kinder to simply make him as comfortable as possible.'

'And watch him die?'

'That is inevitable.'

Titus was trembling as he stood there, silent, digesting this. Domitian embraced his brother and whispered something in his ear. Titus shook his head, but the younger brother whispered again, and I saw the fight go out of his sibling. As Domitian stepped back, the heir of the Flavii straightened.

'Make him as comfortable as you can, Andromachus, and know that we are grateful for everything you have done.'

The physician left, and Titus stood in the centre of the room, shaking. Domitian did what he could, and in turn we all went to the prince and shared our support with him. There was no one in this room who had not known the Flavii all their lives, and all but three were blood relations.

We sat around, then, sharing old stories, Titus and Domitian, Domitia Longina and I, Flavius, his sons Flavius Clemens and Flavius Sabinus, and Julia, Domitilla and Petilius Cerialis. Most of us had known one another for decades, and the stories were apt and often funny. Indeed, we were roaring with laughter at the realisation that of all the astounding things Vespasian had done, history would probably best remember him for his name being given to the public urinal pots around Rome. We were so loud that it took a while for us to realise the slave was standing in the doorway, quietly trying to respectfully get our attention. Finally, Titus turned to him.

'What is it?'

'The emperor is distressed that so many people are laughing and he cannot hear the joke.'

There was an odd silence, broken as Titus laughed again, a slightly sad laugh this time.

The slave gave a nervous smile. 'The emperor says that he still has sufficient strength to eat something and would appreciate it if the evening meal could be served in his chamber and everyone attend. And that someone tells him the joke.'

Thus it was that we spent that night at a strange, bittersweet dinner in Vespasian's bedchamber. The room carried that faint odour of illness, but the slaves had done an excellent job of masking it with scented oils, incense burning in the brazier and garlands of fragrant flowers around. The room had been set up such that the emperor's bed formed the couch at the head of the table arrangement, as though this were perfectly normal.

It took a while for us all to slip into this artificial normality, but even ill and ancient, Vespasian had an easy nature that drew people to him. So within the hour we were laughing with the emperor and telling more stories and jokes. Indeed, while he had trouble propping himself up sufficiently, and hardly touched the food, verbally and mentally the emperor was thoroughly on form, and even ribald at times. Indeed, he seemed his old self in some ways, the Vespasian who was little more than country nobility who nobody could possibly imagine reaching such lofty heights.

There was a strangely thoughtful pause at one point, where things became serious. We had been telling stories of that year of civil war. Despite the terror and the disasters of that time, there had been moments that were palatable and deserving of remembrance, and we did so, Vespasian even ribbing Cerialis over his escape from Vitellian Rome, when he had disguised himself as a peasant and had to mumble and 'ooh-arrr' his way to freedom. Then, as the room fell silent, the emperor cleared his throat.

'There must not be another, you understand?'

'Father?' Titus prompted.

'Civil war. There must not be another. That year nearly ruined the empire. It cannot be allowed to happen again. We have the makings of a dynasty here. As the descendants of the great Julius Caesar ruled Rome for a century, we must do the same. No wars among our own. When I am gone, rule wisely and rule well, Titus. Have a mind for your empire. Do not countenance fools, and deal harshly with revolt and subversion, but make sure that no matter what you do and who you do it to, the senate and the people of Rome still think of you as their benefactor. That has served us well for ten years.'

'I will, Father.'

'But there is more. If we are to have a dynasty, there must be continuation. Titus, you need to take a wife and have heirs. Until that is the case, you should take your brother as your co-emperor as I did with you. Then, there can be no uncertainty over succession. Always have the succession planned, and in a manner that will satisfy all. Then, our dynasty can go on, and there will be no new civil war.'

The room fell silent again, once both sons had pledged to their father that this would be the case. In fact, the silence stretched out long enough that it began to feel uncomfortable.

'And then Cerialis will not have to wear rags again,' Vespasian grinned, breaking the spell. Everyone laughed again, even Cerialis, if rather sheepishly.

Humour resumed, and as the evening wore on, Vespasian seemed to suffer some digestive discomfort. The noisy and lengthy farts that came periodically were the subject of much humour and a lot of pinching of noses.

'Who knew that becoming a god was so pungent,' the emperor laughed, in reference rather darkly to his imminent demise. It could have been a comment that set Titus off, but so good was the humour that night that it passed with the rest of the jokes.

I have seen death many times in my long life. I have seen it come in roaring violence on the battlefield, and I have seen it come from the executioner's blade. I have seen it at banquets in poison form and in noble suicide. I have never witnessed as noble an end as the great Vespasian's. Whatever he might have done to keep Rome in line, and he was no shirker with the execution order himself, Vespasian ruled Rome well, and set a precedent. His easy humour and self-depreciating simplicity was with him to the end.

We had finished the food and it had been cleared away. Slaves had brought more wine and water and then tactfully withdrawn until called, and the ten of us laughed and sighed over wine for perhaps an hour after dinner. We all looked up as Cerialis broke off in the middle of some anecdote about a cavalry officer with an allergy to horse hair, for Vespasian was moving, making odd, groaning noises. There was another wash of pungent wind, and then the emperor's legs slid out of the bed, his veined, almost blue feet slapping down onto the marble floor.

'What are you doing, Father?' Titus asked, leaning to rise.

Vespasian gave a smile, though a somewhat forced one, and waved his son back to his seat.

'Father, you're too weak,' Domitian added. 'I will have a slave bring a chamber pot.'

Incredibly, though Vespasian had only barely managed to prop himself up on an elbow throughout the meal, he rose to a seated position with a smile of satisfaction. With a hiss, he braced himself, and rose from the bed, like Neptune from the waters. We stared in surprise as the ageing, dying emperor stood for the first time in days, swaying a little, next to his table.

'An emperor,' he announced in a clear voice, 'should die on his feet.'

And he did. With that, he fell once more, collapsing back onto the bed. Titus and Domitian were the first up, running from their seats around to their father. Vespasian had been dead before he landed, with his one last gesture. No breath. No pulse. The emperor had, indeed, died on his feet.

The two brothers huddled over their father, both crying, both muttering prayers and promises, making vows to gods. We should, perhaps, have left them to their grief, but then among the rest of us were his daughter and nephews, sons-in-law and old friends. There was no one there who did not have a right to be there. We sat in mournful silence as the brothers consoled one another and hugged their father. After a while, Domitilla was there too, a daughter who had spent much of her life away from the emperor, and then Julia, a granddaughter mourning her grandsire.

I sat quietly throughout it all, as did Cerialis. We were friends, but it was not our place to be quite so intimately involved in this family affair. We waited, and finally the two brothers rose from their father's deathbed, steadying themselves, breathing deeply and stepping away into the centre of the room.

As Titus shook still, the emotions running high, Domitian straightened, his face turning sombre. He reached out and gripped Titus by the shoulders.

'You need to go. First thing in the morning. As soon as it is light.'

Titus frowned, and shook his head. 'No. Father just died, Domitian. He is still warm. There is much to do and it's my place to do it. You know that.'

Domitian looked his brother in the eye. 'Remember what Father said this evening. There cannot be another civil war.'

Titus frowned. 'I don't follow.'

'It's been ten years, but that's only one emperor. A single decade of tradition. And I know you've made a reputation for yourself between Judea and the Guard, but will everyone see you as the natural successor? Remember what happened with Caecina. All it would take is one governor in a strong province deciding he would make a better emperor and suddenly we're back in civil war.'

'You think that won't happen if I'm in Rome?'

Domitian bared his teeth. 'The senate. You need to be there the very moment tidings reach Rome that the emperor is dead, so that the gaggle of flapping sycophants can ratify you and confirm your position. Their approval will go a long way to preventing usurpers in the provinces. Jove knows, it's the only thing the senate is good for, and it's the only real power they have, so you might as well harness it. If you delay to deal with Father, the senate might start to look elsewhere.'

Titus nodded slowly. 'I don't like it, but you're right.'

Domitian nodded. 'Take the others back with you. Their support will open doors, too, especially Nerva and Cerialis. I can make all the appropriate arrangements here, and then you can pay your respects properly when we bring Father to Rome for the funeral.'

'I will have someone prepare the imperial mausoleum across the river.'

'No,' Domitian shook his head. 'It will not do to have him interred with the likes of Caligula and Tiberius. We'll build a new mausoleum, in Pomegranate Street.'

Titus shook his own head in turn now. 'No. The great mausoleum is the very symbol of imperial apotheosis. Father needs to be among emperors, good and bad, not on his own. If it makes you feel better, build him a temple in Pomegranate Street, maybe where our home now stands?'

Domitian pursed his lips for a while before agreeing. 'And there are other arrangements to make. You'll not take a third wife, I presume?'

Titus shook his head. 'No. And you know why.'

'I do,' Domitian answered, his gaze darting briefly to his beloved Domitia Longina. The pair shared a smile. 'All right,' he said, straightening, 'if you won't marry for position, marry for love.'

'What?'

'I did it, remember? No matter how much Father nagged and pushed, I held firm and married my Domitia. Forget Roman matrons if they're not who you want. You're *emperor* now. Bring your Judean princess to Rome and marry her. Have half-Jewish boys.' He laughed oddly. 'Who knows, you might even bring the two peoples together.'

As Titus digested this with a wry smile, Domitian became serious again. 'You need sons,' he said.

'Rome will not accept a foreign empress, even a queen of the Herodian line.'

'I think you overestimate the propriety of the Roman people. They can forgive a lot. She will be the Cleopatra to your Caesar.'

Titus mumbled something into his chest and then straightened. 'I will not wait for morning. You are right. I must be ahead of the news. I will leave and travel through the night.' He turned to the rest of us. 'Everyone else follow on at a reasonable time tomorrow.'

We gathered and paid our respects to the emperor as slaves cleaned him up and laid him in an appropriate manner, while Titus hurried around gathering everything he would need for Rome. Finally, once he was ready to leave and the stable boys were leading out his horse, his escort preparing for the trip, he returned to his father's body and reverently leaned down and removed the seal ring from his finger, the signet of the Flavii that was now his. With one last embrace of his brother and sister, and one last long, sad look at his father, the new emperor of Rome left the villa to claim his imperium.

'You should have gone with him,' I said after a while, directing my words to Domitian.

'Someone needs to deal with the arrangements,' he replied. 'His son, really.'

'You are to be co-emperor,' I reminded him. 'You will help him rule, and until he has a male heir you will be that too. The senate needs to see that.'

The look he turned on me was full of his disparaging opinion of that august body. 'I do not give two figs what the senate thinks. They simply need to ratify Titus and then they can slide back into powerless obscurity,' he grunted.

I nodded, sadly. The Flavian dynasty had now begun, a new family to rule Rome for a hundred years or more. Titus would be glorious, and we all knew it. What we did not know was for how long.

XIX

Everyone's friend

AD 79

Looking back, I can see the differences between Titus and his father as rulers of Rome, though at the time he seemed almost a facsimile, if brighter and more likeable. There had been no argument in the senate over his right to succeed Vespasian, though the senators in general greeted his reign's outset with trepidation. After all, under 'benevolent' Vespasian, it had been Titus and his Praetorian Guard who had dragged disparaging noblemen from their homes and tortured the truth from them before displaying their heads in the forum. There were a number of fears over what kind of an emperor that man might make.

But the fact was that what Titus had done for his father had been nothing more than a job, it did not reflect the personality of the man. In fact, Titus was actually far more benevolent than his father had been, and it took time for people to realise it. Vespasian had spent much of his reign stamping Flavian power on the empire, taxing with impunity and using wily politicking to maintain a façade of easy geniality despite all of this. Titus inherited a Rome with a healthy treasury and stable military and politics. He had no need for vicious taxes, and no need for a war, for he'd earned his triumphant reputation already in Judea. So he settled into his reign easily and with nothing imposed on the people.

Indeed, one of his first acts was to officially repeal a number of laws connected with maiestas and treason, to make networks of informants not only unnecessary but actually illegal, to dismantle such networks and punish the informants. There had been something of a tense time when Domitian, on my advice, approached his brother and admitted to controlling a network of spies of his own. The subject was glossed over without reaching public ears. Titus promised not to punish Domitian's people, and Domitian promised to dismantle his network. Titus lived up to his promise. Domitian did not. He had spent decades learning the value of such a thing, and decades building his web, and he was not about to dismantle it because Titus wanted to prove something to the senate.

Titus was officially acclaimed as emperor, and as the days rolled by it was a relief to all when he received the oath from every province's governor and legions. Once that had happened, the chances of revolt seemed negligible, and Titus' ever-growing popularity made it unlikely that this would change.

Indeed, one night over wine, I had discussed it with Domitian.

'He is trying too hard to become everyone's friend,' he murmured.

'Your father ruled very successfully by being seen as everyone's friend.'

'But *he* never forgot that he was their master. He smiled and shook hands while using the other to take the gold from their pocket, and noting any dissent to pass on to the Praetorians for their ministrations. Titus is all smile and no control. He is too eager to please. I have spoken to the freedmen and the praetors of the treasury. The public Aerarium looks healthy enough, but that is a puddle against the sea of the imperial fiscus, and that sea is almost dry. Do you know that in two months Titus has spent more than Father made in taxes over the last year? How long can he continue to be so extravagant before the treasury is empty once more? What then if suddenly we have to raise legions for war? He is not thinking far enough ahead.'

I had shrugged at that. 'It is the way of emperors. They must begin their reign with such generosity. It will tail off once he no longer needs to secure his rule.'

Domitian sighed. 'I very much hope you're right, Nerva, though I suspect you are mistaken. This is Titus. This is who he is. Do not expect change. It will be our job, his family and his friends, his extended familia and *consilia*, to keep him in line and to stop him going too far.'

There was little I could say to that. Perhaps Titus would prove to be sensible in the end, or perhaps he would be a new Nero with his extravagance. We would never know, for the gods began to intervene.

It began that autumn, only four months into Titus' reign. He had quickly secured a reputation as a golden prince and a good friend to all, a truly benevolent emperor, though his lavish spending continued unabated despite Domitian's insistence. Indeed, the brothers were often at odds that autumn, Titus repeatedly stating his imperium and his right to rule however he felt, Domitian continually nagging at him to think further than his next party. No great gulf opened up between them as had in the presence of Mucianus and Caecina, but certainly their relationship became a little more strained as that season progressed. Despite having been promised it more than once, the official promotion of Domitian to the role of co-emperor never came about. Personally, I believe that to be Titus' answer to his brother's continual opposition over the treasury, though it was, when occasionally pointed out, generally brushed aside as an oversight that would be corrected eventually. In truth, Domitian occupied that role anyway, despite the lack of any official title recognised by the senate. I doubt he cared. Senatorial confirmation mattered little to Domitian anyway.

At length, October came around, and the gods rolled their first dice. We were not present for the disaster, of course, but we had urgent and very detailed reports from the witnesses and, their arguments forgotten, Domitian immediately accompanied Titus as he gathered his consilia and hurried away to Campania. I was part of that consilia, of course, and so I went with them. We took ship for speed and pelted down the Italian coast.

The great mountain, Vesuvius, which towered over Pompeii, had exploded. The reports we had heard were so devastating and horrific that none of us believed them to be true. They had to be exaggerations. The noble Pliny, admiral of the Misemum fleet, had lost his life in the disaster as he tried to organise shipping and save as many of the population as he could. But still, despite all the accounts that reached us in the immediate aftermath, we could not imagine the disaster had been anything like the descriptions.

It was as our ships pulled into Neapolis that the truth insisted itself. Horrifying as they had been, the reports had, if anything, played down the reality. Vulcan, great god in the earth with his fiery forge, had detonated the great mountain, and the scale of the destruction was incalculable. As we crossed the water to the city where we would dock, we realised why it had to be there and not nearer to Pompeii.

There was no longer anywhere nearer to Pompeii to dock. The glorious Campanian coast had been obliterated. Over the centuries, thriving towns had grown here, and the villas of the rich and famous, even Nero's wife, had lain near the seafront along the bay. All had gone. From Neapolis to the furthest visible promontory, the world had been destroyed. Indeed, even the sky was a hazy dark grey; we had assumed that to be inclement October weather, but it transpired that the day was in fact clear, sunny, and even quite temperate. The exploded mountain, however, had thrown so much dust into the air that it was yet to settle, and the sun was but a weak glow through the grey.

We disembarked in a sombre mood, and climbed into carriages that would take us into the disaster zone. As the column moved south along the coast, four carriages with two carts of freedmen and slaves behind, then three carts of supplies, all accompanied by eighty Praetorians on horseback, we witnessed the true scale of the devastation.

Seven months ago we had been here with the ailing Vespasian, in a party atmosphere, enjoying the imperial sojourn among the resorts and spas of the region. Now we were travelling through the charred corpses of those places.

I remembered one *caupona* on the edge of Herculaneum where we had stopped for a happy couple of hours. The owner had been so overwhelmed that Titus and Domitian were drinking his wine that he almost swooned. The locals came in droves to look at the princes in their town, and Titus and Domitian had both bought food and drink by the cartload and distributed it to the cheering crowd.

I had thought to identify the remains of the caupona as we passed the town, but could see nothing. It only dawned on me as the carriages rattled on that this was because the place had gone entirely. Herculaneum was no more. What we were riding across was not road or field, but the debris the mountain had cast down upon Herculaneum. With horror I saw the apex of a roof rising a mere three feet from the ground close to where we rode. My wide eyes slid past it to see the crumbled and battered upper arc of the theatre wall, so deeply entombed that it stood only the height of a man. Herculaneum had been buried alive. For all I knew I was riding across the top of that lovely caupona.

The scale of it all continued to grow in our eyes as we passed the sites of enormous palatial villas that we had visited a few months earlier, some even owned by the emperor, all buried or obliterated, little to see but exploded fragments. Pompeii was worse. This city had not been entirely buried, which meant that we had more of an idea what had happened. Pompeii was entombed in ash and pumice and rocks to roughly the height of a man, the second storeys of the city rising from the detritus, but they were far from intact. Their roofs had largely gone, and many walls were crumbled, and battered, all burned. They were the half-buried, charred skeletons of buildings. We rode in silence and horror as we saw all manner of grotesque sights. Here and there a charred body was half-buried, looking as though it were trying to free itself from the ground in which it was trapped. We saw the corpses of animals and men and women, children too. The survivors had come back to the ruins of their city, a pitifully small number, and were digging into the ash and rubble for the remains of loved ones.

I had witnessed murders, executions and civil wars, but Pompeii that first day crowns every horror I have ever seen in my life. It was the worst thing imaginable. It became clear that healing this land was not going to be a quick job, if such a thing was even possible.

'We will move the court here for a time,' Titus said, his face grave. His gaze slid to Domitian, a challenge in his eyes as he went on. 'The imperial treasury will be made available for the relief of the people of Campania.'

Domitian, for once, did not argue. He simply nodded, eyes shadowed with despair at what we all saw. Over the few days since the mountain had stopped exploding, the survivors had come back, and the naval forces at Misenum across the bay had continued the work they had started under Pliny. No longer required to sail survivors away across the waters, they had bent their efforts to providing a temporary home for them. The fleet had brought timber and canvas from Misenum and constructed what looked like a massive legionary camp, with makeshift wooden barracks and tents all across it in ordered rows to house the victims of the disaster.

Titus took one approving look at the place and praised the fleet. Here, he said, we would make our court while the disaster was dealt with. Rome could do without him for a time. A new compound was set up at the edge of the camp for the imperial party, and cohorts of Praetorians were summoned from Rome. Indeed, over the following months, we set up quite some court here.

Titus placed two ex-consuls in charge of the relief efforts: myself and Lucius Ceionius Commodus. While the emperor and his brother took a prime role in the highest-level decision-making in Campania, the actual nuances of the work were left to Lucius and myself. We did what we could, and as we did, I was acutely aware of just how much of Titus' treasury we were draining. By mid-November our camp had doubled in size, with the majority of the Praetorian Guard and both Roman fleets based here helping with the relief efforts.

All winter we worked amid the charred remains of Pompeii, and Titus' happy countenance remained in place throughout, though anyone who knew him could see that he forced it upon his face on a morning, and then let it fall away like a mask in private at night. He was becoming exhausted, both physically and emotionally, with what we dealt with each day. Spring came around and brought with it a pestilence that seemed to leech from the very earth around us. Many among the court found excuses to return to Rome, and many begged Titus to do so. Titus would not. He would stay as long as it took to repair the damage here. Of course, it was by now clear to those of us doing the actual work that there was no hope for this land. It could never be returned to what it was. All we could do was save what could be saved, help those who had survived to build new lives, and wait until the ground grassed over to start again. New towns would likely grow up over the old, but it would not be now, and it would not be the result of imperial design.

Spring rolled into summer. I caught the illness in May, and missed almost a month of work as I writhed in my bed sheets, expecting to die every day. Somehow, I gradually returned to health. Actually, more than half those who caught the illness survived, but I had become weak and gaunt. Thank the gods that there were already a multitude of physicians on the site, working to heal the people of Campania, for their aid saved many also from the following pestilence.

It was June when things changed again, and not for the better. A messenger was admitted to the imperial command building, a timber structure of impressive size. Titus, care-worn and pale, was seated, his brother close by, while Commodus and I delivered the latest reports. We all turned as the slave announced the messenger and then stepped out, and the Praetorians on duty admitted the dusty man and then shut the door. The messenger approached to an appropriate distance and then dropped to a knee, head bowed, offering a scroll that bore imperial markings.

It came from Epaphroditus, who Titus had retained among his palace staff. It begged the emperor to return to Rome. He was needed with all alacrity, for there had been a disaster. We all looked at one another in disbelief. We were still deep in the throes of one disaster, and now were we told of another?

There had been a fire in Rome.

I watched the despair creep back into Titus' expression then, though he hid it well. Gesturing to the messenger to rise, he spoke solemnly. 'Visit the mess tent and get yourself something to eat, and find the baths and clean up, though you'll find it a poor, makeshift affair. Then ride back to the Palatine and tell them the emperor is on the way.'

The next morning, Titus left for Rome. Domitian went with him, and the brothers took four cohorts of Praetorians with them. Any conflagration that was of such note was no small affair. Commodus and I were left to oversee the efforts here. Thus it was that I never saw the second of Rome's great fires that century. This was nothing on the scale of the Neronian conflagration, of course, but it was still huge and disastrous. I heard about it in reports periodically throughout the remainder of the year. The fire had started in the Campus Martius and had destroyed many of the most important landmarks there, from Pompey's theatre to the Pantheon. It had ruined swathes of housing in the process and had spread once more to the Capitol, where the great Temple of Jupiter burned for the second time in just over a decade. By the time the emperor reached Rome, the fire had been brought under control, and for half a year, the Praetorians lent their hand to the removal of rubble and the rebuilding of a portion of the city.

I did not, thanks to my absence, witness the inevitable arguments between Titus and Domitian, as they opened the doors of the imperial treasury, to find them already echoing with space, and drained them further to help with the fresh disaster in Rome.

I was relieved of my role in Campania during the winter, alongside Commodus, and our replacements arrived just before Saturnalia. We effected a very neat handover of the role to them, for we had already put in place most of what needed to be done and now it was just a matter of making sure things continued at that pace and dealing with any unexpected problems that arose. I was back in Rome for Saturnalia and, had I not put in the appropriate appearance at the palace to announce my return, I might have turned right around and ridden off for somewhere quiet in the country.

Rome was a centre for all-new disasters, and I was sick of disasters now, having spent a year amid the ruins of Pompeii. The city still suffered from the aftereffects of the fire, with many families homeless and either living camped in alleyways or in the fields outside the city. Whole regions of Rome were still little more than charred graveyards, some not even having recovered from the fire of Nero before they were torched once more. But the gods were not done yet.

Even as the ash from the fire settled, so a new plague arose in Rome. In fact, as I soon learned from one of the court physicians, the plague was not restricted to Rome. It had struck in almost every corner of the empire by the middle of the following year, swiftly rolling across known lands from east to west. It brought whole towns low, a black pox that brought blood, pus and worse from its victims.

I spent time at the palace. Titus had need of every available helper that year. My duty was answering the endless requests for aid from the provinces. Governors begged for money, for extra grain rations, for resources to help. Military commanders begged for money and recruits, for martial strength was no defence against the plague, and the disease cut through the military faster than the civil populace, killing almost a tenth of Rome's soldiers in just half a year.

One night, as I sat with Domitian and two of the brighter freedmen, trying to work out how we could use what little we had available to support both Pannonia and Germania, two of the harder-hit spots, Titus staggered into the room. I rose in surprise as the door creaked closed behind him of its own accord. He was drunk. I had seen Titus have a little too much wine once or twice in his life, but I had never seen him so utterly plastered as he was that evening. He staggered over to a chair, a cup of wine in his hand, sloshing and dripping to the floor, and half-sat, half-fell into the seat, where he belched, brought up a little sick, wiped his mouth with his free hand, and then sagged.

'I am cursed.'

'What?' Domitian, his face disapproving, moved towards his brother.

'No, fuck. Stay back. Keep away from me. You'll get hurt. Everyone does. I'm cursed and I'm a curse.'

'What are you talking about?' Domitian replied, waving the other freedmen from the room.

'Father ruled for ten years and suffered nothing. Rome grew and healed and even though he taxed mercilessly, everything went well. I've sat on the throne for less than two years, and Rome is rotting and burning and falling apart around me, and I can do nothing to stop it. I've emptied the treasury trying to save people, and no matter what I do, the gods keep throwing me fresh horrors.'

'These things happen, Titus,' I said soothingly. 'Look at your predecessors. The fire of Nero. The...' I faltered to a stop. In actual fact, thinking back, I suddenly couldn't recall anything on the scale of what Titus was facing.

'I am fated to this. The gods hate me. I cursed Aesculapius, you know? When father was ill. I cursed a god for his lack of care, and this plague is his revenge. But I can't think what I did to Vulcan to bring on such explosions, though I keep wracking my brains over it.'

We let him ramble for a while, and before long he sank into a wine sleep, and with the help of a number of his slaves we had him stripped, cleaned up, re-dressed and deposited in his bed. But the idea that Titus was cursed somehow stayed with both Domitian and me. And it seemed hard to deny.

Later that summer, Titus faced his next threat. A potential usurper appeared in the east. A man by the name of Terentius Maximus. It was said that he was Nero. In fact, reliable witnesses from Asia confirmed that this man looked so like Nero, and sounded so like him, that he had beguiled a whole following into joining him. He was, it was said, Nero who had not died as we'd thought, but had fled Rome to avoid the terrible usurpers. The governor of Judea, Lucius Antonius Saturninus, dealt with the false Nero swiftly, bringing most of his followers to the sword, and it was only by chance that the rebel managed to escape his clutches, fleeing across the border and seeking safety among the Parthians. It was less of a grand disaster than the others Titus had suffered, but for a time, we worried about it. Despite still not having made Domitian co-emperor, Titus decided it had to be done soon. If usurpers were going to rise, everything needed to be secure. He would appoint Domitian officially at the new year when the consuls took office.

In summer that year, Titus oversaw perhaps the one highlight he could claim. The massive amphitheatre begun by his father, situated where Nero's ornamental lake had been drained, was finally completed, and he held games there for a hundred days, with gladiators and wild animals, including the largest boar anyone had ever seen, sent as a gift to the emperor from Agricola, now the governor of Britannia. The day after the final event, Titus came to us. He was looking drawn and pale, more so than ever. He had always been strong, lively and with a smile, but two years of the gods throwing ones in the dice game of empire had taken their toll. He was tired, dispirited and not well.

He had decided that he needed a break from all this trouble. He would take the court and travel north. We would go back to Reate, the ancestral home of the Flavii. There he would visit the baths that his father had so vaunted. He would vow a temple there to Aesculapius and attempt to appease the god. He would put everything right in Reate, rest and recover his body and soul, and we would return to Rome for Saturnalia renewed and ready to begin afresh. Then, with the new year, Domitian would be made co-Caesar and all would be well.

Somehow, I had a feeling that was not our destiny as we travelled north. I had a terrible feeling of foreboding, and I suspect Domitian felt it too, for he was pensive and quiet, more so than usual. That September, in the villa in Reate – gods, but even in the same *room* where we had said farewell to Vespasian – Titus lay wrapped in a fever that would not break. Like his father before him he had tried the spa of Aquae Cutiliae and trusted to the waters to heal him.

They failed.

Titus suffered his fever for three days, each progressively worse than the last, and on that final day no one present in that house believed he would live. Whether it was the gods who had taken revenge for his slights, or the strain of having dealt with so much in such a short reign, whatever the case, Titus simply had neither the strength nor the will to fight back.

He lay on that bed, white and waxy-sheened, shaking and sweating, and looked up as we attended him. He could not talk, for every time he opened his mouth, he went into a series of violent shakes and then folded in on himself for a time. Finally, he managed a few words.

'I have made but one mistake.'

We waited for elucidation, but we would never learn what that mistake was.

Titus died on the evening of the ides of September in his family home, in the same room as his father. He had ruled Rome for just twenty-five months, and doing so had killed him. Some will tell you that his illness was the result of Domitian poisoning him. Do not listen to them. The brothers had been close to the end, and I saw Domitian that day, and saw what the passing of his brother did to him.

Times were changing. Titus had gone, and before word reached Rome, the younger brother would have to run to claim unexpected imperium, for Domitian was now Rome's emperor.

XX

Currents and undercurrents

Rome, 18 September AD 81

One thing that Domitian always held to was a belief that the senate was an entirely antiquated and worthless institution, its only contribution of value and power being the right to ratify a candidate for the throne of Rome. Oh, some ruled Rome without being approved by the senate, notably a certain creature during the civil war, but that never ends well. To satisfy the bulk of the arrogant nobility, the senate has to approve of the emperor who will rule them. I found it highly ironic that, in essence, the senate have the right to choose the man who will control and use them.

This approval is especially important in cases when the succession is not absolutely certain. Most of the descendants of Caesar had little difficulty with the transfer of power, but that year of civil war had shown Rome what a succession crisis can do to the empire. That had been why Domitian had rushed Titus into racing for Rome upon their father's demise. The Flavii were, after all, a new dynasty, and nothing was certain. Similarly, then, when Titus died that night before the ides, despite family propriety Domitian left matters to his cousin Flavius and rode for Rome. I went with him, as did Cerialis and an escort of men, and we barely rested the horses on the way. This was no slow and grand procession, but a breakneck ride to confirm the succession.

In fact, those rumours that do the rounds linking Domitian with his brother's death probably have more to do with his speedy departure than anything else. It is faintly possible, even, that Titus was not quite dead when we left, though there was no doubt in anyone's mind that he was sliding swiftly towards it and it would be an hour or two at most.

We rode into the greatest city in the world on a drizzly grey day and made straight for the palace. It was critical that Domitian address the senate as soon as possible, but if he did it in tunic and boots, dusty and travel-worn, it would not go down well. The senate is a slave to propriety. We climbed to the Palatine and dismounted there, hurrying inside the palace. I say we, and mean Domitian and myself. Cerialis had veered off as we passed the forum to pass the word that an impromptu meeting of the senate was urgently required.

We used the palace baths as swiftly as I have ever done, and hurriedly dressed in clean tunics and togas. By the time we set foot on Caligula's stair and began our descent to the forum, both Domitian and I looked like the conscript fathers of old, republican statesmen. Nothing, of course, could be further from the truth.

If every senator attends a meeting, there are 600 voices in the curia. That no one ever expects a full meeting is clear by the lack of space in the building. If six hundred men met they would have to be stacked three deep. By the time we arrived there, runners had managed to gather a grand total of 103 senators, though a few others continued to drift in once the meeting had begun.

I looked around the place as Domitian and I stepped into the doorway, facing the seated aristocracy of Rome. Few were friendly. One of those seats was actually mine, and so once we entered the building, I wished Domitian good fortune and then crossed to take it. Petilius Cerialis should have had one of those seats, too, but he had his own task right now, for even as Domitian was here, ready to win over the senate, so Cerialis, once the call for the senate had gone out, next raced for the Castra Praetoria to secure the loyalty of the all-important Guard.

I sat and waited in the senate amid the expectant and worried murmur of the assembly. News of the passing of Titus could not realistically have beaten us to Rome, and yet many would suspect it. The young Caesar waited until he had relative calm, and then stepped into the centre of the floor.

'Conscript Fathers, masters of Rome, I greet you solemnly on this most unexpected and unfortunate day.'

That did it. The murmuring began afresh, and I heard Titus' name echoing among the seating. I could see Domitian controlling strained patience as he waited for silence once more. He had ever been an impetuous youth – man now, I suppose – and his temper could sometimes break through the shell of civility. Somehow he kept control, and finally the murmuring died away again.

'Conscript Fathers, the tidings will reach Rome this day that your emperor, my beloved brother, Titus, has ascended to take his place among the gods.'

Another surge of murmuring. I did what I could, calling out, 'Calm, people, let us hear the man.'

It had the desired effect, and Domitian looked at me with a tiny nod of thanks before continuing.

'Though it is hardly seemly for me to address this august body when I should be with my brother preparing him for his final journey, expediency drives me to abandon familial propriety and place myself before you. Though it has been a dozen years, I know that every face in this room looked upon the chaos and bloodshed of the civil war after the fall of Nero, and I do not believe that a single person here wishes to see a repeat of that terrible year. In an effort to ensure a smooth transition of power that will benefit Rome, and not plunge her into war, I stand before you as heir to my brother and ask that this body vote to add its support to my rightful claim to the throne.'

There it was. A claim. A demand, veiled as a request. The senate's voices rose into a susurration of conversation again and this time there was no choice but to wait for it to crescendo and then descend into calm once more. It did so with a single voice ringing out at the end. As the murmur died away, I recognised the tone of Claudius Pollio, echoing out around the hall in an almost challenging manner.

'And what of your cousin, Domitian? For there is no clear precedent here.'

I saw Domitian's eyes narrow, and wondered how close he was to snapping already. Miraculously, he smiled calmly and asked, 'Oh?'

Pollio folded his arms. 'There has always been a *reason* for the succession to be secured without argument. Your brother was raised to be co-emperor and heir by your father. It was clear to all the world that Titus was to succeed him. Yet the blessed and mourned Titus ruled the empire for two years and in that time he did not see fit to make you his co-emperor. I wonder... why is that?'

Domitian's hands bunched into fists in the shadows of his toga. Few will have seen it. I knew he was fighting for control of his temper.

'My brother had vouchsafed that role for me more than once, as numerous witnesses will testify. It was, indeed, my father's wish that he do so. You may be aware that during his two years on the throne, my poor brother had a rather troublesome time. Exploding mountains, burning cities and the like? My elevation was planned for the coming new year, but sadly the gods claimed him before this could happen. You have a reason to doubt my right to succession?'

Pollio looked unconvinced, and a small group of sour-looking faces, including the ever-troublesome Manius Acilius Glabrio, had gathered around him now, risen from their seats. 'There is, perhaps, a member of your family with a better claim,' he said.

He was inscribing his name on a list of targets; I could see that even if Pollio couldn't.

'Oh?' Domitian's monosyllabic reply came out as little more than a breath.

'Young Flavius Sabinus. He is grandson of the great Sabinus who all Rome adored, and husband of Titus' daughter. In some ways one might say he has two claims to the throne, but as the male heir of Titus through marriage, he might naturally expect to be offered the succession.'

I pictured the younger Flavius Sabinus, and I pictured how his father, my old army friend, might react to having been entirely ignored in this potential succession. The youngest scion of his branch of the family was a good and noble lad, but he lacked that vim one needs to rule an empire. He would make a good governor, but an emperor? There was no doubt in my mind that Domitian was far more suited to the role.

'If this is your stance, Pollio,' Domitian replied with a slight sneer in his tone, 'then you go *against* precedent, for did not Claudius have a natural son in Britannicus, just a few short months from official manhood, yet the senate threw their support behind Nero?'

Damning, I thought, and an excellent argument in response. Had he managed to keep the sneer from his voice, he might have won them over directly with that sentence alone. As it was, his manner simply got Pollio's hackles up.

'So we are to give our consent to a man not groomed for rule, who, unlike his brother, was not given a court education, who has no military record or indeed any record of useful service to the state, who was passed over for co-rule by his brother, while we ignore a son-in-law of the last emperor who also shares the family blood? I am not greatly convinced.'

A discontented murmur ran around the curia. Domitian's right hand was gripping now beside his hip, readying an imaginary blade. He was not going to maintain his composure for long.

'How do you know the mind of dead men, Pollio?' A new voice called from across the room. 'Are you a sorcerer now?'

The room fell silent and all eyes, mine included, turned to see the speaker. I vaguely recognised him from times around the court years earlier, but I couldn't quite place him or put a name to that swarthy, dark-haired and leathery fellow. It was only when he was named that the memory fell into place.

'Oh, you're here, Saturninus? Taking a breather from your Jewish catamites, are you?' laughed one of the men behind Pollio.

Of course... *Saturninus*. The man Vespasian had put in charge of vital Judea just before his death, who had squeezed the last

234

silver from the defeated Jews to fund the great Flavian building projects of Rome and had now returned to Rome a hero of the Flavii. The man who had chased down and neutralised the false Nero in the east for Titus. A man with, so far, a very good track record, but for something lurking in the back of my memory that I could not quite put my finger on.

'I would take a clean Jewish boy over your warty old cock any day,' Saturninus laughed, eliciting a roar of hilarity from the assembly and a snarl from Pollio.

'Friends,' Saturninus said, turning with his arms spread and addressing the room, 'this scion of the Flavian line speaks plainly. There are many who know that Titus intended Domitian to share his rule as heir, for he had no male child. Petilius Cerialis knew this, for I have spoken to him on that very subject. Cocceius Nerva over there,' he added, pointing at me, 'he too knows it, and so do I, for I spoke to Titus on the matter directly. And you all know that Titus had little time for such manoeuvrings since he spent his two short years trying to hold our empire together despite a multitude of disasters. Can any of us say with any real belief that Titus did not mean to pass his imperium on to his brother?'

'Domitian is unprepared,' Pollio insisted.

'So is Flavius Sabinus. Indeed, he is considerably *less* prepared. And your words concerning Domitian hardly hold water, esteemed colleague. He has no great military victory to his name yet, but neither had most of his predecessors before they took office, and they did not have to fight for their life on the Capitol against murderous usurpers to get there. And he has no experience of rule? Who do you think kept the worst of Mucianus' barbaric policies in check before Vespasian reached Rome? You do not seem to remember, as I do, how often and how eloquently this young man addressed the senate in that time. How he *was* the Flavian family in Rome for the better part of a year.'

That something which had been nagging at me as the man first spoke finally clicked into place as I thought back over the times I'd heard of him. Saturninus was a name I had known long before his time in Judea. I had come across it more than once in connection with Caecina. Saturninus had governed Hispania Baetica while Caecina had been procurator there, and the pair had been connected time and again since then. I struggled with this. Caecina had been dead set against Titus, far enough to plot his downfall, yet Saturninus had put down usurpers to *save* Titus. There was no real suggestion the pair had worked together, and yet I couldn't help remembering how we'd failed to draw any extra names out of the conspirators. There had to have been others in on it. Saturninus probably was not one of them... but he *had* been a close associate of Caecina.

By the time I was listening to the murmur of the senate again, the discussion seemed to have ended. Someone called for a vote on the succession, and the curia divided the way it does, allowing votes to be counted. Needless to say, I shuffled across to the pro-Domitianic side, where I managed to sidle between yawning old men until I reached Saturninus.

'Your return from Judea was timely,' I said.

He shrugged. 'My work there was done. I finished what Vespasian and Titus started, and now it's just an administrative role. I was brought home and someone more passive was sent to replace me. I can't say I'm sad. Judea is a very dry country, and every brick there is made of one part clay and two parts resentment.'

We stood silently as the count was made, but I was no longer worried. A single glance was enough to confirm that Domitian was going to be the accepted choice. Our party outnumbered the other considerably.

Thanking Saturninus for his intervention, I took my seat as the meeting reconvened. I listened to several eloquent antiques pouring honeyed words in favour of the new emperor. They praised his line, and the young emperor himself. The duty of confirmation fell to the consul present, Carminius Lusitanicus, who rose and gave a long-winded and rather dry speech in favour of Domitian, promising the senate's support and faith throughout his rule.

Domitian then delivered his response, and his genius with oratory was hammered home to me with every line. He managed to make every toga-clad denizen of the room feel valued and noble without actually complimenting anyone at all. He managed to make them feel that he accepted without question his traditional role of *princeps*, first man of the senate, while not once promising anything other than absolute rule. In short he told them one thing, and they heard another. He imposed his intent to rule like a king of old, but because of the terms he couched it in, they expected almost exactly the opposite. Few of us there were immune to his magic. Saturninus, I noted, seemed rather amused by it, and from the scowl on the faces of both Pollio and Glabrio, they had not missed the undercurrent in what their new emperor was saying. But nine senators in every ten gave Domitian a rousing cheer when he finished and stepped back.

The gathering disbanded a while later, and Domitian remained in place, shaking the hands of men he despised, a smile riveted to his face. I waited until the ranks had thinned and then moved towards him. He spent a short time in conversation with Saturninus, and the two laughed several times. As I moved in to congratulate him, Glabrio slipped in ahead of me.

I half expected Domitian to go for the man. It would not be the first time. Twice the senator had invaded the house of the Flavii, once to search for the missing Nero and once to place Domitian and his family under house arrest on the orders of Vitellius. The first time, Domitian had thrown a cup of wine at him, the second he had threatened to puncture his throat with a pen. Their relationship had never been anything but direct hostility. I noted that Glabrio might have been gathered with the opposition in the room today, and certainly voted in favour of young Flavius, but he had most uncharacteristically not opened his mouth to heap insults on Domitian, allowing Pollio that honour. Was the man changing, or was he simply riding the wave of Roman politics as usual? Now that the Flavii were in control he could try and heal the divide and secure his own position, as he had with both Galba and Vitellius.

'I expect you'll be wanting my head,' Glabrio said in a light tone as he leaned in to shake Domitian's hand, the exchange missed by most as the assembly broke out into loud murmuring again.

Domitian continued to shake the hand. He did not smile, and there was no lightness in his tone as he replied.

'I find you a loathsome man, Glabrio, as you know. You and I will never see eye to eye. But what I do now, and what this whole gaggle of flapping hens purports to do, is for the good of Rome. Your record of uncovering and charging false accusations as a praetor of Rome is unparalleled in the history of the office. I intend to have Rome run like one of the machines of Hero of Alexandria. I want a smooth and truly efficient administration. There are many freedmen who are best trained for the majority of the work, but there are still important roles in the city that are filled by senators, and as long as you remain one of Rome's outstanding praetors, I would not deny the city your talents.'

Glabrio inclined his head, his brow furrowed. He was not entirely sure how to take this.

Domitian reached in, grasping his shoulders and pulling him into an embrace. As he did, he spoke in a whisper that only I, standing behind them and waiting, heard.

'But the day you cross me again, you will have outlived your usefulness, and no man since Sisyphus will have suffered as you will. Do you understand me?'

In answer, wordlessly, Glabrio stepped back and bowed his head. 'May you reign long and wisely,' he said, then turned and marched away. I paused for a moment. I knew that Domitian was not a soft man by any means, and that he had a dangerous streak about him, but something about the way he looked after the departing Glabrio made me shudder. Even though I, too, hated him, I hoped for his sake that he stayed on the right side of his emperor. Domitian still retained spies in many houses, and I had absolutely no doubt that at least one pair of eyes and ears paid close attention to Glabrio within his domus. The day he even joked about Domitian, he would regret it.

In fact, it was that very day, with the weight of Titus' edicts no longer hanging over us, that I put my first spy in place, beginning an intelligence web of my own. By nightfall I had a slave in the palace, attending the various altars of the Lares. Domitian was my friend, but I had no doubt he watched me as he watched everyone. I would not be caught out. I would know of trouble coming my way before it raised its head.

'You spoke well,' I said, watching the last stragglers departing the room, leaving us with relative privacy.

'I had good teachers,' he replied with a smile. 'Speaking of which, your career seems to have faltered of late. Is there a posting you desire?'

The question of what yet awaited me arose from time to time in the quiet of a solitary evening. I could try matrimony, of course, but I was rather settled into the single life now. I had achieved the consulship, and might yet do again. All I really lacked was a triumph. I shrugged. 'You could give me a troublesome province and a powerful army so I can become your generation's Corbulo,' I said, with a wry smile.

That, at least, made Domitian laugh. 'I will see what I can do.'

I took a breath, returning to my subject. 'There are currents and undercurrents in the senate. No matter how well you got most of them on side today, the few bad apples among them will start to spoil the barrel. Others will join their ranks. Glabrio and Pollio are simply the most visible. I advise watching Saturninus, too. I doubt you have ears in his walls, since he has been abroad so much, but now might be the time to do so.'

'Oh? The very man who swayed them to my cause?'

I pursed my lips. 'While that is true, and I can see no reason for Saturninus to turn on you, he was formerly a close associate of Caecina. Bear that in mind.'

Domitian smiled. 'I will find uses for him. Saturninus is a wolf, not suited to quiet administration. He needs wars to keep him happy. I will give him wars and troublesome borders to occupy his talents. Indeed,' he added, sweeping out an arm at the now almost empty room, 'I will find somewhere safe to store each and every bad apple where they cannot rot the rest. As Caesar once rebuilt the senate with his own men, so shall I. I will have Rome in the palm of my hand by the time the new consuls are chosen. And may the gods help any man who gets in my way.'

XXI

Rome changed

Rome, autumn, AD 83

I watched with pride and great anticipation as Domitian went to work over the following year and a half. From the very outset, he knew precisely what he wanted to achieve: autonomy. He distrusted the senate as a whole and many individual members of it in particular. I was instrumental in the first month in helping draw up lists of the sitting senators, for while no appropriate governorship had yet arisen, Domitian had shared the censorship with me, granting me the power to shape the senate as I saw fit. Then, with the emperor, Flavius, Cerialis and a couple of the administrative freedmen who Domitian trusted implicitly, we categorised them.

The first column we shuffled people into were those whose loyalty was beyond doubt, such as myself and those drawing up the list. Those of us, less than forty in number out of the grand six hundred, were to be the core of Domitian's senate, shuffled into the primary positions. The second column were the sycophants and cowards, a surprisingly large number, who could be relied upon to obey out of either fear or greed. Their seats were secure, but they would be watched for the first sign of exhibiting a spine, at which point they would move to column three. *That* column held the untrustworthy, perhaps a quarter of the total number. They represented a constant threat of opposition, and thus they could not be relied upon. We worked tirelessly with each name, examining their history and talents. Armed with that information, we could find a posting for them which appeared to be a promotion, but in fact shuffled them far from the curia and any hope of voting in the senate, such as to a governorship of a province with no legions to control. After all, it would be foolish to place a potential enemy in charge of an army. Neatly each one was removed from real power to achieve specific goals. Column four was the interesting one. They were the names that were so clearly enemies that there was no doubt. They were allowed to remain in the senate, for it is always best to have real enemies where you can see them at all times. With the sweeping changes, they could not now call upon enough votes in the curia to make a difference, anyway. The whole process was incredibly efficient and effective and, best of all, no one argued, for they all thought they had been granted a boon, either by being kept around or by being promoted elsewhere.

As the first new year of his reign came about, Domitian's new tame senate voted the emperor as one of the consuls, and, at Domitian's insistence, his young cousin Flavius Sabinus as his colleague, neatly acknowledging the importance of the young man who might well have been emperor had things gone another way. In the palace he placed the renowned Epaphroditus in the position of his personal secretary, the role the man had played so well for Nero, and raised a very efficient freedman by the name of Maximus to be his personal chamberlain. The whole palace was reorganised, the most effective freedmen and equestrians shuffled into positions of authority, often positions formerly held by troublesome senators.

His reforms, pushed through within the first half year with the aid of his obedient senate, were greeted with relief by many. He reinstated the public feasts forbidden by Nero, limited the cultivation of lucrative vineyards in favour of grain for the people, and took a personal interest in the court system, expelling corrupt figures and correcting oversights ignored by his predecessors. In fact, within that first year, a man put through the courts in Rome could count on a fair and honest trial for the first time since the failing of the Republic a century earlier. Such was Domitian's desire for everything to be neat, organised, efficient and correct.

Less favoured were his moral adjustments. The banning of public theatre performances as promoting immorality was not over-popular, and led to him adjusting his ban to allow private performances to continue, where they could not unduly influence the general public. He made it illegal to lampoon someone, which was, of course, a favoured pastime of much of the populace. Perhaps shocking to some, he curbed the increasing immorality of the Vestals. Over the years, Caligula, Claudius and Nero had allowed the priestesses a surprising amount of licence, and their flaunting of ancient laws had become rather public. Domitian reinstated the old laws and the old punishments among them. It was with mixed reactions that the people of Rome that first winter watched lusty men being dragged from the house of the Vestal Virgins and then scourged to death in the forum by Praetorians, while the guilty 'virgins' were led to the Colline Gate to be buried alive.

While Rome was reorganised and brought into line with Domitian's strict moral code, his personal world expanded, albeit briefly. Domitia Longina had settled well into palace life, and gave birth to Domitian's heir in the winter. There was a great deal of rejoicing, and those of us who had seen the effects of an uncertain succession heaved a sigh of relief.

'What do we name him?' Domitian asked over a cup of wine that night as the mother dozed to recovery and the baby nestled in the arms of his nurse.

'You could do worse than naming him after your father,' was my suggestion.

He mused over this, the smile that had graced his face all day making it difficult to sip his drink. 'It has the benefit of recalling my brother also. Titus Flavius Caesar. I like it. I think Domitia will, too.'

That was the first of many evenings of discussion on what the world would hold for the young scion of the Flavii, and the year rolled around with a more positive feel to it than any of us could remember for some time.

We were premature, though, for in little more than a year the infant boy succumbed to an illness and passed away.

Those who did not know the emperor as well as I thought him cold for the way he dealt with the tragedy, organising the burial of the boy and his acknowledgement as living among the gods in deification. Coins were struck with the boy's name and image in memoriam. But the emperor himself went on with his work with little outward sign of grief. I knew better. I knew precisely how much it was hurting him, and his response was to bury that pain in work. Indeed, such was his pain that he sent Domitia away to a grand villa on an island to remove from his presence any reminder of the lost child, though he swiftly realised that her absence did more harm than good, and recalled her.

So Rome changed over those first eighteen months, ancient morals and laws reinstated, corruption halted, the throne secured and dissent reduced, all with an increasing imperial grip on power at the expense of the senate. I was as busy as I have ever been during that time, as one of Domitian's closest advisors. Those of us upon whom he relied had a lot of work to do.

Thus it was on one relatively balmy autumn morning that I was pacing along the corridors of the Palatine with a slave at my heel carrying a stack of reports I needed to go through with Domitian. The emperor had rearranged how the palace worked. He refused to use the remaining structures of Nero's Golden House, much of which had been buried beneath the buildings his father and brother had constructed, and he had begun the process of turning the family home in Pomegranate Street into a temple to the Flavian genius. So the available palace was limited to the old complex of Tiberius and Caligula. With the enormous administration Domitian had created, there simply was not room, and so now Tiberius' great audience chamber was filled with rows of desks at which freedmen worked feverishly. Domitian had taken to using a smaller, more private chamber for most of his meetings, and had laid the plans for a new palace that would occupy the wider breadth of the Palatine and would allow far more space for his enormous administration.

I hurried along a corridor at the end of the palace close to the temple district, and rounded the corner to approach the emperor's chamber, nodding my thanks to two Praetorians who stepped aside to allow me easy access. I stumbled to a halt at the corner at the sight of the man coming the other way.

I have always been weirdly fascinated by the Galli, the priests of Cybele from the Temple of the Magna Mater. They are a weird lot to say the least, and their leader, the archigallus, the weirdest of the lot. Eunuchs all, they dressed as women, though gaudy and over-done. The current archigallus had taken his appearance seriously. The man storming towards me like an angry bull wore flouncy yellow silks and golden sandals, his elaborate crown resting on flowing, wild white-gold hair above a face painted with so much makeup that if he smiled it would surely split his face in half. His right hand was weighed down with an intricate bracelet of authority as his arms circled wildly, and he positively reeked of rose water and incense.

The sight of a man like that in a fit of anger is peculiar and incongruous. I stood in the middle of the corridor, effectively blocking his path, not by design but in stunned fascination. The way he moved was like one of those exotic eastern dancers Nero used to value at his parties, and he swayed to a halt in front of me, face oddly contorted, rage vying with the cherry lips and kohl-rimmed eyes for control of some sort of expression.

'You are in my way,' he snapped in his curiously squeaky voice.

'I am sorry,' I replied politely. 'Is something wrong?'

'Wrong?' he shrieked. I caught sight over his shoulder of two more Praetorians down the corridor grinning like idiots and stifling giggles.

'You seem upset.'

'This emperor is a prude and a prig,' the man snapped, apparently heedless of the fact that Domitian was probably still within earshot of shouted conversation.

'The emperor feels that Rome has slid into a pit of immorality,' I replied calmly. 'I am sure he does not intent to curb excesses within the temples, however,' I added carefully. I wasn't quite so sure. From the rumours I had heard, the excesses within the Temple of Cybele would have made Nero shudder.

'The emperor is to institute a law against castration,' the archigallus snapped.

I blinked. I knew precisely what Domitian thought of eunuchs. Those years of his youth when he had been in my care we had spent much time among them in Nero's palace. Personally, I had always found the imperial eunuchs harmless and generally rather entertaining, but they very much did not fit with Domitian's image of Rome. His view of the perfect empire owed much to our staid agricultural forbears, and more recent sexual excesses were anathema to him.

'Surely there will be a way this can be dealt with,' I tried.

'Oh?' he squawked at me. 'The law is a blanket prohibition. It is a slight on the temple and an insult to the goddess. How am I to staff my temple with such a law? And the other temples across the empire? It is abhorrent.' His voice rose a clear octave. 'It is *wicked*. It is… it is *cruel*,' he shrieked in conclusion, and with that he barged past me in a cloud of heady perfume and a mist of flaking makeup.

I stood there for a moment, still a little stunned, as the Praetorians ahead gave up trying to stifle their laughter. It was a thorny one. Domitian was going to have to make some provision outside his new law to cater for the priesthood, for the ritual castration of their priests was one of the central tenets of the Magna Mater's cult. Palace catamites were one thing, but pissing off goddesses could be dangerous.

Taking a breath, I marched on down the corridor, my slave coughing in the perfume cloud as he struggled with my pile of records. As I approached, the two Praetorians gained control of themselves and nodded respectfully. 'You are expected, senator,' one said, gesturing to the door.

I knocked and at Domitian's summons, pushed it open and stepped inside.

The office was filled with documents and writing paraphernalia, with a table at the centre surrounded by chairs, one slightly higher and more ornate than the others. No man, no matter how important, could attend upon Domitian without being reminded that the emperor was more important still. The emperor himself, dressed in a simple tunic, was poring over a map. My eyes slid to the other occupant of the room and I tried not to be irritated or disappointed. I had no real reason to dislike Saturninus, and indeed he was perfectly pleasant to me and seemed to be highly supportive of Domitian, but there had always been something about him that made me jumpy. I presumed that, since I was expected, their meeting was finished and Saturninus would be dismissed, but my irritation increased a little when I realised he was making no effort to rise. Domitian looked up at me, caught sight of the slave behind me and frowned. 'Court cases?'

I nodded. 'Several discrepancies that might want attending to. I wanted to go through them with you before I made any other move, for some of the culprits are senior senators.'

Domitian brushed it aside with a wave of his hand. 'I will look at them later.' He gestured to the slave. 'Put them on the table over there and get out.'

As the slave did as much, I tried not to be offended by this almost offhand dismissal, bowing my head and making to leave. As I did, Domitian waved at me. 'Him, not you, Marcus. Sit.'

The slave exited, the Praetorians closing the door behind him, and I crossed to the table and took a seat. The map, I now noted, was one of Gaul, Germania and southern Britannia. It was covered with small wooden blocks, some of which were painted with gold coins and some with red flags or black ones.

'Lucius,' I said in greeting to Saturninus. He replied in kind and then sipped his wine as Domitian looked up at me again. 'You seem urgent. Distracted.'

'I encountered an angry archigallus in the corridor.'

'Ah yes, The archi-*freak*. It is long past time that his sort were dealt with.'

I coughed meaningfully. That was a little too sharp for my liking. Moral rectitude was one thing, but one could impose *too* much morality for the good of society. Rome had become used to certain freedoms. 'Your law is... it will be greeted with mixed feelings. I can understand perhaps cutting out the insanities of Nero's palace, but there are some sectors where it will cause a great deal of trouble. The galli...'

'Are a collection of drug-addled hedonistic fools masquerading as priests,' Domitian answered in a flat tone. 'The Magna Mater is an ancient goddess of the corrupt east, a Phrygian import. Her worship does not conform to the expected moral of the Roman character. Why promote such immorality in favour of a foreign god when we have our own gods whose priesthood is an honour for those taken in. Minerva is an Olympian. She is the soul and heart of Rome, more so than Vesta these days, since *her* priestesses have been permitted to fornicate wildly. No. We will have a return to the morality of the Rome of old, Nerva. I am determined.'

I could see trouble in the future of that, but I let it pass for now. 'What is this?' I asked, gesturing to the map.

'I have received reports of trouble brewing among the tribes of the Germanies,' Domitian said, drawing a fingertip along the line of the Rhenus River.

'Oh?' I replied. 'I've heard nothing to that effect.'

'It is not public rumour, Marcus, but the reports of very subtle men I have in position.'

I nodded. I had been partially responsible for that. Any province where the governor had control of a legion now had half a dozen imperial spies at work, for too many provincial governors had had ideas above their station during the civil war. 'Spies.'

'Quite. The tribes are yet to move, but the reports are heavily suggestive that a major crossing of the Rhenus is coming. It seems that the past decade since the war there has done little to improve matters. Food is scarce in the forests of Germania, and the rich agricultural lands of Gallia Belgica lie tantalisingly close across the river. I am rather surprised they have not done something about that earlier. However, I do not intend to allow them the opportunity to ravage our lands. Oh, we would chastise them and have our revenge, but the damage would have been done by then. I intend to strike first before they can invade. Saturninus and I have been planning our moves. I want you involved.'

I nodded my head. 'A pre-emptive strike might be seen as an unwarranted invasion, of course.'

Domitian shrugged. 'I care little about such matters when it is placed against the threat of major destructive raids into the empire's territory.'

I had to give him that. 'So, what has been decided?'

'In fact, most of it,' Saturninus put in. 'Apologies, but we started early.'

'I have messages ready to send,' Domitian said, 'gathering imperial forces in Gaul in a quiet and calm manner. I do not want this to look like what it truly is, lest the tribes realise what is coming. I am having cohorts drawn from every available legion.' He tapped at Britannia. 'Agricola busily conquers the island for me, but his campaign is costly in men. He has four legions for just half a resisting island full of hills and naked tribesmen. I am pulling a number of his cohorts back across the water, including a sizeable portion of the Ninth Hispana.'

I tried to imagine what Agricola, busily marching his legions into wild Caledonia, was going to say when he learned the emperor was pulling a quarter of his manpower away. Still, if it prevented a tribal incursion into Gaul, it was worth it. His finger tapped at other places near the river. 'Auxiliary units and cohorts from each of the legions of upper and lower Germania and of Raetia will be pulled in. Together they will form a sizeable army. I have also given the order that a new legion be raised in Gaul, trained as fast as possible and added to the army. In honour of the greatest of our goddesses, they will be the First Minervia.'

I nodded. It all sounded reasonably well thought out. 'All that will take time, of course,' I said. 'With the gathering force and the training of a new legion, the army will not be able to move until perhaps next summer.'

Domitian leaned back. 'That is our only concern: that we will not be ready before the tribes decide to move. But at this point we can only roll the dice and hope, trusting to the gods that we have done enough. And this is where you come in, Marcus.'

'Domine?'

'I shall lead the army in its entirety, of course.'

I nodded. He had no experience in the field, but he was bright and he was brave, and his study of the tacticians of Rome was unparalleled. Many a general had been commissioned for wars with less skill and knowledge.

'Saturninus here will lead the amalgam of legionary cohorts, using a number of experienced officers as his aides.' Again, I approved. I might not particularly like the man, but he was, as Domitian had once noted, a wolf. His natural place was commanding an army on a battlefield. He was the perfect choice.

'And me?'

'I want you to command the First Minervia. I need someone I can trust and with a good mind not only leading them on campaign but overseeing their founding and training.'

I straightened. I had to fight the urge to smile. It was rather an honour to be granted such a leading role. For most of my career the emperors had focused on my administrative ability and kept me in civil posts. 'Thank you,' I said, simply.

'You wanted a command in a war-torn province, I seem to remember. Do you have any thoughts?' the emperor added. 'Not on the details of the campaign. We shall discuss that in due course, but on the preparations and the makeup of the force.'

I chewed my lip, recalling mention of the Ninth Hispana, and that brought their most memorable commander to mind. No one had mentioned the horse. 'Who will lead the cavalry?' I asked.

Saturninus and Domitian looked at one another with frowns. The emperor shrugged. 'They will be largely small legionary cavalry contingents under their own officers or auxilia from along the Rhenus under their prefects.'

'Give them to Cerialis,' I advised.

'Cerialis is dangerous,' Saturninus replied. 'He is erratic. He is either brilliant or foolish, and one can only flip a coin to guess how it will turn out.'

'He is brilliant, but rash,' I corrected. 'With the emperor and the rest of us around, we can perhaps prevent him from doing anything foolish, but when we actually engage Germans, there is no man better commanding from the saddle, and he is absolutely loyal to the emperor.'

Domitian nodded. 'You are quite right, Marcus. I will send for him and give him the news. Saturninus, Cerialis and I will visit Gaul once the new year is past to finalise matters. I will promote our visit as some sort of fiscal matter, keeping its true nature from unwanted ears. It will be only natural for me to bring a cohort of Praetorians with me, who can join the army in due course. And then, early next year, when we are all in Gaul, we can plan the campaign in detail. For now, Marcus, I will deal with your court corruption cases. You need to put your affairs in order in the city and take ship for Gaul. Make for Samarobriva and there you will seek out Trajan, who I am assigning as praepositus with the remit of raising the legion, and who will be your second. He has experience of the Germanic provinces and a good military record. Have my new legion ready by the spring, Marcus, and we will carve our names in the leathery hide of Germania.'

The rest of the afternoon we hammered out the details of the gathering force. Once I left the office, I realised that I was departing Rome for perhaps a third of a year and leaving Domitian without my influence. The last time I had done that, Caecina had worked his poison. As I left and glanced back to see him and Saturninus so close, I prayed that the former governor would not be a bad influence in my absence.

–

It took me three days to arrange everything, and then to set out on my travels. I took with me the six lictors due my rank, as well as a small army of private guards, servants and slaves. We made for Ostia and there boarded a ship for Massilia. It took the better part of a month to reach Samarobriva in the north of Gaul, seven days to the coast and then twenty across land to our destination.

I arrived, tired, to learn that this Trajan was out of the town currently and would be back before nightfall. Whoever he was, he was clearly efficient, anyway. A new temporary camp fit for a legion had been constructed outside the town, and the whole place seemed a cross between a supply dump and a recruiting office, bustling with small units of men and carts of equipment. I settled into a building in the town, directed there by a centurion, and my staff organised everything for me while I visited the baths and recovered from the journey. By the time I felt human again and was prepared for a meal, a runner found me to tell me that Trajan had returned and was expecting me in the basilica.

I suppose I could have been offended at what sounded a lot like a summons from the man who was going to be my second in command, but I was tired, and this man clearly knew his business. Trying to ignore my growling stomach, I gathered a small entourage and rode through the centre of Samarobriva to the basilica, reminded once more of my increased age as the jolting shook my aching bones. Upon dismounting, with relief I might add, I was directed to an office guarded by two veteran soldiers.

Marcus Ulpius Traianus, or Trajan as you may know him, was a tall man with a wide face and a flat nose. His hair was cut in a current military fashion, short and straight and no-nonsense. His manner was similar, and he was dressed in an officer's uniform. He rose as I entered.

'Marcus Cocceius Nerva, well met. I hear only good things,' he said with what appeared to be a genuine smile. I liked him instantly.

'Trajan? You have been hard at work.'

He laughed. 'You have no idea. But you soon will. If this is to be your command, I will have to fill you in on everything so far. The first thing is keeping a lid on rumour. It is almost impossible to raise, equip and train a legion in secret, yet that is what the emperor asks. I am doing my best, but it's hard. We need to stop stories of what's happening here reaching the Rhenus.'

'You know of the anticipated Germanic action, then?'

He gave me a wry smile. 'I damn well ought. In the next office my adjutant is dealing with Chariomerus. Have you heard of him?' I shook my head, and Trajan leaned back in his chair, hands behind his head, fingers interlocked. 'He is a chieftain of the Cherusci, who's been kicked from his throne by the Chatti. The Chatti are the meanest bunch of bastards you could ever meet. Chariomerus is one of our sources on the troubles. I'll introduce you at dinner tonight. Did you bring armour and the like?'

I shook my head. The last time I had owned armour was ten years ago, when Domitian and I had ridden with Mucianus to deal with Civilis, only to stop in Gaul and turn round without ever having to wear it.

Trajan laughed. 'Then before we eat, we'd best visit the quartermaster and my armourer. Can't have you addressing your new legion in a toga, can we? They might think you're a *civilian*.'

I laughed. I liked Trajan, and it was clear we would work well together. I took a deep breath and steadied myself for a winter of preparations, for when spring came Domitian would be here, and the war would begin.

XXII

Run them down

Germania Superior, summer, AD 84

Some will tell you that Domitian's war against the Chatti was unnecessary. Some will tell you that it was simple vainglory. Some will say that it was to satisfy Domitian's desire for the war he'd failed to wage alongside Mucianus fifteen years earlier. I will tell you now that the war was both necessary and fought for the good of Rome. And for revenge.

The Chatti, as I learned that year spent with Trajan and the First Minervia, are no bunch of German barbarians. Rome has always had a tendency to see the Germanic tribes as mindless savages, and some of them do fit that mould, for sure, but others are a different proposition entirely. Such are the Chatti, as we quickly learned. I should have taken my cue from the fact that this was far from the first time they had posed a threat. They had overrun the fortress of Mogontiacum twice in the past three decades or so, and in some ways we are entirely responsible for creating the problem.

Rome had tried to civilise the Chatti, and our efforts had had plenty of effects, if not the desired ones. What we had tried to do was teach them to want to be part of the empire. What we actually did was teach them to learn from us. And they did. Far too well.

The First Minervia was joined at Argentorate by cohorts sent from Britannia, and moved in the new year, at a dispatch from the emperor, to a large camp at Mirabellum. There we were joined by more cohorts drawn from other legions, as well as a number of auxiliary units. By the time we moved in spring, we had a force of more than twenty thousand legionaries and as many auxiliaries. It was quite some force, and the largest I have ever seen mobilised. The logistics for it all were a nightmare, and I was extremely grateful for the competent presence of Trajan, who seemed able to handle that side of things admirably. As yet, we were far enough from the Rhenus and the Germanic peoples to be confident that word of our work would not reach them, though that would soon change.

In May, Domitian finally joined us, along with Cerialis and Saturninus and a cohort of Praetorians. He had been meandering around Gaul with the court for months now, ostensibly dealing with tax matters, but in fact gathering strength and equipment and planning the offensive as far as we could. From the moment he arrived at Mirabellum, we were on a war footing. He tarried just three days before the entire army moved, and from there we marched north-east towards the enemy.

By the end of May we reached Mogontiacum, which was to be the initial base of operations. A massive fortress there was occupied by the Twenty-first Rapax, who were added to our number. A sizeable town with its own theatre and baths stood nearby, and an impressive bridge marched off across the great Rhenus River to a small bridgehead fortress on the far shore.

From Mogontiacum, any further obfuscation of our plans was unnecessary. The moment we crossed that bridge with the army and marched past the bridgehead, our intent was clear. For a time, spirits were high, and I even began to wonder whether those reports had been wrong, and that there was no real danger from the Chatti. With everything in place, we moved thirty miles into the wilted croplands and scattered woods of Germania in the first two days and then paused, building a series of large camps in the area while Cerialis' scout units covered dozens of miles in every direction. The tidings they came back with were sobering.

The reason everything had been so quiet and peaceful was that the Chatti had left their villages. Their people had gone. Farms had been left untended, the crops being poor this season once more. But what the scouts had found in their place was startling. Armies had been at work here. Not barbarian warbands as we had expected, but proper armies. The Chatti who had been at work in the area had built camps like ours. They had been settled in regiments. There were signs of training grounds. As I said, we had taught the Chatti to learn, and they had learned from the forces watching over them.

From those camps we moved on, slower now, alert.

The first clash came some twenty miles further into Chatti territory. Had we not believed the reports that the tribe were preparing for an invasion of our territory, that march would have changed our minds. Everywhere we saw evidence of units gathering and training, of guarded supply dumps, or manoeuvres. One morning we had been moving for perhaps an hour when the scouts raced back towards us, shouting. We had been moving steadily north-east, deeper into Chatti territory, following a small river along a wide valley between low, wooded hills. We were passing a series of small lakes at the time, which forced us to narrow our column, which was likely the enemy's design. To their credit, the commanders of the army were all veterans and good at what they did, and the moment the scouts came into view, everyone was moving. Saturninus, the longest-serving general among us, held the overall command, and word came down from him as to how to deploy. The First Minervia took the left flank, while the Twenty-first took the right, for the Germans have a history of hitting Roman marching columns in the flanks. The front lines at the centre were formed of the Praetorians and the cohorts from the Ninth Hispana, while Cerialis kept his cavalry back, at the end of the wings, ready to move in against anything as required.

When the Chatti came, we understood finally how much they had learned from us, and what all those training grounds had been for. They were organised like a legion, or perhaps a phalanx would be a better analogy. They still wore their traditional armour, and bore all manner of colours and designs in their shields, but they were moving at the commands of officers, and in perfect precision, with a hedge of long spears.

They came from valleys to both sides, penning us in between the hills and the lakes, and hit us from both sides and in front simultaneously. Essentially, a legionary legate has little to do with battle once he has given the orders to deploy, unless something goes horribly wrong. From there it is the centurions who do all the real work, and I sat astride my horse beside Trajan, only occasionally shouting advice, often at the nudging of my second, who was truly born to command.

Much of that initial engagement's success is owed to the military skill of Saturninus. The Chatti hit us hard, and here and there they occasionally made inroads to our blocks of men, shattering the shell of a shield wall and butchering with impunity within. But each time it happened, reserves were instantly in place and moving to secure the lines. The fighting went on for two hours solid, and at one point I honestly thought we were losing, for a group of Chatti managed to break into the First and were carving a path towards me. I pulled in the cohorts from the flank and reinforced the section in danger, while Trajan moved into the mass, sword out and waving, bellowing encouragement to the men. Soon we had the lines back in order.

It went back and forth until almost noon, and then finally things changed. Cerialis had become impatient with inactivity, and deployed the majority of his horse, who were now carving holes in the Chatti's rear. At last, their commanders decided that they stood no chance of breaking us, and that this fight was over. Undoubtedly they believed they could withdraw and then hit us again somewhere else with a new plan. Their leaders sacrificed a small number of men to save the majority. Lines of Chatti held us in the fight, while the bulk of their force pulled back and ran for the hills to each side of the valley, melting into the trees.

It was no Alesia or Phillipi, no battle to make the history books, but for those of us who were there, it was a brutal, hard conflict, and thankfully a success, due largely to the talents of two men. The losses had probably been roughly even between us, and no real victory could be declared as they held us while their men ran, until the emperor became involved. Seeing what was happening, I turned my horse and rode for the imperial standards, where the senior officers were converging.

'...and they will hit us again,' Saturninus was saying, 'harder than this, and more challenging, for they know the terrain and we do not, and now they have the measure of us.'

'But how do we stop them?' Vibius Crispus, legate of the Twenty-first, said in exasperation. 'They're getting away, and can regroup. Their sacrifices are protecting their flight.'

I nodded. We couldn't catch them in time. They would leave, regroup, prepare, and try something nastier.

'No,' Domitian said, looking around with a grim expression.

'Domine?'

'No. This will not have been fought for nothing. We had the better of them here, despite their plans and surprise attacks, and we will not let them do this again.'

'Domine, how can we stop them?'

Domitian bit his lip, then pointed at us. 'Legates and tribunes, overcome these units they have left to keep us busy. Flank them and keep *them* busy instead.' His pointed finger moved to Cerialis. 'Quintus, take every man you have and pursue their force. Only the cavalry can catch them in time.'

'We cannot ride in woodland,' he replied.

'They will be disordered now in flight. No matter how controlled they were in battle formations, they cannot be so running in woodland. Now we have the advantage. Chase them and dismount at the trees. Your men's legs will be fresh, theirs tired. Run them down in the woods and smash them, Cerialis. Ruin their spirit.'

Cerialis answered with a grin that I knew. There was little the man liked more than being given the freedom to try reckless manoeuvres. In heartbeats we were racing back to our men.

While we tried to enfold the remaining Chatti to stop them interfering with the horse, Cerialis gathered his men and sent half the cavalry towards each of the bordering wooded slopes.

I never witnessed what happened there, for we were busy carving a bloody mess out of the infantry in the valley, but by the time we had completely overcome them and the battle was over, all we could hear of Cerialis and his men was whooping in the distant forests and the faint echoes of panicked screams.

Cerialis returned with his riders only an hour before nightfall. They had suffered losses. Certainly more than one man in around eight had been lost in the woodlands. Some commanders might have upbraided him for that, but this had been the emperor's reckless plan, not his. Cerialis himself was coated with bloodspatter and gore when he returned, his grin a shock of white teeth amid the crimson. However, what he had done to the Chatti destroyed their will to wage such wars. It seemed that Cerialis and his riders had liberally cut a bloody swathe through the forests of Germania, leaving them strewn with Chatti corpses.

We encamped close to the battleground for the tending of wounded and the burial of the dead, and took a day to recover before moving on. We did not want to give the Chatti the chance to recover, since they had been so brutalised and disordered by the joint work of Cerialis and Domitian. Indeed, the emperor now very much had the bit between his teeth.

For much of the next month we moved through the region, causing havoc wherever we went. Cerialis' work had been so good that the Chatti never again attempted to hit us in a major clash. We moved en masse, sweeping up whole Chatti communities and battering their warriors wherever we found them, but their response now was to hit us in small, unexpected strikes. They resorted to charging from woodland and jabbing at us like needles, taking a few men here, a few men there, sometimes laying unpleasant traps for us, and even poisoning water sources we should have been able to rely upon.

The emperor's answer to this was to obliterate the Chatti. Where their warriors took Roman lives, we would then move against one of their communities, for we were now campaigning deep in Chatti lands. When we found a village, no one escaped. Those who struggled died. Those who did not were sold to the slavers who followed us in droves. In a month we must have flooded the markets of Rome with Germanic stock, yet none of what we did seemed to take the fighting spirit out of the Chatti. They would no longer meet us in battle, but gods they were brutal in their hit-and-run campaign.

It gradually turned nasty, too, if a war could be considered anything else to begin with. We kept finding that men had gone missing during the night, and then stumbling across them the next day, skinned, beheaded, and dangling from tree limbs. In response, Domitian gave the order that all standard constraints for humane war be abandoned. Soldiers began to work like monsters, burning farm huts with the family inside, raping those who were not worth imprisoning, slaughtering and torturing. Both sides committed atrocity after atrocity over the space of the next month, deep in the forests of the Chatti.

But they were getting desperate. The simple fact was that they had begun this whole thing because they were starving. By now they had expected to be weighed down with goods from within the empire. Instead, they were still starving, and now being hunted in their own lands. The commander of the Twenty-first began to espouse the possibility of seeking terms. He was of the opinion that we had broken the Chatti and that they would now seek a solution. We could settle the matter.

Domitian refused.

'In Nero's time they came, and then in my father's. This time we stopped them before they could come, but they will *not* come again. I will finish this such that generations to come will fear to cross the Rhenus.'

'How?' Saturninus mused. 'We are doing everything we can, but they will not meet us in battle now. They can play this game of needling forever.'

Domitian shook his head. 'These Chatti are not like the other tribes. They have armies and officers. They build forts and plan campaigns. They have all the marks of a civilised people, their bloodlust notwithstanding.'

'So?' I asked. 'What help is that? Surely it just makes them a more dangerous opponent.'

'Ah,' the emperor replied, 'but a civilised people have a leader, and a centre. Even if the leader is a body of men, they will rule from one place, and that place will be their heart. We find the heart of the Chatti and we stop it beating. That, gentlemen, is how we win this war.'

It was, of course, Cerialis who found our answer. His mounted scouts eventually managed to capture someone who could be made to talk, and they spilled the location of the Chatti's capital, some thirty miles further north of where we were.

Sadly, he was not to see the end of that campaign.

On the morning of the ides of August, Cerialis led out a turma of thirty riders as the legions broke camp. The scouts were already out and about, searching and putting together their reports. Cerialis simply intended to check the next couple of miles of the direct route of march, for we knew there was a small river coming, and it might need bridging to cross. We were in a flat land with scattered low hills, largely forested. As Cerialis rode forth with his men along the wide gap between woodlands, I happened to be sitting on horseback on a small hillock with both Saturninus and Domitian, Praetorians protectively around us at the base of the slope. Consequently we had the best view to be found in the whole valley.

We saw Cerialis and his riders, almost half a mile from camp. We saw them moving without a care, close to the army, simply checking the ground. Later, Domitian noted that the man should have waited for the scouts to all report in before heading forth, but that would not have been the Cerialis we all knew. He was ever headstrong and rash.

We had little time to react as the Chatti emerged in a huge rush from the woods in the narrowest clear area. They outnumbered Cerialis and his cavalry ten to one. The horsemen fought like heroes, but there are some days when the odds are all that count. Our horse took many of them, but that day the Chatti scored a major strike against us. I watched Cerialis fall, albeit distant and hard to make out, and I saw a small group of men crowding around the fallen general and knew what was coming.

Beside me, Domitian was wild-eyed, as angry as I have ever seen him, bellowing orders for the legions to deal with this. Already soldiers were racing forward, as well as more cavalry.

But they would be too late. I saw one of those Chatti warriors coming up with a large orb in his hand, and knew it to be Cerialis' head. By the time our reinforcements reached the scene, half a mile away, the Chatti were gone, melted into the trees. Cerialis' head was never found. We were in the very heartland of the tribe now, close to their capital, and they were becoming either fearless or desperate. Or both, of course.

Domitian took the death hard.

We did not move on that day. The legions camped again, in a very alert state. The scouts, the ones who had not fallen to Chatti that morning, made sure there was no one else anywhere near us. Domitian retired to his tent and refused to see any of the commanders.

I waited until nightfall, then went to see him. I talked the Praetorians into admitting me, despite their orders to keep everyone out, and I ignored the emperor's demands to be left alone as I entered.

'You cannot weather this alone,' I said.

Domitian looked up at me. He was pale. He was also drunk, which did not happen often. He was brandishing a bronze stilus with a needle point, and a dozen torn and screwed up papers lay in front of him.

'This place is filled with flies,' he said.

I was thrown by the non-sequitur until I crossed the room to see that a small black fly shape sat impaled on the stilus. If you have ever tried to catch a fly, you will appreciate how impressive such a strike must have been. All the more, since there were a dozen dead flies on the desk in front of him, each impaled at some point during the day. Sometimes I forgot that he had spent much of his youth practising with a bow, and he had been quite a marksman.

'You're busy then?'

I hoped to raise a laugh. I failed.

'I am trying to work out how to tell young Domitilla.'

I winced. Cerialis and Domitian's sister had a daughter, who should have been married by now, but who had lived with her father and doted on him since her mother died in childbirth. She would be broken with the news. That, of course, was what was truly bothering him most about this. The effect on his niece. I tried not to feel guilty that it had been my recommendation that had brought Cerialis with us in the first place.

'She will bear this with fortitude, like...'

'Like who? My mother, watching as Father dallied with that whore? My brother, who mourned the loss of his Jewish girl so much he could not take a Roman wife? Like Flavius, who stood with you and I on the Capitol and watched his father hacked to pieces by Vitellius' men? No, Marcus, Domitilla will not bear this. It will kill her, I think. But how can I place this task in the hands of another?'

'I have known her all her life,' I said. 'Would you like to pass the burden to me?'

He shivered. 'No. Thank you, but no. This is my task. An emperor must shoulder every burden if he is to accept every acclaim. I will write again, once I have slept. But briefly, and early, for with the rising sun, we are leaving.'

I straightened. 'Not abandoning the war, surely?'

His eyes turned flinty. 'No. *Finishing* it. They killed my brother-in-law before my very eyes, Marcus. For this their capital will burn, and there will be a surge of blood the likes of which the Germanies have never seen.'

I bowed my head. 'I will pass the word to the commanders.'

Domitian waved me out. I knew now that he would be all right. His anger and grief would pass, for he would bury them under Chatti bodies and drown them in Chatti blood. I left the tent, thanking the two Praetorians, and found the commander of the Twenty-first, Vibius Crispus, watching the tent.

'I was thinking of trying to speak to the emperor. Anyone with him?'

I smiled. 'Not even a fly.'

He gave me a bemused look, and I rolled my shoulders. 'He will take this out on the Chatti. There will be no mercy now. We move at first light.'

Crispus nodded, thanked me and hurried off about his business.

We moved at dawn, blades out.

Four days later we reached the capital of the Chatti. Not since the destruction of Carthage has such devastation been visited upon a people or a place. What we did under the emperor's orders that day was nothing short of abhorrent. Cerialis was most certainly avenged. By the time the sun set, Chatti chieftains and kings knelt before Domitian, begging for terms. He was merciful. He let one of them keep his head to tell everyone he met what had happened to the rest.

The war was over. The Chatti would not cross the Rhenus again, and of that we were all sure. Domitian raised temples to Minerva along the Rhenus frontier in gratitude.

The triumph that followed in Rome was a grand affair, but only those who truly knew Domitian could see how the smile he wore never reached his eyes. He adopted the title Germanicus, and of all the acclamations he received in his reign, it was Germanicus that he kept to the bitter end in memory of Cerialis.

XXIII

Punishment

Rome, summer, AD 87

The aftermath of the German war was as one might expect. The people cheered endlessly, and loved their victorious emperor. The triumph was a grand affair and a celebratory triumphal arch was begun in the forum, part of Domitian's grand plan to beautify Rome with many new and magnificent public buildings. The army was content, for they had proved their mettle against one of Rome's most brutal ancient foes, and the emperor had, of course, sweetened the pay pot somewhat for their efforts. Those involved at the highest level were similarly rewarded. I was awarded triumphal honours, with a column and statue in the forum, close to the one Nero had raised for my aid in unravelling the Piso conspiracy. It was rare indeed to grace two plinths in the forum, and so I was rather exalted. Trajan was vouchsafed an important province in due course, but in the meantime was given a series of commands, first on the freshly settled German border, and then with the Seventh in Hispania, an easy and pleasant position. Saturninus, as the emperor's armoured gauntlet in the campaign, was most exalted of all, being made consul following the campaign and then, a few years later, moved to the governorship of Germania Superior. The only voices of dissatisfaction, as usual, were the few members of the senatorial aristocracy who hated Domitian. To them, who had no knowledge of what had been brewing in Germania prior to the war, the emperor's campaign had been one of vainglory and entirely unnecessary. As usual, Domitian ignored them... or so I thought at the time.

The empire rumbled on in its usual manner, though with warfare continuing to form a central theme. In Britannia, Agricola completed the conquest of the island and circumnavigated it with his fleet, landing in far northern Thule in the emperor's name. The fearsome and troublesome Dacians crossed the Danubius and invaded Thrace just as the Chatti had planned to in Gaul, even killing the governor. Domitian had hastily pulled together a sizeable army from the provinces, sadly abandoning the so freshly won conquests in Britannia, and led them across to the east to put the Dacians in their place. Within the year they had recovered all Roman territory, pushed the Dacians back across the river and killed enough of them for Domitian to claim another triumph on his return.

In Rome, great marble edifices arose. Some had been in the works since his accession, others begun more recently, but all were now reaching completion. An odeon, a stadium, numerous temples, half the Campus Martius restored or reconstructed, a forum to complement those of his predecessors and, grandest of all, the new palace on the Palatine, a structure to rival Nero's Golden House, which stated above all that the emperor was master of Rome now, and not the senate. The senate saw that as a bad thing, of course, but the majority of the populace cheered and marvelled.

As for me? A number of provincial appointments had been bandied about connected to my name, though nothing I felt inclined to leap at, and Domitian was not about to force me into a role I did not want, and so life went on. It was nine days before I was due to leave the city and spend the summer in bliss at a seafront villa I owned near Antium. Many of Rome's nobility had already left for the summer, which suited Domitian. He waited for most of them to leave before throwing a lavish three-day series of games in the great amphitheatre, which were mostly attended, consequently, by the ordinary folk who loved their emperor, and not dissenting senators.

I was invited to the games and given pride of place along with a few other luminaries in the imperial box. I watched the morning warm-ups, the procession, the rituals, and then settled into my seat for a repast over noon alongside Domitian and the others, while the crowd visited the concession stands and waited hungrily for the real entertainments to start. Those began with the *bestiarii*, men armed in a variety of manners hunting beasts in the sand, in and out of scenery placed there during the noon break. I watched as the four wild cats were hunted between potted trees and obscuring hedges. The hunters managed to take two of the great cats quickly, but the others proved more wily, and the crowd cheered as some poor bastard with a spear rounded a corner alone and met two cats who turned him into shredded meat in mere moments. The tables turned, and we watched as the cats now began to hunt the men. They caught another and ate the poor soul. Finally, the animals were cornered and trapped, and the hunters made ready to kill them. Domitian, enjoying himself immensely, halted proceedings and, to the adulation of the crowd, granted leniency to the killer beasts. They had so impressed the emperor he had them sent to the menagerie that was being constructed in the new palace gardens, where they would live long and well.

Other beasts came and went and, once the hunts were over, the sands were cleared of scenery. I had wondered why there had been no executions, which are usually the first order of the day, before noon, and had put it down to a feeling of benevolence in Domitian's character that day. I'd been wrong.

Most scenes in the arena, be they beast hunts, executions or gladiatorial bouts, are retellings of ancient stories or myths. The first execution was no different. Some unlucky thief who'd been captured in Illyricum had been presented as the infamous ancient bandit leader Laureolus. As he was released into the sands with just a dagger and a loincloth, the hunters entered at the far side. Four crucifixes had been prepared. I was not sure why four, when Laureolus was alone, but still I watched with the rest as the bandit was chased around the arena and finally caught. He managed to knife one of the hunters, which earned him a few broken ribs in revenge, and finally he was tied and nailed to the crucifix and raised, howling. He would not die slowly like some peasant criminal, though. Moments later the hunters disappeared and a new gate opened.

I learned later that the bear had been a gift from Agricola in Britain, captured in the wild forests and hills of the Caledonii and sent to Rome to celebrate the conquest. It was certainly a fearsome specimen. I am not averse to blood, even for routine entertainment, but even I flinched as I watched the bear go to work on the pinned criminal. It was one of the most gruesome deaths I have ever witnessed. Indeed, I thought Domitian had gone too far for a while as the crowd watched the execution in a silence so complete I could hear the tearing of flesh and the crunching of bones from the spectacle, but when it was over and the bear led away, the crowd roared its approval.

We had little time to rest, though. What was left of Laureolus remained hanging there, dripping into the sand, as three more gates opened. Three new figures were led from the darkness into the bright sunlight and the golden sand. All of them wore togas, and were being led with bound hands. I frowned. If Domitian was trying to be clever and send a message to the senatorial class by executing criminals dressed as senators, he was walking a dangerous line, even with most of the senate absent.

I was stunned to learn the truth.

As the men were led to the centre, an announcer joined them with a scroll, and began to read the charges. These were no random criminals dressed as rich men.

'Gaius Vettulenus Civica Cerealis, senator of Rome and proconsul of Asia, stands condemned of grand maiestas, treason against the emperor of Rome for his support of the *false* Nero Nysicus.'

I had heard of this Nysicus, of course – just one of the slew of men who cropped up on an annual basis out east claiming to be Nero who had survived his fall – but I had not heard of any involvement of the governor. Mind you, I did not quite have Domitian's network of spies, and it had been some time since he had confided all such matters in me. The governor had enjoyed no public trial, and had been condemned directly by the emperor. I shook my head. This was going too far.

'Servius Cornelius Scipio Salvidienus Orfitus stands condemned of plotting to take the life of the divine Caesar Flavius Domitianus, the evidence damning.'

Much too far. The Cornelii were one of Rome's oldest and most prominent families, and had been ever close to the Flavii. My old military friend, Domitian's cousin, had married into their family. Gods, but it had been this hapless victim's father who had sheltered us that day we had fled the Capitol amid the last throes of Vitellian power.

'Lucius Aelius Lamia Plautus Aelianus stands condemned for fomenting risings against the emperor in the form of inflammatory writings.'

Gods, no. Lamia had written lampooning verses. I had warned him against it, but the man was fearless in his risky humour. He'd annoyed Vespasian once or twice, but that emperor was a lot more forgiving than his son. Again, the Plautii had been one of the families tied most closely to the Flavii. This would drive an irreconcilable wedge between the two families. Worse still, Lamia had been the man I had persuaded to divorce Domitia Longina so that Domitian could marry her all those years ago. Even the meanest peasant could make that connection, and might see it as the emperor's vindictiveness.

I turned to Domitian, my heart in my mouth.

'You could have come to me with the evidence, discussed this.'

He gave me a flat look. 'Why?'

But he wasn't expecting an answer. In fact, his gaze left me instantly and returned to the three consular victims standing in the sand. He was making the most dangerous of statements. Oh, I had no doubt that each of these men had done what was said. Domitian was always well informed of any trouble, and his network of informers was parallel to none. Most of all, Domitian was attentive to detail, and I was sure that evidence had been lodged. But evidence meant nothing to most people. They would hear what they wanted to hear. They would not hear that three traitors were being executed for their actions against the throne. They would hear that three men, a powerful governor, a former husband of the emperor's wife, and a man who wrote risqué jokes, had been murdered. That was all people would remember... or so I thought.

I stared in horror. Crucifixion is not the punishment for a nobleman, no matter what he stands accused of. I watched it all. The entire crowd watched it all. It was intolerable, but we bore witness to it anyway. Each of the three men was led to a cross. To their eternal credit, none of the three showed the panic one might expect, though Plautius and Cornelius went so pale it was visible even from the stands as they watched what happened to Scipio.

They call them crosses, but in truth they are more a T shape. Scipio was laid face down on the T, with his face in the dirt above it. His arms were pulled up and over the arms of the edifice, as though he were hugging it from behind, and were then bound with cords. His ankles were similarly bound, and a small footrest attached just below the feet. Then the real agony began as the wrists were nailed into place. As Scipio howled in pain, the cross was drawn upright with ropes, his limbs stretching with the weight, the nails tearing holes in his arms, his feet dancing, slipping this way and that, trying to stay on the footrest to take the worst of the weight. The shriek of agony as the cross dropped into the socket with a thud echoed across the great amphitheatre. Scipio was done. As the others prepared for their own fate, I continued to watch the first victim. Scipio hugged his cross, unable to do anything else, trying to take the weight on his feet and lessen the agony in his nail-torn wrists and the slow dislocation of his shoulders. He would not last long before the legs began to give way. Indeed, by the time the same treatment had been visited upon the other two senators, already Scipio's legs were sagging, accompanied by shrieks as his arms were slowly torn away from his shoulders.

I learned something unpleasant about the Roman people that day. I had known that Domitian had gone too far. This punishment was unfitting for a nobleman, and it was all too much. I had expected the people in the stands to feel the same. It made me shiver to my core that they did not. When the last of the crucifixes dropped into its socket with a scream, the crowd went wild. I had thought they would see the murder of men who had opposed Domitian, as any senators present surely would. Not so the ordinary people of Rome. They were seeing traitors receive the ultimate justice. They cheered and adored their emperor as he made sport of these men. In fact, the momentum of the atmosphere's rise led to the gladiatorial bouts being announced within heartbeats of the executions' end. The first of the matches was brought on, two trained killers battling with precise and practised moves for the delight of the crowd right in front of those three agonised senators dying on their crosses beside the shredded form of a bandit.

Domitian had done something that should be reviled, yet Rome loved him for it. For the first time, I could, in the eye of my mind, see a Rome with Domitian at its head and just a grand administration between him and the people. No senate. No voices of dissent. In fact, would it be a bad thing, even with such displays?

Game after game was held, some of them good, some of them truly exceptional, for with his usual eye for detail and need to manage matters himself, Domitian had carefully selected each match for their complementary skills. None of them were poor, save those that were deliberately designed to be so. Domitian's dislike of the Thracian gladiators generally led to them being placed in untenable positions at the games, but by now the crowd were used to such things and prepared for the entertainment.

Seven bouts in, I heard angry voices nearby and turned to see Domitian's cousins, Flavius and Clemens, the grandsons of the noble Sabinus, rising from their seats. With black looks cast at their cousin, the two young men turned their back on these displays and walked out of the imperial box, a display of their own, standing clearly against what Domitian was doing. The emperor glanced in their direction, and that was his entire reaction before turning back to the fights, but I could see that the stand had angered him. His knuckles tightened and he began to drum a tattoo on the arm of his chair as he watched the fight. Across the sands, armoured men danced their dance of death while three senators slowly expired in unbearable pain behind them.

The eighth bout did little to lift Domitian's angry mood. With unfortunate timing, the Thracians came on, four gladiators with huge, enclosed helmets, short, wickedly curved blades, and small shields displaying ancient eastern images. Domitian's tapping increased at the mere sight of them. Few knew wherein lay his dislike of them, assuming it a personal preference, just as was his favour for the blue teams at the races, though I was privy to the truth of it. Domitian hated treachery and rebellion above all things. He would never again trust the German peoples after what we had faced with the Chatti, and the Dacians had been added to his list for their recent crossing of the Danubius and ravaging of Roman lands. The Thracians he had always mistrusted, for they had rebelled against Rome just a few years before he was born and even now, four decades on, there were regular displays of anti-Roman sentiment in the province, and the amount of pro-Dacian graffiti that had sprung up across Thrace in support of the invaders over the past two years had moved these people to the top of Domitian's list.

Thus it was no surprise when eight *murmillo* entered the arena opposite the four Thracians, each coloured and kitted in close resemblance to the Minervian legion we had raised in Gaul. This was to be a massacre of the serially disloyal Thracians by heroic soldiers of Rome. I have to admit that I enjoyed the bout's imagery, insofar as I was able to enjoy anything with the tension caused by Domitian's simmering anger and the fading cries of the dying senators.

The crowd went wild as the contest progressed. Most gladiatorial bouts were mock fights, with no actual wounding, or at the least a contest to first blood, for gladiators are an expensive commodity and not one to waste wildly. This fight, though, Thracians being present, was to the death. Someone on the planning side of the event had made the mistake of somehow pitting relative newcomers in the murmillo gear against solid veterans in the Thracian. The result was not the walkover Domitian had planned. In fact, within just a quarter of an hour, three of the Thracians lay dead, but they had taken seven of the murmillo with them. Just one man remained on each side, both wounded. It had, in the end, been one of the more even, and certainly one of the more exciting, matches I had ever seen. This did little for Domitian's mood, and I could almost hear his grinding teeth.

I feared an outburst as the last Thracian managed to put his blade into the neck of his opponent and staggered back to raise his hands in victory. In such cases it was traditional to hold the enemy at sword point and ask the emperor's permission for the kill, but Domitian's rules for the bout had made it clear that kills were sanctioned automatically, for he did not want the treacherous Thracians to walk away with public support. As such he watched with a twitching lip as the last Thracian turned slowly with sword held high, to the adoration of the crowd.

I waited, tense. There would be other bouts to witness yet, but the emperor was fuming, and the best place to be, even if you were his friend, was now far away from him. Yet standing and walking out would be a terrible, and possibly even fatal, decision, so I sat, and I tensed, and I watched.

The fool who spoke probably presumed he would go unheard. He was an ordinary man of middle income, seated in the stands close to the imperial box, in a seat that would usually be reserved for a senator were they in the city. His voice raised, he made his pithy comment to his companion, but unfortunately for him, it happened at precisely the moment the din of the crowd faded, and so his words drifted across the imperial box before he could lower his tone sufficiently.

'The Thracian's a match for the murmillo, but I doubt he'd stand against the giver of the games.'

I winced.

Probably he meant it as a compliment, for Domitian's prowess with a bow and his victory in war were well known in Rome, but the tone and the unfortunate timing made it sound awfully derogatory. This was somewhat compounded by the horribly guilty look he wore as he turned, pale, to see that the emperor was looking directly at him. Domitian beckoned to Maximus and as the chamberlain crossed to him and crouched close, the emperor imparted instructions.

I tried not to groan at this fresh display as, in response to the emperor's commands, the hapless man was dragged from his seat and his wrists bound. A placard was placed around his neck accusing him of being a Thracian supporter who had spoken disloyally, and he was escorted down to the arena even as the victorious gladiator was led away, the bodies dragged from the floor with long hooks and the sand raked to cover the blood. He was left in the arena with no words, baffled and terrified, as everyone else cleared out. Then the door opened and the starving wardogs were released. The result was foregone, and extremely messy and noisy. Again, to my dismay, a crowd that I felt should have been repulsed by all this instead roared their bloodlust.

Domitian was still angry, but I had watched enough. I had *had* enough. I rose from my seat and crossed to him.

'Domine, I don't know how many more bouts there are, but I find I have now had my fill of blood. Might I be excused?'

It was dangerous, even for a man who had been almost a father to him at times, but to my surprise, as Domitian turned his face to me, he had stopped tapping and grinding, and his face was calm. He fixed me with a level look.

'You disapprove.'

'I think you went too far. You are lucky the crowd reacted so, and it is only the lack of senators that allows this. See how seats have emptied. Anyone of senatorial blood has left the stands.'

Domitian shrugged. 'Let them learn the hard way if they must that I rule Rome, not they.'

'Still, this was dangerous.'

He turned entirely now, facing me. 'I will have no treason. No plots. No treachery. No risings. I will have a settled and obedient Rome, and in return, their lives will be bountiful and quiet. Any man who endangers the new Rome of the Flavii will be made to pay the price. You think those men were innocent? Gods, Nerva, but if you only knew how deep the rot went, you would rejoice.'

'There is more?' I pictured cohorts of toga-clad victims being led out to their doom.

His eyes narrowed. 'You think I act hastily. I know that. So I place the matter in your hands. I give you control of my spies, old friend. *You* root out the guilt and see it punished, and then I will not have to do this again. I give *you* the responsibility.'

And that was that.

The next day, as good as his word, two cartloads of extremely secret documents were delivered to my house under the control of both Praetorians and the imperial German Guard. Thus I was given the identity of hundreds of imperial spies in the most surprising places, years of Domitian's work and planning, and all evidence thus far uncovered. If it was all true, then perhaps Domitian had been more lenient and careful than I had realised, for he was right. The rot *did* run deep. But along with him I had unpicked treachery before. Now I would do it again. I would find every voice of treason and give Domitian his loyal Rome.

XXIV

Hint of disloyalty

Rome, AD 88

I worked for more than a year with Domitian's network of spies and informers, collating information, tracing connections and family ties, figures of dubious loyalty who had shared pasts and more. The deeper I had dug, the more it became apparent that Rome was a calm mill pond on the surface, but just beneath, pikes and eels lurked everywhere. Indeed, I found that by the next summer I had so many suspects that I was losing track of my goals and didn't really know where to start with it all.

I had accepted that my promised governorship had not come yet, and part of that was from my own indecision, since several had been dangled before me, but now I decided that I would put aside the idea of governing a province until I had finished solving Domitian's problem for him.

Aelianus, the Praetorian prefect, had been commanded by Domitian to act on my orders as if they came from the emperor himself, but I had issued no orders, and would not until I traced the rot from the many shoots and branches right down to the roots, for with any network of treachery, there is always a root.

'You could simply arrest them all, and gradually release anyone who is cleared,' Aelianus suggested over a drink.

I let out an exasperated sigh and scrubbed my watering eyes. 'If I simply order the arrest of every name I have, half of Rome will be locked up. How big is the carcer? Not large enough to hold the senate in chains, I'd wager.'

Aelianus laughed. Humour is a rare thing among Praetorian prefects, I have discovered, and it made this man a welcome colleague.

But he wasn't a man made for the unpicking of conspiracies, and when it came down to the investigation, I remained largely alone in my work. I was becoming familiar by now with the network of spies and informants Domitian had passed to me. I was not, I think, a natural spymaster, but I was always a strategist and a strategist is not a long stretch from an intelligencer. I began to get a feel for the way the flow of information worked. At first I'd wondered how Domitian had ever had time for affairs of state with clandestine reports flowing in every night, yet within just a month or two I had learned what could reasonably be shuffled aside and what needed immediate attention, which sources exaggerated, which were to be trusted most. In short, I learned the job well.

Despite this, as autumn hoved into view and I realised that I'd actually made hardly any headway since early summer, I began to despair of ever managing to pare my list down to less than half of Rome. I was sitting at my desk in one of the Palatine offices one morning when I lost my temper. I thought I was finally on to something, for after months of stilted failure I came across a list that bore names I'd not been working on, and suddenly I had the promise of something that might tie it all together. The realisation, after a few moments, that the reason I'd not been working on these names recently was because this was the very first list I had completed in the previous winter, and that the 'to do' piles and the 'safe' piles had accidentally become mixed, threw me into a rare violent temper.

I bellowed my hatred of the whole damn thing and gathered up armfuls of wooden tablets to throw against the wall. When I ran out of tablets to throw, I began throwing other things, and I nearly caused an incident when the office door opened unexpectedly and I almost hit the emperor with a thrown ink bottle.

'You seem vexed,' Domitian said in a calm tone.

I tried to bring down my breathing and gave him a weak smile. 'How did you ever manage to unpick webs this thick?'

'I never do anything tedious alone, Nerva. The freedmen of the palace are a wealth of expertise. I highly recommend you make use of them before you run out of furniture to break.'

And that was why, a day later, I worked with a staff of three freedmen drawn from other offices. The emperor had been right, of course. With their help it took only three days to get back to where I'd been when it all fell apart. We then began to work on further investigations. As we made our way through the lists of Rome's great and wealthy, I sent in requests and had the three of them permanently assigned full-time to my staff, where I felt their loyalty could not be called into question by other masters.

With their aid, I finally made some progress. We managed to scratch off name after name where any hint of disloyalty was explained readily away as a mistake in the records. In fact, for a while I was wondering whether we would discover in the end that there was no voice of treachery anywhere in the empire. But the core names continued to show up, hints of trouble that could not be denied, even if they could also not be proved.

A whole new period of frustration began then, for we truly did hit a wall in our investigations. By that winter, we had a number of high-profile characters at the top of the list, but just could not work out the connection and find a common root for them.

In truth, as time wore on, our work was somewhat hampered by Domitian himself, for every few months a short-sighted senator would do something to incur the emperor's wrath and suffer the consequences, and more than once I found someone who seemed to be more central in the web, only to find out that he had been summarily dispatched already before I could learn anything from him. That was infuriating, but I persevered.

In some ways I knew I was planning a reign of terror, of proscriptions and executions, on a scale not seen since the days of Sejanus, but I also knew, because I was being careful, and was already experienced in this sort of work, that anyone who fell would deserve it. In my more sleepless nights, when I contemplated what I would bring about, I consoled myself with the thought that this was one grand clearance, like a housewife cleaning her house in the spring, and after that the empire would be safe, further treason unlikely, and Rome could settle to being a calm and content place.

What a dream to have, eh?

The connection came quite accidentally, and from Aelianus of all people.

I had sent the freedmen off to rest their eyes, and was sitting in my office with a set of records on my desk, each detailing the history of one of my prime suspects when there was a knock at the door. I began to close them and hide them, but when the prefect entered, I stopped. He was as trustworthy a man as to be found in Rome, and I of all people knew that for fact.

Aelianus sauntered in, closing the door behind him, and stopped in front of the desk, hands behind his back.

'I've brought in the four spies you named. They're in one of the Palatine cellars under close guard. I presume you want to be there when they're questioned?'

I nodded. 'I doubt we'll get anything more from them, and they are going to learn nothing new now that their masters are wandering the afterlife wondering what they did to piss off the emperor, but it's worth pressing them anyway. You never know what morsel will make the difference.'

Aelianus made a noncommittal grunt as he swayed back and forth gently, hands still clasped behind his back. His gaze was wandering across my desk and he stopped suddenly, brow furrowing.

'Why are you looking into my men? *My* name had better not be on your lists.'

I shook my head, frowning in return. 'I'm not investigating the Praetorians.'

'Then what the fuck is this?' he demanded, leaning forward, arms coming round so he could stab a finger down at one of the myriad lists, probably my most important one, in fact.

'That is my list of prime suspects now. But they're not Praetorians. You of all people should know that, Aelianus.'

'And you should open your eyes a little wider, Nerva,' he replied. 'I know all these names.' His finger stabbed down again. 'Former Praetorian prefect, served a few years back.' And again. 'Former tribune, only transferred out two summers ago. I remember him.' And again. 'This one I know because while he's not in the Guard, he's at every damn party because his brother's a tribune. Need I go on?'

I stared. '*All* of them?'

'I reckon so. There's maybe three names there I can't place, but I'd wager money that a little digging will turn up a connection. Every name on this list has served in the Guard or is closely related to someone who does.'

I blinked, then looked up, a thrill of excitement running through me. 'Then there *is* a connection. I knew there had to be one. I'd looked at the Guard, of course, more than once when a former service came up, but I was assuming that any conspirators would have served together. It never even occurred to me that they might all be Praetorians, but from different eras. No wonder I couldn't find a connection.'

'But,' Aelianus pointed out, 'half the important people of Rome have served in the Guard at one time or another, or are related. How do you tie them together?'

I already knew that, though. I grinned at Aelianus as I rose to my feet, snatching up the tablet. 'They may not all have served together, but if they all served with one man at different times, then he becomes the root for which I've been searching. Aelianus, you are a genius.'

The Praetorian snorted. 'A genius wouldn't have put his underwear on the wrong way round this morning and found it truly complicated going for a piss.'

Laughing, I wrenched open the office door and found one of the palace runners. 'Go find my three staff and bring them here. We have work to do.'

That set me off on several more months of investigation, with the aid of Aelianus and the freedmen, and when we had finally identified one name that could claim a connection with each and every suspect on my list, I sat back with a sinking feeling. My new suspect had no ties to any known treachery, and should have been above suspicion, really. He had never done anything wrong, and had only been of loyal benefit to Domitian, and yet he had served an extended tribuneship in the Guard, second in command to the prefect, late in Nero's reign and at the same time as most of the names on my list. There was no proof of wrongdoing, but the coincidence was too much to ignore.

Saturninus.

The man who had supported Domitian's claim to the throne when Titus died, and who had led the campaign against the Chatti for the emperor. A man given many honours by Domitian, perhaps second only to me. There was no reason to suspect him of treason, and I could imagine no motive for it, and yet his name was the only one that fit at the centre of the web. He had to be the root. I had to get myself close enough to the man to find some confirmation of either his innocence or his guilt.

That was why I conspired to have myself appointed to an extraordinary position. I was sent to Germania. Not the war-hero governorship I had planned, but a provincial appointment that would be of more use.

XXV

Ice

Germania, AD 89

Ostensibly, I was sent to Germania to streamline the tax system, which had been somewhat sporadic and troubled ever since the war with the Chatti. As such, I travelled up to the great river Rhenus for the second time in my life, and there worked alongside both procurators, of Upper and Lower Germania.

I did the job, of course. The important thing to remember with any cover story is to make it real. I actually did resolve many problems with the German taxes over the months I toiled there. But my work brought me close to the two governors, Saturninus in Upper Germania, and Lappius Maximus in Lower Germania, as well as the procurator in Raetia, Norbanus.

I spent months working hard in public, but also digging deep into the truth of Germania. I quickly became convinced that Saturninus was truly involved in something despicable. I could find no overt proof, but circumstantial evidence existed in droves. I spread my net wide and caught more fish. Figures began to emerge in the military and civil commands of both Germanies, and doubt was swiftly cast upon his fellow governor, Lappius. There were connections with every one of the legions stationed in the region, which numbered a hair-raising figure of eight, four in each province. The only one I felt I could rely upon was the First Minervia, my old legion. Worst of all, I recorded Saturninus holding a number of clandestine meetings with tribal leaders from the far side of the river over a period of months, always with some open excuse, but I knew those excuses to be just that from my work with other tribes settling tax issues. Seemingly, Saturninus now had not only a network of allies in Rome who all had something against Domitian, and not only the potential support of a fellow governor and at least seven legions, but perhaps even the tribes of Germania. The potential for a coup was starting to look enormous. Vitellius had successfully seized the throne from this region with only four legions. Imagine what Saturninus could do. And with the record low temperatures that winter, the Rhenus was frozen solid enough to walk on. Without worrying about bridges, swathes of Germans could cross the river at a moment's notice, not to meet Roman steel this time, but to aid the governor in his treason.

Once again, I had no concrete proof of anything, but my suspicions were vast, and the simple fact was that if they were right and Saturninus decided to move before I could confirm them, the entire empire could hang in the balance. I needed proof. And I needed allies.

Swiftly, I began working on the latter as the winter closed in. I put into place everything I could. I could not yet be certain, but I did everything possible. I confirmed the loyalty of the First Minervia and their officers at Bonna, which was a relief. I also took the risk of confiding in Norbanus, whom I had no suspicions about, and who turned out to be a solid man. I also sent off two messages with some urgency. One went to the Praetorian prefect in Rome, detailing my suspicions, but warning him not to move until I could confirm anything. If I was right and news reached Germania that the Praetorians had marched from Rome, we would be forcing Saturninus' hand and putting my worst fears into motion. The other letter was to the only military officer I trusted. Trajan, the young legate who had worked with me in the war, now commanded the Seventh Hispana, the bulk of which was concentrated at Tarraco. Even at a forced march, it would take him the best part of a month to reach us, but it was the best I could do. I also began to turn local tribal leaders to my side with the lure of gold. I had to do what I could to prevent the tribes swarming across the frozen river if the time came.

It was poor luck that brought it all to a head, and great luck that I survived it.

I was in Mogontiacum, the headquarters of Saturninus and two of his legions, prying deeper into troubling matters, when everything fell apart. A letter sent to me had been diverted by one of Saturninus' agents in the city before it reached my desk. It had come from Prefect Aelianus in Rome, and though it contained no direct information about my activities, there was clearly enough in there to set off the suspicions of that agent. The letter was passed to Saturninus, and everything began to move. Soldiers of the Twenty-first Rapax came for me that icy morning. Through blind luck, I happened to be out of my offices, meeting with a man who claimed he could introduce me to a war leader of the Mattiaci, who could perhaps help contain the Chatti if it came to it. I was in a very reputable caupona in the town with him, accompanied by my two slaves, a clerk and two hired guards when another of my slaves, who had remained at the headquarters, raced in, breathless.

'Master... trouble,' he managed, gulping in breaths of air.

'What is it?' I felt a prickle on the back of my neck. Something was dreadfully wrong.

'Some of the German legionaries are ransacking the office. All your staff have been detained and an order has gone out for your arrest.'

Damn it. I'd dug too deep too quickly.

There was nothing I could do in Mogontiacum. If I stayed, I would disappear. I had to leave, and not return to my offices in the meantime. In fact, I took my slaves, my two guards and the clerk, retrieved my horse from the stable to the rear of the caupona, and we moved swiftly through Mogontiacum to the northern edge of town. There I found a livery and managed to buy a second horse. With some regret, I left the clerk, one of my guards and all three slaves to fend for themselves and rode for my life with just one companion. Already the alert had clearly gone out. Horns sounded on the fortress walls, and men were moving at the gates. I managed to leave the place just before the noose closed around me, and put heels to flanks to get as many miles between me and the soldiers of Mogontiacum as possible as fast as possible.

The icy winter wind whipped at me, trying to tear the cloak away and leave me at the mercy of the elements. My horse thundered along the packed-earth road, hooves churning the surface and leaving a spray of half-frozen dirt in my wake. I rode in desperation. I rode away from peril, and I rode towards it, hoping to save both myself and the emperor.

I had triggered exactly that which I had dreaded, or at least the unwitting Praetorian prefect had done so with his letter. Saturninus had been forced to show his true colours. Had he managed to seize me in Mogontiacum, he could have gone on as planned, and perhaps he would have succeeded. Thanks to the gods, and to both good and bad luck, I escaped, and Saturninus knew his time was up. With me alerted and free, his plot would reach the emperor's ears quickly, and he would be undone. And so he moved early.

I rode for Bonna, home of the First Minervia and my only hope. Trajan and his Seventh would be close now, but too far away still to help, and the Praetorians still in Rome. I rode hard that day, cold and hungry, constantly in fear and knowing that Saturninus' men could be at my heel at any moment. As the winter sun set and I reached Confluentes, I found a *mansio*, an official waystation. I worried about entering, but in reality no one could have reached the place faster than me, and so I paused there long enough to warm up and eat a meal. I changed my horse at the stables for a fresh mount, and dispatched several letters using the efficient imperial post system, which would undoubtedly reach their recipients before Saturninus learned enough to intercept them. Whether they would be fast enough to help was another matter. A letter went to Treverorum, through which Trajan would have to pass, hoping to catch my friend and warn him, urging him to move on Mogontiacum with all haste. Another went to

Norbanus in Raetia, who should be waiting for the word, and had assembled a force of auxiliary cavalry and infantry from his province. A third went ahead of me, past Bonna and to Noviomagus. I had to take the chance. I could neither confirm nor refute whether Governor Lappius was in with Saturninus, but without him, the chances of stopping Saturninus in time were minuscule.

That was the situation as I reached Bonna. Saturninus was ready to move. Early, admittedly, far ahead of his schedule, but he could in theory call on a fellow governor and up to eight legions, plus the tribes across the river. Against him there was only a small auxiliary contingent in Raetia, which might not reach him in time, the Seventh on its way from Hispania, but even less likely to make it, the First Minervia where I was, and nothing else. Things looked extremely bleak for me, for Domitian, and for the peace of the empire.

I was escorted to the commander of the First, who greeted me with a worried look.

'We can do nothing yet,' he said.

'If he moves, the empire could fall. We have to stop him.'

The commander fixed me with a look. 'I have four thousand six hundred or so men, a number extra down with winter illnesses in the hospital, and tribunes I'm not sure I can trust, given your news. Saturninus can potentially call on forty thousand legionaries plus as many Germans. If you expect me to walk happily into battle with those odds, you're insane.'

I sucked worried air through my teeth. 'What do we do then?'

'We wait for news from the north. You dispatched letters. You expect the reply here?'

I nodded. He was right. Marching to face Saturninus could involve twenty-to-one odds, and that would be foolish indeed. If the news came back from Noviomagus that Lappius had sided with Saturninus, it was all over. I spent two nights in Bonna hardly sleeping, half expecting to be arrested in my bed by a usurper. I fretted, waiting for a reply to my letter. That none came suggested heavily that Lappius was indeed a conspirator.

One cold afternoon, the answer finally came. My heart in my throat, I watched a massive force of soldiers hove into view from the north, several legions together. I had my horse readied and was prepared to ride for Treverorum to intercept Trajan, but I did not leave yet. Leading the army was the governor himself, Lappius Maximus, and as the commander of the First went out to meet him, I listened in nearby.

'Aulus Bucius Lappius Maximus,' the First's commander said, head bowing.

'Quintus Sosius Senecio,' the governor acknowledged with a similarly bowed head.

I waited, tense. Neither man's face nor manner gave anything away.

'You have heard of events in Mogontiacum?' the legate probed.

Lappius nodded. Again, still nothing given away. 'Is the river still frozen?'

'It is. Only the cold and the fear of Rome keeps the Chatti on the far side.'

Damn it, but I wished one of them would say something to break the tension.

The silence then dragged out. Finally, Lappius must have seen something in Senecio's eyes, for he straightened in the saddle. 'Then let us pray for warmth to keep the bastards at home. Then we only have to deal with Saturninus, eh?'

I almost exploded at the revelation, and I could see from the way Senecio sagged that he too felt the relief. Lappius had brought his legions in the name of the emperor to stop Saturninus. That was four legions that the usurper could not rely upon. We had almost evened the odds.

We spent that night planning. Lappius reasoned that Trajan was several days away at least, and could not be relied upon to help. By his estimation, if Norbanus had moved immediately, there was a good chance that we could meet him at Mogontiacum. All that remained a real worry was the Germans. Lappius was willing to move, but he knew – we *all* knew – that if the tribes flooded across the river in support, we would still almost certainly lose.

The legions marched out the next morning before dawn, 20,000 men ready to deny Saturninus. As I rose in the cold dark and donned the officer's armour that had hurriedly been made available for me, I looked out of the window at the great river Rhenus and the brooding lands of warring tribes beyond and shivered. I did not notice the great boon the gods had given us. It was only as I left the headquarters and joined the army and its officers that news reached me from joyous men.

The past ten days had been as cold as I could remember, colder than Hekate's heart. My extremities had been ice, and so was the river. The Rhenus had been frozen over so long now that it was being used for carts and for sports. That had been one of the most critical of our worries, for the ice granted unlimited access to the empire for the tribes. And though it was still cold, it had not yet registered that it was far *less* cold than it had been.

The river was thawing!

Large areas remained frozen, but now parts were breaking off into bergs and floating off in the current, and slush formed at the banks. If the temperature continued to rise, the river would flow strong, and the tribes would be restricted to their feeble canoes or a few Roman bridges to cross. If that was the case, they could be contained. Finally, the gods had intervened.

It was therefore in high spirits that we moved off south at speed. Legions can move surprisingly fast when the pressure is on, and the four we accompanied made excellent time travelling along the bank of the rapidly thawing river. Again, we camped for the night at Confluentes, and the next morning the temperature had risen once more. The river was in full thaw. No one could cross it now.

We found Saturninus that morning, not far from Confluentes, and that was not the only surprise. We had expected him either to remain tightly shut up in Mogontiacum, or perhaps to march south towards Rome, and so finding him moving towards us was a shock. That he maintained a force of no more than two legions and that we vastly outnumbered him was a second surprise.

Ideally for the traitor, he would have turned and fled with his forces, rallying them elsewhere, but for some reason, despite being outnumbered and tired, as the two legions crested a low hillside, horns and whistles were blown and the traitor's army charged into battle against a superior force.

I was rather frustrated, really, for I had no authority at the top level of command, and it was Lappius Maximus who doled out the orders, but I also had no command of my own, and so Senecio and the other legates took their legions off into battle, leaving me looking very military on a hillside but with nothing to do. It irked me even more as battle was joined that I found myself positioned with the junior tribunes, those largely wet and untrained adolescents in uniform going through their first step on the cursus.

Anyone who tells you that battles are quick is usually lying. If a battle is over in an hour it has been a complete walkover. The battle at Confluentes raged all the rest of the morning and into the early afternoon. Even heavily outnumbered it takes a long time to beat down and cow the better part of ten thousand men.

The battle that day was bloody. The First Adiutrix and Fourteenth Gemina, the two legions under the usurper's command, fought hard, for they knew their fate when they lost would be dire. And lose they must, for they were facing four loyal soldiers to every usurper.

It was not until that afternoon, when it was all over, that we learned why they had charged us. Norbanus, the procurator of Raetia, had brought cohorts and alae of auxilia from his own province, but on his way to the enemy capital, he had passed Vindonissa and Argentorate and had managed to collect the two legions there, both of which were nominally under the command of Saturninus. Now he had 15,000 men, and had caught Saturninus in the process of breaking camp at Mogontiacum. The way south or west cut off by the procurator's army, and east by the river, Saturninus had panicked, and marched north. There he had walked straight into us and found himself trapped between two armies.

By mid-afternoon, when Norbanus and his men had reached us, the land by the river where the battle had been fought looked like the stuff of nightmares, littered with corpses, the grass churned into reddish mud, endless wheeling scavengers descending to tear meat off the fallen even as the greedy passed among them and stripped them of rings and torcs and anything that might fetch a few coins.

The field was also searched for the fallen officers. I had hoped to take Saturninus alive, for he was surely the root at the bottom of my entire tree of treachery, and the information that could have been extracted from him would have cleared Rome of trouble. Sadly, the moment he realised his coup had failed, the governor had taken his own life after the traditional manner of a losing general. His body was not kept, but disposed of with the rest.

The battle over, the surviving officers who had declared for Saturninus were roped together and the entire army made for Mogontiacum. Along with the commanders of the victorious army and a force of speedy cavalry, we went ahead. We seized the city from the small garrison the usurper had left behind, and began to assert control once more, sending threatening messages to the tribes across the river to inform them that the governor had been removed and that any armed force that attempted to cross the Rhenus would be dealt with savagely.

The next morning I went to continue my investigation. Saturninus would have records, and they could only help me uncover more trouble. I strode into the headquarters building and stopped, stunned, in the gateway. The courtyard was ablaze. Huge piles of documents, racks, shelves, chests and cupboards had been formed into a pyre in the centre, which roared in an inferno. I demanded of the soldiers gathered around what had happened.

'Governor's orders, sir,' was my answer.

Bellowing at them to put out the fire, an order they promptly ignored to a man, I stomped off furiously to try and find out what was happening. All around the place I grabbed startled men by the shoulders and demanded of them their commander.

I found Lappius Maximus in a governor's office that was now bare and empty.

'What in Hades are you doing?' I sputtered.

Lappius turned to me, his face deliberately expressionless. 'What good leaders do. I have burned his records.'

'Why?' I gasped. 'Why?'

'Because there would be endless trials, recriminations and the fall of whole noble families. You know that. I suspect you are perhaps *behind* that. The failure of the coup is enough. It will send a message. There will be no other, but there will also be no reprisals.'

I stared at the man. 'And because your name would be in there,' I snarled.

He shrugged. An admission of guilt, perhaps. 'It may have been. But I have proved my loyalty, have I not? As I say, this will be an end to it. Let Rome return to peace.'

Of course, he could not know that I already had a huge swathe of connected names, through which I had come down to Saturninus in the first place.

There was nothing I could do. I could not un-burn the records, and there would be no copies. The insurrection was over, and any further work would have to be done by me, in Rome. I tarried in Mogontiacum for eight more days. I assiduously avoided contact with Lappius Maximus. He had saved Rome, Domitian and myself, but what had burned in that courtyard had surely included proof that his loyalty had been a last-moment decision, and that he could easily have sided with Saturninus. Indeed, I think the suspicion that the Rhenus would thaw soon and the German tribes would be removed from the plot was probably all it took for him to step back to Domitian's side. I spent my time with good Norbanus, and also with Trajan, who arrived, exhausted, from Hispania two days after the battle, fuming that he had not been in time to help.

But we had saved Domitian, and Rome.

I had work yet to do, though, and in the greatest city in the world, executioners' blades were being whetted.

Part Five – Dominion

Let us not praise a man for his good Fate unless he has arrived at his final day having escaped bad Fate

–Sophocles: *Oedipus Rex*

XXVI

An imperial bloodbath

Rome, AD 91

I returned to Rome from Germania with a list of names that I knew were loyal, and a much longer list that I knew were connected to Saturninus and his treachery. I am not a malicious or severe man by nature, and so I made sure that any name for which there was no evidence, or that I was unsure of, stayed off the danger list, including Lappius Maximus, who had proved himself at the last moment, but who had undoubtedly been involved in the planned coup earlier.

Needless to say, my Praetorian prefect friend had apprised Domitian of everything I had told him, and so the emperor summoned me as soon as I returned, and drew from me anything he did not already know.

'You are to be congratulated,' he said, when I had finished. 'Your work has been a thorough success, as I felt sure it must. You have my gratitude for what you have done in preventing that weasel in Germania from marching against us. I had been right to hand the task to you, and so now, I would that you continue in your work.'

I frowned. 'I have every name I am likely to get now. The work is done.'

'Marcus,' he said, putting an arm around my shoulder, 'the work is *never* done. Treason is like goutweed. You may think you have cleared the garden, for all you can see is order and delight, but you know that its roots remain below the surface and it is only a matter of time before it attacks once more.'

'I had hoped,' I sighed wearily, 'to move on to a less clandestine position. Perhaps a governorship somewhere sunny and heroic, if you remember?'

'Marcus, the only way an emperor can ever consider himself secure is while those he trusts maintain an active vigil against those with a grudge.'

A little downcast, I returned to my domus and settled in.

I began working on warrants and arranging trials in the various basilicas of the city, preparing to have Aelianus and his Praetorians begin the slew of inevitable arrests. I had been at the task for a week when I was summoned once more to Domitian. I found him looking irritable, scratching at his increasingly receding hairline in the triclinium of his new palace, which was now rapidly nearing completion.

'What are you doing?' he demanded. No preamble.

'Domine?' I was nonplussed.

'Where are the heads of your traitors?'

I pursed my lips and moved around to stand in front of him as he paced. 'Domine, I am working on it. There will be arrests in the coming days, but there are many cases to be heard, and only so many praetors who can work them. It will be a time-consuming job. But I am confident that the evidence we can produce will damn each in turn.'

He stopped pacing and frowned at me. 'You are tied up in the bonds of bureaucracy. Cut the ropes and get on with it.'

I shook my head. 'If we learned anything with Agrippina or Piso, or even Caecina, it is that things must be done correctly.'

'If we learned anything from Saturninus,' he countered, 'it is that by the time we have evidence, the plot could be in motion. These men, every name on your list, has the potential to be another Saturninus. And now that they must suspect their time is coming, they will likely feel more compelled to do something about it before they meet a blade. Put aside your warrants. Have the Guard round them up and deal with them as a matter of urgency.'

I shook my head again. 'Domine, if you launch into a series of killings without due consideration of the law, you will turn many more senators against you.'

I regretted that immediately. As he turned, he kept his gaze locked on me, and it was becoming angry. 'What do I care for them? It is these very senators who populate your list, Nerva. If their own names are not there it is not for lack of motive, but for the cowardice endemic in their kind.'

'*My* kind,' I reminded him, somewhat bitterly. 'It is dangerous.'

'Then you are a coward like them,' he snapped. 'You did sterling work in Germania, but of what use are you now if you cannot follow a direct command from your emperor?'

I said nothing. I was starting to get angry myself. I had known this man since boyhood, and I knew how he felt, but he was wrong. Yet to press that was to put myself in danger. He knew me, liked me, respected me, but would that save me if I denied him?

'You are relieved of the task,' he said in a flat voice. 'I will handle the matter myself. Go.'

I was dismissed. And if I had not been aware of the fact, it was rather highlighted by the sudden appearance of two Praetorians, urging me towards the door. I left, still seething at being dealt with thus, but also worried for the emperor. If he did not work this carefully, it would not look like a sensible emperor removing treason and treachery from the court, but an imperial bloodbath. The senators should have been dealt with through the courts. They were not.

I retired into a sort of personal exile in the city. I watched as the streets of Rome ran with blood. No cases were heard in the courts, no accusations proven. Senator after senator was dragged from his domus, wailing for mercy, and summarily executed for a crime I had labelled. I stayed out of the way of the dreadful proscriptions. I could see that Domitian was making a name for himself that would do no good, but I also knew that I would never persuade him of that. And, in truth, I now wanted to distance myself from the killings. I did not want my name attached to them. Worst of all, Domitian found gruesomely inventive executions for any senators that he had a personal dislike for. The populace loved it, of course, because Rome loves a bloody spectacle, but the rapidly diminishing numbers of my own class lived in fear and a growing hatred of their emperor.

Months of death passed, and then I started to see deaths of people I knew had not been on my list. At first I put this down to Domitian continuing investigations and finding new enemies, but as time wore on, I came to the inevitable conclusion that either Domitian, or possibly his eager Praetorian commander, was simply adding to the proscription list the name of anyone they disliked or distrusted, regardless of guilt or innocence.

Then members of the imperial family started appearing beneath the executioner's blade. I was aghast when I heard that the head of Titus Flavius Sabinus, Domitian's cousin and the son of my old friend in the army of Britannia, had bounced down the Gemonian Stair. His name had been tied, somehow, to the conspiracy of Saturninus. Personally, I could not believe any such thing. But I did know that Flavius had been the one name bandied about by the senate in opposition to Domitian when Titus died. If there was one man in Rome that might have had a stronger claim to the throne than Domitian, it was he. Surely, then, this was Domitian using a pretext to remove potential adversaries. Such moves were hardly unknown; Nero had had Britannicus killed for very much the same reason. In reality, I am surprised Domitian had left it this long.

Then Flavius' brother, Clemens, joined the proscription list, another of Domitian's cousins. There was absolutely no way that Clemens could be guilty, though. I had cleared him of any ill will during my own investigations, and knew for a fact that Clemens was no traitor. Yet he met his end. When the executioner's blade fell it was not for treason, but for impiety. If the accusation was to be believed, he had begun to openly worship the god of the Jews, and we all know how that goes, for the Jews deny the divinity of the emperor. I personally cannot imagine the accusation being true. No, Clemens was another family member too dangerous to leave alive. Still, I said nothing.

But finally, a name appeared that I could not bear to hear. I had a somewhat estranged relation who carried also the blood of the ill-fated and brief emperor Otho. Lucius Salvius Otho Cocceianus appeared on the list for some spurious reason, and I knew I had to move fast. Those named did not live for long.

I found myself at court for the first time in a year, and Domitian agreed to see me, perhaps wondering what had brought me back after so long. Various lackeys were dismissed and I waited for him to see me alone, but it seemed that was not to be the case. As well as a number of Praetorians standing in position around the room, a trio of freedmen remained at Domitian's shoulder. I recognised them, of course. Parthenius, Domitian's chamberlain, and his two assistants Sigerus and Satur. They had been important in his household since he had taken the throne, but they had always been kept in the background, working like the palace slaves. To see them so close to the emperor in an official audience suggested they had achieved some level of increased importance. Perhaps Domitian had killed enough people that the court had been emptied.

'I have come to seek a boon, Domine,' I said.

He just raised an eyebrow. He did not look angry, nor amused. Just neutral. I took a deep breath. 'Otho Cocceianus.'

'I had wondered if you would stir from your den,' Domitian said, expression still flat. 'Has your family petitioned you? No one has approached the court.'

I shook my head. 'He is a distant relation, but a relation nonetheless, and few will now speak up in such cases for fear they be added to the list.'

That was perhaps ill-advised and a dangerous thing to say.

'And you have no such fear?' Was that a threat? It sounded innocuous, but one could not always be sure with Domitian. 'He is also the nephew of an emperor who was himself a usurper,' he said.

'He is no threat to you,' I countered.

'He sets himself against me, Nerva. Openly.'

'Really?' I could not see how.

'Truly. I summoned him to court. I had planned to appoint him Curator Aquarum. He failed to answer the summons, and do you know why?'

I shook my head.

'Because he was busy honouring the birthday of his uncle, a man who claimed the throne through the authority of the Praetorian Guard and who had Galba killed.'

Before I could stop myself, I was taking a step forward and levelling a finger. 'I seem to remember you and your uncle slinking off in Otho's company that day. Might it not be self-destructive to start looking at Otho's allies?'

His eyes narrowed. Glittered.

'Galba was a terrible man,' he said, 'and a usurper. Otho was actually a good man, but I cannot condone usurpation by anyone. There must be a set succession and control. Without it, the empire suffers, as we all saw when Nero was removed. Celebrating usurpers is bad enough, but doing so in flagrant denial of the reigning emperor is unforgivable.'

'Your *father* was a usurper,' I hissed.

Domitian rose from his seat and took a step forward, face pale. 'Be grateful, Marcus Cocceius Nerva, that I owe you so much and I count you as unswervingly loyal. Many a man would fall for such an accusation.' He slammed a bunched fist on the throne's arm. 'I disagreed with my father's decision. You know that. But there had to be an end to war, and an end to that monster Vitellius. My father did what had to be done. But we have a dynasty again now, and succession. I have appointed Clemens' sons my heirs, you know? He might have turned his back on the gods and suffered for it, but I will have the Flavii go on. There will be a Flavian emperor after me. But it will not be an Othonian. Never again.

Do not test my patience, Nerva. Otho Cocceianus will meet his end, and you will not persuade me otherwise.'

There was nothing I could do. I had pushed my luck and had said dangerous, unforgivable things. I was truly lucky not to have joined the names on that infernal list and a part of myself, of which I am not particularly proud, realised that I was going to have to return to court and inveigle my way back into Domitian's immediate familia. In sequestering myself and removing my influence from court, I had let him go his own way. I could see that no one was guiding him now, and he needed me once again, before he pushed the state to the brink.

In some ways my timing was good. The proscriptions were becoming less common now, and so my return to court meant I did not have to witness many more. Few senators remained who had a bad word to say about the emperor or, rather, those that did were sensible enough not to do so in public. The executions still trickled on, though. Domitian accepted my return with his usual efficiency. The moment it appeared that I would accept his decisions and not argue, I was welcome once more, and in mere days it felt as though there had never been discord between us.

One afternoon there were perhaps half a dozen of us in the palace triclinium, reclining on couches and picking at nibbles. Our conversation drifted to silence as we heard a commotion in the corridor outside. A shrill voice, in near hysterics, was giving an earful of bile to the guards beyond the door. She sounded familiar, but it was only when Domitian sighed and named her that I placed the voice.

'Let my niece in before she starts to savage my guards.'

Domitilla was admitted a moment later, and she was a shocking sight. She had apparently come halfway through her morning makeup and hair routine and her usually neat coiffure would have given Medusa a run. Moreover, she was in a state of apoplexy, her face burning red beneath the half-applied whitener. She stormed towards us in fury, and two Praetorians had to run to intercept her, holding her back some ten paces from us.

'What have you done?' she snapped.

'Calm yourself,' Domitian replied, with just a touch of irritation to his tone.

'Not content with having my husband butchered for some imagined love of the Jew god, which you know to be utter horse shit, now you take my children from me?' Her voice had risen an octave towards the end, and two more guards moved over to her, just in case.

'They are to be my heirs, Domitilla. They will take the names Flavius and Domitianus. They are exalted. I imagined this would please you.'

'To take them from my *house*? Hostages in your palace of death?'

His fingers began to drum on the table and I willed her to calm down before anything untoward happened.

'They will be given a palace education, trained for rule, as is only proper. They are hardly out of your reach.'

'Brought here where they can learn your bloodthirsty ways and train to butcher their own family?'

The drumming increased, and when Domitian spoke his voice was tight. 'Calm yourself. I will not warn you again. Your boys are in the best place for them.'

'You cannot give me back my murdered husband, but give me my boys, uncle, or I—'

He was upright in a moment. 'Or what? What will you do, Domitilla? Do not threaten me. *Never* threaten me. You need some time to think about all of this. Perhaps a year or two on Pandateria.'

I winced. The island of imperial exile, a place where troublesome family members of the Julian dynasty had been sent, often to starve to death. He had not actually given the order, but if she did not calm and apologise, I was under no illusion that he would.

'You bastard,' she bellowed, and suddenly burst from the grip of the Praetorians, hands curled into shredding talons as she leapt at him. The guards were so surprised, she was almost on him before they moved.

302

I stared in shock as Domitian reacted. He crouched as she ran at him, his hand slipping to the cushions upon which he'd reclined and as he rose to meet her, he brandished a razor-sharp short blade. She almost ran onto it, and just managed to arrest her momentum in time. As she recoiled in panic, the guards were on her again, grabbing her arms. Domitian stepped back and lowered his blade.

'My niece is bound for Pandateria. A year of solitude may strip her of some of this hauteur. See to it.'

She was dragged away still spitting bile and calling her uncle some very unladylike things.

'All things considered, she is lucky to be exiled,' he noted darkly as he slid the blade back beneath the cushions. I watched it, still in shock. How long had he been concealing weapons about his person?

XXVII

The mouth of truth

Rome, AD 92

I entered the palace and there was an oddly subdued feeling to the place that seemed weirdly fitting with Domitian's grand new residence. I had been in palaces many times over the years. I had spent time in the old palace of Tiberius and Caligula, where I had seen Claudius die. That complex had been grand, yet strangely austere, reflecting the nature of those early emperors who maintained the fiction that they had some sort of parity with the senate, which hearkened back to the agrarian roots of the Roman character. I had also been in Nero's 'Golden House', which stretched across two of Rome's hills, encroached on the forum and filled the valley between, constructed among the ashes of the burned city. That had been a monument to hedonism, a mass of stately gardens and palaces that fairly glowed with precious stones and metals, artworks looted from Greece, a rotating dining room, and even a hundred-foot-high statue of the man himself.

Domitian's palace was different again. It said three things to the visitor. Firstly, it sat atop the Palatine's highest point, overlooking the circus, facing the forum, beside the ancient Temple of Apollo. It was positioned to make it clear that its owner was the most important figure in the city, closer to the gods than any other man. Its décor, when one stepped inside, was elegant, but muted and somehow staid. It announced at one and the same time that its creator was incomparably rich and powerful, but also old-fashioned and reserved – a true feat of the designer's art. Thirdly, the very architecture had moved on from being residential to being political. The new Flavian palace was cleverly pulled away from resembling in any way the properties of other noblemen and senators. This was as much temple or basilica as it was domus. This was very clearly the home of a ruler, a king even.

Domitian had begun constructions all over Rome, moulding the city to the shape of his will, but nowhere had the emperor's personality been stamped on the landscape better than at the new palace.

The man who lived here was not the first among equals. He *had* no equals.

An ironic man might point out that this was because they had all met the executioner's blade in the past few years.

But it was not the palace itself that made me frown as I passed inside between nodding Praetorians and made my way along the corridors. The new palace had one other feature. The complex was a three-storey edifice, with many grand halls and rooms, but the lower levels and the substructures were a warren of tunnels and chambers given over to the palace slaves and freedmen. Indeed, the massive complex of support structures ran down the hill from the palace to the circus, with schools for imperial slaves, heralds and freedmen. More so than any of his predecessors, Domitian's state ran on the work of thousands upon thousands of talented nobodies, while the upper classes sat twiddling their thumbs, no longer a part of the process of rule.

As such, every morning in the palace there was a constant bustle of life, so many clerks, scribes, secretaries and slaves hurrying round the complex's corridors with armfuls of documents. Not so today. Today there was silence. Each and every man moved with that strange otherworldly drift of a person wishing he was absolutely anywhere else. More than once as I passed, I considered asking one of them what had happened, but for some reason I did not. It made the hair stand up on my neck. I was far from a young man, now in my sixth decade, and I had seen most of what this grisly world could show me in my time, yet somehow I was still capable of being worried at what I might encounter.

I was answering a summons. It was an odd one. All the emperor had said, relayed by one of his endless supply of freedmen, was 'I seek your opinion.'

On what?

The man I was following took an unexpected direction, and I frowned as we turned away from the great aula regia, Domitian's audience hall. We had already passed the imperial residential area, and if I was meeting him in neither his home nor the official rooms, where were we going?

My tension heightened as we moved into a stairwell that I had never seen opened before, and I was led down a flight of steps lit with flickering lamps into a stygian abyss below the palace. I realised, with a start, as I looked around, that we were in the buried rooms of Nero's early palace, partially demolished and used as foundations for Domitian's new one.

We moved through rooms with rich marble floors and gaudy, rich décor and an increasing glow announced our destination as we approached. I began to hear, extremely strange in the circumstances, the gentle plucking of a lyre. I entered what looked to have been a living chamber. Perhaps a bedroom in the palace of that unfortunate emperor. The room was well lit with lamps and torches, and a single brazier burned to keep the damp chill of this buried room at bay.

The room was occupied.

Domitian sat on a simple chair at the room's centre; another opposite him was occupied by the ageing freedman Epaphroditus. A third, unoccupied, seat was presumably meant for me. Other than the two seated men, there were four Praetorians, standing like granite columns at the four corners of the room, and a small gathering of slaves and freedmen, including several of Epaphroditus' staff. I realised, oddly, that the slave playing the lyre over by the wall was plucking a refrain created by Nero himself. It was like an odd historical tableau of Neronian life, buried and damp.

'Ah, Marcus. Good. I was tiring of waiting. Sit. I want you to hear this.'

I did so, uneasy and anticipating something horrible. I could not figure out why. Epaphroditus had faithfully served Nero and even though the emperor was long gone, he had periodically served as the *a libellis* for Vespasian and Titus and so far throughout the reign of Domitian. I had never known him to be anything but loyal and efficient.

'Tell him of the last days of Nero,' the emperor said to the freedman.

Epaphroditus betrayed no emotion in his expression, other than perhaps a little twitch of nerves.

I shook my head. 'I know what happened. And you yourself told me of Epaphroditus' part,' I reminded him, my memory furnishing me with an image of the distaste on Domitian's face as he'd mused over Otho's reappointment of the man.

'I want you to hear it from the mouth of truth,' Domitian replied. 'Not even just a witness, but from the man involved. Tell him, Epaphroditus. What you told me. Leave nothing out.'

Epaphroditus sighed and turned to me.

'We snuck Nero from the palace. The end was coming and we all knew it. This was at about the time the senate was meeting, acclaiming Galba and declaring our emperor an enemy of Rome. We fled with Nero in disguise, dressed in slave rags. Neophytus was with us, as was Sporus. You'll remember Sporus?'

I nodded, eyes darting to Domitian, whose face had acquired a sneer of disapproval. Sporus – nobody could remember what his real name was – had been a palace eunuch catamite whom Nero had taken as his lover, dressing him as his dead wife. It had all been a little peculiar to me. Nero wasn't the first man in Rome to share his bed with a man, but to dress him as a dead woman was pushing the boundaries of acceptance even in those days. Domitian, of course, with his rigid, rather uptight ways, had held Sporus in exceedingly low esteem. Even the memory made the emperor sour.

'Sporus was there,' the freedman went on, 'and Phaon. Of all of us, Phaon had the nearest villa outside the walls. We knew we couldn't stay in the city, and so we raced for Phaon's estate. We spent the night there. Many, many plans were bandied about. Nero kept coming up with increasingly bizarre and unlikely scenarios where we would end up rich in the east, where he could begin again. I suspect it was Neophytus repeating these stories in the days that followed which has led to all the many tales of the false Neros out east. Sporus was no help in planning. He had dissolved into little more than a sobbing heap. Phaon continually proposed that we seek military allies in order to fight back and recover control. So there we were. Nero with insane escape ideas, Sporus whimpering, Phaon planning a war, and Neophytus tossing about the notion of getting the senate to overturn its decision. I was the sole voice of sense. It was over. We had all known it was over when we fled the palace.'

He shifted in his seat, glanced at Domitian, then took a breath and went on. 'Over the following few hours we heard more and more news from the few sources we could still rely upon. It became rapidly very clear that the senate had completely abandoned Nero and there would be no help there. The Praetorians were out, for it had been they who had begun this whole mess. Military aid would not come, no matter what Phaon thought. And with the declaration of Nero's criminality, the entirety of Italia was locking down on us. Nero was being actively sought by soldier and civilian alike, with a reward at stake. We would never make it aboard a ship, and every road and mansio would be watched. There was no way out. There was nowhere safe to go, and no help to be had. Worse, since Nero was being sought, the villas of his allies would be among the first to be searched. We had but hours.'

I nodded, rapt. I knew the tale, as we all did, but Domitian had been right that hearing it like this was different.

'Go on,' urged Domitian, and there was a hard unpleasantness in his tone.

Epaphroditus closed his eyes. Regret? Sadness? Fear? I could not tell.

'It came down to me to destroy their fantasies. We had such a short time before we were found, and then it would be too late. I had to explain to them. I walked Phaon through the holes in his military plan. I detailed the senate's unassailable position to Neophytus. I told Nero flatly that there was no route we could take where he would not be captured, and that could mean a bloody end like that of Caligula. And occasionally I kicked Sporus to stop him sobbing too loudly. There was no way out. And eventually Nero realised what he had to do.'

'That is not how you told me,' Domitian noted, darkly.

Epaphroditus nodded. Took a deep breath. 'I had to explain to Nero that he needed to end his life. I had to reason that there was no other way. He was ever a nervous man. Perhaps even a coward. He could not contemplate such a thing. It took every ounce of my reason to persuade him. Even then, when he accepted that it was the only way, he could not bring himself to do it. He begged me to kill myself first, to show him how easy it was.'

Epaphoditus sagged. This was not a glorious moment for him.

'I explained that we had to be around to make sure that the emperor passed peacefully and was set in a noble position of repose to be found thusly. I promised him that we would follow on immediately afterwards. Still he could not bring himself to do it. In the end he begged my help. I placed the tip of the dagger against his chest and I pushed until it pierced his heart. I killed Nero. I released him. I saved him. But I killed him.'

Domitian unfolded his arms in the pause that followed and reached out. A Praetorian crossed towards him as the emperor turned to me. 'Epaphroditus was retiring his position today. Entellus is stepping into his role. When they were clearing out the former secretary's office, they found this.'

The Praetorian slapped a knife into Domitian's palm, and the emperor held it out for me to see.

'What is this, Epaphroditus?'

'It is the blade that killed Nero.'

'Preserved for posterity in the possessions of the man who wielded it. Treasured.'

'Hardly that,' put in the freedman, rather bitterly.

'I want your opinion, Nerva,' Domitian said.

'On what?'

'On his guilt. I am not quite decided.'

I frowned. 'His guilt?'

'This man killed an emperor he swore an oath to serve. You might say that he was performing a service, that he was doing as Nero asked, but you might also remember that it was this man who persuaded Nero, against his better judgement, that death was his only option. In my experience, as a man who had been trapped on the Capitoline and besieged by an army, there is always another way. It is always worth fighting. An emperor's life is sacrosanct. No man has the right to take it. And above all of this, the man refused to take his own life, even though that had been an imperial command, and then broke his oath yet again by not following up on his promise to do so after the emperor. In every respect, Epaphroditus seems to have failed his master. And he still bears the knife with which he carried out the act.'

I exhaled. It was pretty damning. I'd never considered the whole of the matter. I'd seen him as doing only what he had to.

'In my mind,' the emperor said flatly, 'this man cannot be trusted and is guilty of enough crimes against his emperor he should die half a dozen times. But he is an old man now, with few years left, and he has served me well, standing as an example to the other freedmen in my administration. There might be an argument for clemency, despite my leaning towards a capital end. As I said, I seek your opinion.'

I did not like being put on the spot like this. In many ways, Domitian was right. The man should have died more than once for what he'd done. But that had been more than twenty years ago, and he had been a loyal servant ever since. And he was old. Most importantly, I could not predict what effect his death would have on public opinion. This was no senator whose death would aggravate that august body but cheer the ordinary man in the street. This was a normal person. A servant, albeit a wealthy and powerful one. To execute the extremely well-known Epaphroditus could have far-reaching effects.

It is therefore my own guilt to bear for what I did next.

I could not decide how to answer. Finally I looked up, meeting Epaphroditus eye to eye. He was resigned. I could see it in his gaze that he already prepared himself for the worst. I suspect even now that he had carried his own weight of guilt for twenty-three years and might even have been relieved to learn it was to be lifted with the simplicity of death.

'There is too much guilt there to pass over,' I sighed. *Let the die be cast*, Caesar had once said as he crossed the Rubicon. Well, I had cast my die, and may the gods forgive me.

Domitian nodded. Turning, he reversed the knife in his hand, holding it out by the blade, hilt towards Epaphroditus. The freedman sighed, and reached up, but before he could grasp the handle, the emperor pulled it away and moved his hand, holding it out instead towards Philo, the dark-skinned freedman who had served as Epaphroditus' secretary for so long. He stared at it in horror.

'Nero did not take his own life,' the emperor said in acid tones. 'His secretary did it for him.'

I shook my head. There would be at least something noble about it if Epaphroditus took his own life, like a losing general in a war. An old, traditional Roman way to go. To be stabbed by your servant was something else entirely. Epaphroditus had been prepared to take his own life, but this was not a noble suicide. This had now become an execution. Given the past few years, perhaps I should have expected no less.

The easterner was shaking his head in horror. Domitian pressed the knife into his hand. 'One of the crimes for which your master must die is disobeying an imperial command. Bear that in mind, given that I have issued just such a command to you.'

I was regretting my decision a little already. To command Epaphroditus' death set him among great men, even in death.

To butcher him was something different. But realistically there was no way back. I watched, bleak, as the under-secretary took the knife that had robbed Nero of his life. He turned, quivering, almost falling, tears brimming in his eyes, and took a faltering step towards his master. Epaphroditus had recovered with a stoicism born of decades of serving dangerous rulers. He gave the younger man a single nod that said eloquently, 'It's all right. Do it.'

The under-secretary placed the tip of the dagger over Epaphroditus' chest. It was in the wrong place, and even I knew that from my military days. The former a libellis reached up and nudged his servant's hand, moving the knife to a position above his heart. The young man was crying openly now, heedless of any danger. Domitian watched, impassive. Still, the younger man could not do it. Finally, as the unpleasant tableau dragged on, Epaphroditus did what he had to do one last time. He pushed himself forward onto the knife, robbing his man of the need to stab. The blade had been kept razor sharp for two decades, and slid with ease between the ribs, though not deep.

Epaphroditus gasped, but had the wherewithal to know that he was not done. Pushing oneself onto a knife held in a reluctant hand is no guarantee of death, and the man was forced, even with the blade in his chest, to heave himself forward once again. He let out a whimper of agony. He couldn't speak through his gritted teeth, but his eyes carried a plea to the wielder to push and help him end it.

'Do it,' I hissed.

'Do it,' snapped the emperor, a few feet behind the panicked freedman. The suddenness jerked him into life and the under-secretary pushed suddenly, driving the blade finally hilt-deep, transfixing his master. Epaphroditus hung there for a moment, quivering, gasping, and then exhaled once, slowly, and sagged. His servant let go of the hilt and pulled his hand back, staring at it, as though the knife handle had burned him.

The man who had killed Nero slid slowly from the chair, blood flowing from him to pool on the decorative floor of one of the last surviving rooms of Nero's palace. I stared. I had woken this morning in quite a bright mood, completely oblivious to the bleak horror that the day was to hold. Here I was now, looking at the still body of a man I had known, and actually quite liked, for thirty years or more.

And it had been as much my fault as Domitian's, and it was likely to send to the world an entirely different message to that intended. By turning it from an honourable act into a murder by passing the knife to the under-secretary, Domitian had made another statement, and this one was not going to be limited to the now-reduced senate.

'It should not have been done like this,' I said. Domitian frowned at me, and I shivered. 'The quality of a ruler is better shown sometimes by knowing when to employ clemency, even in a kill. I was not wrong in my accusation, and execution was not uncalled for. But passing the weapon to the lad turned it from execution to murder.'

Domitian shook his head. 'Your instincts told you he was guilty. I only visited upon him the same gift he gave Nero, nothing more. Neither of us went beyond the necessary. For all his usefulness and skills, had I known the full story all along, I would have done this a decade ago. In fact, I almost removed him from office when I took the throne. And had he not kept the knife as a trophy, we would never have found out. He doomed himself.'

I was still twitching, and the emperor fixed me with a look.

'Nerva, you and I… we spent many years saving emperors' lives. We unpicked plots against Nero and tried to save him, and did the same for my father and brother. You continued to do so for me, but what use is it protecting ourselves from the machinations of the rich if we put ourselves at risk with disloyal servants?'

I sighed. Perhaps he was right. Had we not, just as he said, seen decades of plots, conspiracies and murder? We had watched emperors fall again and again, and Domitian had, ever since the time of Nero, held to the sanctity of the imperial person.

But, I reminded myself, he now sleeps with a blade beneath his pillow.

What had become of the bright and promising boy I had met?

I shivered. The boy who had tortured a slave for information even as a seven-year-old...

I left the room feeling hollow and worried. I avoided court for a few days after that, but I kept my eyes and ears on what was happening. The story of Epaphroditus' death rippled out from the palace over the next few days, its source undoubtedly Philo, its form changing occasionally, but always with that core of truth. Domitian had had the former secretary executed for having killed Nero. In essence that was true, but it was also a huge oversimplification. As I had said, though, time and again, what was intended was not always how things were perceived by others, and this had taken Domitian a step away from his earlier troubles. Previously it had always been the senate who would suffer and that body who would panic over consequences or consider reprisals. For the first time, Domitian had selected what appeared to be a hapless victim from among those freedmen who served in the palace.

With Epaphroditus, Domitian had set an example. It was supposed to be an example of how treachery and disloyalty could not be countenanced even among the trusted freedmen. It should have been the guilty suicide of a man who had betrayed his master. Instead it had become, in the minds of the palace, the senseless execution of a man who had served his master to the end, for in none of the tales I heard did anyone mention the secretary's failures.

XXVIII

An assembly

Rome, AD 94

A meeting of the senate had once been an occasion of state grandeur. In the days when Caesar climbed the steps and met his doom, a senate session was signalled by the hundreds of senators attending converging on the curia from across the city, each perfectly turned out and in a pristine toga, each with an entourage of lictors, slaves, guards, clerks, secretaries and more. Every man arriving was like a parade, and the spectacle drew crowds of awed citizens, lining the temple and basilica colonnades as their betters passed.

That summer the senate only met because Domitian sought their ratification on some minor legislation. While the emperor now had almost complete control of the state, and continued to espouse the opinion that the entire senate was a superfluous body, there were still minor aspects of rule that remained within the senatorial sphere, and until these were eventually changed, Domitian still needed a signature here and there.

This was no occasion of state grandeur.

Accompanied by my entourage, not a lot different in reality to the group Caesar would have brought to the curia, I passed through the forum to attend the meeting. The life of Rome went on around me. The ordinary folk bought fish, argued over playwrights, punched one another, threw up, leaned against walls picking their nose, and almost uniformly ignored the senatorial presence in their midst. My guards shoved and pushed a passage through the forum for me. Such was the pomp and grandeur of being part of Domitian's senate.

I arrived at the curia to find the entourages of the other senators gathered in groups around and about the place. The fact that there was sufficient room is rather telling about our diminished numbers. Perhaps it is a little hypocritical of me to complain about the reduced power and size of the senate when I had had such a personal hand in the arrest and removal of so many of its members, but hypocrisy has ever been a feature of the Roman character.

I entered that hall, and though I was only just in time for the meeting to start, the room was so empty my footsteps echoed around the walls. Row upon row of empty seats greeted me as I made my own way to join my peers.

Fifteen.

An assembly of the men who supposedly govern Rome, whose number should count more than five hundred on a good day. I was the sixteenth to attend. One might suspect that there was some grand hold-up, and that most of the attendees were late, delayed somewhere in the city. One would be wrong. The information that had been trickling in from the network of spies Domitian had placed in the houses of the influential had gradually diminished over the past few years, and now very little was reported for the very simple reason that very few of the senators they were watching remained alive and active. The web was all but abandoned because all the flies had died or fled into hiding.

I waited along with the others past the designated time for the session to begin, and a single solitary senator arrived in that time to join our small gaggle of white-clad politicians.

Seventeen in total.

Seventeen.

There was no fanfare when Domitian arrived. A herald entered the curia and announced the emperor, managing to cram in all the man's many titles, and then stepped aside. Domitian walked into the room, making for the chair facing the rows of seating, but paused part way, coming to a halt, forehead creased into a frown, eyes raking the many empty seats.

'So few?' he said, and his words echoed eerily around the large, empty room.

'It would appear these are all the senators able to attend,' I replied, stating the blatantly obvious for want of anything better to say.

'I wonder why I bother to address the senate at all when no one can be bothered to attend.' There was an acidity to his tone that carried threat. He would, I was sure, cite this day for months to come when banging on about the pointlessness of the assembly. 'How many should there be? Five hundred and thirty-five, I seem to remember.'

I remained quiet this time, for there was still nothing of use I could say. Most of my colleagues managed sheepish expressions and looked at their feet. I have to hand it to Claudius Pollio, for it took courage to stand and reply to the emperor that morning. Pollio was angry, and I could see it in his manner, as, undoubtedly, could Domitian.

'A *nominal* five hundred and thirty-five, imperator,' Pollio said. 'We have lost over a hundred members in the past four years or more, and while occasionally proud men are elevated to our hallowed ranks, they are few and far between and the admission of new members occurs at a slower pace than the rolling heads of the old.'

That had been a dangerous angle. I had seen men suffer for such audacity. My mind threw up an image of that hapless man at the games after his comments on the emperor and Thracian gladiators. My gaze snapped from Pollio to the emperor. Domitian had not replied, but oddly none of his usual signs of ire were visible. No bunching of fists, drumming of fingers or clenched jaw.

Perhaps Pollio also saw this, for he took a breath and went on.

'Of the rest, almost fifty are currently in exile outside Italia and forbidden therefore from attending. The lion's share, some hundred and fifty, are in *voluntary* exile, keeping their heads down for fear that the ballista of our blessed emperor's anger take aim at them. Certainly no one hurries back to the city to attend when they can stay safe behind their own walls.'

I was astounded that Domitian continued to show no sign of growing irritation. Still, Pollio went on.

'The sheep who follow you blindly and would do so even into Hades are all elsewhere, for you have given them sinecure roles to fulfil, and they do just that. What is left you see before you. Cowards and sycophants. I shall leave it to your majesty's considerable intellect to decide which of those categories I fall into.'

Breathtaking. Astounding. No one had talked to Domitian thus since Glabrio had been in the senate, and his had been one of the most visible falls of all, for even the cowards and sycophants had come back to Rome for a day to watch their champion's head bounce down the Gemonian Stair. I half expected Praetorians to appear from somewhere and butcher Pollio where he stood. It was interesting that he had labelled himself, along with the rest of us, either a coward or a sycophant, and yet here he was standing up to the emperor thus.

'How,' Domitian said finally, 'how am I supposed to seek senatorial approval of my legislation with so few men? Is there not some required quorum?'

Pollio shrugged. 'This is your senate, majesty. It is of your making now. Can you not just change the law so that you don't need us to change the law? Why make it pointless for us to attend and then expect us to be here?'

I realised now why Domitian was not showing signs of ire. He was already so angry that he was beyond it all. He had passed some invisible line of fury and become coldly peaceful. That, I suspected, was more dangerous than mere anger.

'You will all ratify my legislation if you approve?' he asked, his voice now becoming tight.

Pollio either had not noticed the appearance of strain in Domitian's tone, or was truly brave or stupid. His shoulders slumped a little and he held out his hands to indicate the rest of us. 'Tell us what you wish and we shall do it, Domine. What else is there to do in the kingdom of Rome?'

I winced. Stupid, then. Brave too, but definitely stupid.

Domitian remained still for a long moment, almost vibrating, and then turned with one last black look at us all, and marched from the curia, his business unfinished. Once he had left, white-clad men crowded round Pollio, telling him how brave and yet foolish he'd been and advising him to run to the emperor and bow before the death warrant was issued.

I doubted anything Pollio could say would now make the slightest difference, but perhaps I still could. After all, nothing suspicious had come out of Pollio's house via the spy we had there. Nodding good day to them, I hurried out of the curia and emerged, blinking, into the summer sunlight. Domitian was only a short way ahead of me, having gathered his considerable entourage. He had eschewed any kind of carriage or litter and was making for the grand staircase that Caligula had commissioned, which arced up from the forum to the old palace on the Palatine.

I ignored my own entourage for now, knowing that they would follow on, and that no citizen would be in my way, for Domitian's own German guardsmen and Praetorians had hurried on around him and pushed the people back out of even missile range of their emperor. I tried to achieve a happy medium between speed and stateliness. If you've ever worn a toga, you will realise how impossible this actually is. What I achieved was a laughable high-speed stagger while repeatedly grabbing at folds of white woollen garment as they continually unwound and attempted to fall away to the ground. As such, I was hardly moving any faster than the emperor's party ahead and by the time I caught up we were not far off the palace vestibule at the top of the stair.

Three Praetorians at the rear turned and made to stop me, but the commotion, and probably my own loud, laboured breathing, drew Domitian's attention, and he turned and gestured to his guardsmen to let me pass. Heaving in a few last deep breaths, I hurried to catch up and fell in alongside the emperor.

'Which are you, then?'

I frowned, and he snorted. 'Coward or sycophant?'

'Ah.' I understood. I gave a small chuckle. 'Probably a little of both.'

He did not respond with a laugh as I'd hoped, but his gait had become a little more normal.

'Go easy on him,' I said.

'I need to do something about the senate.'

I held my tongue. Best not to interfere with his thoughts at that moment.

'Either they are of use or they are not,' he went on. 'Either the entire institution needs to be abolished, which is an approach I favour, for I have seen nothing of value come out of that building in years, or there needs to be a decree of mandatory attendance so that when they are actually required to do something there are sufficient members there to do it.'

'Careful,' I advised.

'No.' He stopped and turned to me. 'Cowed they can still be of use. But those who are not cowed remain insolent, and that is counterproductive. They are better not existing than not attending. They seem completely ignorant that their precious republic has been dead for more than a hundred years. They still cling to the fiction that they rule Rome. They forget that it is *I* who rules Rome, with or without their help.'

'Careful,' I said again. 'You have pushed them as far as you can. We have had no reports of potential opposition from any source, but is it that there is no dissent, or is it that all the fools have fallen, and that those who remain are clever enough to hide their treachery well? Push them any further and something will break. Even diminished, frightened and exiled as they are, do not underestimate the senate. Remember how Caligula did as much, and look what happened to him.'

I had a sudden image of half the senate, driven into voluntary exile for fear of their emperor, meeting in conspiratorial huddles in some seaside villa. I shook it off as a fanciful notion, yet it wouldn't leave me.

Domitian gave a derisory snort. 'If you clad every senator in cataphract armour, head to toe, armed them with two blades and mounted them on a dragon, they would still be too few, too weak and too feeble-witted to pose a threat. Believe me, Nerva, no senator will ever get close to me with a knife as they have with my predecessors.'

I toyed with the notion of pointing out that *I* was a senator walking alongside him and that no one had checked *me* for a hidden blade.

'No,' he went on, his tone now businesslike, lacking audible anger. 'The senate can no longer stand against me. You saw what they now amount to, and you yourself have pointed out the lack of troubling reports coming from any of their houses. I should perhaps consider this my Rubicon. A century or more ago, Caesar marched his Thirteenth Legion across that fateful river and went to war against the senate. He marched on Rome and drove his enemies from the city, pursuing them across the empire and defeating them one after the other. His great mistake was to rebuild the senate in the aftermath. Perhaps I should just finish the job.'

I shook my head. 'Unless you intend to execute all the great bloodlines of Rome, that would be foolish. The men would still live, and would harbour an ever greater grudge for having their one glorious sinecure removed from them. Better you keep the senate as Caesar did, but make sure it is stocked largely with those upon whom you can rely. *That* was my aim when I took the job of weeding out your enemies. I did not seek to destroy the senate, but to clear it of treachery, yet even if traitors persist in its ranks, at least you have them in the open.'

'Are you suggesting that it is better for me to have a nest of vipers visible in the curia than to shatter the nest and risk them cropping up in unexpected places?'

I gave a strange laugh. 'Sort of. It is an adequate metaphor. It is worthy of consideration.'

'Hmm.' Domitian tapped his lip. 'Their existence I think still hangs by a thread, but I am intrigued by your opinion. Perhaps we will attempt to bring some sort of mandatory attendance edict in and see if they can still be of use. Not *all* of them, though.'

He turned and beckoned to Entellus, his new secretary, following the demise of the unfortunate Epaphroditus. The freedman hurried to Domitian's side, snapping open his tablet. I noted a look of fear in his eye. The events of that afternoon below the Palatine lived on as a constant threat of violence for the new secretary.

'Entellus, have a message delivered to the Praetorian prefect. Senator Claudius Pollio is to be arrested on charges of... I am not certain. Impiety perhaps. Not maiestas. That would be going too far. His life is forfeit, though I have no wish to strip his heirs of their inheritance.'

I took a deep breath. 'Clemency,' I said quietly.

'What?' His head snapped around from where he'd been addressing the freedman.

'Pollio spoke his mind, but he did not challenge you, and at least he attended. He might have been sarcastic and even bitter, and he was certainly foolish, but he was there, he was ready to do as you ordered, and he has remained remarkably clear of any taint of treason in any of our investigations. Remember back to when you were young. We used to prize men who spoke their mind.'

Domitian pursed his lips, and I rolled my shoulders. 'If there is to be any hope of a senate you can rely upon it is men like Pollio who will be its muscle.'

After a long pause, he nodded. 'Very well. Entellus, draft a different letter to Pollio. Congratulate him on his bravery and inform him that I have vouchsafed the suffect consulship for him. We will judge his value on his reply.'

As the freedman nodded and dropped back, I raised one eyebrow. 'Oh?'

'If his reply is insolent, then he cannot be relied upon, and the letter will go to the Praetorians as I planned. If it is sycophantic, then he is not as honest and strong as he appears, and I will have him exiled for his own good. If he responds with forthright gratitude, I shall consider the matter closed, and put some thought into rejuvenating the senate as an aid to administration.'

Relieved at the possibility at least that Pollio might walk away from this, I accompanied Domitian to the palace and there we went through the day's work. As one of his close *amici*, I was regularly involved in his administrative activities. His attention to detail was impressive, especially in the legal and financial spheres, and we worked all afternoon and into the evening.

In the end, Pollio's consulship failed to manifest. It had taken some juggling of posts and promises for Domitian to find room to appoint the outspoken senator to Rome's highest position of authority, but the foolish Pollio had made some derogatory comment during that time which had worked its way back to the emperor and caused Domitian to put a hold on his appointment. Pollio had been audibly unimpressed. The man never knew when to stop.

–

The days wore on, and as the winter set in, the Praetorian prefect resigned his commission. I had known Aelianus for many years now, and he had ever been loyal to the emperor. Domitian was saddened to accept the resignation, but understood, for Aelianus was now some fifty years old and suffered a little with gout. He wanted to spend more of his time at his villa near Baiae, relaxing, and who could blame the man. In his place, Domitian returned to the old practice of appointing two prefects, for a man seriously diminishes the danger of insurrection in the Guard when he divides the command of it.

Titus Petronius Secundus I did not know. He had been prefect of Aegyptus a few years earlier and had acquitted himself well, but other than that he was an unknown. His co-prefect, however, was very familiar. Titus Flavius Norbanus had been the procurator of Raetia who had run to contain the revolt of Saturninus. He was a man whose track record was one of unswerving loyalty and strength.

My first encounter with the two of them together was quite by chance. I had been at work in the palace, and was on my way out to visit the baths and relax when I overheard raised voices in a nearby corridor. I couldn't make out the details, but as I rounded a corner towards them, Norbanus turned that same corner and almost knocked me from my feet. Without a word, he scowled at me and then stomped off angrily.

I felt the sense of uncomfortable anticipation. Something was not right. Ahead, I could see two figures. Petronius and Pollio. A strange pairing, and not one I would ever have expected. As they realised I was approaching, they separated and Pollio threw me one dark glare then marched off in the other direction. As I slowed, I could see that Petronius wore a weary look.

'Problem?'

He looked me up and down. 'Marcus Cocceius Nerva.'

'I am he.'

'Good. It's nice to see there are senators who can still speak in a civil manner.'

'Pollio caused you trouble?'

'He was apparently told he could expect the suffect consulship, but it has not come about, and now the ordinary consuls are being chosen. He had a number of very vague grumbles that sounded to me a lot like threats.'

'He pissed Norbanus off, too?' I looked back along the corridor to the corner where we had almost collided.

'No, I pissed Norbanus off. I do believe the man thinks he is above me, just because he helped bring Saturninus down. I fear he thinks Domitian owes him for that, and my presence here countering his sole authority is not over popular.'

I nodded, though the Norbanus I remembered didn't seem that sort of man. 'He will settle down,' I assured him.

'I hope you're right.' He straightened. 'You're close to the emperor, and I hear good things about you, Nerva. I tell you this right now: watch both of them; Norbanus *and* Pollio.'

With that he strode off.

The following month added weight to at least one of his convictions. Angered at Domitian's passing him over for the consulate, and perhaps emboldened by the lack of punishment thus far for his outspokenness, Pollio began a small campaign of slurs against the emperor. For a time, Domitian managed to treat this with simple disdain, but gradually the cutting depth of the insults increased, and finally came the comment that condemned him. Someone at a well-attended senatorial dinner during the winter lauded Domitian's achievements against the Dacians, leading Pollio to throw out some acerbic comment about the emperor adding a thousand Dacian heads to the pile of Roman ones he'd made outside the curia. The intimation that Domitian had murdered the senate was a step too far. One of the other attendees reported the event to the emperor, along with the rather unflattering fact that most of the senatorial guests had chuckled darkly at his comment.

They regretted their levity soon enough, when the invitation came to the imperial banquet. I was in attendance, for the invitation went out to every senator found within the city that month. Just over fifty or so attended, some out of duty, some – me included – out of interest, others out of fear. Given that it was common knowledge that the emperor knew of Pollio's little jest, no one decided to refuse the summons.

We were invited several hours after sunset, and our attendants were kept at the palace door, a slave showing us the rest of the way unaccompanied. The great triclinium was usually a bright and colourful place, sporting marbles from around the empire and the most elegantly painted walls, the trickling of the twin nymphaeum fountains echoing from each side. Not so that night. The entire room had been painted black, and all the furniture replaced with ebony facsimiles. On a dark night, we were escorted to a black dining room.

Each of us was shown to our seat by slaves, young boys also painted black, barely visible in the gloom. It was eerie to say the least, and I wondered what Domitian was up to. He never had much of a sense of humour, and when it did manifest it was usually dark. Once we were all in position, much nervous clearing of throats going on as none of us could see one another as more than a vague black shape in the darkness, finally, the night-hued boys lit a lamp at each seat.

It was shocking. The lamps cast little light, for they were the sort of lamp usually found in tombs, used to navigate the shelves of urns. The funereal atmosphere went far beyond the blackness and the lamps, though. Each of us was seated before a marble slab, and each slab had been carved as a burial inscription for the senator sitting in front of it. The message was clear and extremely unpleasant. The emperor was seated in the usual position, and he was the only one without a tombstone. In the dim tomb-light, the black-painted boys danced an elegant funeral dance, then took up positions around us.

It was at that point that I realised Pollio was not among the diners. I found out later that he had been dragged from his house during the evening and escorted onto a ship, sent into permanent exile. I say permanent, in that he was expected to starve to death there soon enough. Perhaps there was more of Domitian's dark humour there, in that Pollio starved while we banqueted. And that was what we did. The black slaves brought out a meal, but it was a very specific one, formed of just the type of dishes one would serve at a funeral, served up on black platters.

No one spoke for some time, until finally Domitian broke the silence. Quietly and at length he pontificated on death. He very carefully and very slowly went through a list of those who had died over recent years, and made sure to ruminate on the manner of their death, the cause, and any charges that had been levelled against them. It was quite a list, and few of them were baseless, I have to say.

Having thus mocked the senators' earlier dinner with his own meal of the dead, including the clear threat that overshadowed us all in the form of the tombstones, when the meal was over we were all dismissed. As we left we discovered that our entourages had been sent home. Instead we were supplied with a small company of black-painted slaves, escorted to a black litter, and then sent on our way. But we were to keep the slaves and the litters as Domitian's gifts, and the next day all the tableware we had used was delivered to us, as well as that tombstone that had stood behind us.

The senate had been warned.

The senate was a dying beast, but a beast is fiercest when it is in danger.

XXIX

Praeneste

Praeneste, New Year, AD 96

Domitian was sombre as the carriage rolled on. He had been like that for most of the month, following an unexpected arrival from Germania, sent to Rome by the governor there, one Lusianus. This visitor was a ragged and odd fellow with wild hair and even wilder eyes. As he was led into the audience chamber by soldiers from the German legions who had escorted him to Rome, a worn-looking courier handed a letter to Domitian.

The emperor had read the document, his face becoming darker as he did so, and finally he finished it and handed it back to the courier. He then looked into the eyes of the wild man, who flinched and looked away.

'They say you have predicted my death,' Domitian said with quiet menace.

The man looked about in near panic.

'Answer me.'

'Yes, Domine.' Good Latin, but with a thick, Germanic accent.

'Are you an astrologer? I do not like astrologers.'

The man shook his head. 'A wise man of my people. A thousand apologies, Domine. It came in a vision, heralded with a dozen strikes of lightning. A vivid dream assailed me night after night. I did not recount the dream with glee to the Roman authorities, but with fear. I informed the governor for I feared for the emperor's wellbeing, and the governor had me sent here immediately.'

Domitian nodded. The growing anger was no longer evident. It seemed this wretch was no sayer of doom or detractor, but rather a loyal and panicked man, assailed with terrible visions. Now Domitian was intrigued, worried even.

'Tell me.'

The man paused, the panic on his face evident. Finally, as Domitian gave an encouraging nod and gesture, he cleared his throat. 'I cannot say who wields the knife. Perhaps I might draw his face, for I recall it clearly from so many dreams. He...'

He drifted off into awed and terrified silence.

'Tell me.'

'There will be a struggle, here in the palace. In your rooms. An assassin with a blade, who will cut you where the bleeding will not stop. I cannot... it is terrible.'

'When?'

'Soon, Domine. Sometime after Iunius, for the Minervia festival will be done.'

I had been silent thus far, standing with Entellus and the freedmen nearby, but now I stepped forward. 'No specifics?' Still I had heard nothing of concern from the ever-diminishing web of spies in Rome's rich houses.

Domitian frowned at me, but then nodded and turned back to the visitor. 'Is that all? Do you know the day? The hour?'

The man nodded. When he spoke it was an inaudible croak. Domitian hissed at him, urging him to speak clearly. Finally, he said, in a miserable moan, 'The fifth hour, Domine. I do not know the day.'

Domitian leaned back in his chair, silent, thinking. The prefect, Norbanus, approached him and spoke quietly, though loud enough for us to hear.

'What will you do with him, Domine? It is not right that he be allowed his freedom, spreading such tidings as he does. He should be executed.'

'Really?' I interjected, noting the way the man blanched. 'It is hardly his fault he dreams. Are *you* responsible for *your* dreams?'

Norbanus glared at me, but Domitian mused for just a moment. 'Let him pray his dream was just that. He will live so long as I do. If it transpires that his knowledge is more than dream, and he is party to some conspiracy to make this happen, then he will suffer for it. If it is but a nightmare and of no true harm, then he shall live long. He is condemned to death, the sentence to be carried out the day after my own demise.'

The man was led away and we went on to other supplicants and other business, but there was a haunted look to Domitian all that day and through the ones that followed. Proculus did indeed create a sketch of the assassin from his dream, but it was somewhat vague and stylised and of little use to us.

As the new year came around, there was an increase in the tension around Domitian. The stranger from Germania, Proculus, as his name was, had specified this year for the emperor's death in his dream-foretelling. As was tradition, we left the city and made for Praeneste, and here we now were, a procession of carriages, accompanied by the German Guard and the Praetorians as well as a small army of administrators and courtiers.

'It is a grand sight, is it not?' I mused, leaning out of the carriage window and taking in our destination.

Domitia Longina followed suit and smiled. 'Magnificent,' she replied.

Domitian simply sat, silent, subdued. He had been thus ever since the revelations of Proculus. I had tried to persuade him that such predictions were thrown around wildly in the forum by charlatans and that only the predictions of priests and augurs were really worth paying attention to. With his usual insight and quick wit, Domitian had reminded me that priests were just men, the same as Proculus, their only divine power being channelled through them by the gods. As such, Proculus was no different to any other priest. Oracles sprang up from odd sources, after all.

I had been unable to persuade him any different.

'I am prepared,' was all he would ever say, though I wheedled from him what appeared to be a plan to counter the prediction.

He would never be in the imperial apartments during the fifth hour, and then the prediction could not come true. Besides, as he reminded me, he slept with a blade to hand, always, and was no novice in a fight. Woe betide the assassin who would come for him.

Yet despite these preparations, he was still dark and sullen.

Domitia and I attempted to cheer him as the carriage trundled and bounced along the road into Praeneste. I watched the great sanctuary as we approached. The Temple of Fortuna Primigenia at Praeneste is one of the greatest marvels of the world. Rising from the town up the steep slope of a vast forested hill, the sanctuary is formed of tier after tier and terrace after terrace of white marble colonnades and grand staircases, arches and arcades, copses of well-tended trees and clear pools, each level slightly smaller than the last until at the apex stands the temple proper atop a small theatre where cult practices are observed.

The people of Praeneste thronged the streets as the cavalcade came to a halt at the base of the temple, cheering for their emperor. Domitian bolted a smile to his sour face as we alighted, and held up his hands to receive the adoration of the crowd. We paused there long enough for Domitian to give a speech to the people and for the representatives of the town's *ordo* to give grand gifts to their imperial master, which were received with grace. Arrival complete, we began the annual climb. At the start of each year, the emperor came to Praeneste and climbed the temple to do honour to 'Fortuna the First-born' and to receive her benediction for the year, and this was no different. Despite my age, I managed to keep up with the younger men, the pace set, of course, by the emperor. A lazier man would have ascended in a litter and let the slaves take the strain, but the climb was part of the devotion and the annual ritual, and so we climbed the seemingly endless series of staircases to the top.

It was with great relief and very achy knees that I alighted upon the temple's top level. The priest and his attendants awaited us within the colonnade of that hallowed sanctuary. Only a handful of us, including the two Praetorian prefects, joined Domitian as he approached the temple.

The priest greeted us with solemnity and honour, and Domitian made the rote replies as expected. Initial ceremony complete, we entered the temple itself. At the far end of that sacred room, the enormous statue of Fortuna sat on a vast throne, imperious and perfect. She held a cornucopia and a symbolic wheel. Before her, altars awaited sacrifice, gifts or libations. Nearby, this year's oracle boy, a five-year-old dressed in perfect white, waited to perform the one duty for which he had been chosen by the goddess, and all along the sides of the room stood the divine racks of prophecy.

Domitian approached the altars, made his own obeisance to the goddess, who he revered almost as much as Minerva, his patron deity, and gave the offerings. The two prefects passed these to him, a bag of gold coins, one minted for each year of the empire's existence, as counted from the date of Augustus' victory at Actium, and a jar of the most expensive and perfect wine available in all the world. These gifts given, Domitian stepped back.

The priest, his head covered as tradition demanded, intoned the usual rites, and we all stood, silent, respectful, until this was done. More rites and speeches and donations followed until eventually we were ready for the main event. Every year the oracle was consulted for Rome and the empire, and every year we had heard the foretelling in this room. Some years it had been a glorious prediction, others satisfactory. The outcome varied with each year. What I knew, for it had been vouchsafed to me by a friend who had actually served a term in this very role, was that there were no negative prophecies. All the negative ones had been removed during the reign of Caligula, who would not have bad tidings for his empire. As such, in a way, this entire ritual was something of a farce, but few knew that truth, including the emperor himself, and probably even the current priest, and so the prediction would be viewed as irrefutable by all. I wondered what we would get this year.

The boy approached the statue, knelt and said his memorised prayer to the goddess, and then rose and began to sing the song he had learned all year for this very moment, an ancient paean to Fortuna. As he warbled out the melody, he walked around the inner edge of the temple, a stately, measured pace. Finally, on his third circuit, he reached the end of the song, and his arm angled out, his hand dipping into the sacred rack he had halted beside. He withdrew one of the dozens of oak rods that lay in the rack and cradled it reverently in both hands, conveying it to the priest.

The hawk-faced, hooded official took the rod and held it level, carrying it to stand above the central, wine-soaked altar and before the statue, then raised it and began to read.

'The year will witness a great...'

His voice trailed off.

Domitian frowned. I stepped forward to join him, as did several others.

'What is it?' Prefect Petronius demanded.

I had a sinking feeling. The priest had gone as pale as a bloodless corpse, his eyes wide. His hands, gripping the rod, were trembling.

'Great?' urged Domitian, gesturing at the priest to continue.

The old man cleared his throat. 'I feel there has been some mistake, Domine.'

'Read the prophecy,' the emperor commanded in a dark, yet authoritative tone.

The priest dithered for a moment, still, but he was committed and he knew it. He could do naught else. He cleared his throat again. 'The year will witness a great cataclysm. A lake of blood rises to drown Rome and her master. Fortuna cannot be of aid this year.'

I coughed in shock. Either the daft old sod who Caligula had commanded to remove all the dire prophecies had missed one and we had had the monumental bad luck to draw it, or the goddess had truly given us a black and terrible miracle. Domitian had gone as pale as the priest. There was frightened murmuring all around the temple.

'I am so sorry, Domine,' the priest flapped. 'I am positive there is some mistake. I shall have the replacement boy brought in and we shall try again. This boy is clearly cursed, and his curse should not be allowed to rub off on the whole empire. He will have to die. He...'

The man jabbered on, but Domitian had stopped listening. He gestured to the Praetorian prefects. 'These tidings do not leave this room. You understand?'

Both men nodded, and Domitian turned, his back to the babbling, panicked priest, and led the small party out of the temple. As we gathered outside, the emperor gestured to each of us. 'This prophecy is a mistake. It will be proved as much, I am sure, but the damage such a prediction could do to the morale of the city and the empire is enormous. As such none of you will ever speak of this. We will descend to the town and spend the afternoon and the night here as planned, treating the entire event as if it had gone as expected. We will all wear contented smiles, and enjoy the festivities, and then tomorrow we shall return to Rome and watch this fail to come to pass.'

I was slightly distracted by the sound of throats being cut in the temple, as any chance of news leaking out was prevented. Only the priest lived, the boy and the attendants and slaves all executed swiftly. The priest managed a cracked smile as we descended to the town. He would not break the charade, for fear of his life. Of course, I was under no illusion that he would survive our departure, with the chance to tell anyone what had transpired. He just needed to be around for the evening's festivities and banquet, for appearances' sake.

We dined and revelled all that day and into the night, as though nothing had gone awry. We watched the ritual play, drank and ate our fill, and the next day we returned to Rome as planned. I have never felt as dispirited and dishonest as I did that evening, hiding the truth beneath a false smile.

Domitian shut himself away for many days after that. Some of those who had been there thought he was brooding on what had happened, but I saw the truth. For days, Domitian ravaged the palace libraries, going through every scroll and book he could find, looking for anything that might help overcome such a doom-laden prediction. Clearly he found nothing, for over further days he had men brought in to consult. He had a particular dislike of astrologers, who he saw as charlatans, and yet he even had their kind brought in to discuss the matter.

I renewed my work with what was left of the web of spies and, indeed, expanded it hugely in those days, seeking any hint of trouble coming from the dissatisfied senators or the disenfranchised and frightened nobles. I even had ears placed in the rural estates of men in voluntary exile in the hope of finding any hint of what was to come, given the prophecy.

Nothing.

No word from any source more than the usual careful grumbles. Rome's powerful and influential remained seemingly loyal and cowed. I could simply not see how any treachery could come about without me hearing of it.

When the emperor did put in an appearance, which was less often now, he looked tired and unhappy. Months rolled past, and Domitian continued to consult and to read, always seeking any solution to the problem. Those days seemed a boon to the senate, who managed to pass their time without interference from the emperor, for Domitian's entire focus was now on the predictions, one of his death by a blade, and one of a lake of blood. Still, even feeling more secure and able to speak their mind, I heard no hint of true dissent.

Spring came around and brought with it fresh signs of disaster. A thunderstorm, far from unknown in Rome at the time of year, settled in for two days across the city, and a freak bolt of lightning struck the Temple of Jupiter on the Capitoline hill, burning once again the sacred house of the great god that had blazed while we fought the soldiers of Vitellius around it in the civil war. As omens go, they really do not come much worse than that.

Domitian's mood darkened again.

Some hapless moron senator at a meeting on the Palatine had the lack of both foresight and sense to make some barbed comment about the temple burnings, connected to Domitian's days hiding on the Capitol. Few senators, even over Domitian's reign, died as badly as he. Once again, the senate slunk back in fear, one eye always on the emperor.

I was waiting one early summer morning in the grand ante-chamber outside Domitian's apartments. The emperor was still abed, but I had been suffering with a bad back – another sign of my ever advancing years – and had consequently risen early. Those of us imperial amici considered trustworthy, and we were few, were allowed to wait for the emperor in this chamber, in comfort and away from the public areas of the palace. The room was decorated in grand style, with comfortable couches and a small table that was always filled with fresh fruit and a bottle of good wine. Outside the door stood two Praetorians on guard, and the connecting door between this room and the emperor's apartments was locked from the other side.

I spent my time reading a few reports I wanted to go over with Domitian, my only companion the elegant statue of Minerva across the room. The goddess featured heavily anywhere Domitian spent time, and since the new year her statues had increased, replacing a number of images of Fortuna, who Domitian would no longer look upon.

I had no warning. Sometimes, on occasions like this, I had heard perhaps a quarter of an hour of muted murmuring and activity beyond the door. Not today. I looked up in surprise, the pile of tablets clattering to the floor, as the connecting door burst open, and Domitian stormed into the antechamber, still in his sleeping tunic, face pale, eyes ringed with dark circles. He didn't seem to even register my presence. He had something else on his mind, clearly. He charged from the doorway straight across the room and reached up to the statue of his patron goddess. For a moment I thought he was going to pray, a supplicant to Minerva.

I watched in shock as he instead grasped the shoulder of the perfect, beautiful statue, and heaved. He rocked the heavy marble creation away from the wall and to a pivoting position. I leapt from my seat now, a warning on my lips. The statue was going to

336

fall. I dived towards it, and nearly ended my days crushed beneath weighty marble. The falling of Minerva was precisely what he had planned.

I jerked back out of the way at the last moment as the goddess hit the marble floor and both tiles and statue broke and shattered, shards of marble flying. I yelped as fragments drew blood from my leg and my cheek. Shards similarly wounded Domitian, who stood, wild-eyed and panting.

The outer door was open now, the two guards outside reacting to the commotion. The Praetorians burst in, hands on sword hilts, perhaps expecting to find me attacking the emperor. Domitian looked up sharply at the two men, and growled.

'Out.'

The Praetorians shared a worried look, but both bowed their heads and backed out of the room, shutting the door behind them.

Domitian was slowly recovering from his exertion, and he seemed to notice that I was there for the first time. I half expected to be ordered from the room as the guards had been, but instead the emperor sagged and plodded, despondent and weary, across the room to slump onto the couch beside the one I had occupied. Concern filling me, I returned to my seat.

'What is it? The oracle again?'

'The gods abandon me, Marcus,' he murmured in a whisper.

'There was some mistake at Praeneste,' I said, my voice consoling. 'I should not tell anyone this, but the bad prophecies were removed by Caligula. That one had been missed was just bad luck.'

'I knew about Caligula's work there, Marcus. If I had ever thought, even for a moment, that there was the possibility of dire warnings, I would have stopped going. You know as well as I that only makes the oracle's prophecy all the more sacred. It should not have been possible. Fortuna has turned her back on me Marcus, but she is not alone.'

My eyes rose to take in the broken statue across the floor.

'Minerva?'

'She came to me this night, in my dream.'

I shook my head. 'Dreams are unstable things. Most of the time they are just fantasy.'

'Not this one, Marcus. I know it. I have worshipped Minerva above all the gods all my life. She has talked to me in my dreams many times. I know her as well as I know you, so I tell you straight that it was the goddess who came to me tonight.'

Hairs standing proud on the back of my neck, I leaned towards him. 'What did she say?'

My eyes slid again to that shattered marble as he replied.

'Jupiter has disarmed her. The father of the gods takes against me now, and disarmed so, Minerva can no longer protect me. All the gods begin to turn their back on me, Marcus, and I have done nothing but honour them all my life. I exalted Minerva. I consulted Fortuna and gave her gifts every year. I rebuilt the great Temple of Jupiter after Vitellius burned it, and would do so again. But still they turn away from me.'

'Go get some more rest,' I advised.

'No. I cannot sleep again now. I go to the Temple of Apollo. The Sibylline books perhaps will tell me how to solve all of this.'

Before I could say anything more, he was up and heading for the door. Still in his sleeping tunic, he pulled it open and left the room, much to the surprise of the two Praetorians. Apollo's temple was nearby, and connected to the palace complex, but still it was terribly unseemly for the emperor to be wandering the corridors attired so.

I caught a whisper of sound and looked up. One of the imperial servants was hovering in the doorway from the apartments where he had been awoken by the commotion and now leaned around the door frame, eyes bulging.

'Find me fresh clothes and sandals for the emperor,' I commanded.

He did so, rushing around and returning with said articles in mere moments. Laden with more appropriate attire, I ran after

Domitian. That morning he consulted the Sibylline books, and the interpretation the priests managed was only a little negative, though I could see how hard they were working to mute the tidings of disaster.

The next month or two saw Domitian consult oracles, books, soothsayers, and any source of prophecy he could find in the hope of reversing what now appeared to be imminent doom. Nothing changed. I put ever more men in place, slaves and servants across the palace, watching over the emperor, keeping an eye on him.

I never recognised the final move in the great game being played, even though I had seen it. Had I been a little more alert that morning of the Minerva revelation, and paid attention to the identity of that servant in the doorway, perhaps I would have realised, and perhaps I could have stopped it all.

But I did not.

XXX

The assassin

Rome, 18 September AD 96

Everyone had seemingly turned against Domitian, from the toga-clad heart of Rome to the Gods high on Olympus. Domitian had tried endlessly to find a way to counter the curse of Fortuna and to mollify both Jupiter and Minerva. Contrite after his initial explosion and the destruction of his patron deity's statue, he had raised new ones to her across the city, and a grand temple and library to the wise goddess was hurriedly constructed between the forum and the Palatine. The fire damage to the Temple of Jupiter was swiftly repaired, and he had new temples raised to Fortuna on the Quirinal and near the Augustan mausoleum, and enhanced the one on the Capitol. Thus he hoped to bring all three of the deities that had turned on him back into favour. The priests of those temples all assured Domitian that the gods were no longer against him, yet Domitian's dreams seemed to run contrary to that, and we all know how likely priests are to lie when the emperor's favour is at stake.

Months of work to repair his relationship with the divine were accompanied by attempts to counter everything else. An almost continuous stream of games and shows across the city and beyond served to improve the mood of the people. There, at least, he succeeded. The hoi polloi of Rome are ever fickle and slights are easily forgiven with a few small treats. Donatives to the army, the urban cohort, the Praetorians and even the vigiles enhanced his reputation with the military, one aspect of empire that had been unswervingly loyal anyway.

That left, to Domitian's mind, only the senate. And while he was disinclined to make any overture to the body of men who had largely opposed him throughout his reign, in private he would easily admit that the rift there was of his own making. He toyed with the idea of simply disbanding it, but that would only make matters worse, as I managed to persuade him. Instead, he attempted to build bridges with those senators who had hidden themselves away for fear of offending him, and lauded those who had actually supported him, few as they were. In fact, I might say that the few desperate months that followed so many predictions and omens of doom were, in fact, the high point of Domitian's relationship with his empire. For once he was not so focused on the mechanism of rule and the security of the throne that he could not see beyond them.

He had done what he could to mollify every aspect of his empire, from god to pleb. What he thought remained was the German soothsayer's prediction of his demise. There he had taken what steps he could. According to the doom that had been spoken, he would die in the fifth hour in his apartments to the blade of an assassin during a fight. As such, ever since the day he had heard this prediction, he had not only maintained the blade he kept beneath his pillow, about which only a favoured few knew, but banned any other blades from the imperial apart-ments. Indeed, he banned all but his freedmen and slaves from the apartments, even as far as myself now. Finally, he would spend the morning in public, and make sure not to return to his rooms until at least the sixth hour.

He had done what could be done. That he had missed some-thing had occurred to neither he, nor the rest of us involved. Because there *was* a conspiracy still, despite my best efforts to find and remove all treachery. A few remaining senators harboured a grudge, and were clever enough and careful enough to know about the spies in their houses and to keep their work quiet. Their money and promises bought a Praetorian prefect and, more importantly, the man we had spying on said prefect. But still there had to be more, for no prefect nor senator was going to get to Domitian armed. Indeed, I do not believe that any of them would have made a move, that any of them were capable of forming a plan and a conspiracy. My network of eyes and ears was too alert, the emperor's preparations and defences too solid. No one we were watching could have made that move, and so, of course, it all fell to those we had not watched.

It had been a chilly autumnal morning, just five days after the ides of September. I had been with Domitian for much of the morning, as well as with a few of the freedmen, working on matters of state. As was by now the norm, we stopped work only when Entellus, Domitian's secretary of petitions, informed him that it was now the sixth hour. Safe in the knowledge that the perilous hour had passed, and made peckish by a morning's travails, we separated. Domitian returned to his apartments, accompanied by Entellus, and the rest of us went about our own business. I was intending to make my way to the baths for a spot of relaxation and a snack, but I would return to my own rooms first, to change and to put away the tools of state administration. Fortunately I did not have to cross the city all the way to my domus, for these days I had a permanent suite given over in the old Tiberian palace for my personal use, and so I retired there to prepare.

I was in the main hall of my suite, discussing tunic colours with my dress slave, when the door shook to a tattoo of knocks. Another slave hurried to the door, pulling it open. There was no doorman here, as there was in a town domus or country villa. These apartments were within the imperial palace, and so there should be no requirement for protecting the occupant. In the doorway stood two Praetorians. I frowned. Praetorians rarely came to me, and when they did it was usually one of the prefects on some business of state. Two ordinary soldiers was a surprise.

'Yes?' I said, approaching the door as the slave stepped aside. As I neared it, I became aware of a noise threading the atmosphere throughout the palace outside my suite. Something had happened. Something was wrong. There was a muted commotion of panic and disaster. The two soldiers had stony expressions, and I could see behind them, along the corridor, slaves hurrying this way and that. My attention focused on one of them I recognised, moving through the flood of people, making for my door, face white as a senator's toga.

'Your presence is requested by Prefect Petronius, senator,' one of the two Praetorians said in an emotionless tone.

I shook my head, cocking it to one side, trying to listen to the currents of sound. That slave was approaching fast.

'Please,' the other Praetorian added. 'Come now. It is a matter of some urgency.'

But I was not moving. My eyes were on the slave. He came to a halt behind the Praetorians, trying to get my attention without drawing the ire of the soldiers, for a slave's lot is ever one of attempting to please all masters.

I gestured to the soldiers to step aside. They looked unhappy about it, but did so regardless. The slave stepped into their place. I knew him for one of the palace runners employed by Parthenius, the emperor's chamberlain.

'What is it?' I demanded of the boy.

'Domine, Cauto begs you join him in the imperial apartments.'

I shivered. Something was dreadfully wrong. Cauto was my eyes and ears in the imperial apartments. How far I had come since the days I condemned Domitian for his spies. I looked back and forth between the two expectant Praetorians and the worried slave. It was at that moment I heard it. It was just the tiniest noise. The clink of a pebble falling into a pot. But in that moment it rang with a knell like a thousand bells. It was the sound of a tomb door slamming shut. The sound of a body hitting the floor. The sound of the gods' dice landing.

I turned, slowly, to look at the water clock that stood in the vestibule of my suite, already knowing what I was going to see.

Sure enough, the pebble marking the arrival of the sixth hour lay, glistening and wet, in the bowl. The fifth hour had just ended.

At the end of our work, Entellus had either been mistaken or had deliberately lied to his master, and told Domitian that the fifth hour was past, when in reality it had only just begun.

The prophecy of the German soothsayer had come to pass, despite all that had been done to ensure that it never could.

I looked back round at the Praetorians. Petronius wanted me. Urgently. Was he responsible? But also Cauto wanted me, and while Petronius was important, Cauto was suddenly more so. Throughout all the years, I had continued to maintain eyes and ears in some places, and ever since that day when Domitian had burst from his rooms and smashed the statue of Minerva, I had put Cauto in place to watch him. The lad was a slave in Domitian's apartments, with responsibility for the altar of the household spirits and gods, but he was also in my pay, and if he had urgent need of me, that topped anything Petronius had to say. I held a hand up to the Praetorians. 'Tell Petronius I shall be along presently.'

'Sir…' one of them began, but I was already pushing past him, bidding the slave to lead on.

We hurried through the palace and out into the grounds. I knew what had happened, even if I had yet to learn how it had come to pass, but clearly most of the population of the Palatine hill knew only that some disaster had occurred. The atmosphere was one of anticipatory panic, and figures hurried this way and that: soldiers, freedmen and slaves. We crossed to the new palace, and though the Praetorians on the great doors were turning away anyone who approached with rough manners, I was well known enough that at my arrival they bowed their heads and opened the doors for me to pass within.

As they shut behind me I was greeted by a fresh atmosphere of disaster. With my heart pounding out a cavalry charge now, I hurried through the chaos with my slave escort, making for the imperial apartments. The first grisly tableau of the day greeted me outside the emperor's private rooms, in that antechamber where Domitian had smashed the statue.

Prefect Norbanus lay in a bloodied heap at the room's centre, and three Praetorians stood close by, along with a centurion, their swords dripping with the blood of their commander. My mind raced. Had Norbanus done the deed and been caught by loyal soldiers, or had Norbanus been rushing to protect the emperor and stumbled across traitorous Praetorians? Whatever the case, Norbanus seemed to have been killed as a separate event, outside the apartments, his body a mangled mess of sword wounds. His death had been bloody and vicious.

I was shaking now, knowing that nothing I was to find was going to be any better than this.

'Sir, don't go in there,' advised the centurion, pointing at me as we crossed the room. I just waved him away with a sweep of my hand as we moved on. Cauto met me in the doorway. He was as white-faced as the rest of them, and blood spattered his tunic, arms and legs, a nasty gash running down his left forearm. As my guide stepped away and Cauto took over, I closed my eyes.

'Tell me.'

'They did not seem to see me, sir,' the slave replied. 'I first was at the altar, cleaning the incense container, and then hidden. I saw it all.'

'Tell me,' I said again.

He did. And as we made our way into the apartments, and I witnessed the horror, he walked me through it all.

Domitian had approached his apartments, and had planned to go instead to the baths, but Parthenius, his chamberlain, had persuaded him instead to return to his rooms. Parthenius, then, had been in on the matter. *Parthenius and Entellus.* Freedmen whose loyalty it had never occurred to us to question…

Domitian, thinking himself safe, had returned to his sleeping chamber to change into a fresh tunic, and had paused at his desk to read a letter that had been left there. He had been absorbed in the words when he heard a noise.

Turning, he'd seen Cauto, head bowed, moving to tend to his private altar, but also, back through the doorway, he could see Stephanus, one of the freedmen of his niece who had been banished to Pandateria. Without a thought, when she was dispatched, her staff had been brought to serve in the palace, and now, as Cauto told his tale, I realised that it had been Stephanus I had seen that day, lurking in the doorway and listening.

Stephanus had been injured recently, and his arm was bound up in a sling. No one had thought twice about the unlucky freedman, and even the Praetorians at the door had barely glanced at him as he stepped through into the imperial apartment.

Stephanus, Parthenius and Entellus. Again, the freedmen…

Cauto watched as Domitian turned, registering first him and then Stephanus. The emperor's brow creased in surprise, but his eyes narrowed as the freedman reached out with his good arm and shut the door behind him. Closed in with the emperor, Stephanus turned and his bandages fell away revealing a perfectly healthy arm gripping a short gladiator's sword.

Dutifully, realising what was happening, Cauto ran at Stephanus to stop him, but he was small, little more than an astute boy, and Stephanus lashed out, cutting his arm and sending him staggering back. The assassin then leapt at Domitian. The emperor, half-prepared for this moment for the past eleven months, ducked back, trying to make for his bed, where the blade was secreted beneath the pillow, but Stephanus was there, circling, getting in the way, razor-sharp blade slashing this way and that. Domitian looked back and forth between the bed and the door. A method of defence lay in the bed, a chance of escape at the far side. Stephanus would not have time to stop him getting there.

Domitian dived for the door of his room and wrenched it open, but fresh doom awaited him in the next chamber. The loyal guards from his apartments had been removed, and a trio of conspirators awaited him there: Norbanus, the Praetorian prefect, Parthenius, his chamberlain, and Satur, that man's second in command. As the emperor stared, they looked at one another and made to lunge. Domitian slammed the door again, realising now that he was trapped, the panic rising, but also his ever-present logic going to work. He was no stranger to the sword. He had but to arm himself and shout for help, holding off the assassins long enough for that aid to arrive.

Stephanus had followed and was still between Domitian and the bed, but he was wary now, and he and the emperor stepped back and forth, the freedman occasionally swiping out with his blade, inexpert but still deadly. Domitian was fast and driven by self-preservation, and he kept dancing out of the way. Terrified, and trying to keep away from the fight, nursing his wound, Cauto had edged around the room and now Domitian looked up, realising the altar-boy was close to the bed.

'My sword,' the emperor hissed. 'Under the pillow.'

This was it. If Cauto managed to get him his sword, Domitian knew he was better than Stephanus and could best him. Then he could surely hold the unarmed rest of them off while help came. Hoping for a solution, Cauto had dashed across to the bed and reached out, pulling aside the pillow.

There was nothing beneath it.

In a panic, the slave tore the other pillows from the bed, leaping onto it and searching among the covers with bloodied hands. The bed was empty. One of the conspirators knew of Domitian's hidden blade, probably from Stephanus overhearing our conversation, he being that very slave in the doorway the day Domitian destroyed the Minerva statue, and had carefully removed it before the plot unfolded. Domitian was unarmed.

The door burst open again, and the other conspirators appeared in the doorway. Panic filling him and unable to help in any way, Cauto had rolled off the bed and dropped down behind it, hiding from view, peering around the corner and watching the struggle.

Time was now of the essence to both fighters. Domitian was bellowing for aid, and there would be plenty of loyal soldiers in the palace, for all the treachery of one prefect. Any moment, guardsmen could appear, coming to his rescue. Knowing his time was up, Stephanus threw caution to the wind and leapt at Domitian, bearing him to the floor of the apartment where he landed with a thud, the breath driven from both men as they struggled on the priceless marble of the floor. The two men fought there, grappling and panting, swearing and stabbing, scratching and cutting. They rolled around by the bed, just a few feet from the terrified eyes of the hidden slave. Domitian managed to get the upper hand, as he knew he must, for he was stronger and better trained. He managed to get his grip on the blade's hilt, but in desperation, Stephanus headbutted the emperor. As Domitian's cranium smacked back hard against the marble, more damage done by the floor than the butt, the freedman regained full control of his blade.

Domitian, head swimming, reeling, tried to bring up his hands defensively, but Stephanus was not going to be stopped in such a manner. Unwilling to chance the emperor getting hold of the blade again, he leaned back and struck. The blade slammed up into Domitian's groin, punching deep into the cavity of vital organs within, sliding easily into that unprotected region. It was not an elegant attack. It would not be a swift death as they hoped for and desperately needed, but a slow, agonising demise. Domitian, knowing he was mortally wounded now, still fought. As his blood flowed from his groin and his manhood flopped aside, half-severed, he roared like some abyssal horror and reached up, grasping Stephanus' head. His thumbs found the freedman's eyes and he pressed, squeezing the orbs until they burst. The emperor did not cry in the pain he must be feeling, but Stephanus wailed the agony of his blinding.

Then the other conspirators were there. Norbanus was the first, and he tore the blade from the hands of Stephanus, then shoved the blind freedman away and towered above the gasping emperor. At the last, as he lifted the blade, he uttered a quiet apology to Domitian. Then he brought the sword down, again and again, each blow well placed and swiftly robbing the emperor of his life. Seven new wounds were delivered before the prefect, panting, rose. He then turned to find Parthenius and Satur trying to help the wounded Stephanus.

'Stand aside,' he hissed.

They did so, wondering what he was up to, and both called out in shock as Norbanus took two steps across and slammed the murder weapon deep into Stephanus' heart.

'What are you doing?' Parthenius gasped.

'You want to be known for killing an emperor? I think not. And you got your wish. Domitian is dead. And now we have killed his assassin. It's over.'

They stared, but nodded slowly, realising the wisdom of the prefect's words. They had it all.

They had not, of course, known of the slave hiding behind the bed.

That was how it had all come undone. A centurion had come to answer the cry for aid, bringing a squad of Praetorians with him. Their commander had met them in the door, but even as the three conspirators tried to spin their lies, Cauto had appeared behind them, blood-spattered and nursing his wounded arm. He had spoken the truth without fear. Had the three assassins had the thought to simply deny it all, probably the prefect could have talked his men around, but Parthenius ruined their chances by turning and demanding to know how Cauto had seen everything. Where had he been?

The plot revealed and the culpability of the three men clear, Norbanus had lashed out with the blade he still carried, trying to fight his way free. He died under a flurry of blows from his own men, while the other pair, unarmed and panicked, were apprehended and marched away.

And then I was sent for.

And here I was.

I walked into the bedchamber, shaking. The emperor's body was still there, soaked with crimson, lying in a pool of blood. Only one other figure occupied that room. Phyllis, the nurse who had brought the young Domitian up over those early years, and who now, even aged as she was, remained loyal and close. The nurse was struggling, slipping in the blood, trying to lift the lifeless body. She was sobbing uncontrollably.

I turned to the Praetorians, two of whom had followed us back in. It took me precious moments to find my voice, and even then it came out as little more than a croak. 'Help her take the body away. Get it out of here before the head ends up on a spear.'

I could not stop shaking.

Domitian had died, in the appointed place, at the appointed time, despite all his efforts to prevent it. A man who had spent his entire reign doing everything he could to secure the throne from danger had, in doing so, brought it all to pass. He had thinned the treacherous ranks of the senate, and by doing so driven the remains into that same treachery. In the last months of his life, he had done everything he could to bring things back into line. He had appeased the gods, he had lavished gifts and honours upon the senators, he had pleased the people, and he had satisfied the army. The one group that had not occurred to him to appease was the one group he had always trusted and relied upon: his freedmen.

For all that senators had been happy to support his downfall, and for all that the Praetorian commanders had played their part, and even that the gods had turned away from him and let it happen, it had been a chamberlain, a secretary and a woman's attendant that had brought Rome's emperor down and ended his reign in a lake of blood, noblemen and soldiers little more than a tool of the overlooked and forgotten. Those too insignificant to have warranted a spy. Those who had lived for four years now with the knowledge that no matter how competent or loyal they might be, they could be dispatched out of hand and in the most ignominious manner at a moment's notice, just like old Epaphroditus.

That string of enemies, Agrippina, Scaevinus, Glabrio, Caecina and then Saturninus, had all come and gone, threatening destruction and yet being stopped at the last moment each and every time. But the last name on that dreadful list the emperor could never have expected, and could never have countered. In setting Rome against himself, the last enemy Domitian had faced had been himself.

Phyllis, with a few loyal helpers, managed to secrete Domitian's body away, and so it was saved the worst of all depredations. With none of the ceremony of a passing emperor, Domitian was quietly burned and then interred with his family in their tomb on Pomegranate Street, his ashes mingled with those of his niece, Julia, to prevent their removal. There he remains even now, alongside his father and his brother in that solemn house of the dead that stands upon the site of the domus where I had first joined the seven-year-old Domitian in unravelling the plot of Agrippina, on the very site of the cellar where Gaius Rubellius Plautus' slave had been beaten.

As the Palatine became a chaotic scramble of men of all ranks, I walked through it like a man untouched, pale and still trembling. The full weight of what had happened was yet truly to hit me, for I was in shock. Everything had gone wrong. After two and a half decades of a fresh dynasty, trying to build a new Rome in the wake of the civil war, now we were staring into the face of a new conflict, a new scramble for the throne. I was tired. I was old. I had seen too many emperors fall and too many plots in my time. I was sixty-five years of age. But I still had one thing to do.

Thus I found myself in the office of Prefect Petronius.

'You sent for me.' A cracked voice. Hollow. Old.

Petronius nodded, frowning, perhaps noting how my hands were trembling, my eyes staring, wide. 'You and I both know, Marcus Cocceius Nerva, that the succession must be dealt with immediately.'

'He has heirs,' I reminded the prefect. 'The sons of Flavius Clemens, his great nephews.'

Petronius shook his head meaningfully. I wondered for a moment how and when the boys had died. Probably this very morning as the emperor was killed, likely to blades wielded by other conspirators, for there would be other names connected in all of this, senators who could not get near enough to the emperor to wield a blade, but who had willingly thrown in their lot with the very freedmen they had once seen as beneath them.

'Then there will be war again,' I said with a sigh. 'Look to the provinces. There, governors will be preparing soon, if they are not already doing so.'

'There cannot be another civil war,' Petronius said. 'Never again. And there need not be. The senate convenes even now.'

'Oh?'

'They await only your presence, senator.'

I frowned for a moment, not quite getting what he was saying, still stunned, still shaking. Slowly the reason for my summoning coalesced. They would hand me the purple? Put me on Domitian's throne? I, who had helped him cut them down over fifteen years? Gods, but his blood had not even cooled. My mind suddenly took me back a quarter of a century, to when I had been consul and had lamented that the only position higher now was the throne. I had never been that ambitious, but it seemed the gods had been on my behalf.

'Me?' I snorted, bleakly. 'I was his friend. His mentor. I am a loyal Flavian. Always have been.'

'And that is why it *must* be you,' Petronius replied. 'You are of the senate, and you have always defended them, you are a friend of the army and the Guard, of the urban cohort too. No governor will take against you, and you have the skill and the experience to rule. You are the only choice. You go now, to the curia, and accept the honour, or there can be no succession, and war will be our fate.'

I sighed and folded my arms. 'And what was your part in this, Petronius?'

He did not even blink. 'I had no part in any of this.'

'Convenient, then, that the senate are meeting before the emperor's blood is even cold. Convenient that your men came to find me before we had even heard the news.'

Petronius simply steepled his fingers. 'I gather that you helped Domitian unpick plots ever since the days of Claudius, that you helped save many an emperor. I would think, then, that by now you would recognise when it is better that a plot stay unpicked.'

I stood silent for a long time, looking into Petronius' unblinking eyes. I wanted to refuse. I wanted to have him killed for what had undoubtedly been his part in the murder of a man I had called friend for forty years. I wanted the gods to take them all for what they had done, and I wanted, more than anything, to run away in my grief and find a villa in which to hide, like those senators who had fled him. I wanted all of that, and more, and I almost did it. I almost refused. But at that last I remembered all that Domitian and his family had tried to institute an unassailable succession, and I remembered that dreadful year before they had brought stability once more. It matters not to a Roman what he wants, when duty has its own demands.

Finally, without acknowledgement, I turned my back on him. I left his office, gathered my entourage, and made my way into the forum, heading for the curia.

Because, no matter how cold and anguished I might be, as Vespasian had said on his deathbed, there could never again be a civil war like the last.

Nerva

I was close to my end.

I could feel it in the autumn morning air.

Domitian had been gone for only a year and yet it seemed I would follow him already.

But much had been done in that year, and I could at last heave a sigh of relief and know that when I passed, all things should be well.

In the aftermath of that terrible day, I was utterly dismayed at some reactions and pleased to see others. The senate was predictable. As they welcomed me and conferred upon me all the power they believed they had to give – I had been subject to Domitian's point of view for so long that I had rather jaded views on that – they cheered the demise of the tyrant who had systematically disassembled the authority of the senate. They welcomed his murder as only those responsible could. I smiled a rigid, false smile and let them give me power.

The people and the military were almost the opposite. The people wailed and mourned their emperor, any small faults forgotten and only his glories remembered. The Praetorians, in particular, were violently angry. They wanted every last man responsible for Domitian's death caught and punished.

I mollified as I could. I abandoned Domitian's new palace and took up residence in a villa Vespasian had favoured in the north of the city to try and keep the senate happy, but I also removed Petronius from command of the Guard, for, regardless of proof, it was clear that he'd had some hand in the plot. Yet the senate wanted more. They wanted Domitian damned, his name struck from history, and the Praetorians wanted even more. They wanted those senators.

I was caught in the middle. I had to try and keep everyone happy. I had learned through bitter experience in my long life that one had to balance it all. Allowing the senate to hate you was a ticket to disaster, as was evidenced with Domitian, but then so was annoying the Praetorians, as Galba had found out. So I dithered and tried small measures as the senators went about pulling down Domitian's statues without permission, and the soldiers were caught watching estates of men they suspected of involvement in Domitian's death.

To damn the man or not. *Damnatio* was more than just a condemnation of a bad reign. It was more than merely preventing an emperor from taking a place among the gods. Damnatio was to say to the people of Rome for every generation to come that Domitian had been so abhorrent that he no longer deserved to exist even in people's memories. Every image of him across the empire would be destroyed, every mention of his name scratched out, his laws undone, his buildings attributed to others, his remains dishonoured. He would not be nothing. He would be less than nothing. He would never have been.

Obviously, for me, there was no question. Domitian deserved his place with his family among the gods. And the people and the army all sought that. But to agree with them was to deny the senate their revenge. Gods, what a problem.

In an attempt to get the Guard under more control, I reinstated my old ally Aelianus, who had helped me with uncovering treachery, but my grand plan failed. Aelianus was more avid than his men in seeking the emperor's assassins. Reinstating him only made them demand it all the more.

I tried to talk the senate out of their desire for damnatio, but all I did was rile them and start to hear questions about my suitability to rule, my age, my health, and, of course, my lack of an heir.

That was going to be a problem. I actually ran down a huge list of the surviving Flavii to see if there was someone appropriate but, despite the greatness of men like Sabinus, Domitian's relations with the senate had killed any hope of the suitability of a Flavian heir.

In the end, I dithered too long, and part of my problem solved itself. The Praetorians came to the palace in force, armed and angry and demanding the heads of Domitian's killers. When I refused, they ignored me entirely, Aelianus delivering a very stark warning about the shakiness of my position. They left me, quivering, in the palace, and took the matter into their own hands. Former prefect Petronius was butchered in cold blood in a very public place, and his remains exhibited to the people in the manner of a traitor. It seems that before he died, the soldiers managed to extract from him a few names. The streets ran red with blood for days as the Praetorians cut a swathe through all those who even knew about the plot against Domitian, though none suffered as much as the chamberlain Parthenius, who had driven the plot. Held down in the forum by four Praetorians, his genitals were hacked off and stuffed into his mouth in gruesome mockery for the blow that had done for the emperor. The freedman choked out the last of his life around his own bloody manhood in front of a thousand witnesses.

To some extent, the Praetorians were finally mollified and, since they had taken the matter into their own hands without my consent, the blame for it did not touch me, and the senate accepted it, albeit bitterly.

A letter arrived out of the blue one morning. I had been receiving the expected letters of support for my new reign from the provincial governors, but I had forgotten about the governor of Upper Germania, and the heartfelt letter of support that arrived settled the matter of the succession. By the end of that same day I stood in all my imperial glory on the Capitol and announced the adoption of Trajan, the man I had relied upon in Germania so many years ago, as my heir. It was a master stroke. Trajan was popular enough with the senate to be acceptable, but the army adored him. He was a man of true martial stuff, and had marched and eaten with the legions for decades.

The Praetorians were mine at last. Their revenge sated and the succession planned very much to their liking, all was good.

Only the senate stood in the way of a quiet reign and a steady succession.

I did everything I could. I tried to persuade them, individually and en masse, to accept that the reign had changed, but that was not enough for them. Of all people it was Trajan, freshly arrived from Germania one afternoon, who laid the matter out in its bleakest form for me.

'You have to have him damned.'

'He doesn't deserve that.' And he didn't. He may not have been the most beneficent of emperors, but he had ruled strong and ruled well, just not for the senate.

'I know he doesn't,' my wise friend said, sadly. 'I remember him in the war. But good men are damned, and bad men are praised, and we do what we must to ensure that Rome goes on. You know that. It matters not about you or I, or even Domitian's memory. The empire comes first. That is what it means to be emperor.'

That is why I knew Trajan was the man for the job, of course. And he was right.

The next morning I accepted the senate's wish and confirmed the damnatio memoriae on my friend, with whom I had shared so many perilous adventures. The statues of bronze and gold and silver were melted down to bolster the treasury and pay donatives to the army and the people and in recompense for the losses of many senators over the years. The great arches Domitian had raised to celebrate his victories over the Chatti and the Dacians were demolished, smashed to pieces. His name was chiselled from inscriptions, his coins scratched and defaced.

I watched with a hollow heart.

He would never sit among the gods.

'Everything, Domine?'

'Everything,' I confirmed with a nod.

'Even the marbles, Domine?'

'Especially the marbles. Any you cannot refashion into my likeness, refashion into dust.'

I sat, pinching the bridge of my nose for a moment, as the workmen began their task. I could feel a headache coming on. I was not looking forward to the hammering and the dust, but this was something I had to force myself to watch. The first of the statues, gathered from around the Palatine, was carried to the centre of the room with some difficulty, and there placed upon a wide sheet. The sculptor looked at the figure captured in cold, white marble, austere face above a torso clad ironically in the togate pose of a senator. The orange-tinted paint of the skin and the purple of the robe had been roughly washed off to allow the craftsman a better view of what could be done with it, leaving almost-red streaks collected in the cracks and folds of the clothing.

I watched as the sculptor's eyes took in that wide forehead and the slightly receded hair, tastefully carved to be considerably thicker and curlier than its subject's true coiffeur. The nose was wide and long, though not unattractively so. Domitian was never unattractive, even when his hair began to recede. All around the room, copies of that familiar face looked back at me, accusing.

It was not my doing.

I felt the guilt, though, and perhaps things could have worked out differently. Still, he was gone, and in the forum below citizens and soldiers alike cried their mourning for their fallen emperor. No one cheered for the new occupant of the throne, not yet, and I wondered if I would be reviled by the loyal people of Rome for what I must do. But it had to be done.

The sculptor shook his head, a decision reached.

'There is insufficient marble for a recarve, Domine. I think this was once a statue of the Divine Claudius, already reworked. If I try again, the head will be too small for the body.'

I nodded my understanding, a tacit agreement.

As the sculptor moved off to another statue, one of the workmen stepped forward to the unwanted marble. The hammer swung and I watched that face crack and shatter, the likeness of the young man I had known for most of his life falling away in pieces.

The last of the reddish paint, like deep rivulets of blood, gathered on the body of the statue, making it an echo of a butchered corpse. It made me shudder, for it brought me back to how it all began.

I am Marcus Cocceius Nerva, Emperor of Rome, and this is how it ends.

Historical Note

There may be a variety of reasons Roman emperors suffered damnatio memoriae after their death, but having studied a number of cases in recent years, it has become clear that there is one grand underlying cause in multiple cases, and that lies in the transition of Rome over a millennium from monarchy to republic, then to principate and finally to dominate. Until the day Tarquin the Proud was ejected, Rome had been ruled by kings. The next five centuries are characterised by the creation of a system of governance created specifically with the purpose of preventing a return to monarchy – rule by a body of men (the senate) making democratic decisions, with two annually elected consuls leading that body so that no individual could have all the power. The only time that could happen was in times of national peril, when a dictator could be temporarily voted in to solve the crisis. This system falters and fails under Julius Caesar, and is effectively replaced under Augustus with something that is monarchy in everything but name.

Augustus, and some of his more careful successors, attempted to maintain the fiction that this new head of state was 'princeps', first among equals, and that the consuls and the senate still wielded power. However, as the years rolled on and it became increasingly obvious that the senate and consuls in fact only wielded the power granted them by the emperor, the more dictatorial heads of state (starting particularly with Caligula) no longer bothered maintaining this fiction, and ruled with absolute authority, sidelining and largely ignoring the redundant republican institutions that served them. This, of course, leads to a large portion of Rome's nobility being pitted against the emperor, for he has the power which they feel should be theirs. And the more the emperor rules solo and downplays the senate, the more chance there is that some disgruntled senator will attempt a martial solution to the problem, in the form of gleaming blades in dark corridors. And, of course, when the dust settled in the wake of a great fall, no matter how actually effective that emperor was, no matter how safe the empire, or how much the powerless ordinary folk or the army loved him, it was those very senators pitted against him who wrote his history, who told his tale, and who voted on whether he should be a god or should be stricken from history. It should not be much of a surprise, then, when the latter happens.

Caligula, as I said, was the first emperor to suffer thanks to this, and I have written his tale, murdered and damned by the senate. I have also told the tale of Commodus, who was murdered to prevent further degradation of the senate, and who was subsequently damned. Domitian, then, fits solidly into this mould. He recognised from the start that real power lay in the hands of the emperor. Heaven knows, he had seen it at work with the reign of Nero. He had lived through some of the most turbulent times in the empire's history, and had watched the senate pull apart emperors time and again. He watched the plot of Piso against Nero, and watched the senatorial Galba usurp him. He watched man after man of the senatorial class deposing emperors until his father settled a new dynasty. That Domitian had little respect for the senate should hardly be a surprise. And while it would appear that his father was more accepting, the picture history paints of Vespasian might not be quite accurate. Vespasian and his administration were clearly masters of spin. He is remembered as one of the best, and even *nicest*, of emperors. Smiley, wasn't he? And had a ready humour? And yet even the biographers that laud him tell us time and again how many men were exiled and executed by him and by Titus as head of the Praetorian Guard. And we are told there were many plots against him, though that of Caecina Alienus is the only one with any names attached, likely because readers of the contemporary writers might well have had relations involved in said plots. There are, therefore, underlying hints that Vespasian actually ruled a lot more autocratically than generally thought, but was clever enough to somehow cover it all up.

So what of Domitian? We actually have very little information on Domitian's early life. Indeed, until AD 68/69, we are only really told a few things. The family were poor (even the paltriest investigation proves this extremely unlikely), and Domitian was not given a court education like Titus. In actual fact, he seems to have had an extremely good education and was exceedingly bright. Even his detractors note that he was a competent poet, wrote books, and was an excellent orator. We are told that there was a suggestion he had tried to sell sexual favours to Nerva because they were so poor. This I have ignored as rather absurd. At that time the family were pretty high profile. When Nerva was around Domitian, Vespasian was governor of Africa, then toured Greece with Nero, then went to govern Judea and put down the revolt there. This not only makes their poverty extremely hard to swallow, but if Domitian (who otherwise never in his life shows a hint of homosexuality) had done such a thing, the family would have been appalled. Homosexuality was not necessarily frowned upon in Rome, but for a man in the position of the Flavii, taking a young boy as a lover might be perfectly acceptable, but *being* that young boy really was not. This, then, seems likely to be just another of those wild tales made up to discredit him.

There is, however, a solid suggestion that Nerva was closely tied to the Flavian family. He was made ordinary consul early in Vespasian's reign, which is a high honour, and one that the Flavii usually reserve for family and close friends. There is good reason to believe Nerva was given temporary guardianship of young Domitian, at the latest when Vespasian went east in 66. I have chosen to make this relationship begin a little earlier in order to facilitate the telling of the tale, and that cannot be proved to be untrue. We can safely believe Nerva was tied to the Flavii and was closely connected with Domitian at least prior to AD 69.

We do not know what part Nerva had in the unravelling of the Pisonian conspiracy, but he must have played an important role, given Nero's response. Tacitus tells us that in the aftermath 'the praetor designate Cocceius Nerva [...] he exalted so far that, not content with triumphal statues in the Forum, he placed their effigies in the palace itself.' Given the likelihood that Nerva was central in the failure of Piso's conspiracy in 65 and that he was guardian for Domitian from at least 66, I have combined these two factors in my tale. There is no indication that either of my principal characters were involved in the plot of Agrippina, but I found the possibility too intriguing to ignore, given the Flavii' known dangerous relationship with that nightmare matron. The inclusion of Junia Silana in this episode is drawn from the Annals of Tacitus.

One other tweak I hold up my hands to is possibly shuffling dates for Sabinus. Domitian's uncle may still have been governing Moesia at the time this story begins. He would have been there in 51 when Domitian was born, after his consulate in 47, and was urban prefect from c.57. There are suggestions that his governorship lasted for seven years, but that is unusually long, and most governorships seem to have been three-year appointments. Leaving the customary two-year gap between positions, if Sabinus was consul in 47 and served a three-year governorship, that could have occupied the years 49–51, and it is this angle I have taken with the book, as a conceit in order to introduce Sabinus at the beginning.

Indeed, Sabinus and Nerva may well have been two of the most important figures in Domitian's early life. Domitian was born in 51 and only really enters the history books in 69. In between, his father was absent in Africa, Greece and Judea from 63, and thus Domitian lacked a father between the ages of twelve and eighteen. We do not know when or how his mother died, other than it was after 51, when Domitian was born, and before 69 when Vespasian became emperor. It seems likely she was gone before 63 as she is never mentioned with Vespasian in respect to his various positions. As such it is quite possible that Domitian also lacked a mother figure from an early age. That Sabinus and Nerva became his prime influences during his formative years is therefore highly likely.

The demise of Nerva's father at the start of this tale is conjecture. We know little about Nerva's life, career and family before his reign, and so I have tied the two families closer together by giving Nerva more or less the same relationship with Agrippina as the Flavii. Certainly this sort of scene was far from unknown in the early principate. The poisoning of Claudius remains an unanswered question, but the version I have portrayed is drawn from more than one ancient source, and the villainy of Agrippina seems unarguable, so I see no reason to doubt this chain of events. It is noted by Cassius Dio that Claudius 'would not endure her behaviour, but was preparing to put an end to her power, to cause his son to assume the toga virilis, and to declare him heir to the throne. Agrippina, learning of this, became alarmed and made haste to forestall anything of the sort by poisoning Claudius.' QED. That the Flavii were present is highly likely. Suetonius tells us that Titus was a good friend of Britannicus, Claudius' natural son, and was sitting beside him when Britannicus was later killed, so their presence at such court banquets is hard to refute.

Nero's attempts on his own mother's life are well attested in sources and though there is considerable variation in the fine detail they are all of a general accord, and both Suetonius and Cassius Dio tell us variations of the collapsible ship story. Given Nero's absolute power and his mother's record, there is no reason to doubt this, and indeed, one might even side with Nero as he plots his mother's death. Her involvement in a conspiracy to bring down her own son might be a step too far, and even the sources only count this as rumour, but the fact remains that said rumour seems to have contributed to her downfall, and so I have made her plot the starting point for my clandestine partnership of the two protagonists. I have dealt with the Pisonian conspiracy already, but will reiterate here Nerva's noted involvement in stopping it, and that Domitian's part is my own invention, based upon his personality, intelligence, and connections.

I will grant you that devoting twenty per cent of the book to the year of the four emperors perhaps draws space away from later chapters in which I could have detailed more events during Domitian's reign. I feel, however, that since this is very much the man's formative years and the most turbulent time in a century of Roman history, the effects it must have had on Domitian, who lived through it all in the very epicentre, must have been vast. I have therefore used the events of these years, all drawn from sources, to show what impressions they may have left on the young man. Certainly his uncle Sabinus, with whom he likely lived throughout these events, is a central figure in the troubled year, and comes across as one of the most noble and heroic Romans in history. For the record, those eagle-eyed among you might have spotted the appearance of a certain young slave from the subcontinent named Philo, who I have included in cameos with the blessing of his creator, L. J. Trafford. If you want the most detailed and entertaining account of the year of the four emperors I have ever read, I would direct you to her quartet of books beginning with *Palatine*.

That turbulent year culminates with the siege of the Capitoline hill on the last day of the reign of the dreadful Vitellius (who no one seems to have a good word for). The presence of Domitian, Sabinus and Flavius on the hill, defending it against all comers, is recorded. The presence of Nerva, specifically, is not, but given his apparent ties to the family, his likely guardianship of Domitian, and his probable presence in the city, his being there is far from unlikely. Indeed, Cassius Dio tells us that the consuls were present on the Capitol with Sabinus along with 'other foremost men', while Tacitus tells us that 'Some women even faced the siege; the most prominent among them was Verulana Gratilla, who was not following children or relatives but was attracted by the fascination of war', but also that present were 'some senators and knights, whose names it is not easy to report, since after Vespasian's victory many claimed to have rendered this service to his party'. I have placed Nerva among them. It seems reasonable. The fighting on the Capitol is recorded by Suetonius, Cassius Dio, and Tacitus, the latter giving us an excellent blow-by-blow account, and well he might, having been a teenager at the time and likely present in Rome to witness events. They all tell us of the burning of the temple, which Domitian would later rebuild as part of his grand programme, only for it to be struck by lightning towards the end. Sabinus' arrest is mentioned by one source, and his execution by another. All three tell us a version of Domitian's escape, though they do not quite gel.

Tacitus says 'Domitian was concealed in the lodging of a temple attendant when the assailants broke into the citadel; then through the cleverness of a freedman he was dressed in a linen robe and so was able to join a crowd of devotees without being recognised and to escape to the house of Cornelius Primus, one of his father's clients, near the Velabrum, where he remained in concealment.'

Suetonius has 'When the enemy forced an entrance and the temple was fired, he hid during the night with the guardian of the shrine, and in the morning, disguised in the garb of a follower of Isis and mingling with the priests of that fickle superstition, he went across the Tiber with a single companion to the mother of one of his school-fellows.'

Dio says 'Domitian and the younger Sabinus, however, had made their escape from the Capitol in the first confusion and by concealing themselves in some houses had remained undiscovered.'

I have drawn my version of the entire event from a mix of the three sources, but for Domitian's escape I have used Kenneth Wellesley's 'Three Historical Puzzles In Histories' from volume 6, No. 3/4 of *The Classical Quarterly*, 1956, which neatly explains a plausible set of events that finds accord with the sources.

The immediate aftermath of the civil war is given to us as an odd mix for Domitian. Even those historians who damn him cannot disguise certain hints of greatness. His dealing with the senate in his father's name was excellent. That he truly wanted to ride out with the army and deal with the Civilis revolt is highly likely and quite understandable. The fact that Mucianus effectively crushed every attempt by Domitian to do anything important or memorable is perhaps one of the most telling markers of the man's future.

Here, it is important to note my position on Caecina Alienus. We know that he was a Vitellian general. We know that the moment he felt the wind shift, he tried to defect with his army to Vespasian, and though that might have cost him his life, he managed to live to become a trusted Flavian officer. Yet towards the end of Vespasian's life, Caecina suddenly, once again, turns on his emperor. He seems to be a serial traitor, and so I felt no shame in portraying him as just that: a man who has survived several turbulent reigns by changing sides when it pays best to do so. He clearly was totally untrustworthy, and so his influence on Domitian could only have been for the worse. As such I have had him wheedle his way in and stay there, a Gríma Wormtongue to Domitian's Theoden, for you Tolkien fans. Mucianus clearly falls from grace at some point during Vespasian's reign (the two men had actually been at odds with one another long before the civil war and their sudden unexpected alliance). How he died we do not know, but he is gone long before Vespasian, and so I have laid his fate at the hands of Caecina. The scene in which Caecina falls is largely drawn from sources. We are told that it is Titus who uncovers the plot, but in my telling, Titus is given the information by his brother. It is not impossible. It is certainly Titus who deals with Caecina at the meal.

A word briefly on the Flavian family and wives. There are many Flavii, even just from the close branches, and purists might grumble at how little screentime I have given most of them. This is simply a matter of expediency. I have concentrated on the characters central to this plot, and streamlined the cast. Otherwise the text would have been vastly complicated by a slew of extra Flaviuses and Sabinuses, with utter confusion about who was who. Every man and his dog was a Flavius at one point. Moreover, there are members of Nerva's family who could have played a part, including his sister, who is the mother of the Otho Cocceianus who falls to a Domitianic blade in the story. Again, her inclusion would only muddy the waters for the reader, and so she has been glossed over.

Vespasian and his wife seem to have had a traditional Roman marriage of convenience, with both families gaining from the union. While they may have shared love, there are hints that she had loved someone before, and Vespasian definitely never lost his affection for Caenis, one of those fascinating women in Roman history who is clever, beautiful and dangerous. Titus similarly had wives taken for their value (the Flavii were very good at this) while his only real love seems to have been for a Judean queen who he could only ever have as a mistress. We are told (rather gleefully) in sources that Domitian had attempted to begin two homosexual relationships in his youth, once with Nerva, and once with Claudius Pollio. I have already explained how the former seems extremely unlikely, and the latter is even more clearly character assassination. Given Domitian's apparent prudishness and uptight sexuality, and some almost severe laws in those regards, it seems fanciful that these accusations could be true. Descriptions like Suetonius' 'He was excessively lustful. His constant sexual intercourse he called bed-wrestling, as if it were a kind of exercise. It was reported that he depilated his concubines with his own hand and swam with common prostitutes' seem out of character with other aspects that are described.

Domitian apparently married for love, something extremely rare. He is noted to have briefly exiled Domitia after the death of their child, but to have quickly brought her back because he could not be without her. I have cut this from the story, largely through space constraints. Domitian clearly loved his wife, and there is no reason to believe it was not reciprocated. Any hint that she was involved in his assassination holds no water, and I have swept aside that possibility, since in the source that tells us of it (Suetonius), she seems to have an identical part in this to that played by Marcia against Commodus, right down to the tablet full of names she finds, which suggests that Suetonius has got his stories mixed up. That an inscription from the time of Hadrian refers to Domitia as 'wife of Domitian' even decades after his death suggests that there was never a great rift between the couple, and certainly does not add up with any notion of her being behind his murder.

I have dealt with the reign of Titus only briefly, in one chapter. It is a fascinating time, and full of tumultuous events, but with only a peripheral role in this tale, and so I have breezed past it largely. There are, similarly, huge events in Domitian's reign that I have been able to afford only marginal space. Agricola's conquest of Britain, the Dacian invasion, the immense building projects in Rome and so on. Sadly, I needed to keep Domitian's life central to this tale, and so have focused on the more personal and political aspects of his reign.

The main accusation in the ancient sources against Domitian is his cruelty, and indeed the series of executions towards the end of his reign is known as 'the terror', a label applied also to the beheading of French nobility at the end of the eighteenth century. But in these stories, a little digging into the identity of the victims often suggests links and reasons beyond mere cruelty. That an autocrat of Domitian's power might be required to be ruthless to maintain control should not be a surprise, but is such ruthlessness cruelty, or simple expediency? And given that this 'terror' largely follows on swiftly after the attempted revolt of Saturninus lends heavily to the suggestion that Domitian was, in effect 'cleaning house' after an attempted coup. Much the same had been done by Nero after the Pisonian episode, after all.

Another regular accusation levelled is based on Domitian's German campaign. In his *Agricola*, Tacitus says of Domitian 'He was conscious of the ridicule that his sham triumph over Germany had excited', Suetonius that his campaign 'against the Chatti was uncalled for' and Cassius Dio says both 'After this he set out for Gaul and plundered some of the tribes beyond the Rhine that enjoyed treaty rights' and 'Next he made a campaign into Germany and returned without having so much as seen hostilities anywhere'. Modern scholarship and archaeology are repeatedly forcing a reassessment of this. There are clear hints that Germanic raiding or threat thereof had led Rome to the decision that something had to be done. The evidence of large-scale military activity suggests there was a lot more to this campaign than the sources tell us, and the fact that Domitian then reorganised and fortified the frontier is suggestive of an ongoing threat. Yes, Domitian probably did not need personal involvement, but by this time it had become the norm for an emperor to prove himself militarily, and Domitian would need a victory to satisfy that. It was far from unusual and unexpected. His father and brother had both had the opportunity to win military fame long before they took the throne. Domitian had tried, but had been blocked by Mucianus, and so he still needed his victory.

In the early days of Domitian's reign, then, I recount a number of his administrative, legal and social reforms, I introduce a number of senatorial characters destined to join the ranks of Domitian's enemies, and then move swiftly into the German wars. These are important in that they show a martial aspect to Domitian that is often overlooked, and also allowed me the opportunity to introduce Trajan and tie him to Nerva. Given what would happen at the end of Nerva's reign, Trajan's inclusion seems important.

I conflate a number of executions into one scene for the sake of brevity. Had I kept those names confined to separate scenes you would probably have been reading this book in more than one volume. The methods of the deaths of Civica Cerealis, Cornelius Scipio Salvidienus Orfitus, and Aelius Lamia are not recorded, and they likely occurred some time apart. They simply appear in sources among the list of Domitian's victims, along with some vague notes on their purported crimes. I decided to have them crucified partially for the grisly effect, partially for the unacceptable nature of such a punishment for a Roman nobleman, and partly so that it blended seamlessly with the episode of the bandit being torn to pieces on a cross by a Caledonian bear, something that is also attested in the sources.

Nerva's part in the revolt of Saturninus is my own inclusion, although his being granted the consulship the following year is highly suggestive of his involvement. Certainly someone seems to have triggered the plot too early. Saturninus had a grand plan that included allies from among the Germans, but when he sprang the plot, the Germans could not cross the river speedily because the ice had melted. Moreover, before Saturninus can really rally an army the size he had probably hoped for, he is brought to battle by Norbanus and Lappius Maximus. We are told that Trajan was on the way from Spain but failed to reach the place in time, and that the Praetorians had set off from Rome with Domitian but that the rebellion had been dealt with before they could get there. It is an extremely interesting and telling fact that Lappius Maximus burns all the traitor's records before anyone can read them, almost certainly tying him to the plot despite his part in stopping it. It is this very 'lost list of traitors' that I have woven into my tale as the cause for Domitian's 'reign of terror'.

Simply, there has to be a better reason for a man whose reign had been relatively successful, if a little autocratic and harsh, to devolve suddenly into mass murder. That this huge list of 'victims' might also be conspirators tied to that burned list was too good a connection to ignore. That I chose to have Nerva involved in all this uncovering of conspirators fits with the angle I have taken on general events over the course of Domitian's life. But when it comes down to it, I am not such a revisionist that I will make Domitian's darkest acts the property of someone else. The reign of terror and the execution of so many, including family members, I leave safely in the hands of the emperor. It is for the reader to judge whether it was necessary or not, justified or not, or whether in perhaps attempting something expedient, he simply went too far.

The simple fact is that in this book I am not attempting to excuse Domitian, but merely to understand and explain him. He does not appear to have suffered from any madness (the 'megalomania' of Nero or Commodus, or the 'darkness' of Tiberius). He does not appear to have been a good man, misunderstood. What he was, quite simply, was a man. He was clever, possibly even brilliant. He was a manager (sadly also a micro-manager), but he was also a sharp administrator. Whatever his detractors can say, his reforms and acts made for a much stronger Rome, and a much healthier treasury. Modern archaeology and research are rewriting his military campaigns, and he might just now be seen as the man who began the great fortification of the Rhine frontier as a permanent thing, and whose Dacian campaigns paved the way for Trajan's conquest. In short, hated though he might be, and cruel and harsh though he undoubtedly was in some ways, he was also a remarkably successful emperor. And one might say that an emperor who managed to hang on to his throne for fifteen years was no flash in the pan. Domitian's reign was longer and far more successful than many a later emperor who was lauded for his time in office.

On, then to the man's fall.

We do not know just how far Domitian's pressure of the senate went. Certainly he killed a LOT of senators, and considered it an institution past its prime. He shifted power to himself and his army of freedmen, away from the old guard. Whether he ever intended to get rid of the senate entirely is questionable, but certainly there must have been a hefty proportion of those who were left who hated him, and an emperor often comes to a sticky end when he has the senate arrayed against him. Incidentally, the funereal banquet is lifted directly from ancient sources and is one of my favourite stories. In sources it is cited as an example of the man's cruelty and viciousness. Here, I suspect it is a better example of the man's black sense of humour and ability to 'put the frighteners' on people.

With the Epaphroditus episode we have perhaps the most direct cause of Domitian's death. We do not have any details of how the former secretary died, other than Domitian first exiled (I skipped this for smoothness) and then executed him, apparently for the crime of killing his emperor. This seems such a weird accusation, when Nero had apparently begged him to do it, and so I was forced to look a little deeper into Domitian's potential reasons. And the more that I looked at what had happened with Nero's flight and death, the more it seemed likely that the freedman was the voice of reason in that small gathering of fugitives. That he talked Nero into dying first is fairly telling.

Gradually, a reason why Domitian might be a little unforgiving of his actions began to form. The death of an imperial freedman for apparently doing as he was told is very possibly the prime reason behind Domitian's own freedmen gathering together and plotting his death, though there are many hints that senators, Praetorian prefects, gladiators, and even, according to one source, his wife, were involved. But the straight line we can draw from Domitian killing freedmen to freedmen killing Domitian is clear, no matter who else might have contributed.

Any emperor, good or bad, biographised by ancient sources, is prey to omens and signs. Any source you read, Dio, Suetonius, the *Historia Augusta*, Herodian, and a plethora of others, will always scatter tales of signs and omens through his tale. Indeed, there are often so many that it would simply be impossible to include in a book like this. Certain of these, though, in the case of Domitian, tie in so well to the picture I have formed that they begged to be part of it, and have constituted almost an entire chapter on their own, centring around the prophecy of a certain German visitor to the court, and then the disastrous prophecy at Praeneste. That all the bad prophecies had been removed by Caligula is my own invention. That after fifteen years of good omens Domitian found a bad one on the year he died comes from the sources. Incidentally, the Temple of Fortuna at Praeneste is still visible in much of its form and is one of the most impressive of Roman monuments. On that note, Domitian has left more visible great monumental remains in Rome than most emperors. His building programme was truly immense, and should you be visiting Rome, look up a list of the monuments he built or restored before you go, and you can wander round and appreciate the legacy of this dark but surprisingly successful emperor.

In the scenes of Domitian's death, I was constrained by the fact that there is no indication that Nerva was present. There have been suggestions of his involvement in the plot, but they are extremely hard to swallow, and so I have given them no room here. Nerva had, until he took the throne, shown no sign of anything other than utter loyalty to Domitian and the Flavii, and even following Domitian's fall, he seems to have been reluctant to damn him. Aurelius Victor tells us of the future emperor 'when Domitian's murderers were being called to execution, he was so consternated that he was unable to keep from vomiting […] he vehemently objected […] But the soldiers, with the princeps ignored, slaughtered those they sought'. However, sources do recount a witness, in the form of a slave tending the altar in the emperor's apartments. Our two main sources, Cassius Dio and Suetonius, disagree on some of the details, but the main chain of events is fairly clear. My telling, then, is drawn directly from the sources, tweaking when they clashed, and seen from the point of view of the slave. Making the slave a spy of Nerva's was, again, my own decision, for that was the simplest way to give the reader a direct view of events even when my narrator was not there.

And so Domitian died in the manner the German soothsayer had warned. There could very easily have been another civil war, and the precise events following the death are very vague and brushed over, leaving us only with the knowledge that the senate turned to Nerva and declared him emperor. History does not relate the fate of the two young Flavian boys Domitian had appointed his heirs, but since Nerva took the throne, I think we can safely assume that they did not outlive their great uncle by more than hours.

Nerva's reign was short and relatively turbulent, and the fact that he passed the damnatio memoriae on Domitian is one of the great puzzles that led me to writing this in the first place. Clearly Nerva and Domitian had been friends, their families allied. Why then had such a thing happened? The only answer, of course, is that Nerva was pressured into it, as I have portrayed here.

Domitian is dead. His memory persists in the public consciousness as a wicked tyrant, but as time goes on, it is being gradually revised to reveal a man, not a monster. He may not have been a saint, but neither does he seem to have been a demon.

Sic transit Gloria mundi.

Simon Turney, January 2022